DANGEROUS GAMES

SUSAN HUNTER

SEVERN RIVER
PUBLISHING

Severn River Publishing
www.SevernRiverBooks.com

This is a work of fiction. Names, characters, businesses, places, events and incidents are either the products of the author's imagination or used in a fictitious manner. Any resemblance to actual persons, living or dead, or actual events is purely coincidental.

ISBN: 978-1-64875-591-0 (Paperback)

ALSO BY SUSAN HUNTER

Leah Nash Mysteries

Dangerous Habits

Dangerous Mistakes

Dangerous Places

Dangerous Secrets

Dangerous Flaws

Dangerous Ground

Dangerous Pursuits

Dangerous Waters

Dangerous Deception

Dangerous Choices

Dangerous Games

Dangerous Betrayals

To find out more about Susan Hunter and her books, visit severnriverbooks.com

For Lorrie Taylor and the amazing staff at the Alma Public Library

When in doubt, go to the library. ~J.K. Rowling

PROLOGUE

The killer waits in the shadows, avoiding the illumination of the small security light on the warming hut roof and the eerie glow from the vending machine. It's cold, and still, and dark, but he doesn't mind. He knows this will put an end to things. Now that he has no choice, he realizes he should have done it long before. No matter. He's taking care of it now.

He lifts his head at the sound of a snowmobile approaching. It's almost time. He peers into the darkness and sees the headlights coming. He straightens up and checks his gun. It's ready. He is, too.

The snowmobile roars up the track, then cuts across the open field. The driver stops just yards away from where the killer waits. He gets off his machine, leaving the headlights on to light his path. He takes off his helmet and puts it on the seat. The killer steps out from the shadows, concealing the gun at his side.

The driver turns and sees him approaching. He shouts a greeting.

"Hey, where's your machine? Behind the hut? I thought you were gonna be late when I didn't see it out front. Man, it's cold as hell tonight! I don't know why we had to meet way out here. Let's get this done. There's a hot girl and a cold beer waiting for me on a Florida beach. I got what you're looking for right here."

He reaches in his coat pocket and pulls out a small cloth bag.

"I showed you mine. Now you show me yours."

"Toss the bag here," the killer says.

"Hey now, you're not getting yours 'til I get mine. We got a deal. Show me the money."

"Toss the bag here," the killer repeats. He raises his arm and reveals the gun in his hand.

"Whoa! Whoa! No need for that. I'm not tryin' to cheat you. Take it easy. We been doing business for a long time. I just want my fair share, that's all. Nothin' more. Once I leave, you're home free. You don't wanta do something crazy now, bring the cops down on you. I know you're too smart for that." His voice is now high-pitched and frightened.

"Toss me the bag. Now."

"Okay, okay. Steady there," he says, his eyes darting around, looking for an escape that isn't there. With a sudden move, he throws the bag hard toward the killer. He turns and runs toward his snowmobile. The first bullet hits him in the leg. He feels a burning pain. He stumbles forward. The second shot hits him in the back. He falls face down in the snow.

The killer walks toward him. He kicks his victim once to see the response. Nothing. He feels for a pulse. Nothing. He turns and walks away.

1

A light snow began to fall as I hurried down the main street of Himmel, Wisconsin, headed to the local bookstore. Holiday wreaths circled the lampposts on the main street. Santas, elves, reindeer, and more invited customers into the stores. The Bloom Room floral shop piped Christmas carols out to the sidewalk, and I felt a surge of holiday spirit. It was a perfect Norman Rockwell version of small-town life, right down to busy shoppers exchanging cheery greetings and happy-holidays goodbyes as they stopped and chatted on the sidewalks.

A group of five or six people milled about in front of Buy the Book when I arrived. At first I thought that the bookstore's line of customers was so long that it had spilled onto the sidewalk. Which, of course, would have been great for the bookstore, but not for a shopping-averse—especially Christmas shopping—person like me.

I was seriously considering leaving and returning later in the day when someone tapped my arm. I turned.

"Leah, are you here for the PPOK demonstration? I hope the *Times* will cover it fairly if you are. All these fake news stories are making PPOK look like a bunch of nuts." Dottie Ellsworth, a solidly built woman in her late fifties, jabbed a red-mitten-clad hand in my direction.

"Oh, hey, Dottie. I'm not here for the paper. I'm just picking up some books I ordered. I didn't know you were part of the Parents Protecting Our Kids group."

I kept my tone neutral in a nod to the season of goodwill and didn't make any snarky remarks about book-banning craziness.

Wait. I should pause and introduce myself. My name is Leah Nash, I co-own the *Himmel Times* weekly, and I write books. At the time, I'd recently completed my first foray into fiction, though it wasn't published yet—a mystery set in Michigan's Upper Peninsula.

"I just joined PPOK few weeks ago. After Ed Wagner told me the school board is against parents having a say in their own kids' education. Well, that's not right," she said.

"Aren't all your kids out of school, Dottie?"

"I've still got grandkids in school. And even if I didn't, I'd be here with PPOK. We have to protect our kids. You're not against that, are you, Leah? That's not so crazy, is it?" Her voice had risen slightly, and her tone was challenging.

When anyone says the group's acronym out loud (*P-pock*), I can't stop the image of a regal, blue bird fanning his gorgeous tail from popping into my head. It was a picture very much at odds with Dottie. Her sturdy body was bundled up in a puffy, black coat, and its hood covered her head, leaving only a few stray strands of iron-gray hair peeking out.

"I've got nothing against protecting kids, Dottie, but I don't really understand what PPOK is protecting them from. And I'm not a fan of shouting people down and threatening lawsuits at school and library board meetings."

"I've known you since I was your Brownie troop leader, Leah. And you've always liked to stir things up. All that talk about PPOK intimidating people and being rude, it's not true. My neighbor Mary Jane, she told me that story in the paper was fake news. We just want to make sure the kids aren't reading things that teach them to go against their parents, or to get ideas that are only going to hurt them in the long run. We're not telling teachers what to teach."

"Really? Because taking books out of school libraries kind of makes it seem like you are. Also, Dottie, just because you or PPOK don't like what we report in the *Himmel Times* doesn't make it 'fake news.' I watched the video of the school board meeting. There was plenty of intimidation and rudeness happening."

She shook her head.

"I wasn't there, and I don't have MyTube, or YourTV, or whatever it is they put the meetings up on. But Ed—he's going to speak in a little while—he said nobody listens unless you get loud. And I agree with him. Protecting kids is a good reason to get loud."

"But are you really protecting them? Or are you putting up barricades to learning about the world outside our very small, very homogenous little town? It seems to me that denying them the freedom to read is the thing that will hurt them in the long run."

"I'd expect you to say that."

She folded her arms and set her lips in a straight line, though more in frustration at my obtuseness than in anger at me, it seemed.

"Look, Dottie, I get that you see this differently than I do. But it's too darn cold to try and educate each other about our points of view out here on the sidewalk. I'm going inside, but if you want to talk more, stop by the paper some afternoon. I'll take you to the break room, and we can chat over a cup of coffee. Maybe you can bring some of your sour -cream coffee cake as part of the peace talks," I said, trying to lighten things up a little.

She shook her head.

"You're wrong, Leah. You're dead wrong. This is serious—we have to step up for our kids and for our town. You're just being blind to what's happening in schools and libraries these days. Well, maybe I didn't go to college, and maybe I'm not a famous book writer either, but I know what's right. And PPOK is doing what's right for this town. You'll see."

"So, I guess that's a no on the coffee cake? Okay, Dottie, but if you change your mind about having a conversation, I'll be around."

2

As I walked through the entrance of Buy the Book, Luke Granger, the assistant manager, was talking with a customer. The three dinosaur books I'd ordered—they weren't for me; I'm more of a dragon kind of gal—were sitting next to the register. I caught Luke's eye and waved to signal I'd be browsing the shelves for a while. He gave me a thumbs-up and continued his conversation with an unhappy-looking woman. I recognized her as Brooke Timmins, the very attractive but very tightly wound wife of our local district attorney.

I headed for the mystery section, looking for a book for my mom's Christmas Eve present. The sound of a favorite Christmas song came over the store's speakers. My mind took me straight back to when I was a kid and my sister Annie was still alive.

Every Christmas Eve, our parents made a ritual of letting us exchange the gifts Annie and I had gotten each other, instead of making us wait for Christmas morning. In true Hallmark family fashion, we sat in front of the fireplace, dressed in our flannel nightgowns—Annie's pink with a kitten print, mine red with the Wonder Woman logo. Mugs of hot cocoa and a plate of Christmas cookies sat on a small table. The flames from the fire, the lights on the tree, and a Christmas candle burning gave the living room a once-a-year special glow. It was magical.

After Annie died and my dad left, there was just me, my mother, and my baby sister, Lacey. That first, hard year when I didn't have anyone to exchange a Christmas Eve gift with, my mother took Annie's place in the ritual, and we started a new tradition. When Lacey got older, the three of us did it together. Mom and I still do. And even at thirty-four, I look forward to it. I perused the shelves for a few minutes and found a Nora Fielding book that my mother didn't have in her collection.

Then I headed for the science fiction section to pick up something for my friend Father Lindstrom. As I rounded the corner of a row of shelves, I cut it a little too sharply. I came close to winding up in the lap of a customer sitting in one of the store's comfy chairs, but I managed to regain my balance. I almost lost it again when I saw who was sitting there. Courtnee Fensterman, the receptionist at the *Himmel Times*.

Seeing Courtnee in a bookstore made me feel like I had stepped through the doorway to another dimension. The only thing that silenced the *Twilight Zone* music running through my head was realizing that she was watching TikTok videos on her phone, not reading a book.

"Hey, watch where you're going—oh, it's you, Leah. What are you doing here?"

"It's a bookstore, Courtnee. I'm here to get some books. Since the only thing I've ever seen you read are your text messages, I'll turn the question back to you. What are *you* doing here? Or let me amend that. What are you doing here at 10:30 in the morning when you're supposed to be at the *Times* office, working?"

"I need to ask Luke if he's coming to Miguel's party, but he's, like, just talking to some lady at the cash register. I've been waiting forever for him to get done with her, but she keeps talking and talking. I'm going to have to leave pretty soon."

"Courtnee, Luke actually values his customers. So, he spends time helping them. It's a concept I'd love for you to embrace at the *Times*."

She flipped her blonde hair over her shoulder and accompanied the gesture with a modified eye roll. We don't pay much at the paper—we can't afford to. Courtnee is the end result of that unfortunate state of affairs. I won't say that she is the worst receptionist in the world, but she'd definitely finish in the top five.

"You don't have to be so condensing," she said.

Fluent as I am in Courtnee speak, out of necessity rather than desire, I knew she meant *condescending*. And I was guilty as charged. Courtnee makes such an easy target, it's hard to resist.

"You're right. I don't. But you give me so many opportunities. You can't expect me to resist *all* of them. But in the spirit of the season of peace and good will, I apologize. So what's the story? Why are you lying in wait to get Luke's party plans?"

"We don't all have a hot boyfriend like you do, Leah. I told you last week that I broke up with Kyle again, and now I don't have anyone to go to Miguel's party with. So I thought I would just make sure Luke knows I'm available now. It might cheer him up."

"Why does Luke need cheering up?"

"Because he can't get the loan to buy the bookstore, duh! My cousin Lonna works at the bank, and she told me the loan committee turned him down. They said he didn't have any experience owning a business, and his credit score is kinda low, and . . . well, they couldn't say this out loud, but the Granger name didn't help any. That's what Lonna said. But if he can come up with thirty percent down instead of twenty, they'll give him the loan. Only he can't."

Although I couldn't condone Courtnee (and her cousin Lonna) spilling confidential financial information, I was definitely curious to hear more.

"But Marcus isn't going to retire until he's sixty-five. Why did Luke go to the bank for a loan now? He's still got almost three years to go."

"Because Marcus's heart attack was really bad. His doctor said he can't come back to work. He has to sell the bookstore now. He's moving to Tucson where his sister lives. So Luke needs the money right away. He didn't have enough saved yet, but he got some from like a friend, or a relative, or something. So he thought he could do it. Only now the bank wants more, and Luke can't get it."

I was surprised by the news, but I trusted her intel. Courtnee isn't good at a lot of things, but she's a pretty reliable purveyor of timely and accurate gossip.

"What's he going to do?"

"Something else, I guess. I don't know."

She shrugged, and her eyes drifted toward her phone screen. Clearly she was losing interest in a conversation not centered on her.

I only knew Luke from my visits to the bookstore, but I liked him. We'd had a few conversations about his dream to own the store, and his plans for when he did. Besides his full-time job at the bookstore, he worked part-time at the library as a night janitor, and he took on any other side hustles he could to earn the money he needed for a down payment. The way he felt about Buy the Book reminded me of the way I feel about the *Himmel Times.*

Courtnee's cousin was probably right that a factor in the bank's reluctance to make the loan to Luke was his last name. The Granger family is a sprawling clan with extensions throughout the county. Its members have some legit businesses, like Ride EZ car service and Way to Mow, a lawn-care company. But they're also involved in a number of shady operations and, occasionally, serious crime-ing. Luke—a smart, hard worker with goals—was a once-in-a-hundred-years phenomenon in that family. I hated to hear that his big dream was going to go bust.

Although Courtnee was too absorbed in her phone to notice, a raised and angry voice drew my attention to the front of the store. Luke's conversation with Brooke Timmins had obviously taken an unhappy turn. Several other customers took note as well. Brooke was so loud that none of us felt the need to pretend we weren't listening.

"I don't want to hear excuses. I need that book now. When I called to check on it, the girl said it was in. And now you tell me you can't find it?"

"I'm so sorry, Mrs. Timmins," Luke said. "Clarissa is new. She must have misread the inventory spreadsheet. It's not here yet, but your book is on schedule for delivery this afternoon. I—"

"That's no help to me. I have dozens of errands to run today. I won't even be back in town until after you close at six."

"I'm sorry. I understand how disappointed you are, but—"

"No. I don't think you do. This book is a present for a dear friend. I've planned an intimate lunch to celebrate her birthday tomorrow with a small group of friends. The author of the book is going to be there as a special surprise. How can the author sign the book if I don't have it?"

"What time is your lunch?" Luke asked.

"Don't try to tell me I can get it in the morning. You don't open until ten, and I need to be at the Edgewater in Madison well before that."

"No worries. I'll bring the book to your house tonight, after I close the store. That way you'll have it for your party tomorrow. How does that sound?"

Luke's calm politeness, coupled with his willingness to make a home delivery on his own time, seemed to pierce Brooke's wall of petulance. She waited a few seconds before she responded.

"Well, if the book actually comes in, I suppose that will take care of things. I appreciate your help," she added grudgingly, perhaps a little shamed by Luke's unflagging patience.

"Good, we've got a plan," he said. "We close at six. I'll be at your house shortly after with your book."

He smiled, and I could see why Courtnee had her eye on him.

"Thank you." Brooke nodded, then left without saying anything else.

As she closed the door, the little bell that rang didn't play "Ding-Dong! The Witch Is Dead," but that was definitely the vibe in the store.

3

"Luke, you hit a new high in customer service there with Brooke. Home delivery is really going the extra mile. Especially after she was so rude to you," I said as he rang up my dinosaur books, plus the Nora Fielding mystery I'd picked out for my mother.

He shrugged.

"Oh, she's okay. I like to keep the customers happy, and it's no big deal to drop off her book before I go to work at the library. Usually it's someone older that I make a home delivery for, but if it keeps Brooke happy, I don't mind."

"Well, you just gave a master class in de-escalation. I know why Marcus values you so much. Hey, I just heard that you're not going to be able to buy the bookstore. I'm sorry. I know how hard you've worked to do it."

"Thanks, Leah. It's been pretty tough to accept. Ever since I started working here, it's all I've wanted to do. Even though most of my family thinks it's a crazy idea. Most of them aren't big on reading," he added dryly.

"No, but they're your family. I'm sure they were disappointed, too—for you, I mean."

And I actually did think that, because regardless of their less desirable qualities, the Grangers are big on family loyalty.

"They were, that's true. But I think my family was part of the reason I didn't get the loan. The bank raised the amount they want from twenty percent down up to thirty percent down. They said it was because of my age and inexperience owning a business, but I'm pretty sure it had something to do with my last name, too. When they hear Granger, most people don't think bookstore owner."

"You're probably right, even though it's not fair. You've more than proved yourself as far as work ethic, smarts, and honesty."

"I appreciate you saying that, but some people don't see it that way. You know Marilyn Karr is on the bank board, right?"

I nodded. Marilyn Karr used to be married to my mother's long-time significant other, Paul Karr. Although he was divorced long before they started seeing each other, Marilyn is convinced that it's my mother's fault her marriage ended. She isn't crazy about me either. Even though I saved her spoiled son Spencer from getting killed last summer.

"Yes, I know she's on the board. And if you're thinking that she did her best to keep the loan committee from approving a loan to a Granger, you're probably not wrong."

"That's exactly what I think. But as it turns out, it might not matter."

"Really? How's that?"

"I don't want to jinx it. But I've been trying to think of a way to get the money and I think I might have it now. What's that saying, when a door closes, a window opens?"

"You're saying you found an open window?"

"Maybe. It's been raised a crack, anyway. I'm going to see if I can push it all the way up. Keep your fingers crossed."

"I will," I said, grabbing my bag of books to leave.

A loud shout from outside caused both of us to turn and look through the large plate-glass window at the front of the store. A man standing on a turned-over wooden planter was leading the PPOK chant: "Protect our Kids!" over and over. Instead of the handful of people who had been outside when I arrived, there was now a sizable crowd.

I shook my head.

"Does this happen often?"

"No, it's the first time. And it's their right to protest, I guess. I just wish they weren't doing it in front of the store, during our busiest season."

"I know a couple of them. Do you recognize anyone?"

"A few. But the people who want to ban books aren't a regular part of our customer base."

Another store patron came to the register. I started to leave again, then turned back and said, "Good luck, Luke! I know things are going to work out for you."

If lumps of coal were given out for being wrong instead of being naughty, my Christmas stocking that year would have been full of them.

I slipped through the PPOK crowd unnoticed. But when I glanced in the direction of the speaker mesmerizing the crowd, I recognized him. Ed Wagner was the guy using the repurposed planter as a platform. During our brief chat earlier, Dottie had said Ed was a founder of the group, so I guess I shouldn't have been surprised. But the Ed loudly declaiming his war on books didn't sound anything like the Ed I knew. He and his wife, Gwen, had owned a shoe store in town that went out of business after a discount chain opened in Himmel.

They were both nice people—Ed had an endless collection of dad jokes, and he had seemed to enjoy chatting with customers as much as he liked making a sale. Gwen was quieter but always pleasant. I'd heard they were hit pretty hard when the shoe store went bankrupt, but that was after I'd left town. I hadn't run into them or heard anything about them since I'd moved back a few years ago.

"Mom, did you know PPOK is protesting outside Buy the Book?" I asked as I walked through the front door of the *Times* and saw her sitting at the reception desk. "Also, where's Courtnee?"

"She had a dentist appointment."

"Oh, really? Because she was at the bookstore stalking Luke Granger. And she left about twenty minutes before I did."

My mother, the office manager for the *Times,* has the challenging duty of supervising Courtnee.

She shook her head. "That girl! I'm going to install a work ethic in her if it kills me. Or her. But no, I didn't know about PPOK. What's going on?"

I updated her on the latest salvo in PPOK's battle to make the world safe from ideas.

"I just don't understand how it's come to this. I know some of the people involved. Gwen Wagner and I both used to volunteer at the food pantry at the Presbyterian Church. I always liked her. It's hard to see her as someone who wants to ban books," my mother said.

"Well, according to Dottie, PPOK is all about people who believe parents should have more direct involvement with the school curriculum. But it looks to me like they want to set it, not just be involved with it. Also, what are they doing outside the bookstore? That's got nothing to do with school libraries."

"I can see PPOK's point about wanting to engage with schools more. And I even agree that parents should be able to opt their kids out of reading some books—though I think it's a rookie mistake. There's no surer way to motivate kids to read something than telling them they can't. But I don't like where all this PPOK business is headed."

"Me either. Look at the chaos they caused at the school board meeting last month, and then again at the library board meeting this past week. Now they're outside the bookstore. They're not messing around."

"It's ridiculous. Fine, you don't want your kids to read Harry Potter. Then don't let your kids read the series, but don't take away the books so no one's child can read it. It's just all so unnecessary."

The door opened behind me, and Courtnee sauntered in carrying some kind of whipped cream-topped beverage from the Wide Awake and Woke coffee shop across the street.

"Leah! What are you doing here? You're supposed to be meeting Miguel at Woke. He's there waiting for you. Oh, hi, Carol," she said, her voice faltering a little as she noticed my mother sitting where *she* should have been.

"Shoot! I forgot all about Miguel! I'll catch you later, Mom."

As I dashed out the door, I heard my mother ask, "How was your dental appointment, Courtnee?"

She asked it in the same tone the Nazi guy uses when he's calling Claude Rains to his doom at the end of my all-time favorite classic movie, *Notorious*.

I knew from personal experience what Courtnee was in for.

4

I zipped across the street. When I walked through Woke's door, I spotted Miguel Santos, our senior reporter at the *Times*. That sounds a little grander than it is. We only have two full-time reporters at the paper. He was there first, so Miguel gets the title senior reporter.

I stopped at the counter to order from Will, my favorite barista.

"Hey, Leah. Miguel ordered for you. Your chai is already at the table. It might be a little cold, though. It's been waiting a while," he added, cocking an eyebrow at me.

"Oh, come on, Will. I come to Woke for the extra spicy chai, not for the guilt. My mother has the franchise on that."

He grinned. "I wouldn't feel too bad if I were you. He's been talking up a storm with everyone he knows. Which is basically everyone. He probably hasn't missed you."

"I'm not sure if that makes me feel better or worse."

Miguel saw me then and waved me over with a big smile. His whole being is always on point—clothes, hair, attitude. In sharp contrast to me. And he loves everybody he meets—also in sharp contrast to me. Maybe that's why I love him so much. He's the yin to my yang. Tall, slender, with long-lashed, deep-brown eyes, a smile you can't help responding to, and a personality few can resist. If I weren't already in a serious relationship—

and Miguel weren't gay (there is that) and ten years younger than me, I would be very interested in him romantically. As it is, he's the younger brother I never had, but definitely should have.

"I'm sorry, I'm sorry. I was at the bookstore, and PPOK was there, and I got talking to Luke, and I forgot—"

"No, no, *chica*, it's fine. You're worth waiting for."

"You are almost too perfect to be a friend of mine," I said. "Let me fix that a little." I reached over and tousled his hair.

"Not the hair!"

He made a face of mock horror and then restored his look with a few quick and practiced movements of his fingers.

"Sorry. Couldn't resist," I said.

"I know. But now tell me, why are you so late?"

I gave him a short version of my bookstore adventure.

"That is bad. But I'm not surprised about the PPOK after the library board meeting last week. They are very mad. When I finish my macchiato, I'll go take some photos and get something up online. I can get more for the print edition after."

In our ongoing quest to hold onto subscribers, the *Times* provides both an online edition that's updated as news breaks, as well as the print edition that comes out weekly.

"Good. I think we're going to be following this story for a while."

He nodded, an uncharacteristic frown on his face, which quickly turned to a smile as he changed topics.

"But I'm very happy Luke will be able to buy the bookstore after all. He is one of my favorite friends."

"Everyone is your favorite friend, Miguel. But don't get too far ahead with your glad-boy happiness. Luke said it was a possibility, not a sure thing. But I hope it comes true. He would do great with the bookstore. You should have seen how he handled Brooke Timmins. She was just half a beat short of threatening to have Luke arrested because a book she ordered hadn't come in. But he got her calmed down without a scene. She thinks she's way more important than she is, just because Cliff is the district attorney and she's on a couple of boards around town."

"It is true, she can be difficult. But her fashion game is very good."

Miguel wasn't wrong. Brooke does have style, and he's always one to appreciate that.

"And," he continued, "she stood up for the library against PPOK at the Library Board meeting last week. Some of the board, they were not so sure. But Brooke would not back down from PPOK, even when they threatened to boycott her business."

"Yeah? Good to know she can use her powers for good as well as evil. But not to be snarky—"

He gave me some side-eye on that because snark is kind of my default setting. I ignored him and went on.

"I don't think most of the PPOK crowd would be customers of Brooke's interior design business. Sophisticated Style Interiors is way too pricey, and she's way too snobby."

"Maybe. But still, she did not agree to the book bans."

"Yes. That's no small thing. Maybe Father Lindstrom is right, everyone has at least a spark of good in them. I think that spark might be just about it in Brooke's case, but because it's the Christmas season, I'll drop it there. Speaking of Christmas, how are plans going for this year's holiday celebration?"

"Holidays," he said, emphasizing the plural *s*. "We will be celebrating as many holidays in the month as I can think of—St. Nicholas Day, Hannukah, Kwanzaa, Winter Solstice, Christmas, Boxing Day, and New Year's Eve!—all at once. It's going to be an open house from seven p.m. until whenever. Also, it will be very dressy. You know I love the sparkle season! I am getting very excited! You and Coop are coming, yes?"

"Absolutely. Though neither of us is really that into sparkle."

"No matter. I will help you find something. And Coop, he has his own style. No sparkle required."

"Oh, and I don't have my own style?"

He looked at me without comment, though his eyes said it all.

When he finished elaborating on his party plans, he said, "I think this will be the best party ever. And I think there will be a surprise for you."

"What? What kind of a surprise? A present? Don't get me a present. I thought we agreed to donate what we'd spend on Christmas gifts to the homeless shelter and just do a big blow out on birthdays this year."

"It's not a present. It's a surprise. But I'm not sure if you will like it or not, but it's happening. You will have to wait and see, like everyone else."

"Like everyone else? What does that mean?"

"It means that it's not all about you, but it's something you want, only maybe not the way you want it."

"Okay, now you have to tell me what it is."

"No. I have to go to Buy the Book and get quotes and some PPOK pictures now. I'll see you later."

He left the table and headed for the exit, turning to wave and give me a wicked grin as he walked out the door.

My significant other, David Cooper, is the county sheriff. He's just about a year into his first term, and he's doing a great job. I may be biased, but it's still true. The previous sheriff was both corrupt and not very bright. He left a hot mess in the sheriff's office for Coop to clean up, which Coop mostly has.

I know that cops and journalists can make for strange bedfellows—in our case, literally. But we have the advantage in what could be a tricky relationship, because Coop and I were best friends for twenty years before our feelings got romantic. Or maybe I should say before we realized they were romantic.

The sheriff's office is a couple of blocks from the main part of town, right next to the Grantland County Courthouse. When I pushed through the door, Jennifer Pilarski, Coop's administrative aide—and my friend since the kindergarten time-out corner—was at her desk outside his office. Almost everything about Jennifer is soft—her comfortable round body, her wavy, shoulder-length, brown hair, her warm, brown eyes, and her soothing voice.

"Hey, Leah. What's going on?"

"Well, there was quite the kerfuffle outside Buy the Book this morning."

"PPOK?"

"How did you know?"

"My cousin Maureen—you know, the school librarian—she said someone from PPOK was in her library last week causing a big ruckus."

"Really? Was it Ed Wagner by any chance? He was outside the bookstore today."

"No, it was his cousin Doug Durfee. He had a list of books he wanted Mo to take off the shelves. She tried to talk him down, but he just pushed past her and started pulling them off himself. Luckily, Phil Stillman—the school board president—was in the building for an assembly or something. He came down and escorted Doug out. But Mo was a little shook. I don't know what's up with those PPOK guys, but I don't like it. I don't want them in my kids' school trying to take books away."

"Well, they're doing it. PPOK is showing up at every school and library board meeting in the county to make their case—usually very loudly. It might help if more people who don't share their point of view made their voices heard, too, instead of just talking about it to each other like we are right now."

"Thank you. I was just thinking I'm not carrying enough guilt around about the things I should be doing as a single parent. Now I can add not advocating for free speech to the list. It's just with a full-time job, and the twins, and going to school—it's a lot. I feel like I'm a hamster on one of those wheels, running fast and getting nowhere. When I have a little free time, the last thing on my mind is going to a meeting to stand up for the freedom to read."

"Hey, I wasn't singling you out, Jen. Actually I was referring more to myself. I haven't paid enough attention. The idea that libraries—school or public—shouldn't have *A Wrinkle in Time* or *Where the Sidewalk Ends* available to kids is crazy to me. I'm not sure I would have made it through sixth grade without *Harriet the Spy*. I'm just starting to think those of us who aren't in favor of censoring books should be speaking out. But I know you've got your hands full right now."

She shook her head.

"Don't give me an easy out. This is important, and I should be doing something about it. Hey, I've got an idea. Let's go to the next school board meeting. They meet on the fourth Monday of the month. And afterward we'll go to Bonucci's for pizza and a glass of wine."

"Sounds like a plan, though maybe we should go for that glass of wine before the meeting," I said.

The door to Coop's office opened in the middle of my response.

"What's the plan, or shouldn't I ask?"

"Leah and I are going to mount a counter-protest to PPOK at the next school board meeting."

"Is that right? Leah, I've asked you before not to plot civil unrest in my office. It's a bad look for me," he said in a mock stern tone.

"Ah, but the key is civil, right? It's not me and Jen they'll have to call the police in to handle."

"Jen, I'm sure of. You? Not so much."

5

"And so, I told Jen that I feel like I need to do more than just tut-tut about it. I have to believe there are more—or at least as many—people in town who don't believe in banning books. It's time we got off our couches and went to a meeting or two. Are you keeping an eye on PPOK? Things are getting a little wild," I said, after giving Coop an account of my bookstore visit.

"We are. I just got off the phone with Roy Jackson from the Omico Police Department. He said one of the PPOK members checked a bunch of books out of the Omico Library, burned them, and marched back into the library and dropped the ashes off at the circulation desk."

"You're kidding! Book burning? Here in Grantland County? I'll check with Maggie and see if she's got anyone covering that for the paper. That's a big deal. A bad deal, but a big deal. Who was it?"

"A woman by the name of Barbara Stevens. She's being charged with a Class A misdemeanor. She could get nine months in jail or a thousand dollar fine."

"But she won't, right? She'll probably plead out."

"I'm not so sure. She might take it to a trial for the publicity. Roy says she looks like a sweet, old-fashioned grandmother, but she's willing to be a martyr for PPOK."

"I hate that this is happening here. Things could get really ugly."

"I'd say they already have. I heard that some of the Himmel School Board members have gotten anonymous threatening phone calls. Nothing specific, just general *watch out or you'll be sorry* stuff. It may not go further— I hope it doesn't. But we have to keep an eye on what could turn into dangerous confrontations. Some of the law enforcement agencies have a joint meeting scheduled to talk about ways to keep public discussions and demonstrations from escalating into something none of us want to see."

"Sounds like a good idea. When's the meeting?"

"This afternoon, actually," Coop said.

"Why don't you come over tonight and tell me what happened? I'll make dinner."

"Sorry, you should have gotten your invitation in earlier. I already told Charlie I'd sub for him at his poker game tonight. I could come by after, probably be around 10:30?"

"That works. I need to get serious about my next book, so I can do some thinking and researching on that until you get there."

"Good. I'll see you tonight," he said.

I got up to leave.

"Hey, wait a second," he said, coming out from behind his desk to kiss me.

"That was very nice," I said. "But I thought we decided on no public displays of affection at work."

"We did. But my door is closed. And since we don't live together, and I don't see you as much as I'd like, I don't want you to forget about me."

"Hmm. That is a danger. You better kiss me again to make sure you're seared into my memory."

When I got back to the *Times* office, I went in through the rear entrance to avoid another close encounter of the Courtnee kind. I headed for the newsroom to give Maggie McConnell, our managing editor, the news about the book burning in Omico. Troy Patterson, the other half of our two-person reporter contingent, was out for a few days. With a staff as downsized as ours, it makes a big difference when one person is gone. As a result, Maggie still does some reporting in addition to her managing editor duties. I jump in now and then, too.

"Hi, Maggie. Hey, I just heard that someone from PPOK, a Barbara Stevens, was—"

"Arrested on a misdemeanor charge for burning library books? Yeah, I'm on it," she barked out. Maggie had stopped smoking years ago, but the legacy it left is a voice that sounds like someone tossed pebbles into a coffee grinder.

She pushed her tortoiseshell glasses up onto her thick, gray hair and looked at me expectantly. "Anything else?"

"Just my admiration for your sources, Maggie. Where did you get that so fast? I just heard about it from Coop."

"Jody phoned it in. She's doing a solid job as a stringer. If we ever get enough money to expand the reporting staff, she'd be a good hire."

We use a pool of stringers to help fill in the gaps and keep our tiny regular staff from being stretched too thin. It helps keep payroll costs down —they get paid on a per-story basis, with no benefits and no guarantee of regular assignments. But that situation makes me feel guilty. I try to soothe my conscience by reminding myself that back in the mists of time, I started out as a stringer at the *Himmel Times*. I found it thrilling, not exploitative. And I did learn a lot about reporting before I had even graduated from high school. Still, I don't feel great about using stringers instead of regular employees.

"Yeah, I've noticed her byline quite a lot. You know, I can cover some things to help out if you need me."

"Oh? How's that new book coming? "

"It's coming. Besides, I've got months and months before the first draft is due."

"Thanks for the offer, but I don't think we'll need you in the newsroom. We're keeping our heads above water."

Maggie had one condition when she came out of retirement to take the managing editor job at the *Times*. The newsroom is her domain, not mine. I agreed because it's the same thing I would want in her shoes. But it's hard to stay away from your business when it's located just two floors below where you live. And when you really care about it. And when you have lots of thoughts to offer.

"Sorry, Maggie I wasn't trying to get up in your business. I just meant—"

"I know."

She nodded, put her glasses on, and refocused on the computer screen she'd been looking at when I came in.

"All right, then. Holler if you need me for anything. Otherwise, I'll see you in a couple of days. I'm going to take a deep dive into the wonderful world of fiction writing."

6

I spent the afternoon and most of the evening working on ideas for my next book. I had just turned in my first attempt at fiction, and it wouldn't come out until spring. But I was having trouble coming up with a plot for the next one. Partly because after years as a reporter and then as a true crime book writer, fiction was a big stretch for me. It seemed like a better idea to wait and see how my first book was received. If no one liked it, what was the point of writing another?

However, my agent Clinton Barnes and my publisher did not feel that way. Apparently in a series, which I was supposed to be writing, publishers like to start promoting the next book as soon as the first one is released.

So, I sat down to stare at my laptop for a few hours. I had one or two vague thoughts that I tried to flesh out by doing some online research. I enjoy that stage of writing. All the possibilities are there, and none of the plot points that won't work out the way I want them to have shown up yet. I stopped only for a quick bowl of cereal for lunch, and to feed Sam, my cat.

I had never thought of myself as a cat person. I've always been more drawn to dogs. But I had inherited Sam, a brownish-gray tabby cat with green-gold eyes, when my friend and business partner, Miller Caldwell, had died a few months earlier. It had taken a while for Sam to warm up to me, but I like to think that I've helped him as much as he's helped me to cope with life without Miller.

By the time Coop arrived, Sam and I were comfortably settled in on the couch, me staring at the flames in my gas fireplace, Sam sleeping. Coop grabbed a bottle of Leinenkugel from the fridge and joined us. When he gently urged Sam to move a little to give him some room, Sam gave him an annoyed look but settled down between us. I scooted back into the corner of the couch so I could sit cross-legged and face Coop directly.

"This is nice," he said, leaning back on the sofa.

"It is. And now you can have the floor first. Tell me about your meeting."

"There were some good ideas. We talked about how sometimes police presence can be more intimidating than reassuring. We want people to feel free to speak up as long as they stay civil. In the end, we decided we need to bring the board and council chairs from around the county together to hear what they think. In the meantime, I'm going to do some unofficial drop-ins on a few meetings myself. Off-duty and not in uniform, to get a better sense of things. Oh, and I talked to Ed Wagner today, too."

"How did that go?"

"We'll see. I just told him that PPOK has a right to demonstrate, and its members have a right to speak up at public meetings. But there's a difference between expressing concerns and intimidating people. He seemed to take my point."

"Good. Hey, different topic, but I've been meaning to ask how Marla's doing."

Marla Jarvis had spent most of her career with the sheriff's office as a road patrol deputy. Over the years, she'd had the ambition knocked out of her by a couple of sheriffs who didn't like girls in the clubhouse. Coop had given her a chance to do more.

"Great. Since she got her promotion to sergeant, she's been shaking things up a little. I like watching the guys try to keep up with her."

"You're welcome."

"I didn't say thank you."

"You should have. I'm the one who told you to promote Marla."

"I didn't promote her because you told me I should. I promoted her because she finally got up the courage to take the sergeant's exam, and she did great."

"Yes, but I was the one who gave you the idea to talk to her about it. When you think about it, that kind of makes me your key advisor. In fact, I'm really the power behind your throne, aren't I?"

"No, you're definitely not."

"It seems like I should be. So, is Marla working on anything major?"

"Could be."

"You don't have to be so tight-lipped. I'm not asking for the paper. I'm asking as your key advisor—and because I'm a concerned and supportive significant other, interested in your work."

"Okay. But you're not my key advisor."

"Deny if you must, but we both know that I am. Now, what's Marla working on?"

"This is just us talking, not to go anywhere else."

"Okay."

"She got a tip on local truckers involved with cigarette smuggling. It's legit. So, now she's getting a crash course in working with the Feds."

"The Feds? Just for cigarettes? Why the big guns?"

"Illegal cigarette sales are a big business. They cost the state millions in tax revenues. Alcohol, Tobacco, and Firearms takes cigarette smuggling very seriously. It looks like the ones in our area are coming in across the Indiana border."

"Are Grangers involved?"

"Maybe, but they're not heading it up. It's a more sophisticated operation than your buddy Cole could run. Marla's working with ATF because she's got good local sources. I think she'll do the Grantland Sheriff's office proud."

"Again, I could take a bow for my excellent advice to you, but gloating would be rude."

"That's one thing I appreciate about you, your commitment to politeness."

"You know, sarcasm is also considered rude by many people."

"True. How about this? I appreciate every aspect of your many faceted personality."

"Better, though I sense a lack of sincerity in your tone. I will, however, let it pass."

"I appreciate that."

He smiled and leaned forward. I met him halfway for a kiss.

"You're welcome. I appreciate *you*," I said and kissed him again.

Sam jumped off the couch as it became apparent to him that we were going to spend the rest of the evening appreciating each other. Which we did.

7

Coop left super early the next morning, and though I tried to go back to sleep, Sam was having none of that. I was already showered, dressed, and breakfasted when my phone rang just before seven. I guessed correctly who was calling, my agent Clinton. As far as I can tell, he never sleeps. To think is to do for Clinton, and he's always thinking.

"Leah, first the good news! Reviews from the advance reader copies of *Blood Moon Rising* are coming in, and they're good. Some of them are great. I'm reading comments like 'a promising new voice in crime fiction,' 'a strong, likable female lead,' 'twists and turns to keep you guessing.' So what do you say now about the revision work you didn't want to do?"

"Really? Are they *all* that good?"

I couldn't keep the surprise and skepticism out of my voice. I'd really struggled with my first attempt at fiction, and my confidence level in the end product wasn't very high.

"Not all of them, but enough. You don't really want all the ARC reviewers to gush over it. That might look like you paid for reviews. There aren't many books that everyone loves, unless maybe if you're Stephen King or Agatha Christie. This is happy news I'm telling you. Why aren't you excited?"

"I am, Clinton. This is my excited voice. Seriously, I'm really glad about the early reviews. And as far as the revisions, you were right. I'm sorry I was so reluctant to tackle them at first."

"Reluctant? That wouldn't be my description. Obstinate, inflexible, intransigent—"

"Okay, okay. Maybe I was a little more than reluctant. But you gave me the room to rethink things. And I came around. So, thank you."

"You're welcome. Second item, I got a call from your friend at the little paper that could."

Clinton is not crazy about my ongoing commitment to the *Times*. It wasn't the first time that he'd likened my determination to keep the paper going to the engine with the impossible task in the kid's book *The Little Engine That Could*.

"Miguel called you? Why?"

"He said he keeps inviting you on his podcast and you keep making excuses not to be interviewed. Why's that? It would be good PR, and it's free."

"Miguel knows too much about me. And he's a very good interviewer."

"So he knows where the bodies are buried?"

"Something like that."

"Well, bury them deeper. We need all the free PR we can get. A small publishing house like Clifford & Warren isn't going to fund any promotional tours, except for their star sellers. You should do the podcast but make it closer to the book launch in the spring."

Clinton's advice had been pretty good to date. Besides that I felt like I owed him for believing in me as a writer when I didn't even believe in myself.

"Fine. I'll tell Miguel I'll do it."

"Good. Now, how's that next book coming?"

"Oh fine, it's going fine. I spent a lot of time doing research yesterday, as a matter of fact."

"But you haven't sketched out a plot or worked on an outline yet, right?"

"I've started in my mind. I just don't have much . . . or anything, really, in writing. What's the big hurry? The next book won't come out until a year from this coming spring."

"Well, that's what I want to talk to you about. Clifford & Warren would like to reopen the part of your contract that references publication dates."

"I don't think so, Clinton. I know how long and how hard I had to work to get the first one done. I need a full year to go from zero ideas to a published book."

"Do you really, though? You've got your characters, your setting, you could pick up on the thread about Jo's younger brother and build out from there. Quite a few writers turn out a book every six months."

"I'm very happy for them. And very envious of their superior production skills, which I do not have. Plus I need to do a lot of research when I'm writing fiction."

"What kind of research? You're writing a mystery not a science book."

"It's the journalist in me. I was trained to fact-check."

"If you were writing nonfiction, I'd say that's great to focus on accuracy. But trust me, most readers aren't going to fact-check you. They just want a story that takes them out of their own lives for a little while."

"I understand that. But I'm already asking them to set aside their logical disbelief that a small county in upper Michigan could have so many murders. If they're willing to accept that basic underpinning and enter my pretend world, I don't want them pulled out of it by careless errors or shoddy research. I want my fictional world to feel real—aside from that whole high-body-count thing."

"Very admirable. But listen to Uncle Clinton. You'll sell more books if you have more books to sell. And that's what you want, right? I know it's what I want. I think the first Jo Burke novel will hook your readers. They'll want the next one, pronto. If they have to wait a year, they may move on and forget to come back. There are a lot of books out there competing for attention. How about this, a book every nine months? Like you're pregnant with a book instead of a baby. Think about it."

"That argument is not selling me on the idea. I'll *think* about it, but I'm not promising my thoughts will be good."

"Tell me what I need to hear. Promise me you'll spend some real time thinking through a plot idea. And I know you can produce a book in nine months. You just have to let your inner writer take the lead, instead of your inner naysayer. You can do this!"

"Clinton, you know the sunny side of the street is not my natural habitat. I really don't think that I—"

"Oh, I've got another call coming in. I'll check in later. I know you'll have good news for me!"

And he was gone. Clinton rarely says goodbye. Or hello, for that matter.

I went to my office, opened my laptop, and started work again in earnest. I tried to sketch out a plot, or at least to do some bullet points for an outline. But I didn't have much success corralling my roving thoughts. Mostly because my process leans more toward random and freeform than to the tidy structure of an outline.

The idea of turning out a book in nine months instead of twelve made me nervous. But I owed it to Clinton to at least think through the possibility of doing it. And I did have a murder idea I liked. If I could come up with a cast of suspects and work through their motives and backstories, *maybe* I could organize things enough to commit to a nine-month deadline. I worked diligently until Miguel dropped by.

"Well, well, well," I said after we were both seated at the kitchen island with the chai latte he'd brought for each of us.

"Well, well, well, what?" he asked, his dark brown eyes wide with faux innocence.

"You know what I mean. I talked to Clinton this morning."

"Oh."

"Yes. 'Oh.' Miguel, why did you call him to coerce me into being on your podcast?"

"I want you to be on my podcast, and you keep saying no. I wanted to know what Clinton thought about it."

"Come on, you knew what he'd think. You wanted him to pressure me."

"No, never. Not pressure you. Just persuade you. Did he?"

"You are incorrigible. And yes, he did, more or less. But not until the spring, right before my book comes out. And before that, we'll be setting some ground rules. This will not be an Oprah-style deep dive into my hidden depths. It will be all about the book, maybe a little about the paper, nothing about my personal life."

"Fine, fine. It will be fun. I know you will like it. But are you mad at me?"

I sighed.

"Miguel, I don't think I've ever been mad at you, and that makes you unique among men. My appearance on your podcast is locked in for the spring. Let's let it lie for now."

He nodded and quickly changed the subject.

"I came by to invite you and Coop to Mikey's birthday party at McClain's tonight. Can you come?"

McClain's is a local hangout that reminds me of a bar in a film noir from the forties. It's old and a little seedy, kind of like Mikey the bartender. I like them both.

"Why are you organizing a party for Mikey?"

"Because he told me last week that he's never had a birthday party, not even when he was a little boy. That is not right. So, we're going to surprise him with a cake."

"Who is we?"

"You and Coop, if you can come. Me, Courtnee, my friend Matthew, Gabe said he would come, and I told him to bring someone if he wants to—also Maggie will be there, and your *mamá* and Paul will be there. I might ask a few more people."

"I'm sure you will. But about Gabe, you said he could bring someone. Is he seeing anyone now?"

"I think he is seeing Kristin from the district attorney's office."

"Really? That's nice."

Before Coop and I got together, Gabe and I were in a relationship. I liked him a lot. But I realized I wasn't the right person for him. Mostly because I finally figured out that Coop had been the right person for me since the day we met. I had hurt Gabe badly, and even though we managed to stay friends, I'd felt guilty about it ever since.

"Yes. I was thinking about them for each other, and while I was thinking, Gabe and Kristin got together. Not everyone needs my expertise in the ways of romance. Not like you and Coop did. That was a hard case, getting you two together. But I did it."

The satisfied note in his voice made me laugh—and protest.

"No, I think *we* got ourselves together."

"Ah, but that is the beauty of my work—it all happens under the surface. It looks like fate, but it's really Miguel. That's why they call me the doctor of love."

"Miguel, I've told you before, nobody calls you that except you."

"Maybe not but they should."

"Since you're so skilled in relationship management, maybe you can do something for Jennifer. I know she's lonely. John was an asshat as a husband, and he's even worse as an ex, but she loved him once. She misses what she thought she had. It would be nice if she could find it for real."

"Don't worry about Jennifer. Dr. Love will come through for her. I am on the case."

"Good. I turn it over to your expert handling, Doctor. In the meantime, I'll come tonight, but Coop can't. He's got a dinner in Hailwell. What time does the party start?"

"Be there by 6:45. When Mikey comes in at seven, we will bring out his cake and sing to him."

I got to McClain's early—as is my way, usually, and sat down at the bar to wait until the others arrived. I had just taken the first sip of my Jameson when someone clapped me on the shoulder.

I turned and looked into a pair of smiling blue eyes.

"Andrew! I haven't seen you in forever!"

I jumped off the barstool so I could give him a quick hug. Then I rubbed my hand lightly over his buzzcut sandy-blond hair.

"Still got that Jason Statham look going, don't you? Sit down, I'll buy you a drink."

Andrew Jones had been a neighbor when I was in kindergarten and he was in high school. He'd been extremely patient with five-year-old me. I followed him like a little duckling whenever I spotted him in the yard and peppered him with a million questions. He taught me how to ride my bike without training wheels. I had planned on having him marry me when I grew up, but he joined the Marines before I reached third grade.

His sister still lives in town, so I see Andrew occasionally, but it had been at least a couple of years since we'd run into each other.

"Sounds good, but I can't stay. I'm only here to drop my dog off at my sister's. Did she tell you I'm not in the Marines anymore?"

"She did. She said you're a project manager or something important like that for a big consulting firm. Is that right?"

"I don't know about the important part, but yeah. I like it. Like the travel too, but it's hard on my dog. I've got a regular sitter, but he had to cancel, so Diana offered to take care of him."

"Oh, come on. You can stay for a little bit, can't you? We're having a surprise birthday celebration for Mikey. You remember Mikey, don't you?"

"Who could forget him? Sorry, I would if I could, but I've still got a few things to do for the trip. And I'm catching a red eye out of Milwaukee tonight. I'll be back next week, though. Let's catch up then. I'll buy you a drink when I get back."

"I'll hold you to that."

"Good! Tell Mikey happy birthday for me and have a good time at your party."

I saw Miguel heading toward the bar as Andrew left. When he reached me, he said, "Who was that man I saw you hugging?"

"Don't get excited. It's not an old flame. It was Andrew, Diana Nielsen's brother. I invited him to join the party, but he couldn't stay."

"That is too bad. The party will be very fun."

And it was. Mikey was both touched and surprised, especially when everyone in the bar joined in on the Happy Birthday song. We ate, we drank, we laughed, we had a great time. Just like the passengers on the *Titanic* before it hit the iceberg.

8

I had been judicious enough with partying that I had no trouble waking up on Wednesday morning and getting right back to work. In fact, the partying seemed to have clarified my thinking. I finally had a workable idea for the murder in my second book. I began the more focused research I needed to do to make sure my killing method would actually work. I'd been at it for a couple of hours when Sam jumped on my desk and began walking across my keyboard—his unsubtle demand for attention.

I stopped to give him some head rubs, but his meowing told me that I had misinterpreted the signals. I looked at my watch and realized he was after a treat, not my affection. Sam's new vet recommended I feed him only twice a day and limit him to one or two treats. I'd been pretty good about it. But as a result, if I'm home, Sam is very insistent on his noontime Fishy Favorites.

"Okay, okay," I said. "Hold on a second. I'll get you one."

He followed at my heels as I went to the cupboard, where sad news awaited.

"Uh-oh, Sam, we're out. I forgot to get them when I picked up groceries. I'm sorry."

He gave me a disgusted stare that clearly said, *"Well, Leah, I see you didn't forget to pick up your Oreos, did you?"*

Then he flicked his tail at me and walked huffily over to the window seat.

"All right. I'll go get some. Seriously, I'll be right back."

He refused to look at me, but I knew if I returned bearing treats, he would forgive me. We're very alike that way. There aren't many disappointments I won't forgive if the apology comes in the form of a brownie.

I really did intend to zip to the store and come right back, but there was a fender bender blocking traffic on my normal route home. The detour led me past the apartment building where one of my favorite people lives— Father Lindstrom, the parish priest at St. Stephens. I don't partake of organized religion myself, but if I were ever to do so, it would probably be because of him.

On impulse, I decided to pop in for a quick visit. Sometimes on Wednesdays he makes sourdough bread that's every bit as good as you can get at Madison Sour Dough—which is very good indeed. That isn't the reason I visit him fairly regularly, but it is a nice bonus.

When I reached his block, I saw Luke Granger walking from the opposite direction, heading toward Father Lindstrom's building. The two of them had kind of a lunchtime sci-fi book club because they're both big fans of the genre. I decided not to stop after all. With the current stressors in Luke's life, he could probably use a little one-to-one time with Father.

"Well, Sam, you're in luck," I said out loud. "I really will be right home with your treat."

Hearing myself speak gave me pause. Talking out loud to myself is a longtime habit. And talking to a pet is very common. But talking out loud to a cat who wasn't even there? Maybe I had skipped crazy cat lady and gone straight to crazy.

As I got closer, I slowed and rolled down my window to call out to Luke.

"Luke! Hey, did you get the money you need for the bookstore yet? I've been sending positive thoughts your way since you told me about it Monday."

He looked up with the startled expression of a person who had been lost in thought.

"What?"

I came to a stop and leaned out as he walked to the car. I wondered if I'd put my foot in it, if the funds he'd hoped for hadn't materialized. Maybe he was on his way to talk to Father Lindstrom about that.

"Luke, did you get bad news? Did the money you were hoping for fall through?"

"No, no. I was just daydreaming. Things are looking good. I'll know by tomorrow. Keep those good vibes coming."

"I sure will. Oops, I'm blocking traffic. I'll see you later."

He smiled then and lifted his hand in a quick wave before he turned and hurried back across the street.

That evening, Sam and I enjoyed a quiet dinner. Coop and I spend quite a few nights together, sometimes planned, sometimes spontaneous, but we each maintain our own homes. I like things the way they are—my space, his space, and regular times when we share those spaces. Coop would like us to share the same place, all the time. There's a line from a poem that my mother occasionally recites, "Something there is that doesn't love a wall . . ." But in my case it's more like, "Something there is that doesn't love a shared house." We've tabled discussion of the topic for now.

Wednesday night, after a hard day's thinking and researching to see if my idea could be made into a plot, I was very content to put on my pj's, make a cup of tea, and sit on my window seat with Sam. It wasn't long before the soft music of the Christmas playlist I'd chosen, the purring of Sam, and the warmth of the chamomile tea conspired to cause my eyes to close and my head to droop. The third time it happened, I gave in.

"Okay, Sam. Time to wrap up another rollicking evening at the homestead. I know it's only nine o'clock, and you've been napping most of the day, but I have to go to bed. You can come when you're ready."

Almost as soon as I pulled up the covers, I fell into a deep and dreamless sleep. I was startled awake by the simultaneous sound of sirens on the

street below and my cell phone jumping around on my nightstand as it
both vibrated and loudly rang.

"Miguel, what's going on?" I asked as I answered my phone.

"The library is on fire!"

"What? Our library? The library is on fire? How bad is it, Miguel?"

I hit speaker so I could keep talking with him as I leapt from bed and
grabbed my jeans and a hoodie. I began pulling them over my pajamas.

"The storage area is fully engulfed. It looks bad, but I haven't talked to
anyone from the fire department yet. They're too busy trying to put it out.
I'm taking photos and shooting video. Some people have started coming to
see what's happening."

"Count me as one of them. I'll be right there."

I glanced at the time and temperature on my watch. Almost 11:30 p.m.
And a chilly twenty-eight degrees. I laced up my boots, put another layer on
before I grabbed my jacket, said a quick goodbye to a disgruntled Sam, ran
out my door, and pounded down the stairs.

9

Multiple fire trucks were at the scene when I arrived. Police had established a perimeter a safe distance from the fire and worked to keep the growing crowd of onlookers behind it. I spotted Coop's SUV but couldn't pick him out in the crowd. I saw Miguel at the front of the barricades, and I elbowed my way up to him.

"How long have you been here? When did the fire start? Is it still confined to the storage area?"

"The call came in to the fire department at 10:55. I got here about twenty minutes ago."

"Have you talked to Al yet?"

Al Porter is the chief of the Himmel Fire Department. Unlike some fire chiefs I've worked with over the years, he understands that journalists have a job to do, too. As long as we don't get in the way, he's always been a cooperative source.

"Just for one second. He told me when the fire is more under control, he'll give me what he can. But Miss Fillhart is here, and I talked to her. She's very upset. The storage area is where they keep janitor supplies, art supplies, gallons of hand sanitizer. The used books for the Library Friends book sale are stored there, too. So are holiday decorations, old files in banker boxes—"

"In other words, once the fire got started, there was plenty to feed it. Poor Claudia, she must be beside herself."

Just then, I noticed the librarian standing alone, staring at the fire, a look of disbelief on her face.

"Miguel, I'm going over to talk to her. I saw Coop's SUV here when I pulled up. He might be able to give you something. I'm sure he's talked to Al. Have you posted anything online yet?"

"Just a short video and that firefighters are at the scene, with more details to come."

"Good man."

~

"Claudia! Claudia!"

I had nearly reached her when I called out, but she didn't turn around. The whooshing sound of hoses being deployed, the pops and loud cracks coming from the burning building, and the excited chatter of the crowd made it impossible for Claudia to hear me until I was right next to her.

When she saw me, she grabbed my arm and squeezed it so tightly I almost yelped in pain.

"Leah, I can't believe it. The library—if they can't stop the fire in the storage area, the whole library will go. All our collections. The historical documents, the old newspapers. The equipment. I told the city council we should have a sprinkler system in the storage area, like we do in the rest of the library. But they said no."

"Why?"

"Budget concerns. They said sprinkler systems are to save people, not things. That no one was in the storage area for any length of time—people just take things out or put things away there. So we wouldn't need it to save a life. Also that the chances of a fire were small anyway, since the wiring in the whole library was upgraded when we built the addition. The council said a sprinkler system in the storage area didn't meet the cost/benefit standard. But if the fire door between the storage area and the main library doesn't hold ... Oh, I can't bear to think about it."

Claudia is usually a calm and steady presence in any situation—unsupervised children running amuck among the shelves, querulous patrons upset when they exceed their allotted time on Ancestry, PPOK members at the circulation desk shouting and waving lists of books they want banned. She takes it all in stride. But the fire at the library was a level of terrible that she wasn't prepared for.

I put my arms around her in a hug. Her breath caught, and then she gave a long, shuddery sigh. I could tell she was trying to hold back tears.

"Oh, Claudia. Hey, hey now, it's going to be fine," I said, patting her gently on the back. "We've got a great fire department. I saw that Omico's department is here helping, too. They'll get the fire out before it breaches the door. I know they will."

I didn't know any such thing, but I tried to sound confident, and I hoped I was right.

She sniffed loudly and pulled a tissue from the pocket of her jacket as she stepped away from me.

"I'm sorry, Leah. You're right. I just needed to fall apart for a minute, but I'm okay now," she said, giving me a watery smile. "It's just such a shock. But if the fire can be kept to the storage area, nothing we lose there is irreplaceable. I'm grateful that it happened at night when no one was in the library. That's some consolation."

"Yes, it is. And see," I said gesturing toward the blaze, "the flames have come down a lot in the last few minutes. It looks like they're about to go into the building."

Claudia got a call on her cell phone then. She looked at the screen and said, "It's Tim, wondering what's happening, I'm sure. He'll be worried about me if I don't take it," she said.

"Of course. I'll catch you later."

Claudia's husband Tim uses a wheelchair to get around, and that was no doubt why he wasn't there. As I left, I spotted Coop in the crowd and headed toward him.

~

Coop saw me coming and met me halfway.

"Coop, what do you know about what's going on? Claudia told Miguel there are a lot of flammable supplies in the storage area, plus tons of paper and used books. That must be why the fire took off so fast. Any idea what started it?"

"How it started is taking a back seat to how to put it out. It could be a while before the cause is determined. But I'll bet everyone on the council is squirming about their decision not to install sprinklers."

"They should be."

"Coop, Coop!"

Claudia was running toward us, a panicked expression on her face.

"What is it? Claudia, what's wrong?" I asked.

"His car. It's in the parking lot. He's not. His mother hasn't—"

Out of breath from her jog over to us, she kept tripping over her words.

"Claudia, take a deep breath," Coop said.

She swallowed hard and tried again.

"I just talked to Tim. He said Luke Granger's mother called the house, trying to reach me. She heard about the fire and went to tell Luke. Only he's not home. She wanted to know if he was here."

"I haven't seen—"

"No, no, that's not it. Luke's car. I didn't notice it before, but I looked just now. It's still here, in the parking lot across the street. That's where he always parks."

I'm here to tell you, the expression "my blood ran cold" isn't just a cliché. I felt as though the frigid night air was pouring through my veins.

"You don't think—" Before I could finish the awful ending to that sentence, a shout came from the crowd watching the fire.

"Look! Look!"

We all turned as one toward the building. Two firefighters emerged carrying something the size and shape of an adult body.

For a moment, everyone was still. Then Claudia's voice broke the silence.

"Luke, oh no, it's got to be Luke. His car. It's still across the street. He shouldn't have been here. He leaves at ten. He always leaves at ten. I don't understand. Why was he still here?"

Her voice seemed to unleash the pent-up horror and disbelief of the moment. Everyone began talking at once.

Coop leaned toward me so I could hear him above the din of the crowd.

"Leah, can you take Claudia to my SUV? There's a blanket on the back seat and a thermos of coffee in the front. She needs to get warm, though it's probably the shock more than the cold that's affecting her."

I saw then that Claudia had begun shivering violently.

"Yes, sure," I said.

"I'm going over to talk to Owen and Al, see what I can do to help. Maybe just get the crowd away from here. Stay with Claudia, would you, until I can get there?"

"Of course," I said.

He tossed me his keys and left to find Owen Fike, the Himmel police captain, and Al. I put an arm around Claudia's shaking shoulders and led her to the SUV.

10

Claudia sat quivering without speaking while I turned on the engine, wrapped the blanket from the back seat around her, and handed her some coffee from Coop's thermos.

"Come on, drink it. It'll help you warm up faster," I said.

She nodded, but her hand was shaky as she lifted the cup to her mouth and took a small sip. She put it down in the console holder and pulled the blanket tighter around herself.

I was shaken at the news about Luke, too. But for me, it was a generalized sense of sadness at the loss of someone so young with so many possibilities ahead of him. It was different for Claudia—she knew Luke very well, and for her, it was a particular and personal loss.

I continued to sit in silence with her, waiting until she was ready to speak.

Finally, she reached for her cup of coffee and took a larger sip. Then she said, in pretty much her normal voice, "Poor Mrs. Granger. I need to call her back. I should—"

"No, Claudia, you don't have to do that. I'm sure, if it is Luke, that Owen or Al will send someone to tell her personally. And they'll have more information to give her. You can call or visit her tomorrow. You've had a major

shock. Give yourself a little breathing space. And we still don't know for
sure that it's Luke."

"Leah, please. You don't have to treat me like I'm made of glass. I know
that so far I haven't acquitted myself very well. But I'm steady now. You
know it's Luke, and so do I. Who else could it be? He was working tonight.
His car is still in the parking lot. He didn't come home."

She paused before going on, but when she did, her voice was strong.

"I've known Luke almost his entire life. His mother used to bring him to
the library for story hour. As he got older, he'd ride his bike here for Lego
Club and the summer reading program. And he couldn't get enough of the
Harry Potter series. He was always a great reader." She paused and smiled
at the memory before going on.

"I didn't see him much when he got to high school. He made some bad
choices after his father died, though that was understandable. When he
came back to town, I think he was looking for a do-over. He was so bright,
Leah. And he was a very kind person, too."

"I didn't know him like you did, but I always enjoyed talking to him at
the bookstore. And I loved it when he and Father Lindstrom would have a
verbal throw-down about the merits of Star Trek versus Star Wars . . . It's
sort of hard to believe he was part of the Granger family."

"Yes, Luke was certainly cut from a different bolt of cloth than most of
the Grangers. You know, I tried to talk him into going to college and
pursuing a degree in library science. He loved books so much. He told me
once that reading saved his life."

"I know the feeling."

"But when I suggested college, he just laughed and said he couldn't deal
with all the BS of higher education. He told me he was pursuing education
on his own. He kept a life list, like birdwatchers do, only it consisted of the
books he'd read and the ones he wanted to read before he died. He said
that was all the education he needed."

She talked about Luke as though she were a proud parent. Maybe, on
some level I hadn't realized, she was.

"No wonder he liked working in the bookstore so much."

"Oh, he did, didn't he? Marcus was so good for him, and to him. When
he offered Luke the chance to buy the bookstore, Luke felt like he'd been

offered the keys to the kingdom. And he worked so hard to earn the money he needed for a down payment. He was crushed when the bank turned down his loan application. I hate to think that the very last days he spent on earth were filled with so much disappointment and unhappiness."

"But I don't think they were, Claudia. I saw him on Monday. He told me there was a good chance he'd be able to get the money. He seemed very hopeful and upbeat. Happy, even."

"Oh, is that really true? I'd like to think so."

"Yes, it's true, Claudia."

"That's good. That's good," she repeated.

We fell silent again. I couldn't stop my thoughts from turning to Miller Caldwell's sudden death a few months earlier. They brought with them the sharp pang of loss that plagued me less often than it had, but still showed up regularly, especially in moments like this.

"I don't understand, though," Claudia said when she spoke again.

"You mean why death is so random? Why someone like Luke, who was on the brink of such a positive turn in his life would be snatched away? I wonder, too. But it happens all the time."

"No, I don't mean from an existential perspective. The thought that keeps coming to my mind now is more practical. Why was Luke at the library when the fire started? His shift ended at ten. The alarm didn't come in until 10:55. Al Porter told me himself."

"Maybe he stayed late to finish up something?"

"The janitorial service we contract with doesn't sanction overtime. Luke has—had—to use an app on his phone to clock in and out for his shift. He got a written warning when he worked overtime once. And I made him promise not to work off-the-clock just to get something done. He didn't make enough money to feel like he owed his soul to S&S Janitorial Services."

"Claudia, you sound surprisingly militant!" I said, teasing her gently.

I was rewarded with a small smile so fleeting I almost missed it.

"My father was a union man to the day he died. Mother said he taught me to say 'A fair day's wage for a fair days' work' as soon as I could talk. That might be a true story, knowing my dad."

"But isn't it possible that Luke might have worked extra anyway, some nights, if he thought it would help you out?"

"Well, yes. I know he did a few times, but that was last year when we were short-staffed on the circulation desk for a few weeks. I'd come in, and the returned books cart that was full the night before would be empty. I asked Luke about it. He said he couldn't be sure, but he thought he'd caught a glimpse of the book-return fairy coming in as he was leaving. I know he worked off-the-clock to help out. But we're in good shape staff-wise right now. There wasn't anything for him to do but his janitor work."

The door on my side of the vehicle opened, and Coop poked his head in. I could tell immediately what he was going to say. Claudia could, too. She began to cry.

11

Much later, back at my place, I fixed a Jameson for myself and one for Coop. He's usually a beer kind of guy, but it felt like the situation called for something stronger. He didn't disagree when I handed it to him.

"I'm not going to ask a stupid question like 'How did Luke's mother take the news?' I'm sure she was devastated. But are you okay? Talking to Ellen Granger must have been brutal."

"Yeah, I'm all right. But I'm never going to get used to delivering that kind of news."

"Why did *you* have to do it? The fire investigation falls under Al and Owen, doesn't it?"

"Yeah. Mostly Al and his team. But I know Ellen Granger. She worked at Family Pharmacy when I did in high school. She's a nice lady. I thought it might help if she had someone she knew tell her."

"Did it?"

He sighed heavily before he answered. "Not really. When you have to tell a mother that we believe her son died in a fire, but his body was so badly burned we're going to need dental records to be sure, there's no way to make it even the tiniest bit easier to hear."

"It's so horrific. What a terrible way to die. But you're a thousand percent sure, right? I mean, there's no chance it isn't Luke? "

"Leah, I know this is really hard for you, given how your sister Annie died. But there wasn't a happy ending for your family then, and I'm afraid there isn't going to be one for Luke's mother either. Mistaken identity plot twists don't happen very often in real life. His car was still at the library. He didn't call his mom to say he wasn't coming home for the night—which she said he always did."

"I know you're right. I just don't want it to be him."

"No one does. Connie will do the autopsy first thing, so Luke's mother can know for sure. Paul Karr has the dental records. That will cinch it."

I remembered the night Annie had died in a fire. And what her death had done to my dad and my mom—and to me. I had nightmares about that night for a long time.

"I hate that Luke's mother will have to know not only that her son is dead, but that he died in such a painful, horrible way. Coop, do you think it's possible someone deliberately set the fire? Just a few days ago, you said that things with PPOK could turn dangerous."

"I was thinking more along the lines of physical violence, not arson. It's a big leap from picketing and shouting to burning down a building. Arson itself is a Class C felony. If anyone dies as a result, that bumps it up to Class B. So, if someone set the fire, they're looking at up to sixty years in prison."

"But if you're really mad, and you think you're really right, and you can't get people in power to do what you want, maybe you're too wrapped up in your rightness to think about the consequences—or to care. Or maybe you do care, but you think you're too smart to get caught."

"I hope that's not the case. That would really tear the town up."

"How long before we know how and when the fire started?"

"At least a couple of days, possibly longer. Maybe never."

Sam, who had been sitting contentedly on the window seat jumped down then and walked over to the doorway into my bedroom. He turned and stared pointedly at me, then let out several loud meows.

"Sam is telling us it's time for bed."

"I agree. I'm beat. There's no point in speculating about the fire. We'll find out more in the next few days."

We did, but what we learned was something no one expected.

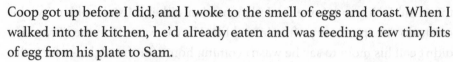

Coop got up before I did, and I woke to the smell of eggs and toast. When I walked into the kitchen, he'd already eaten and was feeding a few tiny bits of egg from his plate to Sam.

"Want some breakfast?" he asked.

"No, I'm not that hungry. I think I'll take a shower now and eat later. Thanks, though. Also, you're spoiling Sam. He's going to expect eggs every morning."

"No, I'm winning him over to my side. We've been discussing things, and he's willing to advocate for me, provided I make it worth his while. The egg is my first bribe."

"What side is that?"

"The side that thinks it would be easier if we lived together, instead of spending random nights with each other and having to keep a second set of clothes and personal items at each other's places."

"Don't try to turn my cat against me. Sam cannot be bought for a bit of egg," I said, though the purring and head-butting he was lavishing on Coop seemed to give the lie to that statement.

"Anyway, I thought we were done talking about moving in together. I love you madly, isn't that enough? But I want to keep my own space. It took a lot for me to get here. I'm not ready to give it up."

"But you wouldn't have to give up your own space. I'd make a space for you that would be just yours, either at my place now or at whatever place I find to buy and fix up."

"Who said I'd move into your house? Why wouldn't you move in here?"

"Is that an invitation? Because if it is, I'd be willing to rent a construction trailer to hold all my woodworking tools, fishing gear, and my other stuff. I could put it in the parking lot here."

"It was not an invitation. You know, you agreed to just let this whole moving-in together thing lie for a while. Why are you bringing it up again so soon?"

"Because the death of a guy just a few years younger than me feels like a flashing reminder that life moves pretty fast. You don't know how many tomorrows you have. I want to go to sleep with you beside me every night, and I want you to be the first person I see every morning. Is that such a bad thing?"

He had put his hand on mine while he spoke, and his dark gray eyes were so serious I knew I couldn't turn the discussion away with a joke.

"That is a lovely thing to say. Thank you. But—"

"There's always a but, isn't there?"

"About this, and for now anyway, yes. Coop, I just know in my gut it's not right for me right now. I'm not ready. But it makes me feel bad to make you feel bad every time I say no. But bottom line is, I just can't do it now. I'm sorry."

He nodded, then leaned over to kiss me.

"Well, in *my* gut, I know it's right for us. But okay. End of discussion." He got up and put his plate in the dishwasher, changing topics as he did. "I'm going to stop and talk to Owen and Al to see what's going on. I'll call you if there's anything significant."

"Thanks. I'm going to call Father Lindstrom. He and Luke were good friends, and maybe he'd like to talk about him a little. Priests need someone to talk to, too, don't they?"

"I think God fills that function for them, but God with a side of Leah might be welcome."

"Thanks, I think. Hey, come for dinner tonight, since you made breakfast."

"Sure. Can I bring anything? A couple of takeout menus?"

"You're hilarious. No, I'm going to make curried cranberry chicken. You love that."

"I love it when your mom makes it."

"I watched very carefully the last time she did. I'm ready to go solo, and you will be eating your words along with your delicious dinner."

"I can't wait."

"I'm going to choose to believe that you're being sincere. I'll see you tonight. You'll be able to find your way here by the delectable smell of the dinner I'll be cooking."

12

When I got to the Elite Café and Bakery for my coffee date with Father Lindstrom, I was surprised to see the place was packed, which was unusual for 9:30 on a weekday. Typically by then, the breakfasters have left and the coffee-breakers haven't arrived. But from the buzz of conversation, I knew people had gathered to talk about the fire.

"Leah, the Father is over in the corner. I bring you chai and apple walnut muffin. Still warm. You will love it," said the Elite's owner, Clara Schimelman, from behind the counter. Her confidence was justified. I've never eaten anything at the Elite that I haven't loved.

"Thanks, Mrs. Schimelman. But I think I'll have a coffee instead of chai. I could use the caffeine boost. It was a late night last night."

"Oh, ya. So sad about Luke. Such a nice boy. Last time I see him, he was so happy. Talking to me all about his books. And he was so handsome, too. So many girlfriends that one had, always with a new one. But," she said with a shrug of her plump shoulders, "he was young. He should have fun. Now you . . . you should settle down, get married to Coop."

"Oh, no. We're not going there today. Anyway, I'm young, too. Why should I settle down?"

"Because Coop, he is your OTP."

"What's an OTP?"

She shook her head at my ignorance. Mrs. Schimelman is very into teen slang—perhaps as a result of the high school crowd that congregates in the Elite after school. Despite living in Himmel for more than thirty years, she still retains a strong German accent, and the contrast between it and the latest buzzwords is sometimes quite funny.

"OTP is One True Pairing. Keep up, Leah, I know I tell you that before. You have your OTP. Now you are just wasting time. Luke, he was still looking. But oh, I feel very bad for his mama. She is a good lady. It is very hard to lose your child. She will never get over it."

"You're right. You don't ever get over the loss of someone you love. If you're lucky, though, you can get through it eventually."

Unexpectedly, her eyes filled with tears. At that moment, I realized I knew almost nothing about her. She was very friendly but, at the same time, very private.

"Ya, for sure you are right. But it is always here," she said, covering her heart with one hand.

A tear escaped and ran down her cheek as she spoke. She pulled the ever-present white dish towel off her ample shoulder and dabbed her eyes.

I reached out and gave her other hand a light squeeze.

She nodded, and when she spoke, it was with a return to her usual heartiness. "You're a good girl, too, Leah. But very *stur*—that means stubborn in German. Good thing for you Coop is very patient. But you are not getting younger. And Coop, he is a thirst trap, that one. You don't want another like Rebecca to find him."

"Thank you for the advice. You know how much I value it. I'm just going to go and talk to Father Lindstrom now."

She laughed and swatted the air in my direction with her towel. "Oh, ya, I

know how you value it. But is okay. I still give it to you for free. You go. I send your muffin and coffee over."

~

Father Lindstrom stood as I approached the table and pulled a chair out for me. He has old-fashioned manners which are very nice.

"Hi, Father. How are you doing? I'm so sorry about Luke Granger. I know the two of you were good friends."

"Thank you, Leah. Yes, we were," he said with a sad smile.

"How did you get to know Luke? Through the bookstore?" I asked as I settled down across from him.

"No, I've known him since he was a child. His family wasn't part of the parish, but his father was a handyman who did odd jobs around the rectory. He sometimes brought Luke with him."

"I didn't realize you went back that far."

"After his father died, I was transferred to St. Mary's. I didn't see Luke again until he came back to the area a few years ago, around the time I came back to St. Stephens after Father Sanderson died. I was in the bookstore, looking for a book on the *X-Files* that my brother had told me about. You know I'm very fond of that show."

"Oh, I do know. I'm surprised you don't carry your coffee mug with the disappearing *X-Files* logo on it with you," I said. We have a running joke about his fanboy devotion to the show.

"I would if I wasn't afraid it would get broken," he said. "It turned out Luke was a fan, too. He helped me find the book. We got into a conversation about the series and then about science fiction books we loved. That's how we reconnected. We had lunch every few weeks, you know, and talked about what we were reading. I enjoyed our friendship very much."

"I'm glad you got to see him yesterday."

"I didn't see Luke. I wish I had. I hadn't talked with him in several weeks. I had to cancel our lunch for this week. We were scheduled to meet next Wednesday instead."

"Oh. When I saw him yesterday, he was right outside your apartment. I just assumed he was going to see you."

His eyes looked so sad that I realized then how thoughtless I'd been. Instead of comforting Father, I'd given him something to "if only" about—if only he hadn't cancelled their lunch; if only he'd stopped by the bookstore this week, if only, if only, if only.

"Wow. I don't always find the right words, but I just hit it out of the ballpark with the absolute wrong ones. I'm sorry, Father. I asked you to meet me for coffee today because you're always there when I need to talk. I thought maybe I could return the favor and listen to you for a change. Instead, I just made you feel bad that you didn't get to see Luke one last time."

"It's not you who is making me feel bad. It's the full realization that we'll never have lunch together again, never argue about the merits of Star Wars again, and the next time I go into the bookstore, he won't be there to greet me. It's the process of accepting the loss of Luke that hurts. And I'm very touched that you reached out to comfort me."

I didn't know what to say, so I didn't say anything. When he spoke again, Father Lindstrom chose to focus on the facts and not his feelings about the tragedy.

"Do you know what happened? How the fire started, and how Luke got trapped in the building?" he asked.

"It was confined to the storage area, so that's one good thing amid the awfulness. But the storage area was the stuff an arsonist's dreams are made of. Lots of flammable materials—plenty of fuel to get a fire going."

"Arsonist? Is there a thought that the fire was set by someone?"

"At this point, it's just my own speculation, nothing official yet. But you know as well as I do that PPOK's rhetoric has ramped up a lot in the last few weeks. It's possible they decided to take some action to shake things up and didn't realize anyone was in the building. Luke wasn't supposed to be. His shift ended at ten, and the alarm came in just before eleven. He should have been gone."

"Oh, I hope you're wrong about PPOK. That would be a grave thing for any of them to carry on their conscience."

Our coffee and muffins arrived just then. Mrs. Schimelman joked a little with us, and when she left, our talk turned to other things. I said something that made Father laugh, and that's always satisfying to me. He said some things that made me think, which I believe is satisfying to him. I hadn't found any profound thoughts to share to ease his pain, but I realized that wasn't what he needed from me. Just being a friend—not giving advice, not trying to fix things, just being there was enough.

13

I bypassed the newsroom when I got back to my place. I didn't feel like hashing everything over just then. I knew Miguel or Maggie would relay any important news to me.

Sam greeted me at the door with a welcoming meow.

"Hey, did you miss me?" I asked as I scooped him up for a quick snuggle. "I'll meet you on the window seat. I'm going to make a cup of tea and sit for a while before I start working. I didn't get much sleep last night."

Sam was already asleep, or pretending to be, when I walked over and claimed my spot. The hot tea in the thick mug warmed my hands, and as I sipped slowly and looked around, the luckiness of living where I do began to relax me a little—or maybe it was the lack of sleep.

My apartment wasn't designed specifically for me, but it couldn't be a better fit if it had been. The exposed brick wall, the smooth wooden floors, the kitchen with its granite-topped island, the gas fireplace in the living room, my office—I love them all. But, like Sam, I enjoy the window seat the most. It sits beneath three tall arched windows and gives me an excellent vantage point on the street below.

From my favorite corner, leaning back against a pillow, I watched cars moving on the street below. I noted a few pedestrians on the sidewalk braving the increasing snowfall, and the steady flow of customers in and out of Woke coffeeshop across the street. The almost rhythmic movements below me had a hypnotic effect. My eyelids began to droop. I put my cup of tea down, and Sam came over to sit on my lap. We both napped for a while.

When I woke up, Sam jumped off me, and I went to the kitchen to make some lunch. After I washed my hands and had opened a can of tuna, Sam began rubbing against my leg and purring.

"Don't think I don't know what you're doing," I said, glancing down at him. "You never look up at me that adoringly unless I'm wearing essence of tuna. You're only supposed to eat two times a day."

He meowed in protest. I ran my finger around the inside of the empty can and picked up a few bits to share. He licked them from my finger with great delicacy. Then he gave me a look designed to melt my heart and result in more treats. When it did not, he abandoned me and went back to the window seat. I had just finished my sandwich when my phone rang. The caller's name on the screen caused me to answer with pleased surprise.

"Charlotte! It's good to hear from you."

"Hi, Leah. I just wanted to let you know I'm coming back to Himmel tomorrow. I'll be there around 4:30 or so. Could you meet me for dinner at Dad's house around 6:30? I'll be staying there until we decide what to do with it. I'd like to get the nonprofit plan for the paper back on track."

"Wow. Okay, if you're ready, I'm ready. But are you sure you want to dive back into things right away? Are you doing all right?"

She hesitated a little before answering. Charlotte Caldwell and her brother, Sebastian, had lost their father, Miller, in the most cruel and unexpected way. I felt the loss of him keenly as a friend and business partner. Obviously, it was an even sharper pain for his daughter.

When she spoke, her voice had lost its practical, let's-get-on-with-it tone.

"To be honest, it's pretty hard some days, Leah. I've tried to be strong for Sebastian and that's helped me hold myself together. I'm glad I decided to go back to Chicago with him. It was important for us to spend some time with each other. But now I need to get back to work, and Baz needs to get back to law school. But I still miss Dad like hell." Her voice quavered a little at the end of her sentence.

"Anyway," she began again, "I guess the accurate thing to say is that I'm okay now, mostly. But sometimes at night, instead of falling asleep, I fall apart thinking about Dad and everything he was and did. I wonder how I'm ever going to take his place in the business, in the family, in the community. It's a lot, and it kind of scares me. I don't want to let anyone down."

"Charlotte, Miller was an exceptional person. His death left a huge hole in the community. But the lucky thing is, he raised an exceptional daughter. Your dad wouldn't expect you to take his place. He'd want you to make it your own place. And you'll do that. Miss your father, mourn him, carry on his work, but don't ever think you have to be him or do things exactly as he would. No one else expects that of you. Don't put that burden on yourself."

I'd been trying to reassure her, but instead I could hear her crying.

"Hey, it's okay, Charlotte. I'm sorry. For someone who uses words to make a living, I've been pretty clumsy with them today. I didn't mean—"

"No, Leah. I'm crying because I still can't help it whenever someone says something really kind and touching like you just did. Thank you. For everything. I'm fine, really."

She blew her nose, and when she spoke again, she was in control.

"And I know I'm not the only one who's missing him, or who has a big load to carry. You, and Maggie, and Miguel, and Troy, and your mother have done a great job at the paper. I know that I basically left everyone hanging when I left town right after making the big pitch to turn the *Times* into a nonprofit organization. But I'm ready to come back now and give the paper the attention it deserves."

"We'll be glad to have you back. But don't rush it. We're still bumping along all right."

"But we're not, not really. You all are doing everything possible—and more. But the financials are still not good. The *Times* meant so much to Dad. I think he'd want me to make that a priority. So, are we on for dinner at 6:30 at Dad's? I'll pick something up for us."

"Sure, that sounds good. Oh, hey, Charlotte did you hear about the fire at the library last night?"

"No! I had so many errands to run getting ready to leave I haven't checked the *Times* website yet. How bad was it?"

"Really bad. The storage area is gone, and someone was killed. Luke

Granger. You might know him. He worked at Buy the Book, but he had a part-time job as night janitor at the library."

"Sure, I knew Luke. I'm so sorry to hear that. He was a really nice person."

"Yeah, he was."

I filled her in with the few details I had.

"Poor Miss Fillhart. She must be devastated. I'll call her when I get back and see if there's something the Caldwell Foundation can do to help."

"That sounds exactly like something your father would do," I said.

"That's the nicest thing you could have said to me. Well, I'll let you go. I still have a lot of packing to do. Oh—wait! I can't believe I almost forgot. I had a call from Marilyn Karr. She heard that we were considering moving the paper to nonprofit status. She's interested in serving on the board. That could be really good. She has a lot of influence in the community and lots of connections we could use in the philanthropic world. What do you think?"

Charlotte's announcement generated many, many thoughts in my head, none of them pleasant. I held back with an effort.

"Wow, that's a surprise! Marilyn doesn't have any journalism experience. It seems odd she'd be interested in serving on the board."

"Well, board members don't have to have direct experience in the field. They won't be making daily newsroom decisions. They'll be there to provide strategic guidance. There'll be others on the board who have journalism expertise. You, for one. Marilyn has plenty of fundraising experience. And plenty of money, too, so that's a plus. I'm sorry, Leah, I've really got to go. We'll have a lot to talk about tomorrow. I'll see you at 6:30. I'm looking forward to it. Bye!"

"Yeah, bye, Charlotte."

14

After the unsettling news about Marilyn Karr, who is the founder and president of the Leah Nash Must Die Society, I couldn't stop thinking about how terrible it would be to have her involved with the *Times* in any capacity. Charlotte was right. Marilyn is a wealthy woman of influence who could do good things for the board. However, I was pretty certain that she would not. And that she could and probably would instead do great harm.

I began doing the prep for my curried cranberry chicken to give my racing thoughts a place to go. I don't cook because I enjoy it. I cook because I like eating things. Most of the time, I satisfy that need with fast food, pizza, the Piggly Wiggly deli counter, or something my mom drops off for me. But once in a while, instead of opting for any of those fine choices, I feel the urge to create an actual homemade meal.

But the chopping of peppers and onion did not settle my mind. We— Miller, Charlotte, and I—had started discussing the possibility of the *Times* going nonprofit just before Miller died. A number of struggling small-town papers have had success with that model. I was open to it, but Miller's death had put the idea on hold.

During Charlotte's absence, I hadn't given much thought to the composition of a board of directors for a nonprofit version of the *Himmel Times*. It certainly never crossed my mind that someone like Marilyn was a possibility. And by "someone like Marilyn," I mean a selfish, mean-spirited, calculating woman.

I sautéed the vegetables and spices, added in the chicken, cranberries, and tomatoes, and then let everything simmer together on the stove. While that was happening, I Googled the role of board members for a nonprofit newspaper. I did not like what I found. Next, I researched the role of a publisher when a privately owned newspaper goes nonprofit. I didn't like that either. In fact, I was beginning to sour on the whole nonprofit idea.

With dinner basically ready, and Coop not due for a couple of hours, I had nothing to do but keep pacing around my apartment and railing out loud about what I feared was an impending disaster for the paper. Sam had enough of me and went to lie on my bed. I put on my coat and boots, wrapped a scarf around my neck, and pulled on a wool hat to take my walking and my worries outdoors.

The temperature had dropped considerably since the morning. It was so cold that the first inhale felt like it had frozen the hair inside my nostrils. The sidewalks were a hopscotch pattern of shoveled and not shoveled pavement. Walking was treacherous, and I concentrated on not falling on my butt as I trudged forward, until I heard someone call, "Nash! Hey, Nash, what are you doin' out in this?"

I recognized the voice immediately and turned to see Charlie Ross pulling over to the curb in his car. I walked over and leaned in to talk to him.

"Hi, Ross. I'm just walking off some frustration."

"You picked a hell of a day for it. The temperature is down to ten degrees, and with the wind chill, it's probably below zero. Your nose is as red as your hat. Get in. I'll give you a ride home."

"Thanks, I'll take you up on that. I didn't realize how cold it was."

Ross is a detective sergeant in the sheriff's office. When I first came back to town, we didn't get along that well. In fact, we detested each other. He thought I was a know-it-all reporter, and I thought he was a know-nothing detective. Over time, he's changed, or I have, and we get along pretty well now. Mostly. The only remnant of our earlier enmity is that we still call each other by our last names. It's kind of become our thing.

"Why are you wearing a paper name tag that says, 'I'm a proud Elm Street School Parnet'?" I asked as I slid onto the passenger seat and reached around for my seatbelt.

He looked down in surprise. "I forgot I had that on. Jennifer's boys made it. It's supposed to say *parent*."

"Back up a little. What are you doing masquerading as a 'parnet' at the twin's school?" I answered my own question before he could speak. "Wait a minute, John backed out of Bring Your Parent to School Day, right?"

"Yeah. That guy's a piece of work. The twins were pretty upset. Jennifer was, too, 'cause she had a big final exam in one of her classes that she couldn't ditch. When she told me about it yesterday, I told her I'd fill in."

Jennifer and her husband, John, had divorced after she discovered John's long-term affair and a number of other things about him. I wasn't surprised he had let his sons, Nate and Ethan, down—again. I was quite surprised that Ross, who can be a bit of a curmudgeon, had agreed to stand in for him. Still, over time, I've discovered a lot of unexpected things about him.

"That's amazingly nice of you."

"Eh," he said, shrugging off his good deed. "I missed a lot of that stuff when Allie was little. It was kinda fun to tell the truth."

Allie is Ross's high-school age daughter. She works part-time at the paper. To his dismay, she wants to be a journalist.

We both fell silent for a minute as we drove past the library.

"Hell of a thing, that fire. Damn shame about Luke Granger," Ross said a block or so later.

"Yeah. You hear anything new on it today? Any thoughts on how the fire happened?"

"Nope. I took the day off to do the twins thing. And anyway, it's not our case. It's for the fire department and HPD to handle. I got enough on my plate. Seems like you do, too. I hear from Coop that you're gonna try to write another book. And from what Allie says, things are still pretty dicey finance-wise at the paper. Seems to me you've got plenty to think about without adding the library fire."

"I do. But I can't help wondering about it. What do you know about PPOK, Ross?"

"Buncha people who are gettin' into other people's business. Why?"

"Well, they've been getting pretty vocal. And they were protesting outside the bookstore on Monday. I'm kind of wondering if the fire was set deliberately by someone from the group to make a point. Someone from PPOK did burn a box of books from Omico's library. Do you think that's possible?"

"Listen, here's what I think. People don't want their kid to read a book, don't let 'em read it. But you don't get to not let anybody's kid read it. I tried talkin' to one of those PPOK guys at the Elks the other night."

"Yes, and?"

"And there's no talkin' to him. They got their minds made up. So yeah, maybe one of them was wrong-headed enough to start the fire. But like I said, it's not my case. So, I'm gonna wait and see, like everybody else. You should think about doin' that, too."

We had just pulled up in front of the *Times* building. I unbuckled my seatbelt and reached for the door to get out. "I'm just wondering, Ross. That's all."

"Yeah? Well, I've seen you wonder yourself into some bad places. Maybe this time you concentrate on your pretend mysteries and leave the real ones to the professionals."

15

When Coop arrived at my place, I barely gave him time to sit down to dinner before I launched into a detailed recitation of all the reasons Marilyn Karr couldn't be on the board of our proposed nonprofit. As well as my newfound doubts that a nonprofit was a good idea at all.

"If the *Himmel Times* becomes a nonprofit entity, besides the board of directors setting the mission—the whole direction of the paper—they'll hire an executive director. And that person will run things kind of like a publisher runs a newspaper, based on what the board wants."

"And?"

"And it's my paper! I didn't sign on to the idea of a nonprofit so I wouldn't have any say in the *Times*. It's my paper!" I repeated, aware of the childish petulance in my voice but unable to stop it.

"So tell me again, slower this time. I understand why the idea of Marilyn on the board is upsetting you. But you knew what having a board and an executive director was all about a couple of months ago, right? Why are you freaking out now?"

"I'm not freaking out. But the thing is, I didn't think through what having a board would really mean on a day-to-day basis. It didn't sink in that I'd be just another board member, and the executive director would be working directly with Maggie."

"And you don't like that because, despite what you say, you really don't want to give up that level of control over the newsroom. You still want to be able to hop in and out and drive Maggie crazy, is that what's really bothering you?"

"No, that's not it," I said, not trying to hide the crankiness I felt at his lack of understanding. "Look, let's go back to Marilyn for a minute. What if we wind up with a whole board full of Marilyns? That could be worse than not having a newspaper at all. I've been thinking that I might tell Charlotte that I withdraw my support for the whole nonprofit idea. And then . . . "

My voice trailed off as I envisioned a variety of progressively worse fates for the *Times*.

"And then what? Keep struggling and cutting back? Lose good staff because you can't afford them? Have all the blood, sweat, tears—and money—you've already put into keeping the paper alive go for nothing? "

"You're not making me feel better."

"Do you want me to tell you what you want to hear, or do you want me to tell you what I think?"

"No. I want to know what you think. But it doesn't sound as though I'm going to like it."

"I'm not trying to upset you. I'm trying to help you consider all the ramifications of pulling out of the plan now. For instance, what will you do if Charlotte says 'Okay, I understand your concerns. But I disagree, and I think we need to go our separate ways'?"

"I guess I'd have to buy her out. It's not like the paper is worth a lot of money. She'd probably even just sign off her interest in it to me. Even if she didn't, I could pull together enough for a loan to buy her out."

"If you did that, would the paper survive without being shored up by money from an external source?"

"You know it wouldn't. I'd have to find investors, or—"

"And do you have the time or the interest in trying to find investors for a business that has a good track record journalistically, but not financially?"

"No, not really."

"So you see what I'm getting at here, don't you?"

"Yes, Socrates. I get that you're asking me all the questions so I can realize I don't have any good options. Okay, fine. So what am I supposed to do about it? And if you ask me another question instead of just answering, I can't promise I won't hit you."

"I won't. I'll take this rare opportunity, at your invitation, to tell you what you could do about it."

"Go ahead."

"Marilyn is a tough person to like. And she probably does have an ulterior motive for getting on the board. But she'll have a hard time doing any serious damage without the support of the other board members. And if you and Charlotte are careful in your picks, she won't be able to do anything that works against the success of the paper. Eventually, she'll get frustrated and leave. Until then, you can benefit from the influence she has with big money donors. And she'll probably give you a big chunk of change herself. She just made a very big donation to the Community Foundation."

"Only because she craves publicity. She doesn't have it in her to be good for good's sake. She just craves the admiration that comes with public generosity."

"Maybe so, but you still get the money you need. Do you see my point?"

"Yes, I hear what you're saying."

"Maybe if you uncrossed your arms and stopped scowling at me, I might believe that."

In a regrettable loss for adult discourse, I made a face and crossed my eyes at him. But I did uncross my arms.

"Fine. I get your point. But it still feels like us inviting Marilyn to be part of the nonprofit governing board is like Dumbledore inviting Voldemort to sit on the board of Hogwarts. She's very devious."

"Agreed. But you can handle Marilyn. I have complete faith in you."

"Thank you. But—"

"I'm not finished yet. You haven't talked this through with Charlotte. You don't even know for sure that Marilyn is seriously interested. She may just have been testing the waters. You're making battle plans for a war that might not ever come."

I didn't answer right away.

"Hey, I'm done. It's your turn," he said.

"I know. I'm just thinking a minute. Okay, so I suppose it's possible—I'm not saying it *is,* just that it *could* be—that it isn't so much Marilyn being on the board that I'm upset about. It's more that I don't want a board at all. The paper is my baby. Maybe I don't want to hand over its care and feeding to a board, even one without Marilyn. How can I be sure that the board, or the executive director, will care enough to make the right calls?"

"I feel like we're back to an old issue here."

"Oh? What's that?" I asked, though I was pretty sure I knew where he was heading.

"Leah, you lost a lot when you were a kid. And you came away thinking the only person you can trust is yourself."

"That's not fair. I trust you, Miguel, my mother, Father Lindstrom—lots of people."

"Yes, but you only trust us so far. And on the one hand, you're right. Trust is a risk. People will let you down sometimes. We're all human, and everyone lets people down sometimes, even you, Leah."

The call from my sister, Lacey, that I didn't pick up the night she died flashed into my mind, along with the sharp pain I feel every time it happens.

"I know that," I said quietly.

"Hey, I wasn't talking about Lacey, if that's what you think. That was a complicated whole other thing. I'm trying to say you're a brave person and you take a lot of risks—more than I'd like you to, honestly. But trusting someone else to do what needs to be done, that scares the heck out of you. I understand why, but that's a tough way to go through life."

"You sound like Father Lindstrom."

"I'll take that as a compliment."

"It's meant as one." I let out a huge sigh before I went on. "Coop, I know that's how I am. But it's one thing to recognize the patterns that have a hold on you, and it's another to change them."

"Leah, I'm on your side, wherever you land on this. I love you. I want you to be happy, that's all."

"You know what makes me happy? You do. Thanks for listening and helping me think. Even though I'm still not sure what to do."

"You're welcome."

"And now our food is cold because I talked so much about my worries, real or imagined. Give me your plate, I'll reheat dinner in the microwave, and we can take it from the top. Only it's your turn to monopolize the conversation now, while I listen."

A few minutes later with our dinner reheated and the two of us reseated, I scooped up a forkful of food. Before I put it in my mouth, I said, "Okay, start with the library fire investigation. What's happening?

The answer he gave literally made me drop my fork.

16

"Luke didn't die in the fire."

I gasped and immediately started choking as a half-bite of food went down the wrong way.

"The body wasn't Luke?!" I managed to get out in between trying to breathe.

Coop shoved my water toward me.

"No, it's Luke. But he wasn't killed by the fire or by smoke inhalation. He was shot."

"What? Way to bury the lead!" I gasped again, moving from choking to coughing. "Who told you, Connie?"

Connie Crowley is a retired physician who serves as the Grantland County medical examiner.

"No. I got it from Owen, but I don't want you to—"

"Yeah, yeah, I know our ground rules. This isn't for publication; it's a personal conversation. So tell me, what happened?"

"Connie found a bullet lodged in Luke's chest. It hit a bone and that kept it from exiting. She knows that's what killed him because there wasn't any smoke in Luke's lungs. That means he was already dead when the fire started."

"Whoa, whoa. That doesn't make sense. I can imagine a PPOK member getting crazy angry and burning down the library, not knowing Luke was inside. But if Luke was shot, that means someone went there deliberately to kill him."

"Not necessarily. Lots of people around here have a concealed-carry permit and they always have a handgun on them."

"That's a scary thought, but go on," I said.

"If someone went to the library to start a fire and Luke surprised him, he might have panicked and used his gun."

I turned the idea over in my mind.

"Okay, so then the arsonist goes ahead and finishes setting up the fire, hoping—or maybe assuming—it will conceal the murder?"

"That would be my guess. People assume a fire will reduce a body to ashes, but it has to be pretty intense to do that. What it can do, though, is make it very hard to find an entry or exit wound. If the damage to the body is extensive enough, it's possible for a medical examiner to miss a bullet. Especially when a fire offers a logical cause of death."

"But not our medical examiner?"

"Right. Connie just finished a course about using postmortem computer-assisted tomography in deaths by fire. They've got the equipment in Selden County, and she got the medical examiner there to help her out. Otherwise, the fire might have worked to conceal the gunshot."

"Score one for Connie. Is Cliff Timmins back in town? Because if he isn't, I'm sure neither HPD nor the prosecutor's office will release the autopsy results yet."

"Cliff's due back from his hunting trip late tonight. He scheduled a press conference for noon tomorrow."

"Figures. Now that he's running for judge, he never misses a chance to be in the spotlight. What does Owen think about it? Does he have any theories yet?"

"Thanks to my relationship with you—and don't get me wrong, I'm very thankful for my relationship with you—Owen doesn't share that much with me. But when we talked, I didn't get the impression that PPOK was his focus. It sounded to me like he's interested in the Granger family."

"The Grangers? Besides the fact that murder isn't really in their wheelhouse, except for Harley Granger, why would any of them come after Luke?"

"Envy maybe. Luke was making something of his life. People liked him and respected him. Most Grangers don't get much of that. Maybe they resented Luke's success."

"I suppose that could be but ... "

"Owen seems to think that maybe Luke wasn't as removed from the family business as everyone thought. And he could be right. Luke was pretty desperate to get money to buy the bookstore. He could have gotten in over his head, and things went wrong."

"No, I don't agree. Luke wasn't like the rest of his family. Do you really think that?"

"It doesn't matter much what either of us think. It's Owen's case. So, we just let him get on with it. Right?"

"But I just think—"

"Leah, you aren't—"

"I know, I know. I'm not involved."

"Just because you don't like Owen, it doesn't mean he's not capable of investigating a murder without your input."

"I don't dislike Owen. Our personalities don't mesh very well, that's all. And I'm not trying to get involved. I'm just eating my dinner . . . and having a few thoughts."

He didn't say anything, just looked at me with one eyebrow lifted.

"What? I can't think?"

"I didn't say that. And I don't want to argue with you either. This is one time when both of us are going to be on the sidelines. Let's finish dinner— which was great, by the way—and do like everyone else is going to do: wait and see what happens. Okay?"

"Yes, okay. You're right."

"Hold on a second," he said, reaching into his pocket. He held up his phone, pressed the record button, and said, "Repeat what you just said, please. I'd like to record it for posterity. I may never hear those words from you again."

I rolled my eyes, but it was *kind* of funny. And possibly true.

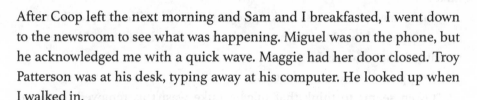

After Coop left the next morning and Sam and I breakfasted, I went down to the newsroom to see what was happening. Miguel was on the phone, but he acknowledged me with a quick wave. Maggie had her door closed. Troy Patterson was at his desk, typing away at his computer. He looked up when I walked in.

"Hey, Troy. Glad to see you back. Anything on Luke Granger yet?"

"It looks like a big story could be brewing, but I can't get any confirmation. When I stopped at the Elite for coffee on my way in, people were saying Luke was murdered, that he didn't die in the fire."

Ah, the Himmel grapevine . . . it's a powerful thing. Much too powerful for Cliff Timmins the prosecutor to control. I didn't violate Coop's confidentiality request, but it wouldn't be long before Troy nailed down the real cause of death.

"Who've you talked to?"

"I called the medical examiner, and she referred me to Cliff Timmins. I called his office, but he wasn't in yet. His secretary said he got back from his Canadian hunting trip late last night. But there's a press conference scheduled for noon. I tried Owen Fike, but he said no comment at this time. I have a couple of other sources at HPD to try. They won't go on the record, but I want to confirm the rumors, so I know what to press the prosecutor on before he cuts me off. When anything big happens, he usually just gives me one shot before he pivots to the TV reporters. Even though they're not local."

Troy is even younger than Miguel, and very earnest. With his carefully parted sandy hair, his freckled face, and his wire-rimmed glasses, he looks more like a high school valedictorian—which he was—than a reporter. I was skeptical that he had what it takes at first, but I was wrong. He's turning into a very good journalist.

"You might try asking him if they're going to be interviewing PPOK members in connection with the fire. They've been kicking up quite a storm lately."

Troy's gaze had shifted from me to somewhere over my shoulder. From his expression, I had a pretty good idea who was behind me. I turned.

"Hey, Maggie. I was just—"

"I know. You're just saving me the trouble of doing my job, right? Troy, thank the nice newspaper owner for her help, and let's get on with our work, okay?"

Clearly, it was time for me to leave.

"Okay. But just so you know, I wasn't bossing things, Maggie. I was just making a few observations. Because *you*, not me, are in charge in the newsroom. I think we all agree on that!"

To prove it, I caught Miguel's eye and mouthed *talk to you later*, as I skittered out the door.

I went back upstairs to do some more work on developing suspects for the pretend murder in my next book, but I couldn't get the real murder in my real town off my mind. I checked social media, specifically the *Grantland County in the Know* page, to see the rumors circulating there. The feed is mainly requests for recommendations for house cleaning, or stump removal, or invitations to participate in multi-level marketing. Occasionally, there are complaints about customer service at a local business. However, when something big like the fire at the library happens, locals who use social media weigh in on *In the Know*.

Discussion on the page had moved beyond the rumor that Luke had been murdered to the fact that he had been shot. The information could have come from a leak in Cliff's office, or Owen's department, or the medical examiner's office. It's hard to keep a lid on news like that.

Regardless of the source, the information had generated a lot of speculation online. The people posting were aligned in two different camps. The first was that Luke was a good guy who was at the wrong place at the wrong time and had just been in the way. The implication was that PPOK was involved, but no one who commented actually named the group.

The second thesis aligned with the "blood will tell" idea that Coop had said Owen Fike seemed to favor. Namely, that the fire and Luke's violent death must have something to do with his family. There was lots of fact-free conjecture from both sides of the question.

I closed the lid of my laptop and went to the kitchen in search of a Diet Coke. Sam heard the refrigerator open and came running from wherever he'd been lounging.

"Sorry, buddy. You know we're supposed to be watching your weight, and thanks to Coop, you got a few too many extras last night. Don't look at me like that. There's nothing here for me either. However, I'm going to exercise my privilege as a human and go get myself something. Maybe when I come back, I'll feel more productive."

17

Jameson is my favorite adult beverage, but in the non-alcoholic class, nothing beats a fountain-style Diet Coke with extra ice. I know it's not a good healthy-eating choice—Troy tells me often enough—but it's a years-long habit that I haven't been able to kick. Though truthfully, I haven't tried that hard. At JT's party store, I filled a large cup up to the top with crushed ice, then pulled the lever and watched as the bubbling brown beverage cascaded into my glass.

After doing a second check to make sure the plastic lid on my Diet Coke was truly secure before I put it in the cupholder—I've learned my lesson on that score—I drove to Riverview Park. It's not the nicest park in town. In fact, it's the most rundown one. But it holds a lot of comforting memories for me. When I was very young, my dad used to take me and Annie there to play. We loved to run around what we called the racetrack. It was actually a small cement circle that enclosed a flower garden. Next to it stood a tall stone tower built to honor a town founder. Annie and I used to pretend we were princesses who lived there. The water fountain it encased produced the sweetest, coldest water I've ever tasted.

Today, the flower garden is nothing but dirt and weeds, and the water fountain in the tower hasn't worked in years. The bandstand and the playground equipment we loved is mostly gone, too. But I don't go there for what the park is now. I go for the memories of what it once was.

I parked my car in my usual spot on the south end. It gives me a panoramic view of the park, and I can also see the train trestle that offers a quick but extremely dangerous shortcut to JT's across the river. Coop still has a zigzag scar on his finger that he got rescuing me from an ill-advised dash across the trestle (my idea) that nearly killed both of us when we were twelve.

I pushed back my seat, stretched out my legs, and left the heater running. The first sip of my Diet Coke was perfection—icy cold and so fizzy it made my nose tingle. I closed my eyes in satisfaction. Until a loud tapping on my passenger-side window jolted me to attention.

I looked up and saw the face of Cole Granger staring through the window with a wolfish grin. He motioned me to let him in.

Against my better judgment, I unlocked the door. He slid onto the passenger seat.

"We can't keep meetin' like this, Leah. Your boyfriend's gonna get suspicious."

"What do you want, Cole? And how did you find me?"

"What I always want, Leah. Just to nurture our friendship. I saw you comin' outta JT's with a big old soda, and then I saw your car headin' this way. I thought to myself, *Leah's goin' to the park.* So I got me my sausage biscuit and come on over."

He stopped to fold back the paper on his biscuit.

"Oh, that's where the nauseating smell is coming from. I thought it was just you."

"Hey, now," he said around a mouthful of the breakfast sandwich. "Why do you have to go and say a mean-hearted thing like that? It's because you're always fightin' our chemistry, ain't it?"

Cole, the default head of the Granger family, usually talks with an Appalachian drawl. It may have once been genuine—he spent some childhood years in Kentucky. But I think he leans into the slower speech pattern now because it makes some people believe that he thinks as slow as he talks. He doesn't.

"Cole, let's just get to it. What do you want?"

"A word of condolence might be nice. I just lost my cousin Luke, as I'm sure you know."

I felt a slight pang of guilt.

"I'm sorry about Luke. He was a nice person."

"I appreciate that. It's what I come to talk about."

"I'm not a grief counselor, Cole. And I'm not a friend. So I can't think why you'd choose me to talk to."

"Because despite your harsh ways, I know you got a heart. And I know you got a brain. I'm hopin' to persuade you to use 'em both to find out who murdered Luke. You do know it wasn't the fire that took him? He was shot."

"I heard. I also know the Himmel Police are investigating. I'm happy to wait and let Owen Fike do his job."

As I said it, I wished Coop could hear me parroting his advice.

"Now see, that's just the thing. Owen Fike's got it all wrong. He was out talkin' to some of the family at our Ride EZ last night."

Like many rural areas, Grantland County doesn't have countywide public transportation. Ride EZ is a car service run by Cole's mother Tammy. It's one of the family's fairly legit businesses.

"After he told us Luke was shot, he started insinuatin' all kinda things about Luke and our family. I won't say no Granger skirts the law, but Luke, he wasn't one of them. Not after he come back a few years ago, anyway. None of us could figure why he wanted to buy a damn bookstore, but he worked his ass off to get money saved for it."

He shook his head at Luke's peculiar ambition before he went on.

"But every time some little untoward thing happens in this county, blame the Grangers is the name of the game. When we was talkin', Fike all but called me a liar, right to my face! And he got mama real upset, too. It's hard to live with that kind of po-lice abuse." He emphasized his disgust by dragging out the word *police*.

"I'm sorry you had to go through that traumatic experience."

He responded as though my comment had been sincere.

"Thank you. I know we got our problem folks, just like any other family.

And Luke, he always was kind of an odd duck. But his daddy was a Granger, and that makes us family. And Granger family sticks together. I don't like Fike and his crew harassin' my family. And I don't hold with him makin' out like Luke was doin' some kind of crimes and that he got himself kilt for it."

"Did Owen say that?"

"As good as. And I'm tellin' you that never happened. I know why he's out there trashin' Luke's memory and my family's reputation."

"Okay, why would Owen do that? "

"Fike, he's fixin' to put the finger on one of us and drag Luke's good name down because he's still pissed that Luke stole his girl."

"What?"

"Luke was like me, quite the ladies' man. When you got it, they just don't leave you alone. Seems as how this girl was seein' Fike, but then she got eyes for Luke, and she dumped old Owen. He didn't take it so well."

Cole, with his close-set, yellow-flecked green eyes, slicked-back mud-colored hair, and small thin mouth, doesn't come to mind when you think ladies' man. Though I suppose some might be taken with the dragon tattoo that starts on his bicep and runs all the way down to his wrist.

"Uh-huh. So who is the 'girl' Luke stole from Owen?"

"Some librarian name of Stella. I never met her. But one of the cousins told me she was all hot and heavy with Fike, then Luke, he comes along, and she don't remember Fike's name. Now, he's got a chance to ruin Luke's good name and the rest of us Grangers, too."

I considered for a moment. Cole has been the source of useful information for me in the past, but playing with him can be a dangerous game. He's the ultimate unreliable narrator, especially about anything to do with his family.

"Cole, even if Owen's girlfriend dumped him for Luke, I highly doubt that set him off on some kind of a vengeance quest."

"I'm not sayin' that's the only reason. But you know what I say is true. If anything bad happens, it's always the Grangers that get accused, first, last, and always."

"I've heard you recount the sad tale of the persecution of your innocent family by law enforcement many times before. But I also know where

Grangers go, trouble follows. I do agree with you on one thing, though. I don't think Luke was involved in anything criminal. But that doesn't mean he didn't know something about a Granger who was. Maybe that's why he was killed."

"I'm tellin' you straight, it wasn't. Grangers don't kill Grangers—with the possible exception of Harley. Why isn't Fike goin' after them crazy book-burnin' PPOKers? I'll tell you why—'cause it's easier to blame a Granger."

A part of my brain whispered that Cole had a point, and what would it hurt to do a little poking around on my own? The smarter part told me to step away. For once, I listened to the smart part.

"Sorry, Cole. The answer is no."

18

"But you don't even want to ask a few questions, *chica*? What could it hurt?"

Miguel had come up to my place when I got back from the park. I had just finished telling him about my encounter with Cole.

"I don't believe Luke was a criminal."

"I don't think he was either, Miguel. I liked him, too. And if Owen really is bent on the idea that Luke was murdered because he was involved in something illegal, I think he's on the wrong track."

"Yes, that's what I am saying."

"But don't forget what I just told you is from Cole's perspective. And we both know he's not the most reliable source. You always have to look for what's going on beneath the surface with Cole, what his real motive is."

"Yes. Cole is not always for the good. But sometimes he is."

"Really? Like when?"

He then proceeded to tell me a story I'd never heard from him before.

"When I first came to Himmel to live with Uncle Craig and Aunt Lydia, not everybody here was so comfortable with the gay Latino boy from Milwaukee."

"People in Himmel were harassing you? Grangers, you mean? Miguel, I'm so sorry."

"No, not Grangers. In fact, it was Cole who saved me."

"That's kind of hard to believe."

"Believe. I was shooting hoops by myself at the park after dinner one night. Two boys who were seniors—I was a junior—showed up. They were a little drunk. One of them grabbed the basketball from my hands. I knew trouble was coming. I tried to get it back and go. But the other said, 'Look, at the beaner, he wants to play!'"

I like to think that kind of thing doesn't happen in Himmel. Sadly, people being people, it does.

"Oh, Miguel, I'm so sorry!"

He shrugged and went on with his story.

"So I thought, *okay, leave your basketball, Miguel, and get out of here.* Two to one is no good. But then the bigger one, he shoved me and said, 'We don't need another queer here. Go back to Mexico.'"

"This is getting worse and worse."

"I said, 'Hey, I'm from Milwaukee not Mexico.' I was trying to make a joke so I could get away. Only then the other one, he pushed me, and I tripped and fell. Then he kicked me. It was getting very ugly. And scary. And painful."

"Ugly? It was criminal!"

"Then suddenly, there was Cole! He pulled the one off me and kicked him hard. The other one just backed away. He told them to go . . . and keep their mouths shut and leave the gay kid alone, or they would get worse. They ran away like little puppies, crying."

"I don't believe it. Cole did that for you? Why? What did he say?"

"He told me to learn how to fight and not to be a pussy."

Although the action was outside what I'd expect of Cole in that situation, his words were pretty much in character.

"I told him, 'Thank you so much' and that if the chance ever came, I would help him too. He said he wouldn't ever need my help and not to tell anyone what happened. He didn't want anyone to think he was soft. And I didn't tell until now. But I still owe him. If you help Cole, I can help you, and that will be my payback to him."

I trusted that Miguel was telling the truth, but I still didn't trust Cole. I'd gotten tangled up in the sticky Granger web of chicanery and lies before. I didn't want to do it again. But Miguel hardly ever asked me to do anything for him, and he did so much for me.

I wavered. "Miguel, I don't know. It just doesn't feel—"

Before I could finish my phone rang. I glanced at the caller ID.

"Just a second, Miguel. It's Mom. Hang on." I answered the call. "Hi, Mom. Can I call you right—"

"Leah, Ellen Granger, Luke's mother is here. She's very upset and really wants to see you. Can you come down right away? She's waiting for you in my office."

Ellen Granger was a middle-aged woman with short, brown hair, lightly threaded with gray.

"Hi, Ellen. I'm Leah Nash. I'm so sorry about Luke."

A shaky sigh caught in her throat as she attempted to speak. She coughed and blinked hard before she tried again.

"Thank you. I want you to find out who killed him."

"Ellen, I—"

She continued speaking as though I hadn't interrupted her. "I know he got into some trouble after his dad died. But that doesn't make him a criminal now."

"What kind of trouble?" I asked, curious. The only side of Luke I knew was the friendly, busy guy trying to save money to fund his bookstore dream.

"In high school, he got caught shoplifting once. But just once, and I set him straight on that. And another time, he got suspended from school for a fight he didn't start. Some kid said something nasty about his dad. Luke wasn't right to fight. I'm not saying that. But he got punished, and the kid that started it didn't, because Luke's last name is Granger. He wouldn't have gotten into any real trouble except for his cousin Brodie."

"What happened?"

"Brodie talked Luke into breaking into a vacant house. They weren't going to steal anything. They just wanted to see if they could get away with it. But once they got in, Brodie started going through the liquor cabinet. He dropped a bottle, and it broke and spilled on the floor and the carpet. Somebody going by saw lights on in the house and called the cops. Both of them wound up with six months in jail for breaking-and-entering. It was a wakeup call for Luke."

"How?"

"He knew he had to get away from Himmel at least for a while. He moved to Michigan. I've got some family there. He stayed a few years, got his head on straight. He came back to help me when I had surgery and couldn't work for a while. I was a little worried he'd start running with Brodie again. He didn't, though. He got that job in the bookstore. Once Marcus told him he was going to retire in a few years, that's when Luke started working two jobs to earn the down payment money."

"You must have been proud of him."

"I was. I still am. That's why I can't sit by and let the police act like it was his fault he got killed because he was up to no good with the Grangers."

"Why are you so sure that's what the police think?"

"They've been asking questions about how close was he to his cousin Brodie, and did I notice if Luke seemed to have extra money. I knew what they were thinking. The Grangers are bad news, and Luke was a Granger, and so he must have done something that got him killed. But his father wasn't like that, and neither was Luke."

"What was Luke's father like?"

"He was funny and smart, like Luke. After we got married, we lived in Michigan a while. Then Josh got a job offer from a high school friend here, and we moved to Wisconsin. I didn't know his family at all. I might have put up a fuss about moving if I had. Josh wasn't like them, but he loved them. I didn't try to keep him or Luke from seeing them. But I kept my distance. I just tried to show Luke there was a different way to be."

"Well, it must have worked. A lot of people are going to miss him. Claudia Fillhart thought the world of him."

"I know she did, and he thought the same about her. I wish that Captain Fike understood that. Maybe then he wouldn't have spent an hour trying to get me to say that Luke sold weed, or stole copper wire, or did the other kinds of things some Grangers do to make money."

"Ellen, I know Luke didn't have all the money he needed to qualify for the bank loan when Marcus had his heart attack. Do you know where he got that $5,000 he pulled together so fast to apply for the loan?"

"I don't. Luke just said that a friend helped him out. I thought maybe Marcus took the price down some on the bookstore so Luke could afford the loan. Luke was so happy for a few days—until the bank told him they wanted thirty percent down instead of twenty. And you'll never convince me that wasn't because his last name is Granger. He was beside himself. I asked him if his friend could help him out again, and he said no. He was really down for a few days, but then he said he thought he had a way to get it, but he wouldn't tell me how. He said he didn't want to jinx it. But I'll tell you one thing, he wasn't planning to get it from stealing."

The last sentence came out as a near shout, followed immediately by Ellen breaking down in sobs of grief and frustration.

"I'm so sorry, Ellen."

She wiped her eyes on her sleeves. "I don't want your sympathy. I want your help. I want you to find out why my son is dead."

"The police—"

"No."

She spat out the word so fiercely that I almost recoiled.

"No," she repeated in a softer tone. "They're fixed on the idea that Luke was a criminal like most of the Granger family. I just don't believe they're going to look at anything else. I don't want to stand by while they drag my son's memory through the mud. His memory is all I have left."

She reached out and put her hand on my arm, leaning in closer as she did, until her face was just inches away from mine.

"I was here when your sister Lacey was killed. I heard all the things that people said about her. But you found out what really happened and gave your mother and yourself some peace. Please, Leah, help me find some peace, too."

Her eyes were bright with tears. I couldn't look away. I couldn't say no either.

"Ellen, I'll do what I can. But once I start, I'll keep going, no matter what I find."

"You won't find anything bad about my son. My Luke was a good man. He deserves to be remembered that way. Thank you."

19

After Ellen left, I went back to my place and called Cole.

"Okay, I'll do it."

"Thank you, that eases my mind a whole lot."

"Well, don't get too easy in your mind. I'm doing it because Luke's mother asked me to. But I'm telling you, Cole, if you lie to me about anything I ask you—"

"It hurts for me to hear that from you after all we been through together."

"All we've been through is why I'm saying it. I don't want to let Ellen down, and that means you don't stand in my way."

"Luke was family. We all want to know why he was killed. And we got nothin' to hide about his murder. If Brodie or any other Granger did it, I'd know. And I don't, so that's not what happened. You just go on and have at it."

"Okay, as long as we understand each other."

"I b'lieve we do."

"But there's something I don't get."

"What's that?"

"Miguel told me what you did for him. He's going to help me investigate as payback to you. What I don't get is why you intervened when those two guys were beating him up. It's not like you to step up if there's nothing in it for you. So, why did you?"

"Like the poet says, Leah, I contain multitudes. And you don't know the half of them. But I got to say that I find people of the gay persuasion can get what you might call a little overdramatic. I don't recall that particular story myself. Let's just move on, and you get down to findin' out who killed Luke."

I made some tea and then I retrieved my favorite thinking tools—a yellow legal pad and a mechanical pencil. Sometimes I use a pen, but I like the flexibility an eraser gives me. I carried everything over to my corner of the window seat. Sam was sleeping in his. Leaning back against a pillow, I propped my legal pad on my knees and got down to business.

First, I tried out the idea that Luke's death was an accidental byproduct of an attempt to burn down the library by PPOK.

The ashes returned to the library in Omico could have been the precursor to a plan to turn a whole library into ashes. But the plan went sideways when the PPOK arsonist was surprised by Luke. A confrontation ensued, things got out of hand, and Luke got shot. Then the fire was set as planned, with the added hope that it would destroy evidence of the real cause of Luke's death.

I needed more information on PPOK interactions with the library. I started my list. Brooke Timmins, because she was president of the library board. Claudia, for sure. I tapped my pencil for a few seconds, then added Phil Stillman, the school board president, to my list. PPOK had been very regular and very loud in their attendance at school board meetings. Ed Wagner was apparently a leader in the PPOK group, so I put him down, as well as his wife, Gwen. That should be enough to get started in what looked to me like the most logical direction.

But I couldn't ignore other possibilities. What if Luke's death was planned all along? What if the fire was incidental, and killing Luke was always supposed to be the main event? That seemed to be the theory Owen Fike was leaning into. Okay, so why would someone want Luke dead?

According to Ellen, Owen was pursuing the idea that Luke might look like an upright citizen, but that was just a cover for his innate criminal nature as a Granger. Consequently, his death was the result of something criminal he'd done. I didn't favor that theory, but I really didn't know Luke all that well. I needed to talk to someone not related to him who did. Claudia could help there, and so could Marcus Scanlon, the owner of Buy the Book. They both had a close relationship with Luke.

But there was another possible reason for Luke's murder. What if Luke hadn't committed a crime, but he knew about one, and the killer was afraid he might tell? Ellen Granger had said that Luke and a cousin had gotten into trouble breaking into a house. Going to jail for it had helped Luke set his life in a more positive direction. But maybe his cousin was still crime-ing and had done something serious. What was his name . . . Brian? Brady? No, that didn't sound quite right. I picked up my phone and Googled boy's names beginning with B. There it was. Not Brady. *Brodie* was the cousin's name. I added him to my must-see list.

Before I went any further, I decided to talk to Coop. I'd rather tell him myself than have him hear through the grapevine that I'd done a 180 on investigating Luke's murder.

"Hi. Are you in the office? Have you got a minute?"

"I am in the office, and for you, I have more than a minute. What's up?"

"I think I'll just run over. I've got something to tell you. See you in a few."

~

"Where are you off to in such a hurry?"

My mother was coming in the front door of the building as I was rushing out.

"I'm going to the sheriff's office for a minute."

"Ellen asked you to investigate Luke's murder, didn't she? And you're going to, right? I knew you would. That's why you're headed out to talk to Coop."

"Yes, she asked me to investigate. Yes, I'm going to do it. And yes, I'm on my way to see Coop. Nobody likes a person who knows all the answers, Mom."

"It's my gift and my curse," she said with a grin as she tousled her short, dark hair to dislodge fast-melting snowflakes.

"Well, I need to let Coop know before he hears it somewhere else. He doesn't have your psychic powers. Oh, I forgot to tell you. Charlotte's due back in town today. I'm having dinner with her tonight."

"You don't sound very happy about it."

"I'm happy to see her, but I'm having second thoughts about the whole nonprofit thing."

"Why?"

"Marilyn Karr."

"What does she—"

"I'll fill you in later. Got to go."

∼

"Okay," Coop said. I had just finished recounting Cole's request, Miguel's unexpected pressure, and the final tightening of the screws on my conscience by Luke's mother.

"Okay? C'mon, that's all you have to say?"

"Pretty much. I already gave you my thoughts on getting tangled up in Owen's case, but I get why you said yes to Ellen."

"But you still think I shouldn't have."

"I didn't say that."

"You didn't have to. You have a tell."

"Really, what is it?"

"When you don't like something I'm saying or doing, you start rubbing the scar on your index finger with your thumb. A minute ago, you were rubbing it so hard you could have started a campfire with the friction. Why are you so against it? Is it because Cole is involved? He isn't really. I mean, I may need him for some background information and things, but it's not like we're partners on this."

"Glad to hear it. You know he's not trustworthy. How do you know he's not playing some angle?"

"What kind of angle would that be? There's nothing in this for Cole."

"Unless he's hoping you'll stir things up enough to muddy the waters, so Owen's investigation goes off the rails."

"I don't even believe you said that. I'm not going to get in the way of Owen's work—or 'muddy the waters' either. If I find something that will help, I'll tell him. Though the odds are he won't want to hear it coming from me. You know, I'm well aware of Cole's intermittent relationship with the truth. I think Owen is wrong about Luke, but if I find something that says he's right, it's not like I won't admit it."

He raised an eyebrow.

"So I might not admit it graciously, but I *will* admit it."

He shook his head, but then he smiled. "It's your decision, and it's a done deal. I hope it works out. Whether it does or it doesn't, and whether or not I agree with you, I support your right to choose. And I'll hold back any I-told-you-so's, even if the opportunity comes up."

"Thank you. You get an A for supportive boyfriend-ing. And I hereby grant you the right to say I told you so, if things go sideways. Hey, I've got dinner with Charlotte tonight, and then I'm planning on a pretty full day tomorrow. How about unwinding with me tomorrow night and have dinner and a movie at my place?"

"Sounds great. Let's do carryout. You're busy all day, and so am I. That way neither of us has to cook. I'll pick up a fajita dinner from Casa Dolores in Hailwell. I'll be out that way."

"Doing what?"

"Just following up on something. I'll tell you tomorrow when there's more time."

"That sounds a little mysterious."

"I read that you should keep your girlfriend guessing."

"Mission accomplished. Expect a full grilling on Saturday."

20

It was four o'clock when I left Coop's. I wasn't very anxious to talk to Owen, but it felt like I should. And I had time before I was supposed to be at Charlotte's for dinner.

Although it was still snowing, it wasn't too cold, and the three-block walk to the Himmel Police Department was actually pleasant.

I'd expected that I'd have to joust with Melanie Olson, the HPD secretary, to get access to Owen Fike, but she wasn't at her desk. In fact, no one was in the reception area, so I sped down the hall toward Owen's office before anyone challenged me. I tapped lightly on the frosted glass.

"Come in, Melanie. That didn't take you long. Did you find the file on—"

He stopped talking as he looked up and realized who he had welcomed into his lair.

"Hi, Owen. I'm sorry to barge in, but no one was out front. Can I talk to you for a minute?"

He didn't exactly scowl at me, but it was clear my drop-in visit did not please him.

"I'm actually in the middle of something, Leah. I'd prefer that you make an appointment."

"Seriously, this won't take long. And since I'm already here . . ."

I could see the internal debate play out across his face. Should he insist I leave? Or just get the encounter over with now? I sidled toward the chair in front of his desk and was already halfway to dropping down on it when he said abruptly, "Fine. Sit down. I only have a minute. What do you want?"

"Thank you," I said. "It's sort of a courtesy call, really. I know you're heading up the investigation into Luke Granger's death and—"

"Do you have information about it?"

"Not yet, no, but—"

"Is this an interview for the paper? I told Troy that District Attorney Timmins is the official point of contact for the press."

"No, I'm not here to interview you. But seriously, Cliff is cutting HPD off from the *Times*? I know he likes to center everything on himself, but it sounds like he doesn't trust you to conduct the investigation. He's not your boss."

I was deliberately trying to push his buttons to goad him into giving me some information. After all, I was going to give him some. Was it wrong to want a little *quid pro quo*?

Owen has the pale skin that usually accompanies red hair. Though his is more strawberry blond. Although he could keep his words neutral, he couldn't control the visible flush of anger that crept up his cheeks as he replied.

"It's not a matter of trust, or of who the boss is. It's a matter of protocol. As the prosecutor, District Attorney Timmins has the authority to give directives on the focus and conducting of an investigation."

"I'm aware of that, but I don't recall him ever forbidding Mick Riley to talk to the press when he was police chief."

"And I don't remember that you were ever a part of internal law enforcement operations. Although as Coop's girlfriend, you seem to think you should be. Now, unless you have something of substance to say, I have work to do."

I confess. I enjoyed seeing the usually unflappable Owen riled. He's very by-the-book and thinks the press has no business knowing anything about police investigations. I've worked—and sparred on occasion—with a lot of cops. We both have jobs to do, and our objectives don't always match, but most of them are good guys, and we work out a reasonable way to share what we can and not get in each other's way. It's how Ross and I work.

But something in a past experience with the press must have gone seriously wrong for Owen because his suspicion level is very high when it comes to journalists. Which is too bad, because as I told Coop, I don't dislike Owen. However, I don't like being dismissed as an annoyance, or considered only in regard to my relationship with Coop.

"Yeah, I do have something 'of substance' to say. Ellen Granger asked me to look into Luke's death. She thinks you've already decided that Luke was involved in criminal activity that got him killed. I agreed to dig into things a little and see if I can turn up anything. Just in case you decide to ignore any inconvenient truths that don't fit your idea about what happened."

"I don't intend to ignore any facts, inconvenient or otherwise. Ellen Granger is a grieving mother. Mothers often don't see their children as they really are. Especially after they're dead. They all become saints then. Men like Luke are good at manipulating people. They use surface charm to fool people, but they're out for what they can get, however they can get it. But sometimes the tables get turned, and they're the ones who get hurt—or wind up dead."

His voice was taut with barely controlled anger. The tell-tale flush had returned to his cheeks.

"So, you think Luke was some kind of criminal mastermind? And that's the reason he was killed? The guy worked two jobs and as many side hustles as he could get so he could buy a bookstore, for God's sake. You've really lost the plot, Owen. Maybe you should ask yourself if you're so hellbent on Luke somehow being the cause of his own murder because he used his 'surface charm' so well that your girlfriend dumped you for him. Come on, admit it. You don't really have any reason to suspect that Luke was involved in anything illegal. You're out to prove it because you're still pissed he stole your girl."

"This conversation is over."

He rose from his desk, his fists clenched in a visible attempt to control himself. I'd hit a nerve. His tight control on his emotions had frayed. I wondered if he planned to throw me out bodily. Given his level of anger, it was possible. I made a calculated effort to see if I could get his temper to unravel a little more before I was tossed out of his office.

"Fine. I can see you're very upset. But be honest with yourself, if not with me. Admit it. You don't have any reason other than your own jealousy to suspect Luke of doing anything criminal. I'm surprised a cop like you would let your emotions sway an investigation."

That did it.

"My 'emotions' as you put it, have nothing to do with this investigation or any other. I always stick to the facts. Fact one, the camera at the back door to the storage area and the one inside the storage area stopped recording at ten p.m. But all the other security cameras were working. It's pretty obvious Luke turned off the cameras in the storage area because he had something to hide. Possibly a meeting with someone. Fact two, about that bookstore. It took Luke three years to save $15,000 toward his down payment for the bookstore. But when he needs $5,000 more right away because of Marcus Scanlon's heart attack, he gets it in less than a week? How does that work?"

I shrugged. "Luke had lots of friends."

"Yeah. Friends who like breaking into places. Fact three, about two months ago, we had a couple of burglaries at the Haven. Got away with cash and a nice haul of jewelry, electronics, prescription drugs—the kind of things easy to turn into cash. The haul from that job probably netted the thieves twelve to fifteen thousand bucks."

"Your point?"

"Those burglaries at the Haven, that down payment money, and Luke Granger's murder are all connected. Bet on it. That's what's guiding this investigation, not personal feelings. And those are none of your business."

He stopped to take a deep breath. I waited silently, hoping for more revelations to come. But his pause both calmed him and made him realize he'd said a whole lot more than he'd planned to.

"In fact, nothing about this investigation is any of your business, regardless of what Ellen Granger wants you to do. I won't be discussing this with you again. Is that clear?"

He walked over to the door and held it open.

"Crystal clear," I said.

21

As I walked home, I considered what I'd learned. The Haven is a small enclave of very expensive homes a few miles outside of the Himmel city limits. Its township contracts with the Himmel Police Department for law enforcement services.

I remembered the burglaries Owen had talked about. They'd happened in the evening when the owners of the homes were away. No one had been arrested. It was the kind of crime one of the Grangers would commit, but it couldn't have been Luke. Aside from my positive view of his character, there was the fact that he worked every evening from seven to ten at the library. However, my idea that Luke hadn't *committed* a crime but *knew* about one could come into play here. I already had Luke's cousin Brodie on my list to talk to. Maybe I should move him up a bit.

It hit me then that I hadn't let Miguel know what was happening. I called him, but he didn't answer. I texted and asked him to meet me at Woke at 8:30 the next morning for a debriefing. Then I double-timed it to my place, jotted down the key points of my chat with Owen, fed Sam, and headed out for dinner with Charlotte.

When I arrived, I hesitated a second before ringing the doorbell. It was the first time I'd been there since Miller was killed. I half-expected him to open the door. When it was Charlotte, I surprised myself by bursting into tears.

Charlotte pulled me inside with a hug.

"I'm sorry, this is so stupid," I said. "It's just . . . it's the first . . . Miller . . ." I had a hard time getting the words out.

"I know. It's the first time you've been here since Dad died. When it was me instead of him who opened the door, it hit you again that he's gone. I know, I know."

She patted me on the back as though I were a child. When I stepped back, I said, "Wow. I did not see that coming. I'm okay, really. You're the one who should be crying. It must have been so tough to walk in after being away for weeks and see everything looking like it did when your dad was still here."

She nodded.

"I do cry, but like it is with you, it just hits me sometimes. I'm doing pretty well today. Just now when you rang the bell, I was going through the papers about moving the *Times* to a nonprofit. I came across some hand-written notes Dad had made, and I felt oddly comforted. Like it was a sign that he's still somewhere, watching and approving what we're doing. I needed to get away for a while, and Sebastian needed me, too. But in Chicago, I felt so . . . so *separated* from Dad, I guess is how to explain it. After being here for a few hours, surrounded by his things, sitting at his desk, I felt connected to him again. Weird, huh?"

"No, Charlotte, it's not weird at all."

"Something smells really good," I said a few minutes later as I followed her into Miller's kitchen.

"I brought us a treat. Whenever we were in Madison, Dad would stop by Teddywedgers for a pasty. It was his secret vice. Baz and I are both afflicted with it. I went a little out of my way to get there today, but I felt the urge to have comfort food tonight. A nice hot pasty and cold weather go together."

For the uninitiated, in this context p-a-s-t-y is pronounced like the word "past" together with the letter "t." And it refers to a small meat pie you can hold in your hand. Made right, the crust is tender and flaky and inside is a filling of beef, potatoes, onion and sometimes rutabaga, if you're a traditionalist. Which I am when it comes to pasties.

"I support that urge," I said pulling up a seat at the already set table as she pulled the pasties out of the oven.

Charlotte opened a bottle of burgundy. I'm not a big red wine drinker, but when she said Miller had insisted it was the perfect pairing with pasties, I didn't decline.

We ate, we drank, I told her Luke's death had turned out to be murder and I was investigating for his mother. Then we shared favorite Miller stories that made us laugh, and smile, and cry just a little. When we had no more to say, she poured what was left in the bottle into our glasses. We each lifted ours.

"To Miller," I said.

"To Dad," she said. As we clinked them together, sitting across from each other in the warm kitchen still redolent with the fragrance of the pasties, celebrating the man we had both loved, I realized my anxiety about the future of the paper had faded. When she suggested we go to Miller's office and talk through the steps we needed to take, I was ready.

"Charlotte, before we start figuring out how to move ahead with the nonprofit, we need to talk."

We were both seated on a soft leather sofa in Miller's den, a pile of papers between us. Charlotte was on her laptop, searching for a spreadsheet she wanted to share. She looked up with a quizzical smile.

"That sounds serious. What is it, Leah?"

"I know you're excited about the prospect of Marilyn Karr—and her money—becoming part of the *Times* board if we go nonprofit. I have a lot of thoughts about that, most of them not good."

"Okay, tell me what they are," she said, closing her laptop and putting it aside.

"I've had a lot of experience with Marilyn, all of it negative. She's manipulative, arrogant, and untrustworthy. And she holds a grudge like

Gollum holds his precious ring—tightly and with no intention of ever letting go. I think the only reason she wants to be on the board is to make the *Times* fail."

"Why would she want to ruin the *Times*?"

I recited an abridged litany of the many imaginary sins Marilyn holds against me, beginning with a run-in I had with her son, Spencer, in high school and ending with his arrest for drug dealing last summer, and the subsequent closure of *GO News*.

"Why does she blame *you* for that? Dad said you saved Spencer from getting killed."

"Yeah, well, Marilyn doesn't see it that way. She's not crazy about my mother either. She thinks Mom is the reason Paul divorced her. It's not."

"I'm not doubting you, Leah. But I've really never seen that side of Marilyn."

"Only because you've never thwarted her plans, I'm sure. I know she has money and connections to offer, and we need them, but—"

"Not just money. She called me this morning and offered us all the *GO News* equipment—computers, printers, copy machines, scanners, desks, tables, lamps, chairs—anything we can use, if we're interested. I thanked her and said I'd talk to you and get back with her. But you and I both know we could use everything she offered. None of our stuff has been replaced in years. And it would be free. And practically new."

I was momentarily distracted envisioning a copier that didn't jam, laptops light enough not to throw your shoulder out while hauling them around, desk chairs without duct tape, a real conference table, not three smaller tables of varying heights shoved together . . .

"Leah?"

I snapped out of my reverie. "Yes, what? Sorry. I missed your question."

"I asked if you'd be open to having Marilyn on the board if we balanced her out. You know, make sure the other board members have a genuine commitment to the mission. I admit it. I'm very interested in what she can bring financially to the table, and I'd love to scoop up that free office equipment. But this is a joint venture. We have to both agree. Like you and Dad always did. He'd want that, I know."

"Coop said kind of the same thing. I hear you, but I don't think you understand just how good Marilyn is at being evil. She really could turn out to be a big problem for us."

"Leah, I've worked with people like Marilyn before. I know they like to play games, and I know that can be dangerous. But if we reject her offer to be on the board, that gives her another grudge to hold against you—and a reason to start a new list with me on it. So, she can be trying to do evil from the inside where we can watch her, or from the outside where we'll have no idea what she's up to."

"My gut is saying no, Charlotte, but . . . "

"Think what a huge morale booster it will be to give the staff access to all that almost-new furniture and equipment. We'll have it as soon as we say yes to Marilyn. And she also comes with the promise of significant financial support. I think it's worth the risk."

I was silent, considering Charlotte's arguments—and also the fact that my intense dislike of Marilyn might be keeping me from seeing things clearly.

"Leah, if you really don't want her on the board, then I'll tell her no. This is a partnership. We need to be in agreement."

"Well, then, go for it, I guess. I just hope we don't live to regret this."

22

"How was your dinner with Charlotte?"

Miguel asked the question as I slid into the booth at Woke with my chai latte on Saturday morning.

"Pretty good. We covered a lot of ground. Just FYI, one of her ideas is having Marilyn Karr on the board."

His expressive face registered surprise. "But is that really a good idea? Marilyn, she can be very . . . " He paused and searched for a word.

"Let me help you out— loathsome, evil, vicious. Is that what you're searching for?"

"No, I think *difficult*."

In Miguel speak, because he likes everyone, or tries to, that was pretty harsh.

"Maybe this will change your mind. Along with Marilyn comes her money, her connections, and her offer to give us all of the furniture and equipment from *GO News*. That means new—or nearly new—laptops, desks, printers, copier, and even—brace yourself—Spenser's ultra-fancy DLSR camera. Now how do you feel about the idea?"

"Like I might faint."

And, in fact, his breath was coming pretty rapidly.

"*Chica*, Spenser's camera is a Leica Q2! "

"Well, that will be yours, my son. Sadly, Marilyn's largesse is accompanied by Marilyn. But Charlotte convinced me it's worth the risk. We'll see. Anyway, I plan on letting Charlotte be the Marilyn whisperer. I've got my hands full right now between figuring out my next book and investigating Luke's murder. With your help, I hope."

"But of course! Now, what first?"

"First is the usual condition. You can't—"

"I know. We keep this separate from regular coverage for the paper. What we turn up isn't for a story—yet. And if we have something that will help the police, we give it to them."

"Exactly. Although after my chat with Owen yesterday, I'm not feeling in a super-sharing mood."

"What chat?"

"Didn't I tell you?"

"No, you did not. Your text just said to meet you here."

I gave him the gist of my conversation with Owen and why he suspected Luke. Miguel zeroed in first on the love connection.

"I didn't know Luke and Stella were seeing each other," he said. "How did I not know that?"

"Maybe you're slipping, Dr. Love."

"Did you ask Owen about PPOK?"

"I would have if he hadn't gotten so mad. They're definitely on our list. Today I'm going to try to see Ed and Gwen Wagner, also Phil Stillman from the school board, and Brooke Timmins from the library board. I want to talk to Brodie Granger, too. He's Luke's cousin, and I hope he can tell me more about Luke—and maybe about the burglary Owen thinks they both committed. If his death isn't the result of a PPOK plan gone horribly awry, then we need to figure out who had a reason to want Luke dead. And I want to talk to Marcus Scanlon about the bookstore."

"You are doing everything! What can I do?"

"You can talk to Stella. She may know where Luke got the original $5,000 he needed. He'd have to spin a lot of straw into gold in just a few days to come up with that. And it's not just that money. We should find out where he expected to get the additional $10,000 he needed."

"Okay, and I—"

Before he could finish the thought, a voice called out his name.

"Miguel! I was just thinking about you!"

I turned and saw Pat Rohn, a friend of my mother's, heading toward us. "We miss you at pickle ball. Are you coming this afternoon?"

I wasn't even surprised that Miguel was somehow part of a mostly over-sixties group devoted to playing pickle ball at the community center gym.

"No, I can't, Pat. But sit down for a minute, why don't you?"

I felt a twinge of impatience. I had a lot of people to talk to, and I wanted to wrap things up with Miguel and get started. But just a twinge. Pat's one of my mother's oldest friends, and I really like her.

"Leah, can't you give this boy a day off?"

Miguel scooched over to make room for her.

"Sorry, the news never sleeps, Pat."

"I guess not! That was quite a story about the library fire the other night. We were at my sister's in Milwaukee when it happened. Didn't know a thing until Thursday afternoon when my neighbor called to tell me. When she said Luke had been killed in a fire, I was shocked."

"Were you a friend of Luke's?" Miguel asked.

"We lived next door to Ellen and Josh Granger years ago. Luke was a nice kid. I always knew he'd turn out fine, even though he got into a little trouble after his dad died. My heart just breaks for Ellen."

She grabbed a napkin and pulled off her wire-rimmed glasses to dab at her eyes.

"Sorry," she said. "It's just hit me hard. And I feel bad, too, that I was so mad at Luke for a while. I wish I hadn't been so quick to judge."

Miguel and I exchanged glances. Pat is an easy-going person. It was unlike her to be judgmental. I let Miguel take the lead.

"Why were you mad at Luke?" he asked.

She shook her head and held up her hand to dismiss the question. "No, no, it was nothing. It wasn't any of my business in the first place. That's why I didn't say anything about it then. Now that he's gone, I'm not about to."

"But Luke's mother, she asked Leah to find out why Luke was murdered. So maybe it does matter, Pat," Miguel said.

"Murdered! Luke was murdered? I thought he died in the fire!"

"Didn't you see the story online last night? Luke was shot. He was dead before the fire started."

"No, Miguel. I didn't. I went to bed early, and I haven't looked at the *Times* yet. Somebody shot Luke? I can't believe it!"

"It's true, Pat. Anything you know, even if it doesn't seem like much, could help," I said.

"Oh, I don't want to be in the paper. And I don't know anything. Not really. It was just something I saw."

"This isn't for the paper. It's for Ellen Granger. She's afraid the police aren't going to look very hard to find Luke's killer. She thinks they decided that because Luke was a Granger, he was involved in some kind of criminal activity that got him killed. Do you think that's possible?"

"Well, no, of course not, but . . ."

She paused.

"Pat, you are a mother. Ellen Granger, Luke's mother, she needs to know why this terrible thing happened to her son. You can help her," Miguel said.

"But I don't *know* anything. I just saw something, and it upset me. I don't want to spread gossip."

"No, no, we understand. We will be very careful with what you say, Pat. But we need as much information as we can get to figure things out. Please, tell us what you saw," Miguel said.

I thought she was going to say no. Instead, she sighed and began her story.

"Maybe four or five months ago, I was in my car in the parking lot behind Blissful Body Massage. I saw two people in the far corner of the lot, near the back entrance to the bookstore. They were kissing. The man was Luke. The woman was Ava Farley."

She'd emphasized the name of the woman as though it was important, but I didn't recognize it. Miguel apparently did.

"Oh, Ava Farley. I see," Miguel said.

"I don't. Who is Ava Farley?"

"She owns Blissful Body Massage," Pat said. "She isn't single. She's married to Ray Bowman, a really nice guy. I thought it was pretty low of Luke to get involved with a married woman. Ray had a rough time of it a few years ago when his wife died. But he adores Ava. I felt so bad for him, seeing Ava and Luke together."

"Did you say anything to Luke?"

"I almost did, but I knew it wasn't my business. Then every time I ran into Ray after that, I felt so bad knowing what I did. I just don't think people should sneak around. You're unhappy? Get a divorce first, then go looking."

"Are you sure what you saw wasn't just a hug like you might give a friend?" I asked.

"Leah, I can tell the difference between a hug from a friend and a passionate kiss."

"Sorry. Point taken. Was that the only time you saw them together?"

"Yes. I don't know when things ended with Ava, but I know they did. Last week, I saw Luke with Stella English at the Daily Grind in Omico. They came in holding hands. They didn't even notice me sitting at a table. The next day at the library, I asked Stella if they were dating, and she said yes, but they wanted to keep it quiet."

"Did she say why?" I asked.

"Stella said she'd been seeing someone else. It was casual for her, but when they broke up, she found out it hadn't been 'casual' for him. The guy took it really hard. She didn't want to make him feel worse by showing off how happy she was with Luke. She's a nice girl. But I don't see how this is any help to you, Leah."

"At this point, I don't know that it is, Pat. But thanks for trusting us with what you know."

"Okay, but remember, I don't want to be the cause of rumors going around town. Ray Bowman may not know anything about Ava and Luke. Why hurt him now?"

"Don't worry, Pat. We have no intention of hurting anyone. And your name will not cross our lips in connection with this. Promise."

I wasn't lying to Pat. I didn't intend to hurt anyone. But you know how the saying about good intentions goes, don't you?

23

My mother was sitting at the kitchen table when I walked in, having her usual second round of morning coffee.

"I see my plan worked," she said.

"What plan was that? Mmm, something smells good."

"That's the plan. You haven't sat still long enough in the past week to have an actual conversation. I thought if I made banana walnut muffins, they might lure you in."

"Hey, I already planned to stop by today. But I can't stay long. I've got a ton of places to go and people to see."

"You can find half an hour in your busy schedule to sit down, eat a muffin, and talk to your mother."

"I just talked to you yesterday," I said.

"Yes, for two minutes on your way to see Charlotte. And that was about the longest conversation we've had all week. Plus you left me hanging about what Marilyn Karr has to do with Charlotte. If you don't have the time, you don't get the muffins," she said.

And because I do enjoy talking with my mother—most of the time—and also because she really would withhold the muffins if I didn't, I sat down at the table. She poured me a cup of tea, handed me a muffin, and joined me.

"First things first, how is Charlotte doing, and what's next for the paper, and the thing I'm most curious about—how does Marilyn Karr come into the picture?"

I filled her in on my talk with Charlotte, including my reservations about Marilyn. "But we're going ahead with it. I just hope I haven't sold my soul for free furniture and equipment."

"And I hope Charlotte's right that good board members and a strong executive director can keep Marilyn under control. But I have my doubts," my mother said.

"Me too. Actually I thought of someone for the executive director spot who would definitely not be easily influenced by Marilyn."

"Who?"

"Connor Rafferty."

My mother has a hard time keeping a poker face, but she gave it a good try.

"Oh? I thought he was working at a paper in Florida."

"*Was* is the operative word. It shut down about a month ago. He didn't see it coming. He called last week and asked me to let him know if I heard of anything. It's a tough time to be a reporter looking for work right now. I'm thinking the executive director job might be a good fit for Connor. He's experienced, he's smart, he's covered all the bases in reporting, and he was a managing editor at one time, too."

"He's also an alcoholic."

"Recovering, Mom. He's not like he was when we were together."

"Unreliable and untrustworthy, you mean?"

"That's not fair. That was when he was drinking. Which he isn't anymore. You're the one who taught me to give people a second chance."

"Not people who hurt my daughter like he hurt you. Leah, he let you down constantly. Why do you want him back in your life?"

"When people are in the grip of an addiction, they let you down. Connor is sober and has been for a long time. Also, he won't be back in my life in the relationship sense. I'm with Coop, and that's not going to change. Connor needs a little help finding a job, and we need a lot of help launching a new version of the *Times*. Anyway, I haven't asked him about it yet. I need to talk to Charlotte. Don't get in a tizzy about something that may not even happen."

"I'm not in a tizzy. I'm in concerned-parent mode. But I realize it's your decision to make. Yours and Charlotte's. Now, let's talk about something else. Anything on Luke's murder yet?"

"Not much, but I've got a full day lined up to find out more."

I ran through the list of interviews I hoped to get to.

"Okay, you win. You *are* too busy to see your mother. From that list of names, it sounds like you're leaning into the idea that PPOK set the fire at the library. Are you?"

"Leaning is a little strong, but I think a tilt in that direction is warranted. What I have to figure out is if Luke's murder was intended, or if he was in the proverbial wrong place at the wrong time."

"You mean someone from PPOK set the fire, got caught by Luke, and killed him to keep from getting arrested for arson?"

"That's the theory. How did you know?"

"I'm sixty, I'm not senile. I can still put two and two together."

"Whoa. That was a little crabby. What's up?"

"Sorry. You got the leftover irritation of a week of run-ins with sales clerks, repair people, and well-meaning strangers who seem to think people my age are ready for a shawl and a rocking chair on the front porch."

I smiled at the image of my fit, active, outspoken mother gently rocking away her days.

"Mom. I think you're overreacting. No one who knows you thinks you're ready for a rocker. Maybe that you're off your rocker, but—"

"What I'm talking about isn't funny, Leah. It's dismissive and demeaning to make assumptions based solely on a person's age."

"You're right. I'm sorry. But I wasn't dismissing or demeaning you. I was just acknowledging your smarts, that's all."

She waited a beat before answering. "No, I'm the one who should be sorry. I don't need to take my irritation out on you. I do need to figure out how to handle those kinds of patronizing interactions, though. For now, let's just move on."

"Okay," I said. Though I knew I wouldn't want to be on the receiving end of whatever it was she decided to do about it.

"Going back to PPOK, I think you might be onto something. They're almost obsessed with the need to ban books. I know Dottie Ellsworth is part of the group. Maybe she'd give you some information."

"I don't think so. I saw her at the demonstration outside the bookstore. She got pretty mad when I tried talking to her there."

"I'm sorry to hear that. She and I haven't talked about PPOK. I think neither one of us has wanted to get into an argument about it. We've known each other for thirty years. But now when I run into her, we just chat about nothing, when we used to actually talk. I'm starting to think if all the weight a friendship can bear is conversations about the weather and how the Packers did, maybe it's not a friendship worth keeping."

"Let's not be hasty, Mom. We might never see another piece of Dottie's sour cream coffee cake," I said.

"Now that's a sad thought. So, going back to Connor for a minute. Have you told Coop about hiring him yet?"

"No. Mostly because I haven't seen him since I came up with the idea. And Connor isn't hired yet. We don't even have our board yet. Also, I don't even know if he'll be interested."

"Okay."

"Why are you saying *okay* like that?"

"Like what?"

"Like you think I'm deliberately not telling Coop because I don't think he'll like it."

"You're reading an awful lot into a two-syllable word."

"That's because you packed a lot into those two syllables. Mom, stop worrying. I'm not hiding anything from Coop. He knows all about me and Connor and our past relationship. He'll be fine. Now, I really have to go. Thanks for the muffin."

"Take one for the road. It doesn't sound like you'll get a lunch break today."

24

When I reached Ed and Gwen Wagner's house, I parked across the street because of a semi-truck cab that was taking up most of the Wagner driveway.

"Yes?" Gwen answered my knock on her door hesitantly, as if expecting a salesperson or a missionary. When she saw me, her expression changed from wary to puzzled. "Leah? My goodness, what brings you here? I haven't seen you in forever."

"Hi, Gwen. It's been a long time, I know. I'm looking for some information, and I hope you and Ed can help me. Have you got a few minutes?"

"What kind of information do you need? You're not doing multilevel marketing are you? Because we're really not interested in that."

"No, no. It's about PPOK—"

Ed suddenly appeared behind Gwen in the doorway.

"Leah, this is a surprise. What brings you here?"

"She wants to ask us about PPOK, Ed."

"Oh? Well, come in, why don't you? It's too cold to stand on the doorstep."

He spoke in the same jovial tone I remembered from his shoe-store days. Gwen moved aside so I could enter.

The door opened directly into the Wagners' living room. A stack of signs, the top one of which read "PPOK—Parents Protecting Our Kids!" leaned next to a sofa that gave off the distinct smell of new leather furniture. The largest TV screen I've seen outside of a sports bar hung on one wall.

"Excuse the mess," Gwen said, pointing toward the dining room table, which held a jumble of bowls, plates, glasses, and other kitchen miscellany. "We just remodeled the kitchen, and I'm trying to put it back together."

Gwen is a wispy sort of woman with a voice so soft you sometimes have to lean in to hear her.

"Please, sit down," she said, indicating the sofa.

I took a seat, and Ed folded his tall frame onto a recliner across from me. Gwen perched, rather than sat, on the sofa next to me.

"Now, what would you like to know about PPOK?" Ed asked. "Is this for a story for your paper? I wouldn't mind setting the record straight. A lot of people seem to have the wrong idea about us." He maintained his friendly tone, but the smile he gave me seemed a little forced.

"No, it's not for the paper. I saw you speaking at the protest outside Buy the Book on Monday, and I heard you're one of the founders of the group."

"That's right, me and my cousin Doug."

"Well, I want to understand what PPOK is all about. And you seemed like the person to ask. Why did you start PPOK, and what do you want to accomplish?"

"It's pretty simple. We want to keep kids safe. We don't want them exposed to things that destroy their respect for family and good moral values."

"And you think books do that?"

"Some of them, they sure do. Like those Harry Potter books. They're teaching kids to believe in witchcraft. Our kids are grown, and thank God they weren't big readers. But we've got grandkids now. I don't want them getting taught the wrong things when they're old enough to go to school."

"Ed, the Harry Potter books are fantasy. And lots of children's fantasy books—like the Narnia series—take their cues from Christian theology. You can make a case that books like Harry Potter, or the Narnia books, actually support religious belief."

"I have to disagree with you, Leah. What you said sounds like that same old college-professor BS to me. These schools and libraries and bookstores nowadays, they have books on their shelves that are just flat-out wrong. You should pick one up and read it sometime. You'll see."

His voice was no longer friendly.

"See what, Ed?"

"That some cute little story about animals is really about telling kids it's okay for men to be women and women to be men. Or they say that Columbus didn't discover America, and we ought to apologize for things we never did. These teachers and school boards and librarians, they think they're smarter than a kid's own parents. They don't want to hear anything we say."

Any goodwill left over from our previously pleasant acquaintance was obviously gone. I might as well get straight to the point.

"Luke Granger's mother asked me to look into his death. I'm sure you've heard that it wasn't accidental—that he was shot, and the fire at the library may have been set deliberately to cover it up."

Gwen gasped. "Luke was shot?" Her hand came up and covered her mouth. Her eyes were wide with what seemed like genuine surprise.

"Yes. He was dead before the fire started."

"But who would do that?"

"Don't be foolish, Gwen!" Ed snapped. "She thinks PPOK did it, don't you, Leah? That's why you're here. You don't want to *understand* PPOK. You want to *blame* us."

He had edged forward on his seat and leaned in when he talked. Ed has a large head, with eyebrows as thick and furry as caterpillars. He brought them together in a fierce frown as he glared at me.

"No, I don't want to blame PPOK. I want to find out what happened. You have to admit your group has been getting more aggressive at the school and library boards. And just this past week, one of your members checked out a pile of books and returned them as a box of ashes. Is it such a big leap from burning books to burning down the source of books, the town library?"

"That was one member—if it's even true—not the PPOK group. People like you try to make it seem that people like us are ignorant crazies. Well, we're the ones who know what's going on. And we're the ones who are trying to save our world, not burn it down. We have a right to speak out."

"You do. And I don't think most people think you're crazy. But a lot of people think you're scary."

"Scary how?"

"Because you want to control access to ideas you don't like. But, Ed, you and PPOK don't get to choose for me. Or for my kids—if I had any."

"If you did, you'd know how the schools, and the internet, and the media, they're trying to change everything that's good in our country. All these gay rights, and minority rights, and women's rights—what about my rights? What about the rights of the majority of people in this country? We're done being told how to raise our kids, and live our lives, and think our thoughts. We're pushing back, and people like you, who've had their way for years, you don't like it."

I could feel my own temper rising to meet Ed's. I knew it wasn't a good thing, but I couldn't stop it. The tension in the room was rising.

"Ed, there is nothing on a library shelf or in a bookstore that you're forced to read. You can choose what you want and leave behind what you don't. But you want to take that choice away from everyone. Your rights don't trump mine. I have to wonder, Ed, how far PPOK will go to make sure their choice is the only choice. Where were you last Wednesday night?"

His fists were clenched, and his body radiated the tension of trying to hold in the anger he obviously felt.

"It's none of your business where I was. But it sure as hell wasn't burning down the library! You need to leave."

"Ed—" Gwen reached out to put a calming hand on her husband's arm. He shook her off.

"Get out of my house, Leah. Now!"

Gwen, tiny as she was, grabbed my arm and practically hauled me off the couch. Then she hustled me out and shut the door behind me. There was very little chance that I'd get a return engagement in the Wagner living room. And I hadn't learned much of anything in my visit. I shouldn't have let my feelings get the better of my judgment. Someday those words will be carved on my headstone.

After I was back in my car, I pulled out my reporter's notebook. I don't always take notes when I'm doing an interview. The sight of someone writing down your every word can have a chilling effect on a conversation. But I try to get key points down as soon as I can. I had just sketched out my conversation with Ed when I saw Gwen emerge from the house. She began running toward my car, waving for me to wait.

"Leah, I'm sorry Ed got so upset. Really, he feels terrible about the library fire. People get riled up, but no one in PPOK, especially not Ed, would want anyone to get hurt, let alone killed!"

"I'm sorry I let my temper run away with me, Gwen. But somebody set fire to the library, and somebody shot Luke Granger. Given its history with books, PPOK seemed like a good place to start asking questions. And frankly, Ed's reaction makes me think I must have hit a nerve."

"You can't seriously think Ed had anything to do with that fire."

"I don't know what to think, Gwen. Ed seems really different from the guy I knew in his shoe-store days."

"He is. That's what losing everything does to you. When the shoe store went bankrupt, our house, our savings, even my car . . . everything went. Ed couldn't find a job—turns out fifty-two isn't a great age to start over. All I could get was minimum wage at the grocery store. It flat-out crushed Ed. I seriously thought he might kill himself. He was that low."

"I'm sorry. That must have been a terrible time."

"It was. We were never religious people, but I prayed every night for God to help us. And He did. He sent Ed's cousin Doug to us. Doug got Ed into truck driving, and that turned things around for us. He's got a good job working for Bingley Transport in Hailwell. When Doug told Ed he was worried about what the school had his kids reading, Ed did the research. He found out Doug was right. Something has gone very wrong in our community schools and libraries. Then Doug and Ed got the idea for PPOK. Having steady work, having our debts paid, having a purpose in life —all that has made a world of difference for us."

"I'm glad for you. It looks like you're doing well now."

"We are, and that's because Ed works so hard. Leah, I can tell that you think PPOK is a bunch of crazies. It's not like that. PPOK isn't anti-books and anti-learning. We're just pro-kids, and we want to protect them. We would never set fire to the library and kill someone!"

"Why did Ed get so angry with me?"

Gwen's expression told me that she was getting tired of friendly persuasion. She hesitated for a second, then she gave up the fight and raised her voice—something I'd never heard her do before.

"Because you insulted him! You asked him where he was Wednesday as though he started the library fire! I'll tell you where he was. He was working! He picked up an extra run that night for Bingley Transport. He takes on extra work whenever he can to catch us back up to where we used to be. And before you ask, I was home. Alone. I don't have anyone to vouch for me. So now I suppose I set fire to the library and shot Luke Granger?"

"Gwen, I—"

"No. I thought you might listen, but you have your mind made up. Ed was right. Don't come back here, Leah. We've got nothing to say to you."

25

My next stop was Sophisticated Styles Interior Design, owned by Brooke Timmins. I hoped she'd be there because I'd rather not run into her husband, Cliff. No doubt Owen had already told our esteemed prosecutor that I was interfering in the case.

It was almost noon when I walked through the door. I'd never been in Brooke's office before. The reception area was furnished with several upholstered chairs and a coffee table. The walls were beige with a few modern art prints in bright hues, bringing pops of color to the room. The decor she'd chosen reflected her personal style—cool, elegant, and contained. Which made me wonder, as I had before, why she had chosen Cliff as her husband. He was none of those things with his pinky ring, his unwarranted self-confidence, and his limited intellect. The heart wants what it wants, I guess.

No one was at the reception desk, but I could hear Brooke's voice. I followed it down a short hall.

A door on the left was partially open. A quick glance revealed a work-table and rows of shelves holding fabric samples. An entire wall was taken up by a whiteboard and smaller cork board. This was obviously Brooke's design studio. I hesitated a minute at the other door because I could hear her wrapping up a conversation.

"That sounds good. I apologize again for having to cancel on Wednesday night. Whatever bug I caught knocked me flat . . . Yes, I'm perfectly fine now. Thank you. Oh, I almost forgot your pineapple finally arrived. I'll bring it with me. . . . Yes, I'm looking forward to it. Goodbye."

I tapped on her door and opened it slightly, poking my head around the edge. "Hi, Brooke. I'm sorry to barge in. No one was in the reception area."

Her office was both functional and stylish. She sat in a black leather chair at a glass-topped desk, upon where there was not a single stray paper. A black-metal credenza behind her must have held all her files. In front of her were two black-leather guest chairs.

"Oh, my assistant must have forgotten to lock the outer door when he left. We weren't busy, so I sent him home early. How can I help you, Leah?"

I had been prepared for her to tell me she was far too busy to see me and that I'd need to make an appointment. I was pleased by her semi-friendly response and decided to try a little small talk to get things started.

"This won't take long, but I have to ask. Are you selling fruit as a side-line? I overheard you promising a delivery."

"What? Oh, the pineapple. A client ordered a brass pineapple for her front porch weeks ago, and it finally came in."

"Sorry, I'm not really into decor. Why would anyone want a pineapple on their front porch?"

She looked at me as though I'd questioned the use of forks when we all have fingers.

"The pineapple is the traditional sign of welcome. You didn't know that?"

"No, I didn't." I held back from adding, "That's why I asked."

"Well, we're all here to learn, isn't that the expression?" From her tone, it was obvious she thought I was in need of some serious remedial education.

"Now, Leah, what was it you wanted? You're not selling ads for the paper, are you? I told your salesman last week that my clientele doesn't come from display ads in the *Himmel Times*. We get most of our business from referrals."

"No, this doesn't have anything to do with the paper."

"Really? Well, what does it have to do with?"

"PPOK. I know members of the group regularly attend the library board meetings. And that they're very vocal."

"That's an understatement. One of them practically leaped onto the table where the board sits at the last meeting when we declined to take action on the list of books PPOK wanted removed from the library. But what's your interest if it's not for the newspaper?"

"Luke Granger's mother asked me to look into his murder. PPOK was demonstrating outside the bookstore last week, and not for the first time. The group has gotten louder and more aggressive. Luke's death took place in the library. I'm wondering if those things might be connected. I'd like to hear any insights you have on the group or its members."

"I see. You know I can't comment on an investigation that my husband is directing."

"I understand. I'm not asking you anything about what the police or his department are doing. I'd just like your opinion of the group in general, and any observations you have. I'm not writing a story. Consider it deep background."

She hesitated, and I could almost read her internal debate on her face. She didn't want to do anything to jeopardize the official investigation, but she had something she wanted to say. I tried to help her come down on my side of things.

"I've talked to Owen Fike. I know he's pursuing a theory that Luke was killed because he was involved in some crime. I don't think that's true, though I can't rule it out. But I think it's more likely that PPOK was involved in the library fire, and Luke's death. I'm not asking you to speculate on the case, just give your impression of the group and its leaders."

"I guess I could do that, as long as this isn't on the record. But I will, of course, tell Cliff that I spoke with you."

"I don't have a problem with that. As I said Owen knows I'm investigating."

"Fine, then ask your questions."

"How long has PPOK attended library board meetings? What do they want the board to do?"

"Ed Wagner and his cousin have become regulars the last few months. Other members of the group show up sometimes as well. At first, they just sat pretty quietly, but the last few meetings they've gotten loud."

"What are they getting loud about?"

"They have a list of 'bad'"—she did the air quotes—"books they got online. They want them removed from the library. We have a formal policy that doesn't allow for blanket removal of books. A person has to file a request, fill out the form, and then the request is reviewed first by the library director, then by the board. The board's decision is final."

"Have you removed any books?"

"No. We don't police what patrons read, no matter what their age. If they're minors, as long as a parent has signed their application for a library card, they're entitled to check out what they choose. It's their parents who are responsible for monitoring and restricting as they see fit what their children read. Neither PPOK nor any other group can dictate what other children have access to."

I have never liked Brooke Timmins. Even before she was such an asshat to Luke at the bookstore. She's delusional about the importance her husband's position as county prosecutor gives her. Also, with her cool blonde looks and high-level fashion game, she reminds me a bit too much of Rebecca, Coop's now-dead wife. Which is a whole other story.

But as she finished speaking, I felt like hugging her.

"Have you had any repercussions from facing down PPOK?"

"Ed Wagner has called for a boycott on my business. I'm not worried. PPOK supporters are hardly the target demographic for Sophisticated Styles," she said with a lift of one eyebrow.

Now see, that's what I mean. The way she made it seem like anyone in PPOK was beneath her notice. I don't like their views on books, but I don't like Brooke's snobbiness either.

"How about personally? Has anyone threatened you?"

"No—well, maybe."

"What do you mean maybe?"

"I was working late one night. When I went to my car—I was parked out front—a truck drove by and swerved very close to where I was standing. Someone yelled, 'Watch out, groomer! You'll get yours one of these days!' Or something close to that."

"Did you report it?"

"No. I mentioned it to Cliff, but I knew the police wouldn't be able to do anything. I didn't see the driver clearly or recognize the voice, other than it was a man. It happened so fast I couldn't remember anything about the truck except that it was black or dark blue. Besides, I didn't take it seriously."

"Do you think it could have been Ed Wagner?"

"It's possible. Or maybe his cousin Doug something. I can't remember his last name."

"Durfee," I said. "Has anyone else on the board been harassed?"

"Not that I know of. But Phil Stillman, the school board president, received some anonymous calls with similar messages."

"Yes, I hope to talk to him today, too."

26

As I drove to his house just a few miles outside of town, I thought about Phil Stillman. I'd covered Himmel school board meetings when I first came back to town, so I knew him a little. There's not much glory in serving on a school board, but there's a lot of work and a fair amount of bashing from unhappy parents, teachers, and the general public. Phil's ego was strong enough to withstand the slings and arrows of outraged citizens, and his temperament was cool enough to act decisively without a lot of drama.

The Haven is a quiet enclave in a wooded setting. A tranquil branch of the Himmel River, which was already frozen over, borders the south end of the property. Snow-capped pine trees and smoke floating from chimneys made the scene look like a Currier and Ives print—except that the homes were far larger and more luxurious. The dozen houses sit on half-acre lots that afford privacy but still offer a sense of neighborhood.

At this time of year, the beginning of the holiday season, most of the houses I passed already had outdoor lights strung and lawn decorations out—Santa for the secular, Nativity scenes for the religious. One house had covered both bases with a scene of Santa visiting the baby Jesus.

When I reached the Stillmans' house, a man was hanging Christmas lights on a tree in the front yard, but he was too short to be Phil. I thought he might be the owner of the snowmobile parked in the driveway.

I stamped my feet against the cold as I waited for someone to answer the doorbell. I was about to ring it again when I heard the repeated rattling noise of someone fumbling with the door lock. At last, a woman with a mass of curly, light brown hair opened the door.

"Sorry, I just can't get the hang of this new security system. I set it off twice this week, so I'm trying to be really careful," she said with a rueful smile.

She was pretty in a doll-like way with wide blue eyes, a slightly upturned nose, and a full pink mouth. She wore a fluffy pink sweater over black leggings. She looked a little younger than Phil, maybe early forties.

"Are you Mrs. Stillman?"

"That's me."

"My name is Leah Nash. Is Phil home? I'm doing some research that I hope he can help me with."

"Leah Nash? Really? I just read one of your books. The one about your dad and the cheerleader. For my book club. Lots of times the ones they pick are kind of over my head. But I liked yours. Phil isn't home right now. He's skating, but he should be back soon. Would you like to come in and wait?"

I was surprised but happy she didn't require any more than my bare-bones introduction to invite me in.

"I'm sorry, did you say he's skating?"

"Yes. It's been so cold the ice is thick enough already. Phil played hockey in college. Skating is his favorite exercise. Not me. I hate the cold! Speaking of that, it's way too cold to stand outside. Please, come in."

"Thank you, Mrs. Stillman."

"Oh, please, my name is Kimberly. Mrs. Stillman makes me think of Phil's mother."

A mock shiver and a slight roll of her eyes conveyed that she wasn't a fan of her mother-in-law.

"This is the most elegant mud room I've ever been in," I said, as I stepped into a heated, well-lit, and airy space that fronted the house. It contained hooks for hanging jackets, a rack for boots and shoes, a small bench, a bright rug on a slate floor, and a basket filled with knitted booties in various colors and patterns.

"Well, our interior designer—Brooke Timmins, do you know her?"

"I do. I know her work is very well thought of."

"Yes. She's a friend of ours, and I really do love what she did with enclosing the portico we had. It's so much easier for visitors than teetering in the front hall trying to get their shoes off. Brooke calls it a vestibule. But I'm like you, I just call it a mud room."

"Where did you get all the booties? The pair with the moon and the stars is amazing."

"Oh, thank you. I knitted those from my own pattern. There's really no one home during the day here in the Haven. Most of the women have careers, so I'm on my own a lot. But my crafts keep me busy. I donate a lot of my projects to the Women's Club Christmas sale. Why don't you take the moon and stars pair home with you? I can always knit another."

"I will, thank you! It's very nice of you," I said as I put them on.

"You're very welcome. I'm happy you like them."

She opened the inner door, and we walked into a large entrance hall where everything was highly polished—the floor, the impressive staircase, the console table holding a winter floral arrangement. All of it gleamed in the light from the crystal chandelier overhead.

The booties were soft and warm. But I had to work hard to keep myself from taking a running start to see how far I could slide on the slippery floor.

"We'll go to the den. I don't usually use it—it's Phil's space, but our living room is all upside down now. Our annual holiday party is next week, and the event planner has garland, and tree lights, and I don't know what all strewn all over the place in there."

The den was a cozy room. Built-in bookshelves flanked the small fireplace and a modestly sized flat-screen TV with a DVD player attached was mounted above it. A cushiony sofa with two wing-back chairs on either side sat in front of the fire. On the east wall a large window looked out on the side yard, where snowflakes had begun lazily drifting down.

Kimberly turned on a lamp before she sat next to me on the sofa.

"This is a great room for reading," I said, starting the obligatory round of small talk while we waited for Phil to return.

"It used to be my crafts room. I liked looking out the window at all the birds that came to the feeders while I did my projects. But when we remodeled last year, Phil wanted to change it over to a den. So I moved my things upstairs. Leah, would you like some coffee or tea? Or maybe some water?"

"Sure, Kimberly. Tea would be great, thanks."

"Oh, good! I'll make us some and be right back," she said, her voice happy and light.

I have no illusions about my personal charm. I wondered if Kimberly was so glad to entertain a random stranger because she was lonely in this big house.

While she was gone, I got up to take a look at Phil's books. I think you can tell a lot about people by the titles on their bookshelves. But Phil's collection stymied me. It was both random and odd for a middle-aged real estate magnate—or at least what passes as a magnate in Himmel. It included *The Complete Works of L.M. Montgomery, Great German Short Novels, Walden, War and Peace, Etiquette for All Occasions,* and most inexplicably, *Heidi.*

I tried to envision Phil Stillman sitting by the fire on a snowy evening, a tumbler of whiskey next him, his well-worn copy of *Heidi* in his hand. Nope. Couldn't do it.

"Here we go!"

Kimberly's cheery voice startled me.

"I was just checking out your husband's library. And trying to figure out his reading taste. The books seem kind of . . ."

"Boring and old?"

"Well . . ."

"That's okay. I agree, they are. But that's because they aren't to read. They're to decorate with. We got them from Books by the Yard. You buy the books by size, color, and the kind of binding. Brooke told us about it."

"Ohhh. Now that you say that, I have heard of it. That makes things make sense. I was having a hard time picturing Phil settling down on a cold winter's night to read *Heidi.*"

She laughed.

"When Phil reads he likes action stories. You know, with lots of guns and explosions. But those are all paperbacks. He keeps them upstairs in our bedroom. Phil spends more time watching TV and his old DVDs in here than he does reading."

I changed the topic to take advantage of Kimberly's seemingly total absence of an internal censor. I wanted to find out more about the burglaries at the Haven that Owen thought were related to Luke's murder.

"Kimberly, you mentioned that you'd just installed a new security system. Is that because there was a burglary in the neighborhood recently?"

"It wasn't just in the neighborhood. It was right here at our house, and at the Martins next door."

"Really? Did the burglar get away with a lot?"

"He did! Or they did, whatever, the police don't seem to know if it was one person or two. They took my engagement ring. It was too loose so I had it in my jewelry box until I could get it resized. And they got some other bracelets and things, some cash Phil keeps in his home office for emergencies, his Rolex, his laptop, my iPad, the TV and DVD player that was in this room. They even took my anxiety medication! The same kind of thing happened at the Martins."

"I'm sorry. Have you gotten any of it back?"

"No. The police said we probably won't. They said burglars usually sell things on eBay or take it to Chicago or Milwaukee to somebody who deals in stolen property."

"How did the thieves get past your old security system. You did have one, right?"

"Yes, but it was one of those do-it-yourself kinds. Phil installed it. He forgot to put a sensor on one of the basement windows. That's how the burglar got in. The system we have now is a lot harder to use. That's why I keep setting it off by accident. Phil is getting really annoyed with me. I think I'm going to turn it off when I'm home in the daytime. But don't tell Phil," she said with a conspiratorial wink.

"Did your next-door neighbors have a DIY system too?"

"They didn't have one at all. Kevin said their dog was enough. But that night, the burglary night, I mean, their dog was overnight at the vet's or something. You'll never guess how the burglars got into their house. Go on, guess!"

"Through the doggie door?"

She beamed at me as though I had just given the winning answer for my high school Quiz Bowl team.

"Yes! How did you know? They crawled right into the Martin's kitchen and then had the run of the house. Just like the Martins' dog, Loki, does."

Suddenly Kimberly's attention shifted over my shoulder to something outside. I followed her gaze to the window. The man who had been hanging lights in the front had moved to a trio of small pine trees in the side yard.

"Oh no! Brodie's stringing the white lights."

"Brodie? Would that be Brodie Granger?" I asked, my ears pricking up at the name.

"Yes. I'm sorry Leah, I have to go out and talk to him. Phil wants the middle tree to be blue. He'll be mad if he gets home and it's not. I'll be right back," she said as she hurried out of the room.

So Brodie Granger, Luke's cousin/friend, worked for the Stillmans. I could see him right after I talked to Phil.

27

I watched through the window as Kimberly instructed Brodie, but I began to wonder if I should go out there, too. If Phil didn't get back soon, Brodie might finish his work and leave before I had a chance to talk to him.

On the other hand, if I went dashing out to talk to Brodie, it would be a little hard to explain to Kimberly. Plus Brodie, who wasn't likely to be very forthcoming anyway, would probably clam up in front of his employer.

I turned away from the window, but instead of resuming my seat on the sofa, I took a detour to Phil's DVD collection. Maybe it was more revealing of his character than the books had been. As far as I know, you can't buy DVDs by the yard for show.

The first two rows spanned end to end on the shelves and were mostly action thrillers in the *Mission Impossible* vein, with a few old Clint Eastwood Westerns and war movies in the mix. The bottom row of DVDs reached only halfway across the shelf and was propped up by a brass bookend to keep from tilting over. The plain cases were hand labeled as Packer games, with dates and the name of the opposing team. My mother is a major Packers fan. I sometimes wonder if the real reason she's with Paul Karr is that he has season tickets for the Packers. But even she doesn't have a library of old football games on DVD. I saw no opportunity to bond with Phil over shared favorite films.

As I was straightening up from my inspection, a male voice behind me said, "Excuse me, but who are you?"

I whirled around to face Phil Stilton. He looked very different from businessman Phil who I was used to seeing in expensive suits and cufflinks. This Phil had cheeks and nose that were red with cold. He wore jeans and a Packers sweatshirt. And his thick, wheat-colored hair was flattened in some places and sticking out in others—evidence that he had indeed been skating . . . and wearing a winter beanie while he did it.

"Leah?"

His voice changed from a little confrontational to puzzled as he recognized me.

"Phil, hi. I'll bet you're wondering what I'm doing in your den."

"I am a little surprised. Where's Kimberly?"

"She went out to talk to the guy doing your lights. I apologize for just dropping in on the middle of your weekend, but I was hoping to talk to you about PPOK. Your wife was nice enough to invite me in to wait for you."

"PPOK? Is this for the paper?"

"No, I'm not doing a story on them. But I am doing some research."

"I'm very aware of the group, as I'm sure you know. But if you're not doing a story, I don't understand—"

"Do you mind if we sit down, Phil? I promise it won't take long."

"Of course, please, sit."

"Thank you. And just so you know, I wasn't being nosy when you came in. Well, I guess I was, a little. I was curious about your DVD collection. I have one of my own, but it runs more to classic films."

He waved away my explanation. "No, no, that's fine. But now I'm the curious one. Tell me why you're interested in PPOK if it's not for a story. You're not planning to join are you?"

I recognized his question as an attempt at a joke. Weak though it was, I smiled. After all, he could have said he was too busy to talk to me.

"No, I don't have any plans to join them. I'm interested because I'm investigating the arson and murder at the library."

"Surely that's a job for the police."

"Oh, it is. Definitely. But Luke Granger's mother asked for my help.

She's very concerned his murder won't be solved, because the police are pursuing the wrong theory."

"What theory is that?"

"They seem to believe that Luke's death happened because he was involved in something criminal—you know, because of his family. His mother insists he wasn't. She asked me to see if I could turn up anything that the police might overlook because they think they already know what happened."

"And you believe PPOK was involved in Luke Granger's murder?"

"I think it's possible that someone from the group intended to set the fire and then may have killed Luke when he caught them in the act."

"Well, that's a little shocking, but not entirely surprising. They've turned every school board meeting into a battleground."

"Is that why you're not running for reelection, because of PPOK?"

"Partly. I was already thinking about not running again—eight years is long enough. And PPOK has definitely taken the pleasure out of public service."

"What do you think of Ed Wagner?"

"I used to have coffee with Ed now and then when he had his shoe store. We weren't friends, but we were friendly. Now he seems to think I'm the enemy. I've invited him out for coffee and informal conversation to try and bridge our differences, but he always refuses."

"Has Ed or anyone from PPOK ever threatened you?"

"Just to have me recalled. So far they haven't been able to get enough signatures on their petition."

"But nothing violent, nothing outside of the meetings?"

"No. Well, I've had a few anonymous calls that I guess you could call threatening."

"What did they say?"

"That if I didn't stop defending pornography, I'd be sorry. Recently someone scratched 'pedophile' on my car during a school board meeting. I've talked to the police, but Owen Fike said there's no provable connection to PPOK. But who else could it be?"

"Phil, what can you tell me about the burglary you had a few weeks ago?"

"I'm sorry, I may be a little dense, but what does that have to do with PPOK?"

He said it in the patronizing tone people use when they don't really think *they're* dense, but they're pretty sure you are.

"The police are considering an idea that Luke was involved in the robberies out here, probably with another member of the Granger family. The burglars had a falling out, they fought, and his partner in crime killed Luke. Then tried to cover it up by setting the library on fire."

"I see. I know they looked at Brodie for the break-ins at the time, but I never seriously considered him as a suspect."

"Because he's too honest?"

"I've never had a problem with him stealing. He works for Way to Mow lawn care. They service all my properties. He's had plenty of opportunities to take tools, or materials, or even cash. But he never has. Also, to be perfectly honest, he isn't bright enough to commit a burglary without leaving clues leading directly back to him. I told Owen at the time he was looking in the wrong direction. I'm surprised he's gone back to it. It makes me wonder if Owen is up to the job."

I wasn't having a lot of happy feelings about Owen at the time, but I don't care for casually unfair judgments like Phil had just made. And like I sometimes do.

"Owen is doing three jobs right now. He's serving as captain, but they haven't filled his old job as lieutenant yet, so he's still doing that. And since Mick Riley retired as chief, he's been doing that work, too. He's doing a decent job, I'd say, considering all that."

"That's a fair point. I was too harsh. But after this conversation, I'm going to bring PPOK to Owen's attention, if he's not already following up."

"If you do, no need to mention me. Owen and I aren't seeing eye to eye on this. I'm sure he'd take you more seriously if my name wasn't part of the conversation."

"Understood."

"Thanks for your help. I'd better get going and let you get back to your weekend."

"I'll walk you out."

~

I had just taken my jacket from Phil and was zipping it up when Kimberly came in from the back of the house.

"Phil! I didn't know you were home. I was out helping Brodie with the lights. He got the blue and the white ones mixed up. Leah, are you leaving already?"

"I am. I've taken enough of your time. But thanks for the tea and the company, Kimberly. And the slippers," I added as Phil got my boots and handed them to me.

"You're welcome. But are you sure you can't stay and have a glass of wine with us now that Phil's home? We'd like that, wouldn't we, Phil?" she asked, looking up at her husband.

He didn't look too excited by the prospect.

"Certainly, if Leah has the time. But it sounds like she might need to leave," he said, putting an arm around his wife's shoulder.

"I do have to go. Thanks again, both of you."

"You should come again sometime. No one is home during the day but me. Most everyone here works, or they're retired and go to Florida for the winter. Here," Kimberly said, pulling out her phone and handing it to me. "Put in your number so I can text you. Maybe you can come over for coffee some morning?"

I didn't see the two of us having much in common, but what would it hurt to have coffee with her sometime? She was so obviously lonely.

"Sure," I said as I entered my phone number. "I'm going to be a little busy for the next while. Why don't I call you when things settle down a little for me?"

"Yes, I'd really like that."

If I wasn't so anxious to catch Brodie before he left, I might have stayed just to observe the dynamics between Kimberly and her husband. I was a bit curious about how someone as friendly as Kimberly and someone as serious and slightly full of himself as Phil had come together as a couple. But that was probably a conversation more suited to have over a cup of coffee with Kimberly.

28

I saw Brodie Granger inside the garage, putting away some tools. I hurried over and slipped in the garage to talk to him, knocking down a pair of snowshoes hanging on the wall. The noise made him jump.

"Sorry, I didn't mean to startle you, Brodie. I'm Leah Nash. You *are* Brodie Granger, aren't you?"

He wore a Carhartt jacket and a knitted green watch cap. Copper-colored hair poked out from under it. His very pronounced pug nose was red with the cold.

I bent down and grabbed the snowshoes to put them back on the wall. He made no offer to help.

"Yeah, that's me. Can you move out of the way? I'm runnin' late, and I gotta get going."

"Oh, sure," I said taking a few steps out onto the driveway. "That's a nice snowmobile you've got there!"

In my experience, men, particularly Wisconsin men, like talking about their snowmobiles.

"You got that right. It's a Ski-Doo X. An 850 E-TEC engine—the thing is a powerhouse! And the handling is amazing."

"How long have you had it?"

"Got it last spring. Been ridin' every day since we got enough snow."

"It must've set you back quite a bit."

"I got a deal, and it was still almost ten grand. But she's worth it."

"Wow. Yard work must pay pretty good."

His eyes narrowed. "What are you gettin' at? Hey, are you with the cops or something? I saved for a long time to get this. Who are you anyway, and how's my sled any of your business?"

"I told you. My name is Leah Nash. I own the *Himmel Times*. I'm looking into your cousin Luke's death—"

"I don't have anything to say to any reporters."

"I'm not reporting on this. It's strictly a personal favor for Luke's mother. Your cousin Cole asked me to investigate, too."

I thought throwing in Cole's name might carry more weight with Brodie than Ellen Granger's.

"You a friend of Cole's?" He didn't bother to hide his skepticism.

"No, not a friend. But we know each other. And Cole knows I'm good at finding out things. He and Luke's mother are afraid the police have already made up their minds that Luke was some kind of criminal and that's why he was killed."

"That figures."

"They seem to think there might be a connection between the burglaries out here and Luke's death. The cops haven't spoken to you yet?"

"I don't know anything about the burglaries except what Fike told me when he tried to blame me for them. He couldn't, though, because I didn't do them. Look, I don't know anything about Luke's murder. I gotta go."

It looked like I'd alarmed or irritated him—maybe both—and he was ready to bolt. I tried a different tack.

"Hang on—can you at least give me some background on Luke? I need to know more about him to figure out what motive someone could have had to kill him."

"No time. My ass is freezing, and my girlfriend is gonna be big mad at me, because Phil wanted his lights turned around and now I'm late."

He pulled on a helmet and straddled his snowmobile.

"It's okay if you don't have time now, but—"

He turned to look at me. "I'm not talkin' to you."

Then he roared off in the direction of the woods behind the Stillman house.

I considered going next door to meet the Martins and get their thoughts on the burglary and who committed it. But when I glanced over, I saw a car pulling out of their garage. It passed me, carrying two people in the front seat, while I was opening my car door. That interview would have to wait.

Well. Phil had surprised me with his openness—and with his choice of a wife. I liked Kimberly, but I wouldn't have put her with him. She seemed a little too flighty for Phil. I felt gratified that Phil hadn't dismissed my PPOK theory.

Brodie's reaction was interesting. I'd obviously made him nervous. I needed another run at him when it wasn't so easy for him to get away. Maybe I could get Cole to intervene on my behalf. My phone rang as I finished that thought.

"Hello, Cole. I was just thinking about you."

"Don't try to sweet-talk me with your flirtin'."

"I was definitely not flirting, and why would I ever want to sweet-talk you?"

"Because I just talked to Brodie. He says you're doin' the opposite of what I hired you for. You're supposed to be provin' that no Granger was mixed up in Luke's murder. Instead, you're out there scarin' the bejesus out of him, tellin' him the cops are after him again for a burglary he already proved he didn't do. You're not followin' our plan darlin'."

"First, you didn't hire me. I'm not getting paid, and I'm doing this because of Ellen Granger, not you. Second, there is no *our plan*. There's just me—and Miguel—trying to find out what happened to Luke and why. Third, what does Brodie have to be scared about? I just want to talk to him about Luke."

"Brodie did not sprout from the smartest branch on the Granger family tree. I don't want you trickin' him into accidentally talkin' about things that got nothin' to do with Luke gettin' kilt."

"You mean things like the two burglaries at the Haven, for which he is hands down the most logical suspect?"

"The po-lice questioned him about those robberies, they checked his alibi, and they never arrested him. If he was guilty, he'd be in jail, right?"

"You're not answering my question. Which means you either know that he did them or you suspect it. I'm doing an investigation here, Cole. I'm going to talk to whoever I want to and ask them all the questions I need to. You're not directing how I do things."

"Mama said you was a know-it-all that I shouldn't invite to be gettin' into our business. I guess she was right. You are wastin' time harrasin' my family. I will tell you this, and I hope you're smart enough to listen. If any Granger was involved in them burglaries, and I'm not sayin' one was, it wasn't Luke. No one in our family had anything to do with him gettin' murdered."

"Cole, I'm not trying to prove that Brodie did the break-ins. That's Owen's concern. I want to talk to Brodie to find out more about Luke. I have to find the why behind his death. At this point, I'm not even sure if it was intentional or incidental."

"Gettin' shot in the chest don't seem incidental to me. It's pretty much the main event, I'd say."

"What I mean is the fire could have been all that was supposed to happen. Luke was just in the proverbial wrong place at the wrong time. In which case, I should be looking at who would have wanted to burn down the library. And I'm doing that. But I have to consider that killing Luke might have been the main plan, and setting the fire was just to cover it up. That means I need to figure out the motives for his murder. So, what is the risk in Brodie talking to me about Luke?"

"I think there's always a risk in talkin' to you, Leah. I'm not sure Brodie's up for it."

"Fine. Tell him not to talk to me. But I'm not going to stop asking questions because you think they're the wrong ones or addressed to the wrong person. I'll get the answers I need. Even if they're not the ones you want."

The sigh he gave came over the phone loud and clear, and I knew I'd won this round.

"Brodie'll be at the EAT Tuesday mornin' at 7:30. You happy now?"

"Ecstatic. Bye, Cole," I said. But he was already gone.

I wrestled for a nanosecond about whether or not to tell Owen about my brief talk with Brodie and the follow-up with Cole. I decided against it. He'd made it clear he didn't need my help and didn't want my thoughts. He was already certain Brodie had committed the burglaries. I didn't have any new information to give him. I turned down Miguel's Street on the way to my own and pulled in when I saw his car in the driveway.

29

"Come in! The door is open!" Miguel yelled in response to my knock.

"Where are you?"

"In my room. I'll be right out."

I walked into the living room and saw that preparations for Miguel's "holidays" party were well under way. A naked Christmas tree stood in one corner. A menorah sat on the mantel over the fireplace. Fairy lights were strung around the window frames and on the ceiling, and mistletoe hung from every doorway. The couch and chairs were piled high with garland and other decorations.

"You're getting a head start on things. Your party isn't for two weeks," I said as Miguel walked in carrying several boxes of ornaments, which he deposited on the floor next to the tree. He was wearing dark-wash jeans, white tennis shoes, and a white button-down shirt with the sleeves rolled up. He looked more pulled together in his Saturday clothes than I did in my Sunday best.

"I need time to make the magic. Will you turn off the lamp so I can see the full effect of the fairy lights?"

I complied.

"Yes, I think the gold lights are right, don't you?"

"I think whatever you do party-wise is just right, Miguel. Everyone always has a good time at your soirees."

"Yes, they do," he said with justifiable self-pride.

"There's no false modesty about you, is there?"

He grinned. "If you've got it, own it. So, how did your interviews go?"

I updated him on my round of chats so far—the Wagners, Brooke Timmins, the Stillmans, Brodie, and my phone call with Cole.

"Something is hinky with the Wagners," I said. "I need to find out if Ed really was doing a run for Bingley Transport the night of the fire. And if he wasn't, where was he? But I'm not putting all my eggs in the PPOK basket. When I talk to Brodie again, I hope he can give me an idea about where Luke got the $5,000 he needed for the down payment on Buy the Book."

"But I thought Luke needed $10,000."

"He did but remember that was *after* the bank said he had to come up with a bigger down payment. At first, he was just $5,000 short of the money he needed. He got that from somewhere. Owen thinks it's from two burglaries at the Haven that Brodie and Luke probably committed together. So what about you? Did you talk to Stella English and get the scoop on her and Luke?"

"I did. Her heart, it is broken," he said.

"I'm sure she feels terrible. But did she know anything? Did she mention Ava Farley?"

"No, not her name. She said Luke was seeing someone, but he broke it off when he found out she was married. Only the woman wouldn't let go. She called and texted him so much he had to change his number. But Luke didn't tell Stella her name."

"Sounds like Luke had a fatal-attraction situation brewing with Ava. Could be sparing Owen's feelings wasn't the only reason Luke and Stella kept their relationship quiet."

"You think Ava could have killed Luke for revenge because he broke up with her?"

"She wouldn't be the first woman to kill an ex for leaving her. Or maybe her husband found out, and he killed Luke out of jealousy."

"I don't think Ray Bowman would kill anyone."

"Miguel, almost everyone is capable of killing someone if the circumstances are right. Just how well do you know Ray, anyway?"

"We used to play darts on the same team at the Hilltop Tavern. And I went to their wedding reception a few years ago. Some people said Ray should have waited longer to get married again, but he was very lonely. And Ava is *muy bonita*. Ray, he is very in love with her."

"It sounds like she isn't with him."

"The heart, it's very complicated. That's why you need someone like me, with a doctorate in romance, to help you understand things."

"Okay, Dr. Love. I may be a simpleton when it comes to complex romance, but take an older man and a much younger wife and add in an attractive younger man. Is it really that hard to imagine Ray Bowman as a jealous husband who killed his rival?"

"You're right. The love triangle, it's an old story. I hope it's not this story, though. I like Ray."

"How about renewing your friendship with him? See what he has to say about life in general and maybe married life in particular? Basically a fishing expedition. But do it gently. If he doesn't know about Ava and Luke, let's let him stay happy in his ignorance."

"*Chica,* I am an expert in affairs of the heart," he said, pointing to his own. "I know how to do this."

"I trust you implicitly. As for me, I think I'll book a massage with Ava in the near future. Right now though, I'm going to take a run back to the Haven and see if the Stillmans' neighbors, the Martins, are back yet. I'd like to hear their take on Brodie and the burglary."

"I will come with you!"

"I thought you had to decorate for your party."

"I do, but I want to go with you, too. Besides, I know Gaia and Kevin Martin. They own the Naturally Good health food stores. They were on my podcast last summer, don't you remember?"

"I didn't make the connection, but now that you mention it, I do. Sure, come along. It's always nice to have a little pre-established rapport going into an interview."

～

It was close to 4:30 when we arrived. Thick, gray clouds added to the natural gloom of a mid-December late afternoon. The Martin home was a modern structure of glass and wood with solar tiles instead of shingles for the roof. I was happy to see that lights were visible in several windows, signaling they'd returned home.

The woman who opened the door immediately enveloped Miguel in a hug.

"Miguel! What are you doing here? Come in, come in!" Although she issued a hearty invitation, she didn't actually open the door any wider to let us enter.

She was attractive, with glossy chestnut hair that she wore in a braid tossed over her shoulder. Her long legs were clad in black leggings, and a blue Save the Earth T-shirt peeked out from under her long, black cardigan. She was barefoot, even though the temperatures were hovering in the mid-twenties.

As she released Miguel, he said, "Gaia, this is my friend, Leah Nash. She owns the *Himmel Times*, and she's a famous author, too!"

I could tell from the look she gave me that Gaia was trying to connect my name with a book title.

"Don't feel bad for not recognizing the name, Gaia. Miguel exaggerates my reach. I'm a writer, but not that famous."

"Do you write biographies? I love biographies. Or fantasy or sci-fi— that's what my husband, Kevin, is into."

"No, so far just true crime. My first fiction book is coming out in the spring. A mystery."

"Oh, that sounds fascinating," she said, but her tone was polite rather than interested.

"We are here, Gaia, because we want to ask you about the burglary at your house a while ago," Miguel said, to get us back on track.

"That's funny! The police were here this morning about the same thing. It seems pointless to me. It's been months, and I'm sure whoever broke in has already sold everything. Well, blessings on them. Their need must have been greater than ours."

"That's very generous of you. Most people wouldn't feel that way," I said.

She shrugged. "We practice non-attachment. But, Leah, are you doing a story about it for the *Times*? Because I'd rather not be part of it. What's done is done. Although Loki can't seem to let go of it."

"That's your dog?"

"Yes, our German shepherd. He was at the vet's the night we were robbed, and when I told him about it, he was very upset. He just hung his head in shame for days. He seems fine now, but Kevin and I are thinking about taking him to a therapist. We feel there's something more deep-rooted going on in his psyche."

"Ah, I see."

I shot Miguel a look that said *you could have warned me that Gaia was gaga*. He gave a quick lift of his eyebrows in response.

"No, no, it's not for a story, Gaia. But could we talk to you and Kevin just for a few minutes? Then we can explain."

"Yes, of course. I'm sorry I didn't mean to keep you on the doorstep. Come in, please."

She led us into an open-concept living room, dining room, and kitchen. The heady smell of pine permeated the room. An undecorated Christmas tree, the source of the holiday scent, stood in between two large, floor-to-ceiling windows. Open boxes of ornaments were on the floor and several chairs. Garland festooned the fireplace mantel and several Christmas tchotchkes sat on top of it.

"This is a really nice space. I love the view you have down to the river," I said.

"Thank you. We spend most of our time in here. I love to look out the windows and watch the seasons change. Kevin is upstairs. I'll go get him."

30

Right after she left the room, a very large German shepherd came bounding our way. He stopped several feet in front of us and began barking loudly.

"I can see why the Martins felt they had an adequate security system before the burglary," I shouted over the din.

"Loki! Hush now. It's me, Miguel. You remember?"

The dog paused for a moment. He looked at Miguel and tilted his head. Then he resumed barking.

"Loki!"

On command, the dog went silent as Gaia and her husband walked into the room.

Kevin Martin was a few inches shorter and quite a bit rounder than his wife. He had curly, dark hair and a beard. His eyes were the same color as the faded-blue denim shirt he wore over his jeans.

He snapped his fingers in Loki's direction. The dog immediately trotted over to his side.

"Sorry, Loki's very protective, he'll bark but he won't attack without a command," Kevin said.

"Good to know. I'm Leah Nash," I added.

We shook hands, and then he turned to Miguel.

"Hey, man, it's good to see you. It's been too long. Gaia and I are planning on coming to your holidays party."

I wasn't surprised the Martins were on Miguel's guest list. He routinely invites everyone within a fifty-mile radius of Himmel to his parties.

"Good! It's going to be very fun."

"Would either of you like some kombucha? We just started carrying a new cinnamon-clove flavor that is really flying off the shelves. Would you like to try it?" Gaia asked.

For my benefit, Kevin added, "Gaia and I own the Naturally Good health food stores. We're up to five now. You've probably been to the one in Himmel."

I hadn't, but I saw no need to say that.

"The kombucha offer is tempting," I said, hoping my insincerity was not too obvious. "But we don't want to take that much of your time. Especially because we can see you're just getting started on Christmas decorating."

Gaia expressed disappointment, but Kevin seemed fine with our quick departure plans.

"Okay, well . . . sit down for a minute anyway, and tell us how we can help you," he said.

After we did, Kevin seemed puzzled.

"Gaia told you, I'm sure, that the police were here this morning to talk about the burglary. Why is there so much interest suddenly in something that happened weeks ago?"

"I can't say for sure why the police were here, but I imagine it's for the same reason we are. We're investigating Luke Granger's murder," I said.

"Murder!"

They both gasped in unison—a little theatrically, it seemed to me.

"I thought he died in the library fire, which is terrible. But he was murdered? That's so awful. Why? He was such a nice person." Gaia's eyes were wide with shock.

"I'm sorry, I assumed you knew. Didn't you read it online? Or didn't the police tell you that when they were here?"

"No offense, Leah, but we don't read the local news that much," Kevin said.

Gaia added, "On the weekends, we need to recharge. We try to stay off electronics. The police asked us about Luke, but only in connection with his cousin Brodie. They wanted to know if Luke ever worked on our lawn with Brodie, if Luke had ever been in the house, that kind of thing," she said.

"Had he?"

"No. Never," Kevin said. "We only knew him from the bookstore. We both really liked him, though. We always said we'd have him over sometime. Somehow we never did. Man, Luke murdered. It's hard to take in. How was he killed?"

"He was shot. It's possible the library fire was set to cover up that fact, but it didn't work."

"Why would anyone kill Luke?" Gaia asked again.

"That's what we're trying to figure out."

"But isn't that a police matter?" she asked.

"It is. But Luke's mother asked me to see what we can turn up. She thinks the police are trying to link Luke to a crime—"

"You mean the burglaries here," Gaia interrupted.

"Yes."

"No, I can't buy into that," Kevin said.

"But you did say you didn't know him that well, right?"

It was Gaia who answered me.

"There are kindred spirits on this plane of existence who you connect with strongly, even if you don't know them well. I believe that's because you've already met on another spiritual plane. It's not how long you know someone; it's how strongly you feel the connection. Don't you agree?"

"Uh, possibly," I said. I am not really into spiritual planes and previous lives. I was, however, very into mining whatever we could from this vein of information about Luke.

"Wow. Just wow. It's blowing my mind that the cops would think Luke would rob us. Brodie now, I can see it," Kevin said.

"If you think that, why do you have him working for you?" I asked.

"I don't think that. If I had good reason to suspect him, he wouldn't be working here. But I can see why the police might suspect Brodie. He's been in the house. He knows the layout. But we've never had a problem with him. I doubt Brodie could pull off a burglary and not get caught. He's really not that bright."

Kevin's assessment of Brodie was quite similar to Phil Stillman's.

"That's unkind, Kevin. Not everyone is gifted with a strong intellect," Gaia said.

"Yes, you're right babe. I'm sorry. Man, I wish I'd followed through on spending some time with Luke. Now I can't stop thinking about the last time I saw him."

"Why? When was that?"

"Loki and I were coming back from a walk a couple of weeks ago. Luke's car was pulling out of Phil's driveway. I waved him down, and we talked for a minute. I invited him in, but he said he didn't have time, he had to get to his night job at the library."

"Was it before or after you were robbed?" Miguel asked.

"After. Why?"

But he answered his own question.

"Wait, I see. If Luke was at the Stillmans' place *before* the burglaries, he could have been checking out their layout. No, it was definitely after. I assume he was dropping off an order from the bookstore. He does—did—that for people sometimes. I told him I'd call soon and set something up. I didn't, though. I was too busy. That's the thing isn't it? We're always saying we don't have time to see a friend, because we think we'll always have more later. But we don't."

The only thing we were getting from the Martins was that Luke was a good guy and Brodie was a dumb guy. Sometimes a lead just leads to a dead end.

I caught Miguel's eye and nodded. We both stood up.

"Thank you so much. We've taken up enough of your time," I said. "We'll let you get back to your decorating. That's a big tree you've got to fill."

I turned to go, swinging my purse back up on my shoulder as I did. Unfortunately, it hit one of the chairs holding a box of ornaments. The box crashed to the floor, and the ornaments all came tumbling out.

"Oh, my gosh! I'm so sorry," I said, dropping to my knees to gather up the fallen decorations. "I hope I didn't break any."

"No worries, they're acrylic. A friend made them for us. They won't break," Gaia said, kneeling to help me.

"Oh, these are cute. Look, Miguel, an idea for your party?"

I held up one for him see. It was an upside-down pineapple, turned so that the leafy crown served as a beard, and the pineapple itself was wearing sunglasses and a tiny Santa hat.

"Is your friend who made them local?" I asked.

"Not *local* local, but she lives in Madison. That's not too far away. I'm not sure she makes them to sell. She gifted them to us. If you're really interested in the pineapples, I could ask her. Are you?"

"Yes, definitely. If she can do smaller ones, it would make a cute holiday charm for my cat. I think my mom would be interested, too."

"Your mother, really? That's amazing," Gaia said, favoring me with a wide smile.

"Sure, she likes quirky things. Doesn't she, Miguel?"

Instead of answering, Miguel began coughing and lowered his face toward his elbow.

"Tickle in my throat. Sorry. I'll step out, thank you both," he managed to choke out as he exited, his cough continuing unabated.

"Well, thank you both for your time. I'd better get out there and see if Miguel is coming down with Bubonic Plague or something," I said.

"Oh, please, take one of the ornaments to show your mother, in case she's interested," Gaia said, pressing one into my hand.

"Thank you! Let me know what you hear from your friend," I said.

Miguel was standing on the doorstep, waiting for me. He seemed to have recovered.

"Are you okay? I thought you were going to cough up a lung in there. That was kind of a bust, but we did find possible party favors for your holidays soiree, right? Gaia gave me one to show Mom," I added as we walked down the driveway.

Miguel again began coughing so hard he scared me. Until I realized he wasn't coughing. He was laughing so much that he was practically choking.

∼

"What? What are you laughing at? What's so funny?"

He tried to tell me, but he just kept losing it and laughing harder. Finally when we were both in the car, I said, "Okay. We are not moving until you tell me what the joke is."

"OMG, *chica*. I can't believe you don't know this."

He started to laugh again, but this time, I put both hands firmly on top of his head.

"I am very serious. If you don't tell me what is going on with you, I will make your perfect hair look like you went through a hurricane. I'm not messing with you."

"Okay, okay," he said, bringing himself under control as I took my hands down. "The pineapple!" He was working hard not to start laughing again.

"What about it?"

"Don't you know what it means?"

"Yes. A pineapple is a sign of welcome. I got that on very good authority from Brooke Timmins just today. Why is that so funny?"

"A regular pineapple yes. But the upside-down pineapple Santas that you love so much, that you want your mama to have, that you want to put on your cat, and give as party favors—the upside-down pineapple is the swinger sign."

"The what?"

"It's a symbol that swingers—people who like to switch partners—use. The regular pineapple, it's a sign of welcome. The upside-down pineapple is for married people who like to party with other couples and change partners. I think you should be ready for an invitation from Gaia to a different kind of party than my holidays party."

"Shut the front door! Stop it. Did you know the Martins are swingers? Did you let me come blithely out here just so you could set me up for this?"

"No, No, I swear," he said, holding up his right hand but renewing his laughter. "Oh, this is such a good story to tell Coop."

"No. You will not be telling Coop. Or anyone else. And if Gaia asks for my number, don't give it to her. I can't believe this. No wonder she thought my mother was so amazing."

"Oh, Carol will love to hear this," he said.

"No. I mean it. Do not subject me to that."

"It's very tempting," he said.

We were still arguing when I dropped Miguel off at his house.

31

When I walked through the door to my apartment I was hit with the delicious combined smells of onions, chicken, peppers, cumin, chili powder, and whatever else is in fajitas. Coop was taking tortillas out of the microwave.

"Perfect timing," he said.

"No, perfect partner," I said as I kicked my shoes off. "I am so hungry, and there you are, placemats on the bar, fajitas on the stove, and plates on the counter. You're very good at the domestic side of our relationship." I gave him a quick kiss on my way to wash my hands.

"I figure one of us has to be."

"You know what? I'm so hungry, and what you said is so true, that I am going to let it pass without comment. Seriously, Coop, thank you for getting dinner together."

"My pleasure. Now, want to tell me what you've been up to?"

"I do, but I'm starving. Let's eat first, then you sit on the couch while I clean the kitchen—it's only fair since you cooked, sort of. Then we can sit in front of the fire, and you can be the one to talk first."

Silently eating and enjoying a meal, pausing only to say, "This is really good," or "Please pass the salsa," after a long day of talking and listening to people is an underrated pleasure.

When I joined Coop on the couch, I scooted to the opposite end, and he took one of my stockinged feet in his hand.

"Let the foot rubbing commence. I am all ears to hear about your day," I said.

"Okay. So, you know I've been missing actual investigative work. All the administrative stuff takes up more time than I thought it would."

"Yes, you've mentioned it one or two hundred times."

"I followed up on an idea Dad gave me."

"About what?"

"About looking into a cold case. Something I can do when I have time, then drop when I don't, and come back to it later."

"Okay, I take it you found one?"

"I did. An arson investigation. Two actually. Both happened before I was at the sheriff's office. One a couple of years ago, and one in Delving last year.

"Are the fires linked?"

"Maybe."

"Linked by a person, or by the circumstances?"

"Both, I think."

"Why are you making me ask so many questions instead of just telling me straight out?"

"I'm trying to build suspense. But you're ruining my narrative flow," he said.

He began massaging the ball of my foot with slow circles of his thumb.

"Keep doing that, and I'm going to start purring like Sam. Proceed with the story at your chosen pace."

He grinned and then continued. "I will. Dad has an old friend, Jiggy Dawson. He apprenticed with him when he first got into carpentry. They stayed in touch over the years. Jiggy retired when he turned seventy-five. He and his wife, Mary, were going to buy a fifth-wheeler and visit every state in the continental United States."

"Okay. I'm loving my foot rub, but I'm just checking in. Are you still building suspense?"

"I'm giving you the backstory now."

"Okay."

"Before they could start their travels, Mary got cancer. They used all their savings on the medical bills, but she didn't make it. When she died, Dad said it took the life out of Jiggy, too. If it wasn't for his cat, Ginger, he might have just given up and died himself."

"This is a very sad backstory. Does it get any better?"

"Afraid not. A couple of years ago, Jiggy told Dad that someone had offered to buy his house and the five acres of land it sat on. The guy wanted the property for a big storage unit complex. Jiggy said no, that Mary had died in that house, and he was going to die there too. The very next week, his house burned to the ground while Jiggy was away for the day."

"What about his cat? Don't tell me Jiggy lost his wife, his money, his house, *and* his cat!"

"I'm afraid he did. Ginger was inside. Later that night, Jiggy had a stroke. It was a bad one, and he couldn't live alone anymore. He didn't have insurance on the house because he couldn't afford it with all the bills from Mary's illness. So he had nothing. He had to sell the property to the guy who wanted it for storage units and move into assisted living. A year ago, he was diagnosed with dementia. The last time Dad stopped by, Jiggy didn't recognize him."

"This is the worst bedtime story ever. Though I can see why it caught your interest. You think the guy who wanted to buy the property for his storage unit might have set the fire to force Jiggy out, don't you?"

"You ruined my surprise ending, but yeah, I think that might be what happened."

"But the original investigator didn't? Wait a second. Was the investigator Art Lamey?"

Art had been the undersheriff in Grantland County for years and then had a brief stint as the sheriff before Coop got elected. Art's term had ended in disgrace and jail time.

"Yep."

"I assume that Art's tiny brain was not able to see a possible connection between the fire and the buyer?"

"I think you might be selling old Art short."

"That's pretty hard to do."

"Art's always been good at seeing the main chance. I think he did make the link between the fire and the property sale. Only he didn't use it to solve the case, he used it to his own advantage."

"You mean he approached the guy who bought it and, for a price, closed the investigation?"

"Well, it was the dream setup for him—no insurance company to investigate and raise any issues, Jiggy was out of action, and there was no family to step in."

"And you said the same thing happened with a fire in Delving a while ago, right?"

"Similar, anyway. A rental property that needed a lot of expensive work to bring it up to code burned down. The owner pocketed a nice insurance settlement, instead of having to spend a boatload of money to put in a new septic system, re-roof the house, and mitigate a mold situation in the basement."

"So what got your Spidey senses tingling about that? Ohhh, wait a minute. Is the guy who bought Jiggy's property also the guy who owned the rental house that burned?"

"Clever girl."

I smiled because Coop had used a favorite catch phrase from our youth.

"Despite the fact that the guy in *Jurassic Park* is talking to a rapacious dinosaur when he says that, I take it as a compliment."

"I meant it as one."

"So, who is the guy who benefits from both fires?"

"Sorry. The story stops there for now. Didn't I tell you it was a serial?"

"You're seriously not going to tell me?"

"I'm seriously not. Not yet. I'm not going to toss the guy's name out there when I haven't done any real investigating. It might not be anything more than coincidence. But if I turn up something solid to go on, I'll give the exclusive to the *Himmel Times*, okay?"

"The *Times* is the only news outlet in the county now, so I'm not blown away by your offer of an exclusive. But, okay, keep your secret."

"Okay? That's it? No arguing, no badgering, no freedom-of-the-press rally?"

"That is a very unfair characterization of me, and the only reason I'm not throwing you out of my house right now is that you haven't finished doing my other foot yet. I'm a persister, not a badger-er. I've explained the difference to you before. Now, don't you want to know how my day went?"

"Absolutely."

I went through everything—except the upside-down pineapple part. I ended with my planned meeting with Brodie.

"I thought you didn't agree with Owen's idea? If you're all in on PPOK, why are you bothering with Brodie?"

"Because even though I think PPOK very likely set the fire, and Ed is definitely the one to focus on, I'm not going to ignore the possibility that I could be wrong. However, I remain deeply suspicious about the extra delivery run Ed allegedly did on the night of the fire. And I will be checking up on that."

Coop didn't say anything.

"Wait, aren't you going to list some of the many times when I've been wrong and remind me that Owen is a good cop?"

"What? Sorry, I just had an idea about something else."

"Oh, nice. What are you thinking about that's more important than the words that fall like rubies from your girlfriend's lips?"

He shook his head. "No, haven't thought it through enough to share."

"That's not quite fair. I've just told you everything I've been doing. You're already withholding information on your cold case investigation, and now you have something else you won't share?"

"I'll share. When I'm sure I have something worth sharing. Anyway, how can I be sure you won't take whatever I say straight to Cole now that you're partners?"

I knew he was teasing, but I didn't find it that funny. I gave him the serious side-eye he deserved.

"He's giving me some help getting to Brodie. I'm not Cole's gun moll, you know."

"I know. You're the sheriff's girl," he said, like a cowboy in a bad Western. He got off the couch then to answer Sam's plaintive meow from the kitchen.

"Sam, what's the problem?" Coop asked, squatting down as the cat butted against him. "You've got water. You've got food. Are you feeling neglected?" He rubbed Sam's head. "That reminds me, I got you a new catnip mouse today. Hold on, it's in my jacket."

Coop is not a cat person, but he is very much a kind person.

"Hey," I said as he passed the sofa on his way to retrieve Sam's treat.

"Hey what?"

"Hey, you bet I'm the sheriff's girl."

32

I woke up the next morning to the persistent tapping of paws on my head at 6:30 a.m. I tried rolling over, but Sam continued his attack, moving it from the top to the side of my head. Coop was still sleeping peacefully.

I threw aside the covers, thrust my feet into slippers, grabbed my robe, then followed Sam's triumphant march to the kitchen. He was waiting confidently by the cupboard where I kept his food.

"You know, I could have slept in today. When you're taking a nap, do I keep pounding you on the head until you get up? No, I do not," I said, putting food in his bowl.

He paused for a fraction of a second, gave a look that conveyed my question wasn't worth an answer, then began eating. I yawned, made myself some tea, wrapped up in the afghan from the back of the couch, and sat down at the bar to make a list of things to do. I'm not the most organized person in the world, but I do love a good list. It's not as much for its organizing properties as it is for the satisfaction I feel when I can cross something off. In fact, sometimes if I accomplish a task that's not on my current list, I add it anyway just so I can draw a line through it.

I tapped my pencil for a few minutes, then began writing. I had just finished when Coop came into the kitchen.

"You're up early," he said.

"Sam decided it was time. Sorry if we woke you."

"That's okay. I've got a few things to do today."

"On Sunday? Doesn't the sheriff get a day of rest?"

"No rest for the wicked."

"Are you going to work on your cold case investigation?"

"That and a few other things. What about you?"

"I just made my list," I said. "I want to call Marcus Scanlon to ask him some questions about Luke—if he feels well enough. I need to check in with Charlotte, see if she talked to Marilyn again about joining our nonprofit board. And then it's all about my next book for the day, so I have something good to tell Clinton when he calls, which will probably be tomorrow. Oh, and I'm going to reach out to a possibility for the executive director position for the nonprofit *Times*."

"Who?"

"Connor Rafferty."

Coop had never met Connor, but he knew all about my relationship with him—the good, the bad, and the ugly.

"He's out of a job. The paper he works for shut down, and he's having trouble finding something."

"You think a big-city boy like Connor would want to come to a small place like Himmel?"

"Well, I did. For the same reason that Connor may want to land here for a while. Jobs for journalists aren't exactly lying around on the ground. Besides, I think he might enjoy the challenge of remaking the *Times* into a viable nonprofit. And I know for sure that he won't be steamrollered by Marilyn—or anyone else."

"What about the drinking?"

"He's been sober for a while now. Yes, it was bad. Really bad. But everyone deserves another chance, don't you think?"

"I'm not against second chances," he said.

"But?"

"I didn't say but."

"I know. I can tell you wanted to, though. Coop, you don't think I still have feelings for Connor, do you? Well, I mean, yes, I have feelings for him, but not in any romantic sense. You know that, right?"

"I'm not worried about your feelings. I'm wondering a little about Connor's, though."

"Well, don't. It's been years since he and I lived together. We've both moved on."

He nodded. "Okay. I've got nothing against the guy. And if you think he's the right man for the paper, then I guess you'd better go for it. And speaking of go, I need to."

"So early? Don't you want something to eat?"

"No, I'll grab something at a drive-through. I want to get to the office for shift change. Marla's on this weekend, and I want to check in with her on a couple of things."

"Okay, I'll talk to you later."

~

It was way too early to call anyone on a Sunday, so instead of tackling the calls I needed to make, I worked on the plot line for the next book in my Jo Burke series. I had a couple of ideas that I tried to make happen to no avail. I typed a few paragraphs, deleted two of them, added a few more, deleted one, and went back to thinking. Not exactly a model of progress, but at last, I could tell Clinton in good conscience that I had begun writing.

It was 9:30 by then, certainly late enough to make a few Sunday morning calls. My first was to Charlotte.

"Leah, hi! I was just thinking about calling you. I talked to Marilyn. She's very happy to serve on the board, and even though we don't have things set up yet, she's putting in motion her gift of office equipment and furniture for the *Times*."

"And she does know that I come along with the deal, right?"

"Of course she does. She even said something nice about you."

"Uh-oh. Don't fall for the siren song of a sweet Marilyn. If she's saying anything remotely nice about me, she's planning something."

"Well, even if she is, she can't execute her plan without cooperation from the rest of the board, and that won't happen, because you and I are in charge of who else we invite. Which reminds me, Nora Fielding has moved to the area. She's living at Kipp Lake."

"You're kidding! I love her writing. In fact, the first mystery I ever read was one of hers. My mom is a big fan. What the heck is she doing in this area?"

"She inherited her grandparents' cottage at Kipp Lake. Apparently she spent a lot of time there as a kid. Now she's renovating it as a year-round residence for herself."

"That's amazing. I'd love to meet her."

"Well, Marilyn is the link to her. She met Nora at a women's retreat or something. She suggested Nora as a board member for the *Times* nonprofit. What do you think?"

As soon as Charlotte coupled Nora Fielding's name with Marilyn, my initial excitement took a nosedive.

"I think we should be very cautious about any board-member recommendations from Marilyn."

"After what you've told me about Marilyn, I agree. That's why I think *you* should approach Nora, not Marilyn. When Marilyn said she'd be happy to do it, I told her I felt that was something *we* should do instead. And by we, I meant you. You're a writer; Nora's a writer. You could just invite her to lunch or whatever and see if you think she'd be a good fit."

As Charlotte spoke, I was thinking about how much I'd like to talk with an author like Nora—to pick her brain about writing mystery fiction. Regardless of my feelings about Marilyn, this was an opportunity too good to pass up.

"Yes. I'll do it. Text me her contact information. Having someone with her reputation and—let's get real—her money and connections on the board could open a lot of doors."

"I'm glad you feel that way. I was afraid that since the idea came from Marilyn—"

"Hey, I'm not going to let my feelings about Marilyn get in the way of what's good for the paper. But I'm also always going to be cautious about any of her ideas. This one seems like a pretty good one, though."

"Great. And I have another idea for the board. How about Phil Still-man? I'm impressed with how he's stood up against the book-banning movement. Plus he's got board experience, and we can use that," Charlotte said.

"I think it's worth talking to him. I'll give him a call and set something up. Also, back to the reason I called you, I've got someone in mind who might make a good executive director."

I gave her Connor's credentials and his current situation, as well as a brief overview of our backstory.

"He sounds like he's got the kind of experience we're looking for," she said, but I heard the hesitancy in her voice.

"You sound like you have a few doubts."

"Not doubts about Connor. But I wonder if we should have the board in place and have them be part of the selection process. Whoever we hire is going to be carrying out the vision and direction the board sets for the paper, so . . ."

"I can see that. But we want to get things moving as quickly as possible, right? How about this? I'll contact Connor and see if he's even interested in applying. If he finds something before we're ready to hire, well, yay for him. But if he doesn't, he'll jump into the pool with everyone else who applies, and we'll see."

"Yes, that sounds good."

"I have one caveat."

"Which is?"

"Don't tell Marilyn that I have any connection to Connor unless and until we actually hire him. I don't want her to try and sabotage his candidacy."

"You really think she'd do something that petty, Leah?"

"I really do."

"Okay. I'll defer to your judgment. So we stand at you, me, Marilyn, possibly Nora Fielding, and possibly Phil Stillman for the board. If both Nora and Phil say yes, we'll still have two spots to go to bring us up to seven members. I know my dad thought an attorney friend of his, Gavin Braddock, would be good. He lives in Minneapolis, and he served on a public broadcasting board for a long time. Dad never got the chance to talk to him about it, but I'd like to give him a call."

"He sounds great."

"I have another local member I'd like us to consider. Ray Bowman. Do you know him?"

Although Miguel was gathering intel on Ray through his prior connection, Charlotte had just given me a legit reason to approach him and do my own assessment.

"I don't, but I've heard good things about him. I'll call him."

"Leah, your plate is pretty full. You're investigating a murder, plus you've got Nora and Phil to talk to. I can call Ray."

"I know you can, but talking to a few people is not a big deal to me. You're already doing most of the hard work for the nonprofit transition. You're figuring out the financing model, meeting with other nonprofit news organizations, consulting attorneys, drafting the organizational structure, plus you're contacting the Braddock guy. In fact, now that I list it, I have to wonder what exactly *I'm* doing. Let me at least make a few calls and take a few local meetings, okay?"

"I am a little overwhelmed at the moment. If you're sure . . . "

"Consider it done. You know, Charlotte, I think we're really going to make this happen."

"I know we are."

After I hung up with Charlotte, I called Miguel and asked him to hold off on contacting Ray Bowman until I had taken a run at him, using the board position as my point of entry.

"Okay, but I want to help."

"I know you do. And you have and you will, but this will give me a chance to form my own impression of Ray. I'll fill you in, and then we'll see what comes next."

33

Next up was a call to Marcus Scanlon.

"Marcus, hi. This is Leah Nash. How are you doing?"

"Hello, Leah. I'm doing well, thank you. Just getting used to a new normal. The worst part is the food. My sister Eleanor is here, and she's in a conspiracy with my doctor—walks every morning, no steak, no ice cream."

"I'm glad someone is looking out for you. Marcus, are you well enough to talk to me about Luke for a few minutes? His mother asked me to look into his death."

"Yes, I heard about that. I'm happy to talk to you. I'm glad you're pursuing this, Leah. I talked to a detective from the Himmel Police Department yesterday. He asked a lot of questions about Luke's finances. He wanted to know how Luke came up with the extra money he needed to get a bank loan for the bookstore."

"Funny enough, that's my question too. Do you know where he got it?"

"No, I don't. It never occurred to me to ask him. But I'm sure he didn't steal it, which is what the police implied."

"What about the additional cash he needed when the bank told him he needed thirty percent down instead of twenty? Luke was pretty optimistic about getting it the last time I saw him, so I thought maybe you two had worked out a deal. You lowered the price so the amount of the bank loan would be less, and then Luke could make the higher down payment the bank wanted. Then over time, he'd pay you the difference between the original price you asked and what you'd taken it down to. Was a deal like that in the works between you two?"

"No, I'm afraid not. I wish I could have afforded to do that. I'd already set the amount as low as I could. Luke knew that. He never even raised the question. I feel very bad I couldn't, but . . ."

"No, no, Marcus. Don't feel bad. I don't mean you should have. I'm just casting about for answers. What else did the police ask you about Luke?"

"If I'd ever had concerns about his handling of the money at the store. The answer is a firm no. They asked if Luke had been working the evening of October sixth. Of course he wasn't because the store closes at 5:30 except during the holiday season. They wouldn't tell me why they wanted to know."

"I don't know for sure, but I can make a guess. There were two houses burglarized in the Haven a couple of months ago. The cops are trying to figure out if Luke was part of that. I'm guessing the date they asked about was the date of the break-ins."

"Ridiculous. Absolutely ridiculous. Luke would never do something like that!"

"It doesn't seem likely to me either. Marcus, I'm trying to figure out the motive behind Luke's death. Do you have any idea who might have had a reason to kill Luke?"

"It's very hard for me to imagine one. I honestly can't think of anyone who didn't like Luke. In fact, I used to tease him about his fan club."

"His fan club?"

"Yes, there were some women who I never saw in the bookstore until Luke started working there. Louise Scott was always bringing him cookies. Nancy Albright knitted him a scarf last Christmas. And then there were the high school girls stopping by after school. They came in giggling and asking him for book recommendations. I used to tease him about being a loss leader for the store. I said that customers came in for him, but they wound up buying something off the shelves . . . It was just a little joke we had," he said wistfully.

"Did Ava Farley come into the bookstore much?"

"Ava? No, not regularly. Why?"

"Marcus! It's time to go. Are you ready?" a voice called.

"Excuse me just a minute, Leah."

He must have covered the phone because his voice was muffled, but I heard him say, "I'm on the phone, Eleanor. I'll be right there."

Then he came back to me.

"I'm sorry, that's my sister. It's time for her to walk me. She always wanted a dog when we were children. Since my heart attack, I'm starting to feel like she's using me to make her dream come true."

I laughed.

"Well, older sisters can be a bit bossy, but I'm glad you have someone who loves you taking care of you."

"Truthfully, I am too. I'm sorry I wasn't much help. It's very hard to contemplate anyone being angry enough at Luke to kill him. I just feel so terrible about this whole business. " As he finished, his voice trembled, and he suddenly sounded very old and very sad.

"I know, Marcus. I know. You take care of yourself—and listen to your sister!"

Marcus was right. He hadn't been much help, except to eliminate the only idea I'd had to explain how Luke got the original $5,000 he needed. Follow the money might have worked for Woodward and Bernstein, but it wasn't doing a thing for me.

My phone pinged with a text from Charlotte. Nora Fielding's contact information.

I'm not great at asking people for favors, especially people I don't know. But getting Nora Fielding on the board of the *Himmel Times* would be amazing. I punched in her number before I talked myself into procrastinating the ask.

"Nora Fielding speaking."

Her voice was lovely, deep, and rich. My own came out sounding like a breathless fangirl. Which I basically was.

"Hi, my name is Leah Nash. I love your books. *Death Play* was the very first mystery I read—grown-up mystery, I mean, once I'd gone all the way through Nancy Drew. I've read every one of your books since then. I'm a huge fan."

"Thank you, Leah that's very kind of you. I'm so glad you enjoy my work."

"Oh, I do. My mother does too. In fact, I have a copy of your latest, *Love Lies*, to give her for Christmas."

"That's lovely to hear. But while it's very pleasant for the first phone call of the day to be so flattering, I wonder if there's another reason you're calling?"

I was mortified.

"Oh, geez, yes, there is. I'm so sorry for babbling. I forgot to say that I'm co-owner of the *Himmel Times* newspaper. We're in the process of moving to a nonprofit status. One of our board members, an acquaintance of yours, Marilyn Karr, suggested you might be interested in learning more about the project and perhaps joining our board. But I absolutely understand that you must be very busy, and you haven't lived in the community for long, and you probably don't have much time to give to—"

She laughed and said, "I'm sorry to interrupt, but I have to put you out of your misery. I'm going to assume selling is not one of your core strengths. I'm familiar with the direction your paper is taking. I'm very interested in the idea."

"You are? That's wonderful. I'd love to buy you lunch and tell you more about it."

"I'd like that. But can I suggest that we don't go out for lunch? Could you come to my place on Kipp Lake? I think it will be easier to talk here. You can be the first guest in my just finished house."

"Yes, absolutely. I would love to. When would you like to meet?" I was gushing like a broken water pipe, but I couldn't seem to stop myself.

"I have a couple of speaking engagements this week and some book business to attend to. What about the week after . . . say, Wednesday? Would that work for you?"

"Yes, sure," I said without looking at my calendar. Anything on it, I would happily rearrange. "What time?"

"Let's say around one o'clock."

"That's fine."

"A week from this coming Wednesday it is. I'll text you my address. I'm looking forward to meeting you."

"Thank you so much. I'll see you then."

After hanging up with Nora, I tried to reach Connor to talk about the executive director position. When he didn't pick up, I left a detailed voice-mail. Then I realized I had one more call to make.

"Mom, guess what? I'm having lunch with Nora Fielding in ten days!"

"What? No. I don't believe it! Why? How? Tell me everything!"

Her excited response was everything I'd hoped for. I'm a fan of Nora Fielding. But my mother is a super fan. I quickly gave her the details.

"Can I go with you?"

"Sorry, the invitation didn't include a plus-one. But if we hit it off, who knows? I might be able to wangle an introduction for my elderly mother, whose life is only brightened by the ongoing presence of me in her life . . . and a stack of Nora Fielding books by her rocking chair."

"Fine. Go ahead and say whatever you need to in order to get me included in a future lunch with Nora."

"And here's a thought to hold close to your heart. If Nora joins the board, you'll be able to see her semi-regularly, because the board will certainly meet in the *Times* conference room."

"Be still my heart. You know, Nora and I are about the same age. And if she's living in the area, she may want me to introduce her to some organizations and people she'd enjoy. I wonder if she'd like to do something with the Himmel Community Players? Or I bet she'd like to join the Himmel Library Friends. Or—"

"I'm going to hang up, Mom, and let you plan play dates with your imaginary friend Nora. I'll talk to you later."

34

By Monday morning, I had a plot line for my next book. Rough and sketchy though it was, at least I could respond truthfully that I'd been working on it when Clinton called to check up on me. I returned my focus to Luke's murder with an early-morning call to Bingley Transport. I knew that if I just asked directly whether or not Ed Wagner had picked up an extra run the night of the fire, the company wouldn't tell me. I worked out a small story to get the information I needed.

"Bingley," said the gruff male voice that answered my call.

"Hi. Listen, I've got a 40,000-pound load for expedited delivery to Eau Claire tomorrow night. A friend told me to call you guys and ask for Ed Wagner. He said Ed handled a run for him last Wednesday night, got there early, helped unload, and everything was in good shape."

"Cost on that would be around $600, plus a twenty percent premium for expedited runs. And . . . this ain't a pizza place. You don't get to pick off the menu what's on your pie. We send out whoever's on rotation. And your friend musta got it wrong, 'cause Ed don't do night runs. And we didn't even have any runs goin' out last Wednesday night."

"Oh, are you sure?"

"Lady, I been runnin' dispatch here for fifteen years. I think I know who my drivers are and what they do and when we roll. Now, you wanta schedule somethin' or not?"

"Not. Thanks for your time."

I hung up with a smile on my face. I had proof that whatever Ed Wagner was doing the night of the fire, he wasn't driving a truck as Gwen had told me.

Then I read through a chunk of my notes and an idea that had been flitting in and out of my mind finally came into focus. It gave me a theory for what had happened at the library the night of the fire.

I called Claudia Fillhart.

She picked up on the first ring.

"Good morning, Leah."

"Hey, Claudia. How are you?"

"I'm fine, Leah. Still a bit shaken and shocked by Luke's death. There's so much to do here that I haven't had time to fully process everything yet."

"You said 'here.' Is the library open already?"

"Not for the public, no. But the admin offices weren't badly affected by the fire. We got the go-ahead to come into the building yesterday."

"That's good. Listen, I know you've got a lot on your mind right now, but if you have a minute, I'd like to come over and touch base with you on something."

"I've got a meeting in about an hour with the city manager, but if you can get here before that—"

"I'm on my way."

A smoky smell still lingered in the air at the library. But if it weren't for the trucks, dumpsters, and clean-up crews, you might not know anything had happened there. I found Claudia in her office. She looked up with a smile when I walked in, but there was a weariness in her eyes.

"I'm so sorry, Claudia. I know this has been awful for you."

"I shouldn't complain, Leah. The restoration company has made the library a priority. There was no water damage to this building, and just minimal to the annex. They say they'll be finished with the clean up by the end of this week. I'm grateful for that. But grappling with Luke's death and the way it happened has really weighed on me."

I had taken a seat next to her desk, and I reached out to cover her hand with mine.

"I'm sure it has. How could it not? You've known Luke since he was a little boy."

"It isn't only that. Al Porter told me there's no doubt the fire was deliberately set. The thought that someone in our community could harbor so much animosity toward the library, that's what's shaken me so. We've all worked so hard over the years to make this a welcoming space for everyone in the community. And now these senseless fights over books have—"

"You think that PPOK is responsible for the fire?

"I don't want to think that. You know, some of the PPOK group were very big supporters of the library in the past. Ed Wagner and his wife Gwen used to be members of the Himmel Library Friends. I always thought we had a very good relationship—a friendship really. I don't understand how it could all just evaporate."

"I feel the same way. I always liked Ed and Gwen. I don't *not* like them now. I just don't understand them. But I didn't come to psychoanalyze the Wagners. I came because I hope you can plug a hole in a theory I'm working on."

"How can I help?"

"It's about the security cameras. Owen told me they were working fine in the main areas of the library the night of the fire. But the cameras in the storage area—the one outside at the back door and the one inside the storage area—stopped recording at ten p.m. The cops think Luke turned them off because he was expecting a visitor, and he didn't want their meeting recorded."

"Yes, so I gathered from Owen. I suggested it could just be that the cameras shut down because of a power surge or a problem with the cameras themselves. Owen didn't think much of that explanation. He told me it was impossible to check because the cameras essentially melted in the fire."

"I'm not thinking power surges or mechanical failure—or that Luke tampered with them. I'm wondering if instead of someone coming to the library after hours that night, someone was already *in* the library, not to see Luke, but to set the storage area on fire."

"You mean they hid somewhere when we closed for the evening?"

"Is that possible?"

"Certainly. There are some dead zones the security cameras in the main library don't reach—that cubby by the children's area, for instance. And the night of the fire, we had a very well-attended program on birding. Someone could have slipped away from that and hidden. Although they'd have to know where the cameras are stationed to avoid being recorded."

"But a little reconnaissance could easily tell you that, right?"

"Yes. And if they made their way to the storage area before Luke arrived for work, there are plenty of places there to hide. Is that what you think happened?"

"Maybe. Our security cameras at the paper have an on/off switch on the side. Anyone can turn them off manually. Do yours?"

"Yes."

"Thanks, Claudia. You're like my personal search engine. I know you've got to get to your meeting, and I need to go home and do some more thinking."

"It's true, I do need to leave. But I'd like to hear your theory when it's ready."

"Don't worry. If it works out, you'll hear it, and so will Owen."

On my way back home, I called Miguel.

"Hey, are you at the office? I have a couple of things to run by you."

"I am. Come to the break room."

"Why don't you just come upstairs so we can talk without everybody else around?"

"I will but come to the break room first. I have a surprise for you."

"What is it?"

"It won't be a surprise if I tell you."

"Okay, fine. I'm in the parking lot now. But you know how I feel about surprises."

35

Everybody—my mother, Maggie, Troy, Miguel, Courtnee, even Allie, who had the day off from school—was in the break room when I walked in. A large, white bakery box sat in the middle of the table.

"Okay, what's going on? Is there a birthday I don't know about? A national holiday I haven't heard of? An anniversary of something I forgot?"

"Miguel said he has a story to tell us, but you have to open the box first," Courtnee said.

I gave him a puzzled look.

"Miguel, what's up?"

"No, no, you must open the box, and then you will know."

I shrugged. "Okay."

I lifted the cover, and inside was a very beautifully made cake. But not just any cake. A pineapple upside down cake. I knew what was coming next.

"Miguel, I swore you to secrecy!"

"No, you tried to buy my silence by threatening my hair. But the story is so funny that I will make the sacrifice if I need to."

Then he launched into the story of my exchange with Gaia Martin about her cute upside-down pineapple ornaments. When he got to the big finish, he could hardly get the words out.

"And then—" He had to pause because he was laughing too hard. He tried again.

"And then Leah, she told Gaia that you, Carol, would love the little Santa upside down pineapple because you are into quirky things. And that I, that I—" He had to stop and compose himself again. "That I should hand them out for party favors at my holidays party, oh, and I forgot—she wanted to get a little one made to put on Sam's collar!"

That did it, everyone was howling.

"Oh, Miguel," my mother said, when she recovered. "Thank you for giving me such great ammunition the next time Leah teases me about being an out-of-touch boomer."

"Did you really not know that Leah?" Allie asked.

"*Et tu*, Allie? No, I really did not know that. And I am considering telling your dad that you *do*," I said. "And as for you, Miguel—"

"Oh, don't be mad, *chica*. It was just too funny. I had to share."

I shook my head. "Well, at least you didn't invite Coop."

"Oh, I did. But he couldn't come, so I told the story over the phone. He enjoyed it very much."

I groaned.

"Well, it looks like the joke is on me, and the cake is on Miguel. Go ahead and enjoy, you guys. I'm not a big fan of pineapple cake. I'm going upstairs to get some work done. Come up when you're finished, Miguel. I have something to tell you."

"It's not, 'You're fired,' is it?" Miguel asked.

"No. It isn't. But don't expect me to feel the same if I hear you recounting this story on your podcast."

I received a shot of semi-solidarity from an unexpected quarter.

"Leah?"

"Yes, Troy?" I said as I turned to leave.

"Don't feel bad. I didn't know what it meant either . . . But it is funny."

"Thank you, Troy. And, yes, it is a little funny."

～

When Miguel arrived upstairs, I was sitting at the kitchen bar with my legal pad full of notes and my head full of a plausible theory of the crime. I hit him with it as soon as he walked through the door.

"Miguel, listen to this."

"Are you going to yell at me for telling the pineapple story?"

"I am not. Though it's only fair to warn you that something wicked your way comes—when you least expect it. Now, I'm going to tell you that I think Ed Wagner set the fire at the library, and how he did it. Here, take my stool. I want to do a little pacing while I think out loud."

Once he was seated and looking at me attentively, I began.

"Gwen Wagner told me that Ed was doing a run for Bingley Transport the night of the fire. I called Bingley this morning. He wasn't. So, why the lie?"

"Because he was at the library setting the fire? But how would he get in, and if he got in, how would he get around the security cameras?" Miguel asked.

"He got in with everyone who was attending an event at the library that night. It would be easy to blend in with the crowd entering the building."

"But the camera at the door would still record you."

"Yes, but it was cold that night, and people would have been bundled up. I'll bet if we could get the security footage, which we can't because the police have it, that it wouldn't be that easy to identify anyone."

"Okay, yes, that's true."

"I think Ed went to the library with everyone else at the birding program that night. But he didn't leave. He slipped away during the program and went to the storage area."

"But he wouldn't be bundled up then. He would show up as himself walking to the storage area."

"Not if he knew where the cameras were placed. From what Claudia told me, it's possible to avoid them. And when he got to the storage area, he turned off the inside camera and the one over the outside door. Then he waited for Luke's shift to be over to set the fire."

"And Ed just shot him?"

"No, not just in cold blood like that. I think Luke came into the storage area, and Ed was taken by surprise. Maybe he panicked and took out his gun to threaten Luke, and he shot him accidentally."

"But how do you know he even has a gun?"

"I don't, but it won't be hard to find out. And tons of people have concealed-carry permits. They take their guns everywhere. After Ed shot Luke, he went ahead and set the fire—not just for PPOK purposes, but in the hope that the fire would cover the crime. What do you think?"

"I think you might be right, but there is still more to find out to know for sure."

"There is. And Owen is the person who can find it out. It will be easy for him to check on whether or not Ed has a concealed-carry permit. And if he gets Ed's gun, they can compare ballistics with the bullet found in Luke's body. Plus, they can take another look at the front door camera footage to see if Ed was part of the crowd that came to the birding program that night."

"Do you think he will do that?"

"I do. The theory might not be right, but it makes sense. Owen will check it out—even if for no other reason than to prove I'm wrong."

I felt good thinking I might be able to give Luke's mother some peace of mind, and Claudia, too, and Marcus Scanlon, and yes, even Cole.

Then my phone rang.

~

"Leah, this is Gwen Wagner. I just want to say that I hope you're happy. Ed's been arrested, and it's your fault!"

I was stunned. Had Owen been traveling the same road I was?

"Arrested? For the library fire?"

"No! I told you he didn't have anything to do with that. They arrested Ed for smuggling cigarettes! What does that even mean? Why would anybody smuggle cigarettes? You can buy them at any gas station. Ed was just driving an extra load for Bingley's to make some extra money. What's wrong with that? But nobody will listen to me. The police just came in here and took him away. Doug, too! Ed doesn't even smoke!"

"Gwen, I—"

She went on as if I hadn't even spoken.

"This is on you. You just went to your sheriff boyfriend and told him lies about Ed because you couldn't prove that PPOK had anything to do with the library fire. Because we didn't! All Ed and I and Doug and everybody in PPOK has tried to do is save the children. We never did one illegal thing!"

She finally paused to take a breath, and I jumped in.

"Gwen, I don't know what's going on or why you think it's my fault. I had no idea Ed was going to be arrested, certainly not for cigarette smuggling. I'm sorry that you're—"

"Oh, don't even try to apologize."

Actually, I wasn't. I was trying to get her to calm down enough to give me information instead of a diatribe.

"Everything was fine, our life was good, the money was coming in— because we worked hard, not because Ed was some kind of pirate or something! Then all of a sudden you come out here, and everything goes to hell!"

"Gwen, come on. I don't even understand what's happening, because you're not making sense. I'm not involved in Ed's arrest. I—"

I stopped mid-sentence, because even as I was telling Gwen I had nothing to do with Ed's arrest, I realized that, in fact, I did. Several things flashed through my mind—my conversation with Coop about a cigarette-smuggling ring in the area; his loss of attention on Saturday night when I was in the middle of talking about Ed and his mystery truck run on the night of the fire; Coop's sudden need to go to the office Sunday morning to catch Marla at shift change.

The picture came into focus. Marla was following a lead and working with the ATF on a cigarette-smuggling operation that involved local truckers. I had told Coop that Ed and Gwen seemed to be doing quite well financially. I'd also told him that Ed's alibi for the fire was that he was driving an extra run for Bingley Transport.

Coop had passed that tip on to Marla, and she had found out the same thing I had from Bingley—no doubt before I had. A call from police doesn't require subterfuge and doesn't have to wait until Monday morning during regular business hours. Marla had combined that information with whatever the smuggling investigation had already pulled together, and Ed was arrested.

I realized then that Gwen was still talking. Or, more accurately, yelling and crying. I broke in again.

"Gwen, instead of yelling at me, I think it would be wise to find a good lawyer for Ed. I'm sorry you're going through this, I mean that. But—"

"Just stop. People like you think you know everything, and we don't know anything. When we tried to fight back, to wake people up to what's going on in our schools and our libraries, you couldn't stand it. This isn't about cigarette smuggling; that's just a made-up charge so you all can take down PPOK. Well, you won't. We're going to fight this, and we're going to expose you, and you're the one who will be sorry in the end!"

Abruptly, she ended the call.

"What is happening? I couldn't hear what she said, but I could hear her yelling. Why is Gwen so mad?" Miguel asked.

"She's not just mad, she's hysterical. Ed Wagner wasn't at the library setting it on fire on Wednesday night. He was smuggling cigarettes. Now, you've got a big story to follow up on, and I've got no workable theory for Luke's murder."

36

As soon as I filled him in on what I knew about the cigarette-smuggling activity in the county, Miguel left to talk to Maggie and start working the story. I called Coop.

"Why didn't you tell me you suspected Ed Wagner was involved in cigarette smuggling? I was just about ready to go to Owen with my theory that he set the library fire and killed Luke. You do know how much he would have enjoyed telling me I had it all wrong, don't you?"

"Listen, slow down a minute, will you? I didn't even know you had a full-on theory ready. On Saturday, when you told me it looked like the Wagners had come into some money, and Ed was driving a truck, it started me thinking. I mulled it over for a while and I put it together with the smuggling investigation Marla's been working on. I talked to her on Sunday, and she took it from there."

"And you couldn't say a word to me about it?"

"Hey, I told you about the cigarette smuggling last week. You had the same information I did. You just didn't put it all together."

I paused. He was right. He did tell me about the smuggling. I'd shelved it in some back corner of my mind because it didn't seem related to anything I was doing.

"Yeah, okay, that's true. But you could've let me in on what you were thinking."

"I could have. But it wouldn't have been the right thing to do. It's not my case. It's an ATF operation with Marla helping out. I can't give out information that might jeopardize all their work."

"Oh, nice. You think I'm so dumb or so lacking in judgment that I would run up to Ed and tell him not to worry about being arrested as an arsonist because he's about to go down for smuggling?"

"Come on, you know I don't think that. And I know you can see my point. You're just too mad to admit it. This isn't a new topic for us. Sometimes I can tell you things, and sometimes I can't. It doesn't have anything to do with how smart you are or your judgment. It has to do with me respecting boundaries and staying out of a case that isn't mine. I'm sorry you're upset. I really am."

I sighed. "Fine. I accept your apology. But I'm still mad at you."

"That does not surprise me. How many hours do I have to rub your feet before you're not mad?"

"I'll let you know."

After I hung up with Coop, I began the regrouping process. Ed Wagner was out, so who was in? As I started rethinking suspects, I remembered that I needed to set up a meeting with Ray Bowman.

"Bowman Boats, Ray Bowman here."

The greeting threw me off a little. I'd expected to talk to a secretary who would do her best to keep me from bothering her boss.

"Uh, hi, Ray. This is Leah Nash from the *Himmel Times*. I'd like to schedule an appointment with you."

"What about?"

"It's a little hard to explain over the phone, but in brief, my business partner, Charlotte Caldwell, and I are making a major change at the paper and—"

"What's that got to do with me?"

His question was direct, but his voice was friendly.

"We're moving to a nonprofit news model, and we're looking for members for our board. Charlotte said her father thought highly of you. You've got deep roots in the community, people like and respect you, and we think you're a voice we need on the board of directors."

He laughed. "Flattery like that will get you a hearing from me, anyway. My secretary went home sick this morning. It's why I'm answering the phone. She keeps my calendar, but I'm pretty sure tomorrow morning is open. How about 9:30 at the Elite? You can buy me a cup of coffee. If Betty tells me tomorrow won't work, she'll give you a call and reschedule. How's that?"

"Great, thanks! I'll see you tomorrow."

While the newspaper board was on my mind, I put in a call to Phil Stillman, too.

"Leah, what can I do for you? Is this more about PPOK?"

"No, Phil. It's about a big change we have coming at the *Times*. One that I hope you'll consider being part of."

I gave him the same basic spiel I'd given Ray Bowman. "So, I'd appreciate sitting down with you to explain things in more detail."

"I see. Well, it's an intriguing idea, Leah. Who else is on your board?"

"So far, it's me, Charlotte Caldwell, and Marilyn Karr. I've approached Nora Fielding, but we haven't met yet. I'm seeing Ray Bowman about it tomorrow. Charlotte's contacting a retired attorney friend of Miller's from Minneapolis. He was on a public broadcasting board for a long time, so that would be good experience to draw on."

"I don't recognize the name Nora Fielding."

"Really? You must not read a lot of mysteries. She's pretty famous. She has some family ties to the area and moved here recently."

"I'll have to look her up. I'm very open to meeting with you, but of course, I can't make any commitment until I know more about things."

"Of course. Do you have any time tomorrow?"

"Let me look at my calendar."

He was quiet for a minute, presumably scrolling through his phone, and then he said, "About the only thing open is tomorrow at 11:30. I'm booked the rest of the week. I'd say we could talk one evening, but I've got meetings at night Tuesday through Friday."

"Your 11:30 time slot will work fine for me. Thanks, Phil."

"Not at all. See you then."

Next up was sitting down, armed with my thinking requirements, to reconsider my investigation. It was too early for a Jameson and too cold for a Diet Coke, so I made some tea. I also toasted a pop tart to help soothe my deep sadness at being so very wrong. Then I grabbed the afghan off the couch, turned on the fireplace, and settled in on the window seat with my legal pad and my pencil. Time for some serious reworking of my suspect pool.

But before I could begin, my phone rang again.

"How is plot planning coming? And have you thought about agreeing to nine months instead of a year for your next book?"

"Hello to you, too, Clinton. The plot planning is coming okay. I have a victim, a motive, and I'm working on suspects. I need to do backstories on everyone and some research to see if the murder method I'm thinking about is plausible. I can promise you that I will have a loosely organized—very loosely and subject to change—plot ready in the next few weeks."

"Few weeks? I was really expecting the next few days."

"You're funny. I could tell you I'll have it and then let you down. Or you can accept that I will really, truly produce my version of an outline by three weeks from today. Which do you prefer?"

"I'll take three weeks firm, but it's not sparking joy for me. You didn't answer me on moving to a nine-month schedule instead of a year."

"I'm still thinking about the idea. But not very favorably. I don't just put a quarter in the imagination machine and an idea for the next book pops out. It takes a while for me to get my brain in gear when I'm making things up out of thin air."

"Is that really the problem? Or is it the arson and murder at your local library?"

"How do you know about that?"

"I happen to be a subscriber in good standing to the digital version of your little paper that could. It's the best way for me to keep track of you and the excuses you have for not moving things along."

"I don't know if I like you looking over my shoulder like that."

"Don't think of it as me looking over your shoulder. Think of it as adding to your subscriber base. The more your paper succeeds, the more time you'll have to focus on your career as an author. Not as the Joan of Arc of small-town journalism," he said.

"No need to be sarcastic. That dream is inching closer. We're putting together a kick-ass board for the nonprofit version of the *Times*. Guess who might be joining? Never mind you'll never guess. Nora Fielding."

"You know Nora Fielding, and you've never told me? What is the Duchess of Death doing in the back of beyond?"

"Himmel is not the back of beyond. It's the metropolis of Grantland County."

"I don't care if Himmel is the Alexandria of the new world. Tell me about Nora Fielding."

"She lives here now. Not here in Himmel specifically. Her house is in Kipp Lake, a little community not far away. Someone on our board suggested her as a possibility. I'm going to meet with her next week to talk about it. If she says yes, that would be amazing wouldn't it?"

"It would. But if you can get her to write a blurb for your book that's coming out in the spring, that would be even more amazing. What are the chances?"

"I already have to ask her a favor—to join the board for the paper. I don't want to ask her another one. I don't even know her."

"Do you want to get your book off to a great start? Do you want instant credibility as a mystery writer?"

"Sure I do, but—"

"Fortune favors the bold, Leah. You need to become Nora's new best friend. Her guide to all that Himmel has to offer. And then you need to give her your manuscript to read and ask the nice, famous author to recommend your new book. What's the hesitation?"

"I don't like asking for favors. Especially for one that's so self-serving."

"The publishing world runs on favors. In fact, the whole world does.

Think of it this way. Nora does a favor for you now, and some day when you're famous, you'll return the favor to another new writer. It's the circle of life. Stop making excuses. It's a great opportunity. Take it."

"Well, I guess I could try."

"Excellent. I'll be looking for your plot summary very soon."

And as usual, he hung up without saying goodbye.

37

When Clinton signed off—or didn't—I finally picked up my pencil and legal pad and started thinking.

So, Ed and his cousin Doug were out of the picture. And with them gone, so was the idea that Luke's murder was a tragic but unplanned consequence of setting the library on fire.

I had to start looking at his death as the objective, and the fire as the attempt to cover up the murder. That being the case, Luke was targeted because of something he'd done or something he knew. I tapped my pencil on the side of my pad as I considered that idea. Under the *something he'd done* category, Ava Farley had a reason to kill Luke. He had dumped her. A classic woman scorned motive.

It seemed pretty safe to assume the mystery woman who had plagued Luke with texts and messages after a breakup was Ava. But assumptions are tricky things. A stop at Blissful Body Salon to talk to Ava in person was definitely in order. As I picked up my phone to find the number, it rang.

"Charlotte, hi. What's up?"

"I just wanted to let you know that Gavin Braddock is very interested in our board—in the whole project, really. He invited me to come to Minneapolis to meet with him and then stay over with him and his wife

Gloria. I'm going on Tuesday, not just to talk about the board, though. He said he has some photos of Dad from when they were in college together, and some stories to share. It will be nice to see him and his wife again. So, how's your day going? Did you have any luck connecting with our other prospective board members?"

"I did. All three. I've got a meeting with both Ray and Phil tomorrow morning. And I talked to Nora Fielding. We're going to meet next week."

"Wonderful! How about Connor Rafferty? Is he interested in the executive director position?"

"I had to leave a voicemail, and I haven't heard back yet."

"Okay, there's no rush on that. Hey, I ran into Miguel a few minutes ago. He said we've got a big story on cigarette smuggling coming for the *Times*."

Although Charlotte has made it clear in many ways that she intends to carry on with her father's support of the *Times,* I still find it reassuring when she references the *Times* reporting as something that "we" are doing.

"We do. But it means my favorite theory about Luke's murder is DOA."

"I don't get the connection."

I explained.

"So now where will you go?"

"I'm just figuring that out."

"I'd love to catch up on that. Leah—"

She stopped.

"What?" I asked.

"No, never mind."

"Okay, no. You don't get to start to say something, then say 'never mind.' Because that always means there's something that I should be minding. What were you going to say?"

"I just hope you know that you can trust me with anything related to the paper—or to you—the same way you trusted Dad. You don't have to hold back."

She sounded a little hurt.

"Hey, I know that. I'm sorry if it sounded like I don't. When I said I'm just trying to figure out my next step, it's true. I'm not sure what's next. I invested pretty heavily in PPOK being the cause of the library fire. Now I have to regroup. I need to do a little more digging and get things straight in my own mind. So I'll turn things around and ask if you trust *me* as much as Miller did. Do you?"

"Yes, I do."

"Okay then. We'll talk more later. Are we good?"

"Yes, we're good."

I had decided not to make an appointment but, instead, to visit Ava's business in person. When I entered Blissful Body Salon, I was greeted with a faint scent of lavender oil and the soft sound of ambient music. The small reception area held a desk, a couple of chairs for clients, a tropical fish tank, and a water cooler.

No one was at the desk.

"Hello? Is anyone here?"

A tall woman with wildly spiraling blonde curls hurried into the reception area.

"How can I help you?"

She sounded slightly harried, and I noticed the top she wore was mis-buttoned and had a spot on one sleeve. She must have noticed me noticing, because she looked down and said, "Oh, for heaven's sake!"

She quickly unbuttoned and re-buttoned her shirt as she talked. "Frankly, I'm surprised I even remembered to put a shirt on this morning. It was crazy last week, and this week isn't starting any better. I'm Pam Dixon. I'm the facialist here. I hope you're not looking for a massage today because Ava isn't in."

"Hi Pam. I'm Leah Nash. Actually, I was hoping she could squeeze me in. I have a knot right below my left shoulder that's really giving me problems. I don't suppose you do massages, too?"

"Facial massages, yes, but Ava is the only body massage therapist right now because Danielle is out on maternity leave."

"Well, will she be in tomorrow?"

Pam shrugged. "She told me this morning that she would, but I can't guarantee it. She hasn't been in regular for the past week," she said as she opened an appointment book on the desk. "She's got time at eleven o'clock, will that work? Just remember, I can't promise she'll be here."

"I'll take a chance." As she wrote my name in the book, I said, "It must be tough on you being the only one here and having to take care of all the bookings and cancellations. Listen, if Ava doesn't come in, just text me—don't worry about a call. I've worked short-staffed before. I know what the pressure is like."

I put as much empathy in my voice as I could, trying to use Pam's obvious irritation with Ava to my advantage.

"Thanks. I'm glad somebody understands. It's really wearing me down. I've got my own clientele to handle, and I'm spending way too much time every day apologizing for appointments Ava asked me to cancel. Her people are getting pissed and going elsewhere."

"It's really stressful to deal with angry customers, isn't it? Especially when it isn't your fault."

Pam nodded so vigorously in agreement that it set her spiral curls bouncing.

"It's not just that. Now I'm starting to lose clients on account of her."

"Why's that?"

"Because lots of people see both of us. We offer a package discount. Ava does the body massage, and they come to me for a facial massage or a deep cleanse or whatever. It works great . . . when Ava's working. But clients are leaving the salon because she's been out so much. I don't blame them. But if they go to another salon, that means I lose them, too. They get their facialist work done at their new place."

"Oh, I see what you mean. Well, I'm here, and I've never had a facial massage. Could you fit me in today?"

"Hey, I wasn't trying to make you feel sorry for me so you'd make an appointment. I don't always keep my mouth shut when I should. You don't need to hear my problems."

Her cheeks had flushed red with embarrassment.

"No, no. That's not why I want an appointment. I was just thinking that maybe a facial massage would relax me a little and help turn down the stress in my body."

"Oh, it definitely will. Tell you what, I was going to close early because I don't have any appointments booked for the next two hours, and we don't get many walk-ins. If you'd really like a facial massage today, I'll charge the discount rate for a package and put you down for a massage at the package rate with Ava tomorrow. But like I said I can't promise she'll be here."

"Thank you, I appreciate it."

38

"I'm just going to do a cleanse before the massage to remove any oil or makeup," Pam said.

I was lying back on a comfortable reclining chair. Both the chair and small space it was in reminded me of being in a dentist's office. Except that the lighting was much lower, there was soft music in the background, and my hands weren't sweating in fearful anticipation. I'm not a very good dental patient.

As Pam wiped my face with a soft cloth, then applied some lovely-smelling serum to my forehead, I felt like I could become a very good facialist client.

"This is heavenly," I said as she began massaging my forehead .

"I'm glad you're enjoying it. A massage is so good for your face. It stimulates collagen growth, increases blood flow, and really helps you look younger. Not that it's a worry for you now, but it's best to start young. I didn't realize that myself until I took facialist training when I was in my forties," she said.

"When you were in your forties? I would've said that you were forty at the most. If that's what facial massage does for your skin, I'm in," I said.

She smiled. "I just turned fifty last month."

"Really? Well, you're an excellent advertisement for your work. Have you ever thought of just setting up on your own?"

"I'd like to, but I don't have the start-up money I'd need. And my credit rating took a nosedive when I got divorced. But we won't get into that! I've been happy renting space from Ava, until lately. We used to get along really well."

"But now you don't?"

She had moved from my forehead to the area around my eyes, which she was massaging with a gentle circular motion. If this kept up, I'd be so relaxed I wouldn't be able to formulate a question.

"Oh, I was spouting off a little before. I get frustrated with Ava and the way she's been acting."

"You mean not showing up for work and leaving you to pick up the pieces? I'd be pretty frustrated, too."

"Some people don't realize how good they've got it. I'd give anything for a husband who thinks I walk on water," Pam said.

Okay, now we were where I wanted to be. But I had to tread delicately to keep her from shutting down.

"Well, based on my experience with marriage, which I admit isn't extensive, that kind of husband is hard to find."

"Tell me about it. But Ray—that's Ava's husband—he thinks she's God's gift. And I admit, she's a gorgeous woman. But Ray Bowman is a great guy. He deserves someone who feels the same way about him. Do you know Ray?"

"Only the way you *know* a lot of people in a small town. I know who he is, and I've heard people talk about him, but I've never met him. A good friend of mine, Miguel Santos, is a friend of Ray's."

"Miguel? Oh, I love him."

"Everyone does," I said.

"He used to be the shampoo boy at his aunt's salon when he was in high school. He was so much fun," she said. "Then we moved, and when I came back, he was working at the paper. I hardly ever see him, but I love listening to his podcast. He's so funny, but his advice is really good."

"He mentioned Ray to me the other day. Said he hadn't seen him in a while and wanted to reconnect."

"I hope he does. Ray could use a friend, I think."

"Why's that?"

"I don't think he's very happy just now. My grandmother used to say, 'marry in haste, repent at leisure.' That's pretty much what happened with me and my husband, and I think it's what happened to Ray. His wife died, and then in a few months, he goes off to Las Vegas with Ava and they come back married."

"And it hasn't worked out?"

Her deft fingers moved from the delicate area under my eyes and began working with firmer strokes on my cheeks.

"Well, no one on the outside really knows what goes on inside a marriage, right? I don't know how Ray feels, but I don't think Ava treats him right. She has it made. Ray is so crazy about her that he remodeled a whole building for her because she wanted to live in a loft apartment."

"Ray redid a building for them to live in? Now that's love."

"Well, not a whole building, I guess that was an exaggeration. But he converted two apartments into one for her. It's fabulous—a skylight, a big picture window, fancy kitchen. It's in that brick apartment building on Oak Street, the one with the iron fencing out front."

That was Father Lindstrom's building.

"I know the one you mean. A friend of mine lives there."

"On top of that, he pays all the medical and living expenses for Ava's sister. She's got a real bad kind of depression."

She lowered her voice to an almost whisper. "She tried to kill herself last winter. Had to go to some residential treatment place to get better. It cost like $20,000—a month!"

"Wow. Ray must be a really generous person."

"He is. I don't think Ava gets it, though. To my way of thinking, she takes him for granted. If I was her, I'd be doing everything I could to keep a guy like Ray happy. Maybe Ava's just too young to know men like him don't come along that often. She should be grateful for what she's got, not looking for something better."

"You mean Ava's having an affair?"

Her fingers stopped their movement. I opened my eyes to look at her.

"I didn't say that," she said.

"You're right. I shouldn't have asked. I was just getting caught up in the story. It's none of my business whether it's true or not."

"Oh, it's true," she said, apparently unable to stop the tide of information she shouldn't be sharing.

"How do you know?"

"This room shares a wall with Ava's massage room. Let's just say I've heard things."

"You mean you overhead Ava hooking up with someone?"

I managed not to say "eww" at the end of that, but overhearing someone else's romantic tryst is high on my list of things I never want to do.

"No, what I heard was the opposite of that. It was a big fight. I couldn't hear anything the guy was saying, just his voice kind of rumbling. But Ava was crying and shouting, and it was pretty clear he was breaking up with her. After a few minutes, he left and slammed the door on his way out. Ava ran after him."

"Did Ava know you overheard?"

"She never said anything about it. Neither did I. I'm not sure she knew I was in here."

"Was that just recently?"

"No, a couple months ago, maybe. She wasn't herself for a few weeks, but then she got back on track. Then the last week or so, it started up again, even worse. Last minute canceling on clients, totally unfocused—one day she came in hung over so bad I told her to go home. I'm mad at her, but I'm worried, too."

"Have you said anything to her husband?"

"God, no. I don't want to be the one to hurt Ray like that. I haven't said anything to Ava either. She'd just tell me it's none of my business. And she'd be right. It really isn't. I just don't like the way she's treating Ray. He deserves so much better."

She stopped abruptly—both talking and massaging.

"What's wrong?"

"Leah, I haven't said a word about this to anyone. I'm not sure why I did now. I guess I've been holding it in too long. Please don't spread it around. I should have kept my big mouth shut."

"Pam, I don't know either Ava or Ray. I don't have any reason to tell anyone what you said. I won't spread it around."

Although that wasn't strictly true. I needed to recalibrate some of my thinking, and to do that, I'd have to share what I'd just learned with at least a couple of people.

～

When I got back and wrote up the notes from my chat with Pam, something jumped out at me that hadn't clicked while we were talking. I called Miguel.

"Can you come up? I want to share a new theory with you."

"Give me half an hour. I'm finishing up a sidebar to the cigarette-smuggling story."

"Okay. Hey, I bet you didn't stop for lunch today, did you? I can feed you early dinner while we talk, if you're hungry."

"No, I'm good. I already had Honey Nut Cheerios for breakfast."

"That's not as amusing as you think it is. Also, Honey Nut Cheerios are appropriate for any meal. Actually, I was going to serve you one of your favorites—Mom's vegetarian chili, but—"

"Did she make corn muffins, too?"

"She did. But given your very unkind comment, implying that I only offer my friends cereal for meals, I don't think I want you to come for lunch."

"No, no, I beg forgiveness. And I love your way with cereal. But I really, really love Carol's chili and corn muffins."

"Apology accepted. I reinstate my invitation. See you shortly."

39

I put the chili on the stove to reheat and the muffins in the oven, then worked on organizing my thoughts until Miguel arrived. After he was sitting down with a bowl of chili and a buttered muffin, I put my theory to the Miguel test.

"Okay, here we go. While you've been following up on the smuggling operation, I've been mourning the demise of my favorite theory. But I've also been rethinking the possible suspect list."

"And?" he asked as he buttered a cornmeal muffin.

"And I went to Blissful Body today to see Ava. She wasn't in, and according to Pam Dixon, the facialist, she's been out more than she's been in lately. I made an appointment to see Ava tomorrow, but I had a facial massage from Pam today—along with a very interesting conversation."

"Oh, Pam! She goes to Making Waves. In high school, when I was shampoo boy there, she was one of my clients. She spills a lot of tea, but she has a good heart."

"That was my experience."

I did a quick run-through of my talk with Pam.

"So, what do you think?"

"I think Ava has been gone so much because she was in love with Luke, and she is very upset that he died in the fire. Also, I think Pam is in love with Ray."

"I agree. And I put those thoughts together with some others, and here's my theory. Jump in if something doesn't make sense. This is the first time I'm pulling it all together out loud."

"I'm ready."

"Here we go. We know it took Luke three years to scrape together $15,000 toward a down payment on a loan for the bookstore. But if it took him that long, how did he suddenly raise another $5,000 in less than three weeks after Marcus had his heart attack?"

"I don't know, *chica*. This is your theory."

"That was a rhetorical question. Owen's idea is that Luke and Brodie committed the robberies at the Haven, and $5,000 was Luke's share of the proceeds. But the robberies took place weeks before Marcus had his heart attack. Luke didn't know he'd need the rest of the money right away at that point. So why would he suddenly turn criminal and go on a burglary spree with Brodie?"

"He wouldn't. But what is your idea?"

"Ava gave it to him."

Miguel's look conveyed that he thought I was out of my mind.

"Hold on a second," I said. "It makes sense. Luke is desperate to get the bookstore. Ava has access to money. He can't see any other way."

"But why would she say yes?"

"Because she hopes Luke will come back to her if she helps him. And maybe Luke encouraged that hope."

"I don't think Luke would do that. He was a good person."

"Sometimes good people do bad things. We have to look at everything, not just what fits the way we want things to be. Consider it from Luke's perspective. He found the thing that everybody wants—a way to make a living doing something he loved. He loved books, he loved reading, he loved talking about books with other people who felt like he did about them. Owning the bookstore would be like living a dream life for Luke. And he put everything he had into getting that dream. It was within his grasp, until Marcus's heart attack. He had to get that money."

"But that would be so cruel to Ava."

"Agreed. But we can talk ourselves into doing some pretty bad things sometimes if we can convince ourselves there's no other choice to get something we really want. Desire is a powerful motive—for money, for love, for a bookstore, maybe."

Miguel turned that over in his mind for a minute.

"Okay, maybe," he said. "But the $5,000 wasn't enough. The bank wanted more. How did he get the $10,000?"

"I think he went back to Ava. On the day of the fire, I saw Luke. I stopped to chat for a minute, and I asked if the money he needed had come through yet. He said things were looking good and he'd know very soon."

"But that doesn't mean the money was coming from Ava."

"But there's more. When I saw Luke, I thought he was going to see Father Lindstrom. I didn't know until Pam told me today that Ava and Ray live in the top floor of the building—that Ray Bowman owns it."

"And you think Luke didn't go to see Father Lindstrom, he went to see Ava?"

"I know Luke didn't see him. Father told me he hadn't seen Luke that day. It didn't strike me as significant until after I talked to Pam. That's when I realized Luke wasn't going to see Father Lindstrom.

"So with that in mind, what about this? Ava summoned Luke to give him her answer on whether or not she'd give him the money he needed. He convinced her that he truly, madly, deeply loved her. And they arranged for her to deliver it to him at the library that night."

"Why wouldn't she just write a check to him right then?"

"Pam said Ava has a sister who tried to kill herself last winter. Ray had paid for some very expensive care for her. Maybe Ava wasn't ready to leave Ray until her sister was in a stable place emotionally. She didn't want to risk him finding out about Luke before then either. Because then Ray might walk out on her, and she wouldn't be able to pay for her sister's care. Writing a check for $10,000 to Luke Granger would definitely raise a red flag for Ray."

"But then how could she get the money? "

"From her business account. Even during the toughest times, Miller insisted we keep three months' operating expenses in reserve in the *Times* account as a buffer. Ava may have done the same thing."

"Okay, then why did she have to go to the library to deliver it?"

"Well, she wouldn't want to keep that much cash at the house even for a short time. Ray might find it and ask her what was up. She wouldn't leave it at her business where it wasn't secure. And Luke didn't want her to deliver it to the house, because he lives with his mother. The library was a good place to hand it over—no one would see them after hours. That's why Luke turned off the security cameras—so their meeting wouldn't be recorded. But something went very wrong."

Miguel sat quietly for a few seconds, processing what I'd suggested. When he got up, I knew he was moving more toward my hypothesis, literally and figuratively. He prefers to think complex ideas through by doing a reenactment.

"*Chica*, I can see it. Ava thinks they are back together. Her lover has come back to her! She goes to the library so happy that night. But then he says something that makes her know he has been lying to her. He doesn't want her. He just wants her money."

As he imagined the conversation, Miguel became increasingly animated.

"She is very angry. And very hurt. She says she will not give him the money. Luke tries to calm her, tries to explain. She won't listen. The more he tries to talk her down, the more angry she is. She cries. She calls him a liar. She cries more!"

Miguel was fully into the scene, so I sat back and let him act it out.

"Ava asks him, 'Why won't you love me?' Luke says he is sorry. He didn't want to hurt her. But he had nowhere else to turn. Ava says, 'I loved you, but now I hate you. I hate you, and I wish you were dead!' Then, she pulls a gun out of her purse. Luke begs her to be reasonable, but Ava is beyond reason. Luke tries to get the gun. They struggle. It goes off. Luke falls to the ground. Luke is dead!"

Miguel flopped back down on his seat, drained. I took over, with less dramatic flair.

"That's when Ava realizes what she's done and what it means. She'll be arrested and go to prison. She won't be there for her sister. What if Ray quits paying for her treatment? Her sister tried to kill herself once. What if she tries again . . . and succeeds? It will be Ava's fault. She can't let that happen. She has to cover up what she's done. She tries to hide the murder by setting the fire."

"It does fit," Miguel said.

"Yes, but I don't know if it's the right fit."

"What do you mean?"

"I'm a little gun-shy—no pun intended—after I went all in on Ed Wagner. There are more answers to get. For one thing, we don't know if Ava has a gun or access to one. And we don't know if she withdrew money from her business account. And I'm sure—"

My phone rang. I saw who it was and picked up.

"Hi, Claudia, what's going on?"

"Leah, can you come to the library? There's something I think you should see. It's to do with Luke's murder."

"I'll be right there. And I'll bring Miguel. He's working on it with me."

40

Claudia was in her office, and when we entered, she motioned for us to come around to her side of the desk.

"I pulled up security video from the storage area. I'm trying to itemize what we lost for the insurance company, and I needed to refresh my memory," she said as I looked over her shoulder at her computer monitor.

"I thought the police took the video."

"They did, but just for the day and evening of the fire. This is from the day before. I want you to see something."

She zipped through the video until she hit the spot she was looking for. The time stamp read 9:30 p.m. The footage was from the camera at the outside back entrance to the storage area. At first, there was nothing to see except falling snow and a plastic bag skittering across the ground in the wind. Then a dark-clad figure, hood up and head down, came into camera range. A bulky down coat and a scarf wrapped around the neck and up over the nose made it impossible to determine if the person was male or female.

Once at the door, the figure knocked. After half a minute of waiting and stomping feet, the visitor knocked again, harder and longer. Another thirty seconds went by, and the door opened from inside. Luke Granger came into view. He stepped out, but kept one hand behind him holding the door, presumably so it didn't slam shut and lock him out.

He was taller and broader than his visitor, and his body obscured our view. All that was visible to us were the gloved hands of the unidentified person as they gestured, presumably while speaking. At one point, Luke shook his head as though responding no to a question. The visitor put a hand briefly on his arm, though it was hard to tell whether the gesture was pleading or threatening. After a few more seconds of conversation, Luke nodded. Then he stepped back inside, closed the door, and his visitor turned and walked away.

The entire encounter had taken less than a minute.

"Do you have any idea who that was?" I asked Claudia.

"None. I'm not even sure if it's a man or a woman."

I nodded. "Well, Luke was what, five-ten or so"? The person was a few inches shorter. It could be a tall woman or a short man. The standard Wisconsin winter wardrobe makes it pretty hard to tell. It doesn't seem like Luke was expecting anyone. If he had been, it wouldn't have taken him so long to answer the door."

"Do you think it could be Ava?" Miguel asked.

"Who is Ava?" Claudia asked.

"Someone we think Luke was seeing before he got together with Stella."

"Oh, the woman you said had a hard time letting go?"

"Yes. But if it was her, I need to think some more about how that fits in with an idea I'm working on."

"Leah, I know you and Owen are going at this investigation from different perspectives. And I don't think he's right in thinking Luke was involved in something criminal. But the video suggests to me that he might have been hiding something. I hope you understand that I have to turn this over to Owen."

"I understand. He's the official investigator. I'm just the interested amateur. Plus Owen has access to equipment that can enhance the video. He might be able to tell who the person is—or at least if it's a man or a woman. But I'd appreciate it if you didn't mention Ava to him. If I'm wrong in what I'm thinking, she and some people she loves could get badly hurt for no reason."

"Of course I won't say anything. I just wanted you to have a chance to see it in case Owen doesn't want to share after I give it to him."

"Thanks, Claudia. I appreciate it. And I don't think there's any 'in case' about it. Owen isn't interested in sharing anything about Luke's murder with me. Although when I see him next, I expect he'll have a lot to say about my major miss on Ed Wagner."

"Ah, yes. I read the story about Ed and his cousin online just before you got here. I was shocked. Getting involved with a criminal ring and smuggling cigarettes for money—well, I never would have expected Ed to do something like that."

"But, Claudia, you thought maybe Ed set fire to the library and killed Luke because of his PPOK ways. Isn't that even more shocking?" Miguel asked.

"It's far worse, yes. But I can understand how PPOK captured Ed's imagination and that he would do whatever he thought he had to do to support his beliefs. What's so surprising to me is that Ed would do something illegal like smuggling cigarettes just for money. There weren't any beliefs or principles involved. It was just greed. I thought Ed had more of a moral compass than that."

She sighed. "Well, people are surprising in both good and bad ways, I suppose. I should call Owen now, I think. You can certainly stay if you want, but—"

"No, that's our cue to exit stage right."

$\sim$

"From the height of the person at the door compared to Luke, it could be Ava. She is tall. Also it looked more like a woman walking than a man walking in the video to me, don't you think?" Miguel asked once we were back in the car.

"I think if the person was Ava, that throws my theory off quite a bit. Why would she have summoned Luke to see her about the money on Wednesday if she'd already seen him the night before at the library? I'm going to have to ponder this a while. I've got a massage with Ava tomorrow morning and a meeting with Ray. Maybe I'll learn something that makes things hang together better. Or not. Oh, and I have a breakfast with Brodie Granger tomorrow, too."

"But how does Brodie fit in now?"

"I don't know that he does, but it's a lead that needs to be followed," I said as I pulled into the parking lot behind the *Times*. I noticed Coop's car parked a few spaces away, and it made me smile. I always feel a little lift when I see him—or know that I will shortly. Even when I'm kind of mad at him—which I really wasn't anymore.

"Okay. Call me tomorrow after all your meetings."

"I will."

When I walked through the door of my apartment, I saw Coop's coat on the hook, but no sign of him.

"Hello? Coop, where are you?"

"Back here!"

I followed the direction his voice came from and found him kneeling on the floor with a bucket beside him, wringing out a towel.

"Hey, I was pretty mad at you for keeping me out of the smuggling loop, but you really didn't have to scrub my floor on your hands and knees to apologize."

"This isn't an apology. It's a rescue operation. Sam figured out how to turn the faucet in your bathroom sink on. But not how to turn it off, it seems. When I walked in, water was streaming out into the hallway," Coop said.

"Oh, no! He's never done that before."

"He's definitely got the hang of it now. You'd better be extra careful to make sure the bathroom door is shut when you leave. If I hadn't arrived when I did, you could have had a really big problem."

"Thank you! I owe you. And I owe Sam a good talking to. Where is he?"

"Probably hiding on the top shelf of your closet."

"I'll deal with him later. I'm sorry you had to do the mopping up—literally. I didn't know you were coming over. Are you hungry?"

"What have you got?"

"I could make spaghetti. I have a jar of Mom's homemade marinara sauce and a loaf of Italian bread in the freezer. How does that sound?"

"Great. Oh, do you have any of that pineapple upside-down cake left? Miguel told me you guys had it for a treat this morning. It would hit the spot as a dessert. Funny though, I didn't know you had a thing for pineapples until Miguel told me this morning."

He managed to say it with a straight face, but I could tell it was killing him.

"All right, all right. Get it out of your system. Come on, hit me with the jokes, and let's get this over with."

He tried to contain himself, but the laughter came out anyway.

I rolled my eyes, but I didn't really mind that much. Coop has a dry sense of humor, and he doesn't burst into laughter that often. I enjoy it when he does—even when the joke is on me.

41

"Okay, let's trade updates," I said as we sat down to eat. "You go first. What's going on with Ed and Doug and the whole smuggling thing? Is Gwen in trouble, too?"

He shook his head.

"There's no evidence Gwen knew Ed was doing anything except what he told her, that he was making extra money for them by doing night runs for Bingley. She should be okay."

"As far as legal issues go, maybe," I said. "I'm not sure how okay you can be when your husband is headed for prison. Or do you think Ed and Doug will get a deal?"

"I'm sure they'll try. But they were both on the bottom rung of the operation. They may not know anything valuable enough to make prosecutors want to offer them one."

"So is Marla done with the investigation, now that she turned up the local truck drivers for the ATF?"

"Yes. The big players are outside of Grantland County. Her asset to the team was her local knowledge. Now that piece is wrapped up, I need her here. She did get her moment in the sun, though."

"Yeah? How?"

"Cliff Timmins had a press conference this afternoon. He made it sound like he was the one directing the ATF operation, which is no surprise. But he did single Marla out for a little praise, and that was nice for her. I saw Troy there, so you can read all about it in the *Times,* I'm sure."

"Was Owen there?"

"He was."

"Did he say anything to you about his investigation?"

"He did mention that he was glad to see he was right about PPOK not having anything to do with the fire."

"You mean he gloated. I hope you stood up for my honor."

"I did. I told him PPOK was just one of several lines of investigation you were following, and you're on to the next one now that PPOK is eliminated. Are you?"

"I am."

I updated him about my new focus on Ava Farley and explained my theory that Ava had been the source of the extra money Luke needed to buy the bookstore. "So, what do you think?"

"It's possible, yes."

"But?"

"There wasn't any 'but' in that sentence."

"It was implied. What don't you like about it?"

"It's not a matter of liking or not. But you've got some loose ends."

"I know. Like was it Ava Farley on the video Claudia showed me and Miguel? And if it was, why was she there? And if she wasn't, who's in the video? Plus, did Ava withdraw money from her business account, and does she have access to a gun?"

"Those are some good questions."

"And I'm going to get some good answers. I've got a massage booked with Ava tomorrow morning, and after that, I have a meeting with her husband Ray Bowman."

"Why Ray?"

"You sound like you know him."

"I do. He donated a new boat for the marine patrol unit, on condition that we not publicize it. He's a good guy. Are you talking to him as a source or a suspect?"

"I don't know yet. Miguel thinks he's a nice guy, too. Pam, the facialist who rents space from Ava at her salon, thinks Ray walks on water. Also, I think she might be in love with him. So, counting you, that's three people who have testified to what a good person he is. Still, even a good man can get very jealous."

"You mean like I would if I found out that you and Troy were having a torrid affair?"

"You would? I'll remember that next time I start one. Though I have to say putting torrid and Troy together in a sentence is very unsettling to me. But back to good guy Ray. I think that a man whose pretty wife is twenty-five years younger than him might be driven by jealousy to kill his perceived rival. But there's no indication that's what Ray did. I'm seeing him tomorrow because Charlotte thinks he'd be a good board member. I'm using that as my entry point, and from there, I'll see what else I can find out about him and his doings on the night of the fire."

"I assume you'll be using your massage appointment to do the same kind of thing with Ava."

"Yes. I'm hoping she won't realize I'm poking around for information while she's prodding my trapezius—or whatever muscles are in your back."

"What about Brodie? Is he still on your list?"

"He is. I have breakfast with him tomorrow. Now I'm very interested in what he was doing the night before the fire."

"Why's that?"

"Because the person who visited Luke at the library on Tuesday night is the right height to be Ava Farley, according to Miguel. But Luke's visitor was also the right height to be Brodie Granger. So, maybe Owen was onto something when he linked Brodie and Luke together. You know, I really don't care who solves this murder, me or Owen."

Coop raised an eyebrow.

"Okay, okay. I do care. I want to be the one. But more than that, I want the truth. I just hope whatever it is gives Luke's mother comfort and not more grief."

"If Owen's favorite theory is right, that Brodie killed Luke over the proceeds from a robbery, that's the exact opposite of what Ellen Granger wants to hear."

"I know. I warned her things might not play out the way she wants them to. But I'd rather not be in the I-told-you-so position on this one. Wait. Are you trying to tell me something without telling me? Did Owen drop some hints about where his investigation is going, but you're being a loyal law-enforcement bro and not telling me?"

"The only thing he said about the case was that Cliff Timmins has been micromanaging it, and he's frustrated. Any detective would be when the DA decides he knows better how to do work in the field."

"Getting super involved in a case this early doesn't sound like our Cliffie. He likes to throw his weight around, but he usually doesn't do any actual work. He swans in after everything is done and holds a press conference to tell everyone what an amazing job he did directing the investigation," I said.

"Well, it seems to be working for him. Judge Keene's early retirement means someone will be appointed to fill out his term. Cliff's in the running. He might be hanging over Owen's shoulder to pump up his profile and keep himself top of mind for the spot."

"Good point. If he can get appointed to the vacancy, he'll be a shoo-in when the regular election comes. Brooke is probably measuring the judge's chambers for new curtains,"

"It wouldn't surprise me," Coop said.

"I hate the thought of a blowhard like Cliff moving into the judicial ranks, but if he does, it could be a good opportunity for Kristin. Do you think she wants Cliff's job?"

"She's never said anything to me about it. But she's the best prosecutor in Cliff's office. And I imagine she's getting tired of Cliff swooping in to take credit for what she's doing."

"I would be," I said.

"Hey, you haven't said. Did you call Connor about the executive director job?"

"I did, but I had to leave voicemail. I expect I'll hear from him tonight or tomorrow. Now, I feel like I took up way more of the 'How was your day, dear?' portion of our evening than you did. Tell me, what's going on with your off-the-books fire investigation? You haven't mentioned it. Is that because you haven't had time to work it or because it turned out there's *nothing* there?"

"Oh, I think something is there. I've turned up a few interesting facts."

"Well, this is sharing time. So, share."

"No, I'm not quite ready. Getting closer, though. I'll let you know."

"Fine. Keep your secrets. You earned your silence by cleaning up after my cat. Thank you again for that. As a boyfriend, you have a lot of pluses."

"Would you like to see a few more?" he asked, pulling me closer to him.

"Why, yes . . . yes, I would."

42

I fed myself breakfast at home before meeting Brodie at the Eat. The diner has great coffee, but the best thing that can be said about the food is the portions are generous. At 7:30 on a Tuesday morning it was a very quiet place. I spotted Brodie alone in a booth toward the back. He was mopping up the runny yolks of two eggs with a piece of very dark—close to charred—toast. Bacon congealing in its own grease, pancakes, and a mountain of hash browns completed the Eat It All breakfast special.

"Good morning, Brodie," I said as I slid into the booth.

The waitress, a tired-looking woman with a V-shaped frown line between her dark eyebrows, approached with a menu.

"No thanks, I'll just have coffee. Oh, and put his breakfast on my bill, if you would, please," I said, pointing to Brodie.

"He already said you were paying," she replied and walked away.

I turned back to Brodie. "Thanks for meeting with me."

In response, he shoveled in a huge forkful of ketchup-drenched potatoes. He chewed for a minute until he was able to speak without having food drop out of his mouth—mostly.

"Yeah. Cole said I had to. But like I told you before, I don't know anything about Luke getting killed."

"But you did know Luke. That's what I want you to help me with. I'm trying to get a better handle on who his friends were, any relationships he was in, that kind of thing," I said, trying to lull him into a sense of ease with me.

"I can't help you there. We did a lot of stuff together when we were kids, but we didn't really hang out much once he moved back from Michigan." He shrugged and put another fork load of food in his mouth, then washed it down with a swig of orange juice.

"Why not?"

"Luke was different when he came back. Kinda boring. Didn't like to do the stuff we used to do—riding snowmobiles, drinking beer, playing cards. Once in a while, him and me got together at McClain's or watched a Packers game, but he didn't have that much free time. What he had, he used it on the ladies."

"What ladies?"

"Luke liked the chicks. They liked him back, I got to say. Everybody's always sayin' how Luke was so smart, and Luke worked so hard, and all that. But I'll tell you what, he found plenty of time to get himself some, if you know what I'm sayin'."

His attempt at a leer fell short, in part because of the clump of egg yolk clinging to one of his teeth.

"Was he serious about anyone?"

"If he was, he didn't tell me. But there was one chick who was super serious about him. He told me he changed his damn phone number because she wouldn't quit textin' and callin' him after he broke up with her."

"Do you know her name?"

"Eva or something like that."

"Could it be Ava?"

"Yeah, I guess."

"Do you know if Luke had any enemies, anyone he'd been in a fight with, or who thought he'd cheated them on a deal, or anything like that?"

"Not that I ever heard."

I tried a different tack to see if I could shake something out of him.

"You got awfully nervous the other day at the Haven when I was talking to you. You couldn't get away fast enough when I mentioned the burglaries and tried to ask you about Luke's death. Why was that?"

"Not nervous. Pissed. I don't know anything. I didn't do anything wrong. I didn't steal anything. I already talked to Fike. I told him where I was and what I was doin' when the burglaries happened. I don't like bein' harassed by cops or by somebody like you. I give 'em an alibi that they couldn't break. That should be the end of it."

"What's the alibi?"

"That when I finished at the Stillmans' place that day, I went back to Way to Mow to drop off some stuff. I clocked out at 5:40. I got home just before six. You can see all that on my phone. I ordered a pizza for delivery, then I took a long shower. Extra-long, because my girl Shayna showed up and washed my back and did a few other things for me, if you know what I mean. I don't think your boy Owen is gettin' much lately. He seemed real interested in hearing the details. How about you, do you wanta get the whole story?"

"About your shower, no. About your alibi, go on."

"Your loss. It's a real good story. Anyway, we got out just before the pizza came. My hair was still wet when I answered the door. You can check who was delivering that night. He'll remember. I was in a good mood after spending that quality time with my girl, and I gave him a real good tip. I was home all night with Shayna. She can tell you that, and my phone will prove it. I never left the house. Fike checked out my story, and he couldn't disprove a word of it."

He ended with a self-satisfied smile.

His specificity about each thing he did after leaving the Stillmans' place —and his confidence that location tracking on the phone was his friend— seemed highly suspicious. It sounded like a carefully crafted alibi planned in advance. I was inclined to believe that Owen was right about Brodie being the burglar. But it didn't follow that Luke had been involved.

"Actually, all that the location information from your phone proves is that *it* didn't leave the house, not that *you* didn't. And maybe all Shayna's story proves is she's a loyal girlfriend. A good burglar can complete a robbery in under ten minutes if he knows the security system and the layout of the house. You were in a position to know both for the Stillmans and the Martins."

"I got no idea how long a burglary takes because I never done one. I do know the cops got no prints, no DNA, no witness, no stolen goods traced to me. I'm not worried."

His cocky grin seemed to confirm that.

"Fine. Let's go back to Luke. He was on track to earn the money he needed for the bookstore over the next few years. But Marcus Scanlon's heart attack put him in a bind. He needed $5,000 more to qualify for the bank loan, and he needed it fast. Do you know where he got it?'"

"His fairy godmother?"

"This isn't funny, Brodie. Luke is dead. Somebody killed him. Don't you want to help find out who did it?"

"I don't know anything about it. How many times do I got to tell you?"

"I'm starting to think you don't know much of anything, Brodie," I said, letting my exasperation at his stonewalling get the better of me.

"You're wrong there. I'm a real smart guy. Maybe I'm not book smart like Luke, but there's other things that make you smart. Trust me, I know plenty of them. In fact, you'd be real surprised how much I know about a lot of things. Fike's never gonna touch me for them burglaries."

"Maybe not. But you make a nice addition to his suspect list for Luke's murder. Or aren't you smart enough to realize that?"

This time, I was deliberately trying to get a rise out of him.

"Now wait a damn minute. I didn't do any burglaries, and I sure as hell didn't kill my own cousin. And if that's what you think—"

I pressed on. "You don't need to worry about what I think. Owen's the one coming after you for murder. And I can easily imagine how his theory goes."

"Yeah? How's that?"

"You and Luke did the burglaries together. He did the planning because you're not smart enough. You took the real risk and did the burglaries. You split the profits, but you had to take all the heat from the cops. You decided that wasn't fair. Luke just blew you off. You got so mad that one night you went to the library to have it out with him. You argued, it turned into a fight, and you killed him. Then you set the fire to cover it up."

"That never happened. None of that happened. I didn't do the burglaries, and I never killed Luke."

"Okay, fine. So tell me where you were the night of the fire."

"Home. I went to work, I clocked out, I went home." His voice was sullen, but I detected an undertone of fear.

"Can anybody verify that?"

A panicked look had come into his eyes. It was one thing to be suspected of a burglary that was hard to prove. It was something else to be a murder suspect.

"Can anyone confirm that you were home that night? What about Shayna?" I prodded again.

"No, she can't. I wasn't home. I was at a club in Madison. I met a girl at the bar. She had some coke. We went out to my car in the parking lot and had a little fun. She went back in, and I went home. It was after eleven when I left."

"Will she confirm it? What's her name?"

"Kelly or Katie or something like that."

"What about her last name?"

"I don't know. I wasn't asking her to move in with me. We just hit it off and went out to the car for some fun."

"You are in deep trouble, my friend. You need a better alibi than that. And if you think your phone will prove where you were, remember what I said a few minutes ago. Your phone will show where *it* was, but that's not proof that you were with your phone. I hope you have something better than that to get you out of a murder charge."

He surprised me then by reaching out and grabbing my wrist so tightly it hurt. His small eyes had tightened to rage-filled slits, and he shouted at me loud enough for the waitress and a customer at the counter to glance our way.

"And you need to shut up. You keep poking around in what ain't your business, you're gonna be sorry. You hear me?"

He flung my wrist aside so hard it struck the table before he stood and stomped out of the diner.

The waitress looked at me sympathetically as I paid the bill.

"You know, honey, you don't have to take that. I saw him grab your wrist."

"Oh, it's not what you think. He's not—"

"I don't think anything. I'm just gonna tell you that I had a man like that once, and it only gets worse. You take care now," she said as she handed me my change.

43

When I got to my car, I jotted down some notes and then sat for a few minutes replaying my encounter with Brodie. I was taken aback by the level of his anger and the fact that it had escalated so quickly. Maybe the story I'd laid out for Brodie wasn't a story at all. Could Owen's original theory be right? But the timing of the burglaries still didn't make sense. The burglaries happened weeks before Marcus had his heart attack. Luke hadn't known then that he'd need money so badly. Why would he suddenly partner up with Brodie for a burglary?

I looked at my watch and realized I had to get moving or I'd be late for my meeting with Ray Bowman. But my phone rang with a call from him.

"Hi, Ray, did you need to reschedule?"

"That depends on you, Leah. I've got a repair situation at home, and somebody has to be there to wait for the washing machine guy to come. My wife, Ava, can't work remotely like I can, so I'm it. We can still talk if you don't mind meeting at my place and maybe getting interrupted by the repairman."

"That's no problem."

"Okay. We're at 221 Oak Avenue. It's a brick apartment building, top floor. There's no apartment number on our door, but it's the only unit on the third floor. Don't worry, there's an elevator."

"Good to know. I'm on my way."

"I'll put the coffee on."

Ray Bowman opened the door to his apartment before I even knocked.

"Good morning! I'm Ray. I saw you getting out of your car from my kitchen window. Come on in."

Ray was a fit man in his fifties, with thick salt-and-pepper hair and black-framed glasses. When he shook my hand, I was surprised his was so calloused. He must have noticed.

"I have to spend a lot of time in my office. The price of success, I guess. But whenever I get the chance, I like to work with my hands."

"I know you have a boat factory, but what do you do, build them by hand?" I asked with a smile.

He laughed.

"I would if I could, but I don't build fast enough. I've got a workshop at the industrial park where my factory is. My dad taught me how to build sailboats. It's not scalable for production, but it's very satisfying to the soul."

"That's amazing. How many have you built?"

"With my dad, two before he died. On my own over the last thirty years, three of them. The one I'm working on now I've been at for five years. It's going to be a beaut, though. I'm hoping to have a son—or a daughter—and I can teach them how to one day." He stepped back and swept his hand toward the foyer. "Come in, please, Leah."

He led me into a living room with blue-gray walls and bright white trim. Pale-yellow sunlight streamed through east-facing windows. Below I could see a courtyard bordered by tall evergreens hanging heavy with snow so perfectly placed it could have been sprayed on for a stage set.

"Those big windows were Ava's idea. Nice view, huh? The priest who lives downstairs asked if he could put up some feeders. I was never one to pay much attention to birds. But now I really enjoy seeing the little guys hopping around down there. But they go through a lot of birdseed. Those cardinals eat like linebackers!"

I followed him through the dining room to a small kitchen. It wasn't much bigger than mine, but it was well laid out and filled with the latest appliances. Which is why it surprised me when, after seating me at a kitchen table, Ray poured me a cup of coffee from an old-fashioned tin pot that looked like one my dad used to take on fishing trips.

"Ava, she likes all the modern stuff—she can even turn on the microwave from her phone! But me, I like to keep things simple. This is the coffeepot my grandpa always used. It still makes the best coffee, I say. What do you think?"

I'm not a coffee connoisseur, but I know coffee people take pride in their coffee-making skills.

"It's very good, Ray, thank you."

He smiled. "Now, how about you tell me about this newspaper board idea. How does this nonprofit thing work?"

I gave him the short version of small-town newspapers in America—the struggle to stay afloat as advertisers turned from print to digital platforms, the shrinking reader base, the predatory hedge funds who buy up papers and leverage them into oblivion.

"When Miller and I bought the *Times*, we had a decent business plan, but advertisers aren't coming back, and people's reading habits have changed a lot. We've tried some new things like bumping up our online coverage and starting a podcast with Miguel Santos that's pretty popular."

"Yeah, I listen to it sometimes. He's a pretty entertaining guy. I like the online edition of the *Times* because I'm on the road a lot. I've got another factory near La Crosse and one in Michigan. But I can still keep up with what's going on at home. In fact, I've got kind of a funny story about that."

"I like a funny story, what is it?"

"Well, it's not ha-ha funny, maybe *odd*'s a better word than funny. I was in Indiana when the library fire happened, on my way back from Michigan. I'm going back there this afternoon. Anyway, the night of the fire, I was on my way home and got about halfway here. It started snowing when I hit the Indiana state line, and it just kept coming. It got so bad I could hardly see. I pulled over in a rest area around ten o'clock to wait for the snowplows to come through. Once I bundled up in the sleeping bag I keep in my truck, I was out like a light. Didn't wake up until 7 a.m. When I did, I checked my phone first thing, and I looked at the *Times* online."

"That's what I like to hear. We need to get a few more readers who do the same thing, first thing."

He grinned. "Well, I saw the library fire story. I called Ava to find out what was going on. She didn't even know about it! Slept right through everything, she said. I was hours away, and I was the one giving her the news! Weird, huh? But that's technology for you. I felt bad for telling her, though. She was pretty shook up. Luke Granger was a client of hers. She's got a massage studio downtown."

I love talking to extroverts. You have to do a lot less work to get information. Ray had offered an alibi I hadn't asked for—he was out of town. I also knew now that Ava's story for the night of the fire was that she had slept right through it. And that she had been upset over Luke's death.

"Actually I have an appointment for a massage with Ava right after I finish here."

"Is that right? You'll love it. She's got the magic touch. I'm pretty proud of her. After my first wife, Jean, passed away, I just didn't have the heart for anything. I was even thinking about selling the business. Then I met Ava, and all that changed."

His eyes had softened as he talked about her. It made me wish that I didn't know what I did about Ava.

"How long have you been married?"

"Three years in January."

"It must be hard for her, having you gone so often."

"I like to think she misses me," he said with a smile. "But her studio keeps her busy, and she's got a sister she's really close to. Mandy. She's had some rough times. Ava is with her a lot. Well, hey, you didn't come to hear my life story. Tell me more about your plan for the paper."

"When Miller Caldwell died recently, his daughter, Charlotte, became my partner. She's the one who came up with the idea and convinced me the best way to keep the paper alive is for the *Times* to go nonprofit."

"I'm not trying to be cute, but it sounds like you already are. Nonprofit, I mean."

"You're right, in one sense. But our plan is to be the sustainable kind of nonprofit. We're getting 501(c)(3) status, and we'll be relying on donors, grants, sponsorships, and still subscriptions to some extent. We need the right mix of people for the board, and that's why I'm asking you to join us."

"I'm not sure I'm who you're looking for. I have a little experience with a 501(c)(3). I was on the board of the homeless shelter for a while, but that's pretty different from what you're trying to do."

"It's not journalism experience we're looking for from you. We want you because you've got strong ties to the area, and you care about what happens here. That's perfect for community journalism."

"Can you explain what community journalism means? I'm not familiar with the term."

"Community journalism focuses on what matters to the people who live here. Local schools, local government, local events. All the things that can bring people together."

"Well, I'm all for that. But bringing folks together is a tall order these days. Lotta different ideas out there—some pretty crazy ones, too. And people are laying down lines that make it pretty hard to cross from one side to the other. You really think a newspaper can change that?"

"I do. It's not about making everyone agree. It's about providing information people trust. People may still disagree over what to *do* about things, but at least we'll all be working from the same underlying set of facts. We get to that point not just by solid reporting—which I believe we do—but also by having people on our board the community respects. People like you."

I can get pretty wound up talking about community journalism. When he didn't respond immediately, I wondered if I'd put him off by being a little too intense.

"Sorry, I didn't mean to hard sell you. I'm kind of an evangelist when it comes to the power of local journalism."

"You didn't. I just like to turn things over in my mind a while. Can I get a look at your business plan?"

"Funny you should ask."

I reached into my bag for the copy I'd brought and handed it to him.

"Thank you, Leah. I'll read through this and get back to you with my questions."

"Please do, Ray. Either Charlotte or I would be glad to talk with you."

44

My phone rang as I drove to my massage appointment.

"Is this the Leah Nash Employment Agency? I heard you had a spot for an out-of-work reporter."

"Connor, hi. What do you think? Are you interested in applying for the executive director position? Did you read the email I sent you about it?"

"I did. And I'm interested. In fact, I'm at the stage where I'd be pretty interested if the local knitting club offered me a job writing their monthly newsletter. I've got some questions for you, though."

"No problem. I have some answers."

"You always do. Can we set up a FaceTime meeting to talk more about the job?"

"Sure, but let's do it on Zoom. I'd like my business partner, Charlotte, to sit in, too. I'm on my way to an appointment right now. Let me check with her and get back to you."

"Sounds good."

"Great! I'll text you the details."

"Thanks, Leah. And, uh, thanks for reaching out. The job market is pretty tight for unemployed recovering-alcoholic reporters."

"I've been there. Not the recovering-alcoholic part, the can't-get-hired reporter part. But I should tell you that we plan to advertise and interview other candidates. I think you're a strong one, but we're going to open it to all qualified comers."

"Absolutely. I understand. I'm just glad to get into the candidate pool. Thanks for the opportunity."

"Okay. I'll talk to you soon."

~

When I pushed open the back door at Ava's studio, I almost fell into the hallway as someone on the other side pulled it to leave.

"Oh, excuse me! I'm so sorry," I said as I regained my balance. Brooke Timmins stepped back so I could step all the way in.

"Are you okay?" she asked.

"Yes, I'm fine. Are you?"

"Absolutely. I just had a fabulous massage. I've really missed my weekly de-stresser with Ava. You, too?"

"No, this is my first time here."

"Really? I'm glad to hear Ava's picking up new clients. Just between us, a few of my friends have given up on her. Which is a shame because she's very good. Hopefully, she's put her emotional entanglements, shall we say, behind her."

"What emotional entanglements?"

"You haven't heard anything? Never mind. Forget I mentioned it."

She said it the way people do when they're pleased they know something you don't, and they want you to beg for more. I didn't mind obliging in this instance.

"Come on, Brooke. You can't throw that out there and then leave it hanging. What emotional entanglements are you talking about?"

"Oh, it's just a rumor. The usual kind of thing people say when someone like Ava marries a much older man."

"What does that mean?"

"You know, a pretty, young woman and a lonely, wealthy, older man. I don't blame Ava for pursuing him. Not everyone can wait around for a love match. Though Ray obviously adores *her*. Some people are saying that Ava's interests lie elsewhere."

She shook her head and made a deprecating gesture to indicate she wasn't one of those people, though clearly she was.

"Do you mean she's having an affair?"

Brooke's impression of a shocked expression was pretty good, but I detected the sly light of a once-and-forever mean girl in her eyes.

"No, no. If it's anything it's probably just a little flirtation. Please don't pass it along."

"No worries. I'm not going to feed the rumor mill."

"Good."

She paused for a second and tilted her head as she looked at me closely.

"You're looking very tired, Leah, especially around the eyes. You should ask Ava to schedule a facial with Pam. It does wonders to diminish those dark shadows and lines. None of us are twenty-one anymore, are we?"

Few people can wrap an insult inside faux concern the way Brooke Timmins can. I considered a response that would incorporate the fact that I was a lot closer to twenty-one than Brooke was but decided against it.

"Thanks for the suggestion."

She patted my arm with her perfectly manicured hand.

"I hope you're not stressing because your theory about PPOK was so wrong. You shouldn't feel embarrassed. It was perfectly reasonable to consider PPOK. As you know, I did, too. But Cliff has things back on course."

"What course is that?"

"Oh, Cliff never tells me specifics about an investigation. It wouldn't be ethical. But from the little he's said, it sounds like we'll have answers soon. Now I really do have to run. Good to see you, Leah. Don't forget to book a facial. You'll be amazed how much it can help."

I doubted Cliff had done anything but get in the way and wait to claim credit when an arrest was made. If the investigation was close to making an arrest, it would be down to Owen, not Cliff. Had he returned to Brodie as his chief suspect? Or had he picked up the same information on Ava that I had?

When Brooke had gone, I walked down the hall to the reception area. No one was at the desk, but a small card propped up on a crystal bell read: *Please ring if no one is at the desk.*

As I did, I noticed a photograph of two young women—girls, really. I picked it up to study it more closely. One of the girls looked about twelve, the other a few years older. They were going down a waterslide. The picture had caught my eye because I have a very similar photo of my younger sister, Lacey, and me doing the same thing.

"Leah?"

I turned and saw a grown-up version of the older girl in the photo.

"Yes, hi. You're Ava, right? I didn't mean to be nosy," I said, putting the photograph down.

"No, no, that's fine. If I didn't want people to see it, I wouldn't leave it on the front desk. It's me and my sister, Mandy, taken about ten years ago at the Dells. And yes, I'm Ava Farley," she said holding out her hand to shake mine.

I'm not sure exactly what I'd expected her to look like—but it wasn't this. She was very pretty, as I'd been told, with large, dark eyes and shiny, dark hair. But the light freckles across her nose and cheeks and her friendly smile made her seem more like the girl next door than the unfaithful femme fatale my imagination had constructed.

"Let's go back to my office. Since it's your first time here, there's some paperwork to fill out, and I always like to hear a little about what brings new clients here."

"So," she said, once I was seated in a chair in front of her desk, "Have you had a massage before?"

"I have, and it really helped when I was going through some stress at work. My shoulders are telling me it's time for another one."

"I'm glad you listened to your body. Massage can be an important part of staying healthy, mentally as well as physically."

She pulled out a form from her desk, ticked off my answers to a series of questions, and then passed it over for me to sign. Her cell phone rang as she did. She looked at the screen and said, "I'm sorry, I'll just be a minute, but I need to take this."

She stepped out in the hall, but I could easily hear her side of the conversation as I dated and signed my name on the form.

"Mandy, everything okay?"

A pause while she listened.

"Oh, sweetie, that's wonderful! I'm so glad Dr. Kincaid agrees. I'm proud of you, Mandy. Mom and Dad would be, too."

Another pause.

"Hey, don't give what Chelsea said a second thought. People say dumb things sometimes when they don't know what to say. You're ready. To celebrate your big step forward, I'm going to take you out to lunch. I'll pick you up about 12:30. Bye."

Although she'd sounded upbeat on the phone, when Ava came back in the room, she looked upset.

"Is something wrong? Do you need me to reschedule? It's no problem."

Her face crumpled, and her eyes blinked rapidly. She grabbed a tissue from a box on the desk and wiped the tears away.

"Sorry," she said. "This is ridiculous. I just got some really positive news, and all of a sudden, I'm all weepy. It's my sister, Mandy. She's gone through a really hard time with treatment-resistant depression. Last April, she tried to commit suicide."

"I'm so sorry! But she's doing better?

"She is. So much better. I don't know why it's making me feel like crying."

"Relief, probably."

"Maybe. It's been such a struggle. And really, really expensive. But Ray —that's my husband—he hasn't blinked an eye at the cost. They finally found a med combination that seems to work. She met with her therapist today, and that call was to tell me she's ready to go back to college."

"That sounds great."

"Hearing the happiness in her voice is great. We've had so many ups and downs this past year. I worry about her a lot. But I'm a little scared still. I don't want her to go back to that dark place ever again—and I don't want to go there either. Even though she's made so much progress, if she doesn't answer the phone, if she's late, if she doesn't return a text, I get a little panicky until I can get in touch with her. I know it's not good for me or her, but I can't seem to help it."

She stopped, shut her eyes briefly, then, "Whoa. That's a little too much information, isn't it? I didn't mean to blurt everything out like that. But sometimes I feel like I'm in pretty deep water—and I'm not a great swimmer."

I hadn't expected to, but I liked Ava a lot in that moment.

"Hey, I understand. I had a sister, too. In fact, the photo of you and Mandy on your desk reminds me of one I have of my younger sister, Lacey, and me—also at the Dells. Maybe on the same waterslide," I said with a smile.

"You said you *had* a sister. Do you mean she—" She stopped abruptly.

"Yes, she died in an accident. It was a long time ago."

I didn't tell Ava that I actually had two sisters who had died. That's a real conversation stopper in an ordinary exchange of information. For Ava in this situation, it would be way too much to hear.

"That must be awful. I don't know what I'd do if I lost Mandy. But I'm sure you felt that way about your sister, and it happened anyway, didn't it?"

Her lip quivered as she finished, but she didn't give in to tears. I felt like crying, too.

"Like I said, it was a long time ago, Ava. And my story isn't yours. I'm sure you and Mandy have a lot of good sister time ahead of you."

I wasn't sure of that at all. Depression is a beast to fight, and severe depression can have a really bad outcome. But sometimes you just need to give a person a little boost to help them make it through the moment. I was rewarded with a broad smile from Ava.

She was still smiling when the police arrived.

45

Owen Fike hadn't bothered to ring the bell at the reception desk, and now he loomed unannounced in the doorway of Ava's office. I watched as the smile faded from Ava's face. Her worried look returned. I was right. Owen's investigation had led him to the same idea I'd had—that Ava was a strong candidate for Luke's murder. I should feel vindicated that he was on the same track I was.

But my predominant emotion was dismay. I'd put together a theory of the crime using secondhand knowledge about Ava and Luke's relationship. Pat Rohn had witnessed credible evidence of an affair. Pam Dixon, Cole, and Brodie Granger, even Brooke Timmins had supplied other details, delivered with a dollop of speculation. Their information had led me to hypothesize that Ava had killed Luke because he'd broken up with her. But now that I'd talked with and observed her myself, I was a lot less enamored of my own theory.

Ava swallowed hard and licked her lips before she spoke.

"How can I help you, Captain Fike? I told you everything I know when we talked the other day."

"I have some follow-up questions."

"I'm sorry, I'm with a client, as you can see. I could call you later if—"

"This is a murder investigation, Ms. Farley. That takes precedence over your business appointments. I'm sure your client can understand that."

Owen had noticed me but had chosen not to acknowledge me.

"Is it really critical that you speak to Ava this very minute?" I asked.

I knew Owen couldn't force Ava to talk to him unless he arrested her on the spot, which I doubted he was ready to do. And I wanted the chance to talk to her more myself.

"I'm investigating a murder, not coordinating a book club meeting. I've already extended the courtesy of coming to see Ms. Farley instead of asking her to come to the station." He turned away from me to look at Ava. "Would you rather do that, Ms. Farley?"

"No, no, here is fine, Captain Fike. Leah, could I call you later to reschedule?"

"Yes, of course."

"Thank you. I need to make a call before we talk, Captain. Is that okay?" she asked.

Owen hesitated, probably wondering if the call was to an attorney. He's a good interviewer, but no cop wants a lawyer by a suspect's side during questioning. I was certain, though, that the call Ava wanted to make was to her sister. She'd need an excuse for not meeting her for lunch.

I stood up. "While Ava is on the phone, can I have a quick word, Captain? It's important."

Owen's response was to give me a death stare, but he took a step into the hall to make room for me to get out. Probably so he could kill me. I closed Ava's office door behind me.

"Owen, why are you questioning Ava? I thought you were all in on Brodie Granger."

"I told you before that I don't go all in on one idea. I follow all the leads. What are you doing here?"

"It's a massage studio. I'm here for a massage, which it now looks like I won't be getting, at least not this morning. Which lead brought you to Ava?"

"I'm not going to answer that. I'm surprised you're still asking questions. After your PPOK theory fell apart, I thought you might want to back off a little."

"I was wrong about PPOK, I admit it. That doesn't mean I'm giving up. Since you won't say why you're here, let me guess. You found out that Ava had a relationship with Luke Granger, and it didn't end well. So did I. You think that gives her a motive to kill Luke. I did too. But now I'm not so sure."

"Yeah? Why's that?"

"I talked to Brodie Granger today. He wasn't very cooperative. In fact, he got quite upset with me."

"I can understand that."

"Come on, don't be like that. I'm starting to think you might be right about him and the burglaries. And, possibly, about him as a murder suspect."

"I can't tell you how much your validation means to me. No, wait . . . yes, I can. Nothing. I'm not looking for your approval, I'm investigating a murder. I'd be grateful if you'd stay out of my way."

"How can I stay out of your way if I don't know which way you're going? And I think if you're going after Ava, you're heading in the wrong direction. What makes you so suspicious of her?"

He shook his head. "I'm not going to give you any information that isn't available at a press conference. The only thing I'll say is I've got solid evidence that makes Ava a person of interest."

"What kind of evidence?"

"Are you kidding me? I just told you I'm not giving you anything about the case."

"You got Luke's phone records, didn't you? And there were a lot of calls and texts from a number that turned out to be Ava's. And Brooke Timmins passed on a rumor about Ava having an affair and you put those things together. You probably have something else, too, but it's still not enough for an arrest. You don't have to look at me like I read your diary, Owen. Despite what you seem to think, I do have a brain that I like to use now and then."

"I don't doubt your brain. But you've got a pretty big imagination, and police work is all about the facts, not the speculation. I'm not giving you anything except a little advice. Maybe you should schedule a massage with someone else. Ava could be unavailable for quite a long time."

Because of Owen's untimely interruption of my meeting with Ava, I had about an hour to kill before my appointment with Phil. I made a quick call.

"Coop, have you got a few minutes?"

"I do. I've been working on the budget all morning. I could use a break. What's up?"

"Lots. I'll be there in about three minutes."

Ross was walking out as I was walking into the sheriff's office.

"Hey, stranger. Haven't seen you much the last week or so. I hear you're givin' Owen the heartburn you usually save for me. How's life as Cole Granger's personal private eye?"

"I'm not his PI. I'm doing this for Luke's mother. And if Owen has heartburn now, wait until he has to eat his words when I solve the case."

"Big talk there. You must be onto something."

I gave up the facade.

"I wish I was, Ross. I thought I was on the right track, but after Ed Wagner's arrest, I've had to do some regrouping. I had what I thought was a pretty good idea, but now I'm not so sure. But I just saw Owen, and I don't think he's got it right either."

"You never think cops have it right."

"That's not true. Once in a while, you stumble across an idea I can get behind. In fact, any time you want to partner up again, just let me know. I'm ready to jump in."

"I know. That's what scares me."

"Stop. You know you wish I was your full-time partner. You're just too shy to say."

"I'm gonna let that pass on account of this is the season of peace and goodwill."

"So what are you working on?"

"It's kinda slow. The holidays are like that—mostly fights, drunk driving, and stolen lawn decorations. Gotta love that Christmas spirit. I'm doin' some legwork for Coop on a cold case right now. In fact, I gotta go. If you're here to see Jennifer, she's off today. If you're lookin' for Coop, his door was open when I left. I'll see you later."

46

I tapped lightly on Coop's open door and walked in. His usually tidy desk was littered with spreadsheets from which he looked up and smiled at me.

"Hey you. Pull up a chair. I could use a break. You want something to drink?"

"Not unless it's Jameson's."

"That kind of day, huh? Sorry water, coffee, or tea is all I have."

"I'll skip it and go right to confused speculation and regrets."

"That sounds more interesting than spreadsheets. Tell me."

"This morning, I've seen Brodie Granger, Ray Bowen, his wife Ava Farley, and I had bonus run-ins with Brooke Timmins and Owen Fike. And I'm having new thoughts."

"About Ava?"

"Yes. I don't think she killed Luke."

"Okay. Why did you change your mind?"

"Well, first of all, I think I made assumptions about the kind of person Ava is that were filtered through my own experience as a cheated-on spouse. I projected onto Ava all the worst characteristics of Nick—entitled, arrogant, selfish, superficial. But after I met her, I realized that wasn't fair, and it wasn't good investigating either. Ava isn't my ex-husband. I think she's basically a good person."

I told him about Mandy, and Ava's struggles to help her, and her constant, low-key anxiety that Mandy might fall back into another black hole of depression.

"Mandy is alive today because of the care Ray paid for. That probably wouldn't have happened if Ava had left Ray for Luke. She had a motive to kill Luke if you accept that she wanted revenge. But I think her love for Mandy is her strongest motivation. Ava wouldn't do anything that could send her to prison and leave Mandy adrift. The threat of Mandy's depression coming back will always be there. That's why Ava will want to always be there."

"You just said a minute ago that you projected your feelings about Nick onto Ava before you met her. Do you think, after hearing Ava's story, that you might be projecting another set of your own emotions onto her?"

"You mean because of Lacey? Because I wasn't there when she needed me?"

"I do mean that."

I sighed. He wasn't wrong. I'd felt an almost visceral connection to Ava from the moment I saw the photo of her and Mandy.

"Possibly. I get that there are some parallels between her situation with Mandy and mine with Lacey. But even if I'm projecting, it doesn't mean I'm wrong. I feel really strongly that Ava would not abandon Mandy under any circumstances. If that wasn't true, she would have left Ray when Luke said he couldn't be with a married woman. She didn't."

"Okay."

"*Okay* I convinced you, or *okay* you think I'm wrong, but you don't think you can change my mind?"

"Okay, I see your point, but I still think you're letting your feelings, not your thinking, take the lead."

"It's not just feelings that changed my mind."

"What else have you got?"

"The library security video from the night before the fire. I told you it could be a man or a woman, and at first, I thought it was Ava. Now I don't. I think it has to be Brodie Granger."

"Brodie? I'm starting to get whiplash here."

"Well, buckle up while I take you on a wild ride through my thinking process."

"I've been on that ride before. I prefer the Maxx Force at Six Flags. But go ahead."

"I'm serious, Coop."

"I am, too."

"Just listen. I told you I saw Brodie this morning. I didn't tell you how it went."

I explained how cocky Brodie had been initially and how that had faded when I pointed out that Owen wasn't considering him just for the burglaries, but also as a suspect in Luke's murder.

"He coughed up an alibi about hooking up with a woman in the parking lot of a club in Madison. But he doesn't know her first name, let alone her last. I think Brodie panicked and made up the story on the spot."

"Could be. Although that story is pretty on brand for Brodie."

"But if it was true, why did he get so angry at me that he stormed out of the diner? He was so mad the waitress thought he was my abusive boyfriend."

"Sometimes fear comes out as anger."

I gave him an exasperated look. "So when did you join the Brodie Granger defense team?"

"I'm just helping you test your idea. I'm not saying it's wrong. Go on."

"Fine. You know part of my Ava theory was that Luke went to her for the money he needed and either told her or let her think that he wanted to get back with her. Looking at it again, the premise doesn't hold."

"Why?"

"Ava made Luke's life very messy when he broke up with her. Would he really risk restarting that chaos in his life and possibly dragging his new girlfriend, Stella, into it, too, after Ava found out he was just leading her on for the money?"

"Go on."

"And Miguel made a good point earlier. He said Luke going to Ava for money and planning to dump her after he got it wasn't like Luke. I sort of dismissed what he said. But I shouldn't have. Nothing in what I've learned about Luke indicates he was a cruel person. And it would have been very cruel to pretend his feelings for Ava had changed and then to break up with her again after he got the money. I'm not sure that he would have done that to her again, even to get the money he needed."

"Did you ask Ava about Luke when you saw her today?"

"I would have, but I didn't have time to get that far before Owen showed up. She and I had a pretty good rapport. I'm going to rebook my massage. She might open up more if Owen scared her enough. Even if she doesn't, I want to make sure she knows she should have a lawyer with her the next time Owen interviews her."

"No doubt Owen will be very happy for your help in that area."

"Listen, if he didn't always think I was going to mess things up for him, I *would* be happy to help him. I told him when I saw him at Ava's that he might be mostly right about Brodie. He wasn't too excited about it."

"Explain 'mostly' to me."

"Owen's first idea was that Luke and Brodie committed the burglaries together, fought over the split, and Brodie killed Luke, right? But the burglaries happened weeks before Marcus had his heart attack. Luke didn't have any idea he was going to need more cash, fast. Why would he suddenly turn his back on everything he'd worked so hard for and start a life of crime with Brodie? He wouldn't," I said, not waiting for Coop's answer.

"Okay, so where is the part where you agree with Owen? And if Luke wasn't involved with them, what motive would Brodie have to kill him?"

"Brodie pulled off two burglaries alone without a hitch, and he walked away with enough jewelry, electronics, and cash to make for a very lucrative evening. And he didn't get caught. Brodie would have to brag about that to someone. He chose Luke because he didn't think Luke would turn him in. And Luke didn't, maybe partly because no one was really hurt except the insurance company. People find it pretty hard to work up sympathy for a corporation."

"Agreed," Coop said.

"A few weeks later, though, Luke's circumstances changed. He needed money, and he knew Brodie had some. So, he asked him for the first $5,000 he had to have to buy the bookstore. Brodie gave it to him, possibly because he recognized the threat underneath the ask—that if Brodie said no, Luke could turn him in."

"Yeah, Brodie might have felt giving $5,000 to Luke was worth it to keep himself out of prison," Coop said.

"Exactly. But then the bank raised the down payment on the loan by $10,000. Luke went back to his cousin. But this time Brodie balked—he had taken all the risk and done all the work on the burglaries. He didn't want Luke to take all the money. He realized then that Luke would always have a hold over him, at least until the statute of limitations ran out. He got rid of the risk by killing Luke."

"Not bad. But it's going to take some actual evidence to tie Brodie to Luke's murder."

"Okay, so we're back to the library security video from the night before the fire. Luke was talking to someone I thought was Ava. But it could have been Brodie telling him he'd bring the money the next night."

"That's pretty weak. Why wouldn't Brodie just text him?"

"It's a start, Donnie Downer. And don't forget Shayna, Brodie's alibi for the burglaries. She might rethink her story once she hears about Brodie's parking-lot alibi for the night of the fire. It's one thing to risk jail time for your boyfriend. It's another to risk it for a cheating bastard. And if both his burglary-night alibi and his fire-night alibi fall apart, I think lots of things will start falling into place about Brodie."

"I think you should take another run at Owen."

I opened my mouth to protest, but before I could, Coop went on.

"I know. He hasn't been very receptive. But just because he won't tell you anything, it doesn't mean he's given up on Brodie's trail. He's got more resources available to him than you do. You should share what you've put together."

"So you *do* think Brodie is a better suspect than Ava?" I asked.

"Yes and no. You've got a pretty good hypothesis, but some parts are a little weak."

"Like what?"

"Well, would Luke really blackmail his own family member to get what he wanted? That seems out of character."

"I think it's possible. We all have to decide at some point which lines we'll cross. Buying the bookstore was Luke's big dream. He might have convinced himself it was all right to take from Brodie what Brodie had taken from the Stillmans, the Martins, and their insurance company. Or at least threaten to. Or he could have been bluffing and didn't actually plan to go through with it, only Brodie didn't know that."

I glanced down at my watch.

"Whoa! I need to go. I've got a meeting with Phil Stillman."

"With Phil? What's that about?" Coop asked.

"The *Times* board."

"I didn't know you were a fan of his. In fact, I think I've heard you refer to him as a pompous jerk."

"Now, does that sound like the sort of harsh judgment I'd make? Don't answer that. I'm not a big fan, it's true. But Charlotte thinks he'd be good. And he's done a decent job handling the book-banning issues at the school board. I don't want her to think I'm against every person she suggests."

His phone rang then.

"Go ahead and get that, I've got to leave, or I'll be late. Talk to you later."

47

I was about two minutes late when I drove into the parking lot at Stillman Realty and Property Management. I hate being late.

I hurried into the reception area where the woman at the desk was frowning into a small compact as she applied a very vivid shade of red lipstick. I recognized her immediately. Mrs. Mary Louise Myerson, the bane of my high school years. She snapped her compact shut and looked up.

"Mary Louise, hi. I didn't know you worked here. When did you leave the high school principal's office?"

"I've been here for two years, Leah. I'm surprised you don't know that. I would think a reporter worth her salt would be aware of what was happening in her own town."

I bit back a harsh response. No sense in getting into a throw-down with someone who no longer had the ability to report me to the principal. Instead I said, "We try to report all the news, Mary Louise, but we must have missed your career change. So, do you enjoy working as a receptionist for Phil?"

"I'm not a receptionist. I'm Phil's assistant. I have my own office. I'm only at the desk because the receptionist took an early lunch. But yes, I do enjoy the work. It's a very busy office. And there are no unruly students or complaining parents," she said with a sniff.

"I see. What keeps you busy?"

"Phil trusts me with a lot of responsibilities. I schedule showings, coordinate with title companies, prepare paperwork, serve notices to quit, all kinds of things. It's very interesting."

"You serve notices to quit? You mean you evict people."

That seemed like something Mary Louise could really sink her teeth into.

"Law enforcement evicts people. I give them notice that they need to leave. Usually for nonpayment of their rent."

"That must be difficult sometimes. Seeing people at their lowest ebb, I mean—no money to pay the rent probably means they don't have money for food, or gas, or much else either."

"I don't find it difficult at all. People need to live within their means. If they can't afford the rent, they should move somewhere else, not expect the landlord to carry them."

"Rents are pretty high right now, and there isn't a lot of choice in this area. And if you get sick, or lose your job—"

Mary Louise gave me a withering look and uttered a response pretty close to something Ebenezer Scrooge would say.

"That's what homeless shelters are for."

I changed the subject. "I don't want to keep you from your work. I have an appointment with Phil."

"I know you do. But he's with his wife. She dropped in unexpectedly."

She spoke as though Kimberly popping in to say hello to her husband was a serious violation of office protocol. Her lips were still pursed in disapproval as the door to Phil's office opened and Kimberly came out. I almost did a double-take. She looked so different from the woman I'd first met. She had dark circles under her eyes. As she got closer, I could see the tiny petechiae—little red dots on her eyelids—that are the sign of some long ,hard, crying. Even her curls had lost their bounce and lay dull and loose on her shoulders.

She looked at me, but there was no recognition in her eyes.

"Kimberly, hi. Leah Nash. We met at your house last weekend."

"Leah? Oh, yes, Leah. Hi. I'm sorry, I have a very bad headache. Excuse me, please."

She rushed out of the office without waiting for a response.

The phone on Mary Louise's desk buzzed.

"Yes, I'll show her in," she said into the receiver.

She led me to Phil's closed door, knocked once, then opened it for me to enter.

~

Phil stood and came from behind his desk to greet me.

"I'm sorry you had to wait. Kimberly stopped by, and I had to spend some time with her."

"Is she not feeling well? She looked really tired when I said hello to her out front."

"Did she? No, she's fine. Physically, anyway. She's got anxiety and panic disorder issues. I thought we had them under control, but they've come back again. I've tried to make her life as easy as possible, but it doesn't seem to help."

"I'm sorry to hear that. The day I was at your house she mentioned having problems with that in the past. I hope she feels better soon."

"Thank you. We've been through it before. Hopefully she'll be able to pull herself back together again. But I'm afraid Kimberly's visit threw my schedule off. I'm interested in the board position, but I'm going to have to cut this short. Do you have some material you can leave with me to review?"

The fact that Phil seemed to view his wife's issues through the lens of his own convenience made me think he might have a bit more in common with Marilyn Karr than I'd realized.

"Yes, certainly," I said as I pulled a folder out of my bag and handed it to him.

"Thank you. I'll read it carefully. How soon do you need a response from me?"

"Sometime in the next couple of weeks would be fine."

"That's good. I've got a lot on my plate right now. I'll get back with you as soon as I can."

"No rush," I said.

"I appreciate your understanding."

What I understood was that the longer he took, the more likely it was that Charlotte and I could find a better candidate for the board.

"Oh, Leah, I saw the story about Ed Wagner and the cigarette smuggling. That was a shock. Does that mean you're no longer looking into PPOK as the source of the library fire?"

"That's right. It seems unlikely now that PPOK was involved."

"So your investigation is over?"

"No, not yet. Do you know the saying, 'You have to kiss a lot of frogs to find your prince'?"

"I've heard it, yes. But I must be missing something. I don't see how it relates here."

"Well, when you're investigating, whether you're a cop or a journalist, sometimes you have to try out a lot of ideas before you find the ones that fit. I'm doing that now."

"I see. Do you have one you favor?"

"I'm regrouping. Now that I am, I should ask, are you still convinced that Brodie Granger didn't commit the burglaries at your house and your neighbor's?"

"I'll admit I'm not as sure as I was."

"Why, has something happened?"

"Nothing definitive, but I just noticed that Brodie's been driving a very nice snowmobile. I priced the model out for myself last year, and I know he doesn't get paid enough to afford one. I'm wondering where the money came from. As I told you, I've never had reason to doubt his honesty before, but it seems a little odd that he suddenly has the money to buy a machine like that."

"I see. Have you spoken to Owen about it?"

"Not yet, but I'll be doing that shortly. Or maybe I'll go right to Cliff. I told you before I'm not convinced Owen is up to the job. He hasn't been in contact with me about the burglary at all. I understand he's busy investigating Luke Granger's murder, and that takes precedence, of course. But I'd expect Owen would at least let me know that he's put the case away unsolved. And now that I know Brodie's driving an expensive new snowmobile, I think that should at least be looked into."

The phone on his desk buzzed.

"Excuse me—"

"Sure. Thanks for your time, Phil."

"You're welcome."

When I walked to my car, I noticed Kimberly sitting in a white SUV parked next to it. She was staring straight ahead.

She didn't even see me until I tapped on the window. She gave a small jump, then rolled it down.

"Kimberly, are you sure you're okay?"

"Yes, it's nothing. I had a panic attack this morning. It just threw me a little. But like Phil said, I've had them before. I should've stayed calm, and it would've gone away. I'm fine, Leah. I mean, I'm not fine, but I know there's nothing really wrong. It's just that a panic attack can really shake you up, even when you know what's happening. I get this overwhelming sense of fear. I can't think straight, I can't catch my breath, I try to say my mantra, but I can't focus. I—"

She stopped and shook her head.

"That sounds awful," I said.

"It is. It really is. Especially when the things you're supposed to do don't work. I tried to focus on breathing. I kept saying *I'm in control, I'm in control* over and over, but it was terrible. I couldn't stop shaking. When I finally did, I just needed some reassurance from Phil."

"Can I do anything? I could drive you home, if that would help. I'm sure someone from Phil's office could take your car home later."

She made an effort to smile, but it looked more like a grimace of pain.

"No, thank you. I always feel pretty drained after one of these. I called my doctor, and he changed the dose on my anxiety medication and renewed my Xanax. I'll just pick those up at the pharmacy and get on with things."

"Well, if you're sure . . . "

"I am. Thank you, Leah."

48

I went home to write up some notes and sort out my thoughts on my meeting-filled day so far. Sam demanded a treat and a little attention when I walked in, then settled down in a sunny spot on the window seat. I grabbed a quick sandwich, then joined him with my legal pad and a cup of tea.

After I got down the main takeaways from my interviews, I put my pencil down. I closed my eyes for a minute as I leaned back against the cushion to think about what I'd written. Instead, I fell asleep and woke up to the insistent ringing of my phone.

"*Chica*, I need you."

I couldn't stifle the huge yawn as I said hello.

"Are you sleeping? It's daytime. How can you be sleeping?"

"Well, I'm not now. My day started pretty early, Miguel, and it's been a little intense."

"Why, what happened?"

"This is going to take a minute."

"For you, I have all the minutes. What is going on?"

I explained the shift in thinking I'd made from Ava to Brodie.

"Cole will not be liking this."

"I'm aware. If I'm right, that's two hits to the Granger family reputation

—such as it is. Not only does Brodie look like Luke's killer, Luke is basically a blackmailer. I'm not so happy about it myself. And if it's true, I sure don't want to have to tell his mother. I could understand Luke not turning Brodie in if he knew Brodie had committed the burglaries—though I'd like to think he wouldn't lie for Brodie, if it came to that. But it's way harder to think Luke would actually exploit the knowledge and use it to get money."

"But maybe he was just bluffing? You know, he would say to Brodie that he was going to the police so he could get the money he needs, but he wouldn't really do it."

"Yeah, that's what I said to Coop. And maybe it's right. The only way to know is to get Brodie to admit it—or to find someone else who knows the story."

"How will you do that?"

"That's what I'm trying to figure out. My first priority is to get Ava to trust me enough to tell me everything. I'm hoping she has a kickass alibi, but I doubt it. Owen wouldn't be so high on her if that were true. I need to talk to her again, and soon. After that, we'll see. But that's enough of my stuff. What did you need me for?"

"To go on a snowmobile ride with me tomorrow morning. I have to take some photos of the warming hut the Winter Warriors donated for the snowmobile trail."

"I'm sorry, you must have the wrong number. I hate riding snowmobiles. It's freezing, they're loud, and they go too fast to enjoy the scenery. Also, why do you need me there?"

"Because Corky Donovan had to cancel, and I can't find anyone else to go. I need a person in the photo, not just the building."

"Oh, so I'm last choice? Well, I would've gone, but after an insult like that, I just can't."

"Stop. You know you're always first with me. I only called other people because I know you are so busy—and because you did not have very much fun when I took you before. Please. I promise it will be fun this time. I know the way now."

"What time are you going?"

"Early. I will pick you up at 7:30, we drive to my friend Clark's house— he lives right off the trail. And he said I can use his machine, and his snowmobile suits, and helmets. You will be warm, and the ride is less than fifteen minutes to the warming hut. The time we went before, it was all snowing and blowing, and I got us a little bit lost, but this time—"

"A *little bit* lost? If we'd been going in a straight line instead of in circles, we could've crossed state lines into the UP. Worst of all, while you and I were freezing our butts off trying to get out of the Forest of No Exits, everybody else was sitting in the Kipp Lake Bar, eating hamburgers in front of the fire."

"That will not happen tomorrow. The trail is groomed, it's marked, and I know exactly what I'm doing this time. Also it will be a fun friend adventure—no, no, not an adventure, because I know exactly what I'm doing this time. It will be a fun friend activity. We haven't done anything together for a while. Come. Please."

"Okay, I'll go. I do have a good time with you—usually."

"This will be a very good time. I promise."

"I'll hold you to that. How about a drink at McClain's later today? You can help me process."

"Excellent. I have to do an interview with the new city manager in Hailwell. Meet you at McClain's at 5:30?"

"See you then."

After I hung up with Miguel, I couldn't stop wondering how Ava's interview with Owen had gone. I wanted to give her time to come down from it, but I also wanted to get to her before she put up any serious defenses. Finally at 3:30, I called her.

"Blissful Body Salon, Pam speaking."

"Pam, hi! This is Leah Nash. Is Ava there?"

"Nope. She called me to come in because she had to leave. I guess you know that. I saw from the appointment book that she cancelled your massage. She's not coming back in today. Did you want to reschedule?"

"No, not now anyway."

I could hear the sound of a bell jingling on Pam's end.

"My appointment just got here. I have to go. Do you want to leave a message for Ava?"

"No, that's okay. Thanks."

Was Ava not coming back in because she was at the police station with

Owen? Or had she taken the day off to pull herself together because the evidence he had scared the bejesus out of her?

I knew Ava's husband was somewhere on the road to his factory in Michigan. I drove over to her place to see if I could get the answers.

～

Ava looked understandably surprised when she answered my knock on her door.

"Leah? What are you doing here?"

Her eyes were red, and her mascara was smudged. She was clutching a tissue in one hand.

On the way over, I'd tried to think of a way to explain why I was barging in on her at home, when I knew she'd had a tough interview with Owen. I decided to just lay it out with no frills and hope she didn't shut the door in my face.

"I'm here to be straight with you, Ava. I didn't just want a massage today. I know about your relationship with Luke Granger. I wanted to size you up as a suspect in his murder."

"Join the club. That's what Captain Fike thinks, too. I spent two hours with him after you left, trying to convince him I didn't kill Luke. I didn't succeed. I don't feel like going through another grilling. You were just pretending to be sympathetic about Mandy, weren't you? Captain Fike said you were after a story. I don't have to talk to you."

"No, I wasn't pretending about Mandy. And despite what Owen said, I'm not trying to get a story. Luke's mother, Ellen, asked me to look into his murder. You don't have to talk to me, that's true. But you know as well as I do—better, I guess—that Owen is focusing on you. But if you didn't kill Luke, I might be able to help."

"How?"

"Tell me the truth about everything—your affair with Luke, how it ended, and where you were the night he died."

"What good will that do? I already told all of it to Captain Fike. He wasn't impressed. In fact, he advised me to stop lying and come clean. I didn't kill Luke, but I don't have an alibi. At least not one that anybody will believe."

"Try me."

She shook her head and began to close the door. I took my last shot.

"Ava, I don't think you killed Luke. I don't believe you'd do anything that would force you to abandon Mandy. I think Owen is pretty close to arresting you. If you're honest with me, I might be able to stave that off. But I need to know what you know first. This isn't for a story, I promise. I'm not going to report it out."

I didn't know if it was the appeal to her devotion to her sister or the promise that I wasn't going to use what she said for a story, but she opened the door wider.

"All right. I'll tell you, but even I can see why the police want to arrest me."

49

She didn't lead me into the kitchen as Ray had done. Instead, she pointed to an L-shaped sofa in the living room. We both sat down, and she plunged right in.

"I met Luke late last spring. I gave him a massage. He was very nice."

I nodded but didn't prompt her.

"A few days later I was at the Elite. It was crowded. I was trying to find a table when Luke spotted me looking around. He waved me over to his table. We had fun, talking about music we liked—oh, and we found out we were fans of the same bands, liked some of the same books, and that we both liked hiking at Devil's Lake. Ray was away for the week. Mandy was still in treatment at a residential facility. For the first time in a long time, I just relaxed and had a fun conversation. When he asked if I wanted to join him for a hike that weekend, I said yes. We just went on from there."

"What does that mean?"

"Just what you think it means. We started seeing each other."

"He didn't care that you were married?"

I knew the answer from what Stella English had told Miguel. I wanted to see if Ava would tell me the truth.

"He didn't know. I don't wear my wedding ring at work because of all the oils and lotions that I use. I kept my maiden name when I married Ray.

At first, I didn't tell Luke I was married because I didn't think it mattered. I didn't plan on having a long-term relationship with him. I wasn't planning at all, really.

"But you must have been unhappy with your husband, right? Why was that?"

"When I met Ray, his wife had just died. My fiancé had left me for someone else. We were two lost people who would never have come together if we weren't both hurting so bad. It was fine at first. Ray is a good man. I told myself that was enough. And it was, for a while. Ray was gone a lot. I was working hard to build up my business. But as time went on, I realized we didn't have much in common.

"We didn't like the same music or movies. I love eating out and trying new foods. Ray's idea of a fun night is eating his favorite hot dish and watching a Badger's game. I love hiking. Ray hates it. He loves the water. I'm afraid of it. He has a tight circle of old friends and their wives. They have the same history, the same jokes, the same stories about the good old days when they were in high school together. Some of them resented me because Ray and I got married so soon after his first wife died. I didn't fit in. I tried to, but it didn't work. I realized that even though it would hurt Ray, I had to leave."

"But you didn't."

"I was on the verge when Mandy tried to kill herself. Everything else went out the window. I had to make sure she would be all right. She needed expensive medications and lots of therapy, and at first, she had to be in residential care. It took a long time for her to start coming around. Ray paid for it all. I was so miserable. I was worried sick about her and, at the same time, drowning in guilt because after all Ray was doing, I still wasn't in love with him. I couldn't be honest with him and take the risk that he'd stop paying for Mandy's care. I was an emotional wreck. And then I met Luke."

"I'm still not understanding why you weren't honest with him at the start of your affair."

"That's the thing. I didn't think of it as an affair. It just felt good to have a small space where, for a little while, I could forget about everything else. I could pretend all the other things in the real world weren't happening. It was like a daydream you know won't come true, but you enjoy it while you're in it. Only I fell in love with Luke. By the time I realized that, Mandy was doing much better. I could see a light at the end of the tunnel. Once she was truly stable, I could leave Ray. That's when I told Luke about Ray and Mandy, and everything."

"How did he react?"

"He was really upset I hadn't told him sooner. He wasn't okay with seeing a married woman. I told him I'd leave Ray when I could, that Mandy was making progress and I just needed to be sure she was really going to be okay. We just had to wait a little while. I thought he'd be happy."

"But he wasn't?

"No. Luke said it was over. He wasn't mean or anything about it. He said he liked me, but he wasn't in love with me, and he didn't feel right having an affair. I couldn't believe it. I was sure it was just the shock of finding out about Ray. I thought Luke would change his mind. That he'd miss me, and we'd talk it through together and figure things out. But he cut me off completely. He wouldn't return my texts or phone calls. But I kept texting and calling anyway. Finally, he came to my studio. He told me he was changing his phone number and his email address. He told me that I should get help, that I needed to accept that it was over. He was so cold. I knew he meant it."

"So you stopped?"

"I did. But I didn't stop hoping that when Mandy was really better, we could start over. I was obsessed. I admit it."

"Did you know Luke started seeing someone else after he broke up with you?"

"No. I wish that I had. It would have helped me face reality. Instead, I kept my hope alive by telling myself that once Mandy was well, and I had left Ray, Luke would come back to me."

"Ava, there's library security footage from the night before the library fire. Someone visited Luke at work, and they spoke for a couple of minutes. Was that you?"

"Captain Fike asked me the same question. They have the video. They have Luke's phone records, too, and they show my phone number calling and texting him dozens of times right after we broke up."

"What did you tell Owen?"

"The truth. He already knew the calls were me, the texts were me, and I confessed that the person in the video was me, too."

"Why did you go to the library that night?"

"To tell Luke that I was ready to leave Ray. Mandy is so much better. Ray is in a good place, too. He's doing a major expansion at his Michigan factory. He's really excited about the new line of boats they're going to be making. He's happy, Mandy's happy. I thought, *okay, this is the right time to tell Ray the truth. This is my chance to be happy, too.* I went to see Luke at the library. He was surprised, and he wasn't very pleased. But he agreed that we could talk the next day. I went home feeling hopeful."

"What happened?"

"Luke came over here on Wednesday, the day of the fire. He was so angry I could hardly get a word in. He said he was with someone else. That he was in love for the first time in his life. That he wouldn't let me ruin it. If I didn't leave him alone, he was going to report me to the police. He said he had never loved me, that he would *never* love me. And that, in fact, he was as close to hating me as he'd ever felt toward anyone. I was stunned."

"Ava, did Luke ever ask for, or did you ever offer to get him, the money he needed to buy the bookstore?"

"What? No! I didn't even know he needed it until after he died."

"So, what happened after Luke told you there was no hope for your relationship?"

"I cried a lot. I drank some vodka. I fell asleep. When I woke up a few hours later, I drank some more vodka, and then I had a great idea."

"What was that?"

"I'm sorry, Leah. I need some water to drink. And to splash on my face after all the crying and talking I've done today. I feel so ashamed and so humiliated saying it all out loud. I'll tell you everything about the night Luke died when I come back."

50

I used the short break to quickly take down the details of Ava's story. It wasn't a pretty one, but it felt like a true one to me. When she came back, she handed me one of the two bottles of water she held in her hand.

"Unless you want something stronger? It can't be easy listening to me purge myself," she said.

"No, I'm fine with water. And I'm sorry you have to tell your story to a virtual stranger, but I really need to know everything."

"I understand. And it's not really hard—in fact, it's kind of freeing to finally let it all out."

"Good. Just start in again when you're ready."

"I'm as ready as I can be. My great, drunken idea was to drive to Luke's mother's house. I knew he lived with her. I used to drive by sometimes, after Luke and I broke up, in the hope that I might see him working in the yard or something. Like a high school girl with a crush. Anyway, I went over there, and I parked a little way up the street, and I waited for him to get home."

"Oh, Ava. What were you thinking? He'd just told you he'd go to the police if you didn't leave him alone."

"I finally got that he didn't love me. But I didn't want him to hate me. I wanted to tell him I'd stay out of his life forever, but I couldn't stand it if he hated me. Drinking and great ideas don't mix, I guess."

"What happened?"

"I got there a little before ten o'clock. The lights were out, except for one on the porch. I parked and I waited. But I'd had a lot to drink. I guess I fell asleep. I woke up when someone started tapping on my car window."

"Who was it? Do you know what time it was?"

"I don't know the time. I was disoriented. I didn't even know where I was for a few seconds. I rolled down the window. A guy was standing there, and he asked me if I was okay. I said yes. Then he asked if I needed someone to drive me home. I guess he could smell the alcohol. I said no, and I just took off. When I got home, I lay on the couch and fell asleep again. I found out Luke was dead when Ray called early the next morning to ask me about the fire."

"That must have been pretty awful."

"Worse than you can imagine. I had to pretend I just felt normal shock, like you would about something bad that happened to someone you didn't know well. As soon as Ray hung up, I fell apart."

"Can you describe the man who knocked on your car window?"

"Not really. It was dark, I was drunk. He was tall with buzz-cut hair. That's all I remember."

"You told Captain Fike everything you just told me?"

"Yes. But he said I was lying. He told me they knew I was at the library the night of the fire, because they can tell from cell tower records. But I wasn't there. And my phone was on the garage floor when I got home. It must have fallen out of my pocket. So that proves I wasn't there. I knew he was the one who was lying. He can't do that, can he?"

"I'm afraid he can. The police are allowed to lie when they're trying to get a suspect to confess. And I'm sorry, but even if records show that your phone was here when the fire happened, that won't help you much. It just proves your phone wasn't at the library, not that you weren't."

I'd very recently said the same thing to Brodie. It was ironic that my two prime suspects both shared the same misconception that the location of their phones could save them.

She lowered her head and put her face in her hands, moaning softly for a minute.

"Captain Fike said he talked to the woman Luke was seeing," she continued. "She said Luke told her I was obsessed, and I wouldn't leave him alone. That they kept their relationship secret because Luke was afraid I might start harassing her, too. I don't know, maybe I would have. It's like I was crazy for a while. Oh, God. I don't know what Mandy will think, and Ray. Poor Ray. What a mess I've dragged him into."

"Ava, please tell me you don't have a gun or access to one."

From the stricken look on her face, I knew she couldn't tell me that.

"I don't have one, but there's one at the cottage. I don't even know what kind it is. Ray bought it because our place is pretty isolated. I've never used it. I refused to learn how. Captain Fike didn't ask me about it. Maybe it's because he already has it. Leah, I didn't kill Luke. You have to believe me. Somebody has to believe me."

"Ava, I wish I could say everything will be fine, but I won't lie to you. You're in a lot of trouble. You have a strong motive for killing Luke—jealousy and revenge. You have an alibi that's pretty hard to believe. And you had access to a gun."

She started to cry. And with good reason.

"Ava, if you didn't kill Luke—and for the record I don't think you did—you need to stop crying and start fighting."

"How? How am I going to do that? You just said I'm in trouble. I don't have any way to prove I didn't kill Luke."

"If Owen had enough evidence, you'd be in jail right now. So hold on to that thought. But he'll be talking to Ray and to Mandy soon, if he hasn't already. If I were you, I'd call Ray and I'd call Mandy. You don't want them to hear your story for the first time from the police. Then get a lawyer and take the advice you're given."

She stared at me, a look of utter despair in her eyes.

"Ava, don't give up hope."

"It's hard not to."

"Listen, there's another suspect who I think has a motive as strong as yours, and an alibi that's not any better than yours—maybe even worse. I'm going to see what I can dig up."

"Who is it?"

"Sorry, I'm not there yet. I need to do more thinking and more checking."

"Leah, why are you doing this for me? You don't even know me. And after what I've told you, you probably don't even like me. I wouldn't."

"I'm not doing it for you, Ava. I promised Luke's mother I'd try to find out what really happened and why. I can't stop now. As far as not liking you? I know how hard it can be to love someone who's struggling with their mental health, and the toll that can take on your own. I'm not judging you."

"I want you to know I didn't kill Luke. I could never do that."

51

It was only five o'clock when I got to McClain's for my 5:30 meetup with Miguel. I ordered a Jameson over ice and sat at a table in the back to sort out my Ava-versus-Brodie thoughts while I waited. Ava had a real motive that others had testified to and that she had admitted to. Brodie had one I had assigned to him—that Luke was blackmailing him about the burglaries. Which only worked if I was right about it.

Ava had the means—the gun at the lake cottage. It's not as easy as cop shows make it seem to match a bullet and a gun. But if the bullet found in Luke was even the same caliber as the bullets for Ava's gun, that would be a pretty big problem.

A hand touched my shoulder as a voice said, "Hey, how about that drink you promised me?"

I looked up and into the smiling face of Andrew Jones, my long-ago neighbor.

"Andrew! I didn't expect you back so soon. How did you know where to find me?"

"I stopped by the paper, and your mom said you were here."

"Pull up a chair and join me."

"Let me get a beer first. Do you need a refill?"

"Not yet. I just got started. But tell Mikey to put your beer on my tab."

As soon as Andrew finished his first sip of beer, he asked, "So, my sister was telling me that half the library burned down and someone was murdered since I left last week. What's going on around here?"

"The storage area is destroyed, but the rest of the library is okay—or will be after the restoration work is done. But yeah, someone was killed. Not by the fire. He was shot before it started."

I gave him an abbreviated version of what had happened and why I was involved.

"So, is there a suspect?"

"Yes, but I think the police have the wrong one. Though I understand why they like her for it. She has an alibi, but it's a stretch to believe her. I do. They don't."

"Can you say what it is?"

Without naming names or giving much detail, I relayed Ava's story of waiting in the car for Luke to come home and then leaving after a mysterious stranger woke her up and offered help.

"Wait a minute. Wait just a minute. That's me! I'm the guy. I'm the mysterious stranger!"

"What? You weren't even here. It happened the night you left."

"But I was! I saw a white Lincoln Navigator parked on Valley Avenue as I was leaving. I noticed because it was a pretty upscale model for the neighborhood. When I looked closer, I saw someone slumped over the wheel. I stopped to see if they were okay."

My pulse had quickened as soon as his story started. It was racing now.

"I knocked on the window. The driver was a woman . She kind of shook herself awake and rolled it down. I could smell the alcohol. I asked if she was okay. She said yes, but I could tell she'd been drinking. I offered to call someone to pick her up because she shouldn't be driving. But she just took off."

"What time was this?"

"About 10:45. I'm sure because I was cutting it close to catch my flight, and I checked the time after she drove away."

Ava had said she got to Luke's house around ten o'clock. The video from the night of the fire showed that Luke was still alive at ten. The fire alarm had gone off at eleven. There was no way Ava could have been shooting Luke and setting the fire at the library, because she was parked in front of his house.

"Can you describe her??"

"She was pretty. Long, dark hair, brown eyes. She had on a green coat. As soon as she took off, I called 911 to report a possible drunk driver, I didn't stick around, though, because I didn't want to miss my flight."

"Central dispatch will have a record of the call and how it was handled. Andrew, I'm sorry. I have to go."

"Was it something I said?"

"It absolutely was. You might have just saved a woman from an unjust murder charge. I'll talk to you later."

I jumped up and ran for the door, almost knocking Miguel down as he came in.

"Where are you going? I'm not even late. It's not 5:30 yet."

"Sorry, I have to check something out that looks like really good news for Ava Farley. I'll call you. Oh, see that guy at the table in back? It's Andrew Jones, my old neighbor you saw me with last week. Go introduce yourself to him and buy him another beer, would you? He deserves it. He just might be Ava's alibi."

"What? But—"

"Sorry, I'll call you soon, I promise."

∼

I called Coop as I ran to my car.

"Hey, can you check with Central Dispatch and see if they recorded a call around 10:45 p.m. the night of the fire? And also what the follow-up report says?"

"I'm sorry. Who is this?"

"You're very funny, but Coop, this is very serious. I think I've got proof of Ava's alibi."

I filled him in on my conversation with Andrew.

"Yes, sure. I'll go right down the hall and check on it. I'll call you right back."

My phone rang as I parked behind the *Times* building.

"Well?"

"Yes, a call came in at 10:47, reported a possible drunk driver in a white Lincoln Navigator heading north on Valley Avenue. Dale Darmody was dispatched from HPD. He didn't see any sign of the vehicle when he got there. He drove around the area but didn't turn up anything. Not long after that, all hell started breaking loose at the library fire, and Darmody was sent there for crowd control."

"Oh, that's great!"

"Want to give me a few more details now that I've followed orders and successfully completed my mission?"

"Come over to my place and I will. Also, if you bring me a #3 special from the Burrito Palace, my love for you will only grow stronger."

I saw a light in the *Times* hallway when I walked in through the back door. Coop wouldn't arrive for at least half an hour. I walked down to my mother's office to see if she was the one working late. She looked up with a smile when she saw me standing in her doorway.

"Didn't Andrew find you?"

"Oh, he found me. In fact, he gave me some key information about Luke's murder."

"What? How could Andrew know anything about that? He wasn't even here when it happened."

"Ah, but he was, and that's the key information."

"Stop talking like the Cheshire cat and explain to me in English I can comprehend."

I did as I was told.

"You know I heard something yesterday about Ava having an affair, but it was from Courtnee, so I thought she must have it wrong," my mother said when I finished.

"That is generally a correct assumption where Courtnee is concerned, but give the devil her due, she's usually spot-on when it comes to local gossip. I hope Ava talks to Ray really soon. Otherwise, he's going to hear it on the street from some 'kind' soul."

"So if Ava isn't on your suspect list, and Ed Wagner was already crossed off, who's left?"

"Sorry, Mom. Still working on it, but I'm getting pretty close, I think."

"That's good. I saw Ellen Granger yesterday. She's pretty much a mess—who wouldn't be? Have you talked to her recently?"

"Geez, Mom. Even when you're not trying to, you can make me feel guilty."

"So I'm guessing you haven't called Ellen to tell her how things are going? You really should, Leah. She's all alone—well, she has the Grangers, I guess, but I can't imagine there's a lot of comforting going on there."

"I know I should, Mom. And I will. But I doubt it will make her feel any better. In fact she might feel a lot worse."

"Not much could be worse than having your only child murdered."

"Unless he turns out not to be the kind of man you thought he was."

"Leah? Have you found out something about Luke? Something bad?"

"I've turned up some things that are pointing in a not-great direction. I don't want to say any more right now. But you're right, I owe Ellen a call. There's just not much I can tell her at the moment. And I can't tell you anymore either.

Although I did owe a call to Ellen, Ava deserved my first one. I phoned her as soon as I walked through the door of my apartment, eager to give her the good news. The phone rang and rang and then kicked over to voice-mail. I had to leave the bombshell good news in a message, with the admonition that if she didn't have a lawyer, she should get one imme-diately.

Next I made a quick call to Miguel, who not surprisingly was still with

Andrew. I filled him in and asked him to share the news with Andrew that the police verified his story—but to still keep Ava's name out of it.

I had to call HPD to reach Owen, because for some reason, he doesn't want me to have his cell number. He wasn't in, but I left a message that I had new information on the Luke Granger case that he needed to know. If he called me back, I'd tell all. If he didn't, then he could find out on his own the next time he spoke with Ava—or preferably with Ava's attorney.

Then, my duty as a good citizen ready to help the police at any time done, I called Ellen Granger.

52

"Ellen? Hi, it's Leah Nash."

"Leah, have you found out who killed Luke?"

Her voice was filled with such a mix of hope and anxiety that I wished I hadn't called.

"Uh, no. Not yet. But I've eliminated a few suspects. I just wanted you to know I haven't been sitting on my hands. I've interviewed a lot of people, and I'm checking alibis now. Have you heard anything from the police?"

"No. I called Captain Fike to ask what's going on, but he hasn't returned my call."

"I'm sure he'll let you know as soon as he has anything. I did want to ask you something, though. Did Luke have a lot of girlfriends?"

"I suppose it depends on what you mean by 'a lot.' Girls have always liked Luke, and he liked them back. But there wasn't anyone serious. Or at least I never met her if there was. Why?"

She was going to hear about Ava soon. The gossip about her and Luke was already low-key circulating. It would go the Himmel equivalent of viral once Andrew's story got out. But at this point, I couldn't give her any of the details she'd want to know. I opted to keep silent and move on. But Ellen had a question of her own.

"Have you talked to Brodie?"

"Yes, this morning, actually. Why?"

"I've been trying to get in touch with him. He broke a promise to me— not that it hasn't happened before. But now he's not returning my calls. I don't know why I ever asked him for help in the first place."

"Help with what?"

"Cleaning out Luke's storage unit. He rented one when he moved in with me. My house is pretty small—no basement, no attic, a one-car garage. Luke had some things we just couldn't fit in here. I forgot all about it, but the manager at the storage place called Saturday to say the rent was due and did I want to pay for another month or come and clean it out."

"Didn't the police go through Luke's storage unit?"

"No. They came and searched the house and his car right after he died, but they didn't ask about his storage locker. And I was in such a state, I didn't even think about it. I probably wouldn't have remembered it at all, except for the manager wanting the rent. Brodie was here when the man called. He said he came to pay his respects, but I think he was just hoping for some of Luke's things. When I got the call, I told him if he'd go clean out Luke's storage space, he could have whatever was in it. All I wanted was any photos he found there. Luke used to take a lot of pictures, and I thought there might be some from when Josh was alive and we were a family."

"But he didn't do it?"

"Oh, no, he did it right away. He came by when he finished and said there weren't any print photos. But he found an external hard drive or storage disk or whatever you call it. He said there might be some pictures on that. But I don't have a laptop, and the police have Luke's. Brodie said he'd take it home and check. He promised to print them out and bring them over if there was anything on it, but I haven't heard a word from him since."

I was thinking I'd like a peek at that hard drive myself.

"I plan on talking to Brodie again soon. Would you like me to get it back from him? I could print any photos out for you."

"Oh, I'd really appreciate that. I should have known better than to count on Brodie."

"No problem. I'll get on it and let you know one way or the other if there are any photos to be found."

"Thank you. And you'll let me know as soon as you find out anything new about Luke's murder?"

"Yes, of course. As soon as I have something to report, I'll call you. Bye, Ellen."

∽

I thought about calling Cole, but before I had made up my mind, my phone rang, and his ID came up.

"Leah, now I been real patient, but I'm gettin' tired of waitin' and wonderin'. I thought you'd be better than the police. But as far as I can tell, you're gettin' nowhere fast."

"Cole, I don't work for you, and I don't have to give you a report of what I'm doing."

My voice was sharp, probably because his complaint stung a little. I was very happy that Ava had a solid alibi, but also very frustrated that, so far, all I'd been able to do was cross people off my suspect list without making any tangible progress. I was hoping I had it right about Brodie, but I certainly wasn't going to tell that to Cole.

"Hey now, no need to get huffy with me. I'm just sayin' it don't look like you're workin' too hard to clear the Granger family name."

"That's not what I'm trying to do. I'm trying to find out who killed Luke. You ought to consider that if I do, it might not be what you want to hear."

"What's that supposed to mean? I already told you nobody in my family killed Luke."

"Maybe you don't know everything you think you do about your family," I said. He was really starting to annoy me. I don't do my best thinking when I'm irritated.

"I talked to Brodie today," I continued. "His alibi for the night of Luke's death is about as lame as they come. And he was really unhappy when I pushed for details."

"You said you wanted to see Brodie to get some background on Luke, so's you could find someone with a motive to kill him. Brodie ain't got to prove an alibi to you. What are you sayin'? Did the cops get to you? Now you think he did it?"

"I don't know if Brodie did it. And I don't owe you any insights into my thinking. But I will say that for an innocent man, Brodie got very mad, very fast."

"And I will say that I don't need you messin' in my family's affairs."

"Really? Because you asked me to do just that. You know what they say, be careful what you wish for. If Brodie did it, I'm going to find out. If you don't like what comes out when I do, that's your problem. Goodbye."

My phone rang immediately again. I switched it off. But I was mad at myself. I shouldn't have told Cole that much. But at the end of a very long, very up-and-down day, I didn't have much of my usually sunny temperament left. Still that was no excuse. If Cole thought Brodie was in danger of being arrested—which at this point, he wasn't—he might urge him to leave the area. And it would basically be my fault for tipping Cole off.

53

"So, what do you think?"

Coop and I had finished our burritos—well, he had, anyway. I had done most of the talking, so half of mine was still left.

"I think Owen isn't going to have a very good day tomorrow. I feel sorry for him. Cliff is going to come down on him hard for wasting time on Ava," Coop said.

"But Cliff is the one who pulled Owen away from focusing on Brodie when the investigation started, isn't he? And I'll bet he's the one who got Owen going on Ava. When I saw Brooke today, she couldn't wait to tell me about the Ava-and-Luke rumor, so I'm sure she put the idea into Cliff's head."

"Well, to be fair to Brooke, someone has to put ideas into Cliff's head. He certainly doesn't have anything to furnish it with himself."

I laughed because it was true and because he delivered the line so well.

"Coop, I think I should tell you something. I don't want to, but I probably should. I talked to Cole Granger just before you got here. It didn't go very well. I got kind of annoyed with him, and I let my temper get the better of me. I told him something I wish I hadn't. If it turns out badly, I don't want you to be taken by surprise if Owen and Cliff give you grief because of me."

"That sounds a little ominous. What is it?"

I went over my exchange with Cole, finishing with, "And so now I'm worried he'll run to Brodie. In fact, I'm sure he will. And if my theory is right and Brodie did kill Luke, Cole might help him get away."

He nodded, but he didn't say anything for a minute.

"Well? Do you think he will? If he leaves the area, it could take a lot of time, money, and personnel to find him again. I should've just kept my mouth shut."

"Or hung up on Cole a little sooner. I don't know if Brodie will run. But I don't think it's your fault if he does. He's got to be tracking the investigation. When he hears Ava is in the clear, which I'm sure he will fairly soon, he could decide not to stick around and become suspect number one again. Whether or not he's guilty. Don't take that on yourself. Though Owen may want to hand it to you. He hasn't racked up any wins so far, and you might make a convenient target for his frustration."

"I can't believe you said that. Don't get me wrong, I'm happy you did. But you're always telling me not to get in the way, not to do anything that could mess up a police investigation. Which I don't think I do very often. But I can see where this might be one of those times."

"I don't think you've done anything to harm the investigation. In fact, you helped it by finding Ava's alibi. Nobody wants to solve a case by arresting the wrong person. Including Owen."

"Wait. Are you praising my excellent investigating skills? Be still my heart."

"I never said you didn't have skills. I just think sometimes you move too fast."

"That's fair. I did jump at PPOK, but given the fire at the library and the recent ramping up of their activities, I stand by looking at Ed Wagner as a logical suspect. And please note that I didn't ignore Brodie. I questioned him, and I kept him in reserve. But Ava did make a strong suspect for a while."

"I'm glad you're not as changeable about your boyfriend as you are about your suspects."

I knew he was teasing, but it hit a little close to the bone. It did feel like I'd been switching horses quite a bit suspect-wise.

"I'm not changeable. I'm just open to possibilities when they appear. Oh, wait, what's that I see over the horizon?"

I put my hands on his shoulders and leaned to one side as though trying to see something in the distance.

"Is it? Yes, it is— a possible new boyfriend. I may have to make a change."

He wrapped his arms around my waist and pulled me down onto his lap. Then he kissed me. When I sat back up he said, "Still think you see something better ahead?"

"Actually, it's gotten a little foggy. I can only see a few inches in front of me. Let me stand up and see if I can see farther."

I slid off his lap and put my hand over my forehead as though shading my eyes the way you do when you're looking at something far away. I shook my head.

"Nope, you're all I can see. And I mean that both literally and figuratively."

I leaned in and kissed him lightly.

"But you could admit that you do the same thing when you investigate. You ask questions, you form a hypothesis, you test it, and if it doesn't hold, you adjust. Sometimes it takes a lot of hypotheses to get to a solid theory. As Courtnee told me once, 'It's not over until the opera starts.'"

"I'm surprised to hear you quote Courtnee, and I have no idea what that means."

"That's because you're not fluent in Courtnee-speak. She meant it's not over until the fat lady sings. But the point I'm making is that a lot of new things have come up in this investigation. I've had to adjust so that I'm fitting my theory to the facts, not ignoring some facts because they don't fit my theory. And now speaking of theories, tell me how your cold case investigation is going while I shut up and eat my cold burrito. Are you ready to reveal all to me?"

"Not quite, but it's getting close. Charlie turned up something interesting today—"

"See," I said, trying to talk around the large bite of burrito I'd just taken. "And you're adjusting for the new information. Just like I do."

"Nobody does things just like you do. The information isn't really new, it just confirms an idea I've been working on. I've got a meeting tomorrow in Hailwell with the fire chief. His department handled the fire at Jiggy Benson's house, and the one at the rental in Delving. I want to get his take on both fires and see if he agreed with Art Lamey's decision to write them off as undetermined cause. And I'm trying to get hold of the investigator at the insurance company that paid out on the rental house. What I find out from them could confirm my theory. But either way, I'll tell you all tomorrow. How's that?"

"Fine. I'll hold you to that."

54

"I don't know how you convinced me to come out in minus 900-degree weather, Miguel."

I grumbled as I zipped up the bright-orange snowmobile suit that had awaited me in the garage of Miguel's friend Clark.

"Because you love me. And it is twenty degrees, perfect for snowmobiling. The sun is shining, it's a short ride to the warming hut, the air is so clean and crisp, and we will have a fabulous time. Be happy!"

"I'm happy to be with you, but I would be happier if it was indoors somewhere," I said, as I waddled toward the snowmobile in multiple layers of clothing and my well-padded suit. I clambered on behind Miguel. He started the engine, disengaged the parking brake, gave the throttle a little bit of gas, and we took off.

I had to admit that Miguel was right. Despite the cold, it was a good day for a snowmobile ride. I settled in with a firm hold on the handgrips as we rode past snow-covered pines. A white-tail deer in the woods pricked up its ears and sprinted away as we zoomed past, and a flock of birds took to the air. We'd had a light snow the night before, so although the trail was well groomed, we were the first to make tracks that morning. As the miles fell away beneath the machine's skis, I felt some of the tension slipping away from me as well. I still didn't like the loud roar of the engine, but our helmets had built-in microphones and speakers so we could communicate easily despite the noise.

"See, you are having fun, aren't you? The trail is in perfect condition, and the woods—it looks like a Christmas card, yes?"

"Yes, it does. And yes, I'm having fun. Thanks for inviting me."

"Sometimes, it's good to get away from work for a little bit. Now, when we go back, all the pieces of the Brodie-and-Luke theory will fall into place. Dr. Miguel has the right prescription for stressed investigators."

"I thought you were Dr. Love with the right prescription for finding romance."

"I am a man of many skills. Oh, look, I can see the warming hut. I told you it was a quick ride."

In the distance, I could see the small wooden structure. I saw something else as well.

"Hey, doesn't that look like a snowmobile near the hut? Maybe Corky Donovan made it, and you didn't need me after all. I don't mind not being in a photo looking like the orange Michelin man in this snowmobile suit."

"I don't think it's Corky. His snowmobile is black. That one is red."

"Maybe he got a new one. But it's even better if it's not Corky. You can get photos of someone who's actually using the warming hut instead of a setup picture with me or Corky."

"You are right."

But as we got closer we both realized at the same time that I wasn't right. In fact, I was very wrong.

"Over past the snowmobile—that looks like a person in the snow!" Miguel said.

"Someone must have had a heart attack. Hurry!" I said.

Our snowmobile had barely come to a stop when Miguel and I both jumped off and ran to where someone lay face down in the snow. It was then I saw the jagged, blood-stained hole that marked a bullet's exit wound on the back of his snowmobile suit.

"Holy shit, Miguel! It wasn't a heart attack."

We each reached out instinctively to turn the body over. It was literally frozen. And the man was someone we knew.

Brodie Granger.

We stared at each other for a second, then Miguel pulled out his phone and called 911.

My mind was reeling. If Brodie had killed Luke, who had killed Brodie? And why?

"It will be a little while before the sheriff's office gets here because they have to use the snowmobiles," Miguel said. "They don't want us to go to the warming hut because it's part of the crime scene."

"Yeah, sure, of course. They're not going to be very happy that we turned over the body and disturbed things."

"But we couldn't just look and not do anything. We had to see if he was still alive. I didn't even think, I just did it."

"I know, me too."

We trudged back to our snowmobile with eyes cast down, trying to stay in the tracks we'd already made to avoid messing up the scene even more.

"What do you think Brodie was doing out here?" Miguel asked.

"It looks like he was coming to meet someone who wasn't very happy to see him. I definitely did not see this coming. I feel like I'm batting in the negative numbers on this investigation. It's not PPOK, it's not Ava, it's not Brodie—then who *did* kill Luke? Why can't I figure this out?"

"But just because Brodie is dead, it doesn't mean he didn't kill Luke. It could still be as you said—that Luke wanted the bookstore so bad he black-mailed Brodie, and Brodie got so mad he killed Luke. Then this—" he paused and pointed in the direction of Brodie's body. "This is something else."

"It's something else for sure, but what? Unless it means . . . "

"Means what?"

I shrugged.

"I don't know. I was hoping that by the time I came to the end of that sentence, my brain would supply an idea. But I've got nothing."

We fell into silence until Miguel asked, "How long do you think Brodie's body has been here?"

"He's frozen pretty solid, so at least four or five hours, I'd say. It was in the high twenties last night. Do you know what time the trail gets groomed at night?"

"I don't, but the Winter Warriors Snowmobile Club posts it on their website. Let me look."

As he scrolled through his phone I tried to make the information in my head sort itself into a new perspective on Luke's death, but my thoughts remained a disorganized jumble with no discernible pattern.

"Okay, here it is. A team of people from the club start at ten p.m. to the north of the warming hut, where the trail curves, come down this way for five miles, and then back. It takes a little over an hour to do it."

"Then he had to be killed sometime after eleven; otherwise, the trail groomers would have spotted him. We'll have to wait for the autopsy to narrow that down. And that's going to present some challenges. They'll have to thaw the body first. That can be tricky to do without damaging tissue. At the moment, I'm less interested in how and when he was killed than why and who did it."

We lapsed into silence again. The wind was picking up. It gusted and tossed a spray of light, powdery snow in my face. I blinked rapidly and reached up to wipe it away. As I did, my eyes caught sight of a set of footprints that went from the warming hut to Brodie's body. I hadn't noticed them before. I stared for a minute.

"That's weird."

"What's weird?" Miguel asked.

"See those footprints leading from the hut toward Brodie? They look really big—like Sasquatch big. Can you put the zoom lens on your camera so we can get a better look without tramping around out there?"

Miguel mounted the lens and focused it.

"Oh, I see why. Those tracks, they aren't footprints from boots. They are snowshoe tracks—you know, more oval and longer. They go out to the body and then back again. There are boot prints, too. They go a little toward the hut and then back a few feet to where Brodie is. They aren't ours because we came from the trail and ran over diagonally to his body."

He handed the camera to me so I could see for myself. He was right—the big tracks looked like snowshoes. I did a sweep of the camera around the front of the hut, looking for tracks leading away. I spotted them.

"Miguel, there are snowshoe tracks leading from the hut toward the north. They cut over to the snowmobile trail, and then I can't see anymore. But the wind is blowing the snow so much they won't be there for long. Can you take some photos so we can give them to the police?"

When he finished, Miguel asked, "What are you thinking?"

"I'm thinking that Brodie is wearing snowmobile boots. But his boot tracks don't go all the way to the hut. It looks like the killer waited there for Brodie to arrive and get off his snowmobile. Then after just a few steps, Brodie turned and tried to run back to his snowmobile, but the killer shot him. Then he walked out to make sure Brodie was dead before he left. But there aren't any snowmobile tracks around except Brodie's. The killer must have snowshoed in."

"But why would they meet way out here? And why would the killer walk out here in snowshoes instead of riding a snowmobile?"

"This is the perfect place to meet if you don't want to be seen. The trail-grooming times are posted on the website so anyone can find out when the trail is basically shut down. If you wait until after the trail grooming happens, you could be pretty sure no one else would be around. And maybe the killer used snowshoes because he didn't want anyone to hear his snowmobile taking off in the middle of the night. Or didn't want anyone who lives near the trail to hear him roaring his way here."

"Well, you can go very fast in snowshoes. Last year at Winter Fest, Will did the 5K snowshoe race in twenty-seven minutes!"

"Are you suggesting that Will the barista at Woke is a stone-cold killer?"

"No. I'm just saying if he did it, he could get away really fast."

55

"Now, why am I not surprised to find you two here?" Charlie Ross asked as he got off his snowmobile and headed toward where Miguel and I were waiting. He was the first to arrive, but a team of people were roaring up behind him.

"Hey, I was just out for a happy snowmobile adventure with Miguel. I didn't expect to find a dead body. But can we answer your questions really fast and then leave? With the sun gone and the wind rising, it's really cold out here."

"Fine. Let's start with why you're here, when you got here, and what you did."

We went through our story and received the expected criticism for flipping the body—though even Ross had to admit it was a natural reaction.

"Ross, I thought I had Luke's murder figured out finally. I was pretty sure Brodie did it, but now I don't know. I can't figure out why he was killed. It doesn't fit, and that means I'm missing something."

"He coulda been cheatin' somebody in a drug deal, or he owed somebody money he didn't have, or he was involved in somethin' else he shouldna been. It doesn't have to have anything to do with Luke's murder. Playin' the kind of dangerous games the Grangers do, when you lose, you lose big. Like maybe Luke and Brodie did."

"Do you know something I don't about Luke's murder?"

"All I know is what I read in the paper. Speakin' of which, I don't wanta see anything online except a body was found on the snowmobile trail, the name's bein' withheld pending notification to the family, and more information will be available after the autopsy. Nothin' about how he was killed."

"Ross, you know we don't need your permission or approval to run a story. Can't you ever just trust that we're not going to run anything that jeopardizes an investigation?"

"I trust that you won't do it on purpose. I'm just makin' sure you understand what the lines are, so you don't cross any of them."

"Okay, fine. It's too cold to stand here and argue with you. I'll see you later."

"Miguel, can you come up and help me think?" I asked as we drove into the parking lot at the *Times* building. "My mind is very jumbled right now. I can't figure out why Brodie was killed, let alone who did it."

"I will, but first I have to check in with Maggie, and I have to update the online site. But I can't stay very long, because I have a photo shoot at one of the elementary schools."

"I'll take what I can get, and you leave when you need to. I'll start working on trying to make sense of things. Come up whenever you're ready."

Sam often greets me at the door, but he was nowhere to be seen when I walked in. However, I did hear the faint sound of running water. I dashed down the hall to the bathroom, where the door I hadn't closed tightly was now ajar. Sam was sitting on the edge of the sink, drinking water from the tap.

"Hey, I thought we talked about this? Yes, I know I'm supposed to keep the bathroom door shut, but sometimes I forget. That's not an invitation for you to play water ballet in the sink."

I turned off the faucet, swept Sam up in my arms, and closed the door firmly as I walked out. Sam doesn't like to be carried, preferring to decide for himself where he wants to go. Don't we all? He squirmed, and when I set him down, he ran to the window seat and sat down on his blanket in his favorite corner.

I grabbed a legal pad, a pencil, and settled into mine. I stared out the window at the snow gently falling. The wind in town wasn't nearly as bad as it had been on the trail, and the flakes meandered down in lazy sweeps. The snow was just starting to accumulate on the sidewalk below. Sam crept over and settled down beside me, nudging me to pet him. As I stroked behind his ears, he relaxed, and I did, too. When I wasn't trying to force the ideas to come, they began to pop up on their own. Then several of them collided, and I saw connections I had missed before. I retrieved my laptop and checked the *Himmel Times* archives, searching for a story on a residential fire in Delving eighteen months ago. When I found it, I made a call.

"County assessor's office. Betty Jo speaking. How can I help you?"

"Hey, Betty Jo. This is Leah Nash. I've got a quick question for you."

"Well, let's see if I've got a quick answer for you, Leah. What's up?"

"I need the name of the person who owns the property at 716 Third Street in Delving."

"There's no house there, you know. It burned down last year."

"That's okay. I just need to know who owns the lot. Oh, also can you get the name of the person who owns the Full House self-storage facility near Bear Creek?"

"Can do. Hold on a sec, and I'll pull it up for you."

The clacking of keys ensued, accompanied by Betty Jo softly humming what sounded like "The Wreck of the Edmund Fitzgerald."

"Ah! Here we go. You got a two for one here, Leah. Both properties have the same owner. Stillman Realty and Property Management."

"Betty Jo, you're wonderful. I love you! "

"Why, thank you, Leah. I'll let Bill know I have options the next time he gives me an electric can opener for Christmas. You have a nice day now."

I called Coop, but it immediately went to voicemail. Which was probably a good thing. I should calm down a little before we had that conversation.

There was a light tap on the door, and Miguel walked in.

"Perfect timing. I've got some ideas that I'm trying to string together into a theory that makes sense. I need some help. You sit. I'll pace."

56

"Now, I'm just roughing this out, jump in if it doesn't make sense, okay?"

He nodded.

"So, we're going to start back a couple of years or so ago. Bear with me, the backstory is important. Brodie Granger works for his cousin at Way to Mow lawn services. They have a contract to take care of Phil Stillman's home as well as his business properties. And Phil, he's always expanding his properties. Back then, he wanted to buy land in Bear Creek to put up a big storage facility. The land and a house on it were owned by an older guy named Jiggy Benson, who refused to sell. But then Jiggy's house—the one he'd lived in all his life, the one he wanted to die in—burned down. He had nothing to keep him there anymore. He sold the land to Phil, who built his storage units."

"How do you know the story of Jiggy? Do you know what happened to him?"

"He's a friend of Coop's dad. Jiggy had a stroke after the fire. He had no family, so he had to move into a nursing home, and now he has dementia."

"Oh, that is so sad!"

"Yes, it is. It's wicked, too, but we'll get to that shortly."

"Now we move to about eighteen months ago. Phil Stillman has a rental house that needs very expensive repairs—new septic, new roof, mold remediation, and so on. But before the work starts, the rental burns down. Phil collects $75,000 in insurance money instead of having to lay out a ton of cash for repairs."

"Phil is very lucky with fires, isn't he?"

"Indeed. But I think he made his own luck in both cases. I think he hired someone to burn down Jiggy's place, and it worked out so well that he hired the same person to set fire to his rental house."

"Brodie Granger?"

"Clever boy! Yes. And that sets the scene for our burglaries at the Haven."

"What do the burglaries have to do with the fires?"

"I'm now at the totally speculative part of my presentation. But I think when all the facts are unearthed, they'll support it."

"Just tell me, you don't need to sell me. I'm not Owen or Charlie."

"Thank God. Okay, so Phil got what he paid for from Brodie. But Brodie wasn't satisfied with his end of the deal. He ran through the money he got pretty quickly. And then he hears that Phil collected $75,000 in insurance money for the rental house Brodie burned down. Brodie figures Phil didn't give him a fair cut. After all, he's the one who took the risk and did the work. He asks Phil for more. And Phil says no. Brodie threatens to go to the police and tell them that Phil was behind the arson. Phil says, *try it. I'm not the one the cops will go after.*"

"Because Phil is an important man, and Brodie is not?"

"Sad, but true. Phil is a big deal around here. He has a lot of money. He donates generously. And given Brodie's track record, if Phil says Brodie is making the arson stuff up because he's a disgruntled employee who wants revenge, odds are the cops will believe him, not Brodie. And Brodie knows that. But he's still determined to get what he thinks is his due for the work he did."

"So he breaks into Phil's house and steals. Yes I can see that, but why did he rob the neighbors, too? Wait, so that it wouldn't look like Phil was targeted, right?"

"Exactly. So, yesterday when I talked to Brodie, he bragged about how smart he is and how he knows things—things people would be very surprised by. I thought it was just big-talker BS. But now I think Brodie got away with something even more valuable than the cash and electronics and jewelry he stole. Information."

"What information?"

"Well, that's the gaping hole in my story. I'm not sure yet. I don't think it's evidence of other financial crimes or shady deals that Phil's involved with. Brodie doesn't have the background or the knowledge to recognize something like that. Not unless it was in a folder labeled *Phil's White-Collar Crimes*. I think Brodie found evidence of some personal secret that would be very damaging to Phil if it got out."

"Like what?"

"Maybe Phil was a porn star in his youth, or he's trans, or he has a wife and five little Phils in another state. Whatever it is, Brodie finds it and knows it has blackmail potential. But he can't exploit it himself."

"Why not?"

"Because having the secret information links Brodie directly to the burglary. Phil will know for sure that he committed the burglary, and if he goes to the cops, Brodie will go to prison for both extortion and burglary. And he knows Phil will pull out all the stops to fix the case against him."

"I don't understand. If it is so important to Phil to keep his secret, how could he go to the police and say Brodie is extorting money from him without telling the police his secret he doesn't want anyone to know?"

"That's where Phil's influence comes in. He can go to Cliff first and explain his dilemma. They're good friends. Phil has donated a lot to Cliff's efforts to become the next judge, and maybe he'll throw some more dollars Cliff's way. Cliff could prosecute Brodie for the burglaries plus come up with something other than extortion to pin on him, something that will send Brodie to prison for a long time."

"But do you think Brodie is smart enough to think all that through? That doesn't sound like him, from what you say."

"The thing of it is, Brodie may not be a genius, but I think he's crafty enough to see how things could blow back on him if he tries to blackmail Phil. And don't forget, right after the burglary, Brodie's got all that money from selling what he stole. He's feeling pretty flush. He does the smart thing. He leaves the secret alone."

"And so, are we all done with the idea that Luke blackmailed Brodie about the burglaries?"

"We are. Luke didn't blackmail Brodie. When Luke tells Brodie that he's $5,000 short on the money he needs for the bookstore, Brodie sees an opportunity. He's run through the burglary money pretty quickly, and he'd like to get more. That's when he tells Luke about the burglaries and, more importantly, about the secret and what a moneymaker it could be for both of them. Under normal circumstances, I don't think Luke would have anything to do with it. But he is desperate to get that $5,000. He agrees to be the front man and make the blackmail demand to Phil."

"But wouldn't Phil know that the secret came through Brodie, who got it from whatever he stole from Phil's house?"

"He probably suspected it, but he couldn't prove it. And the ask probably wasn't too high—enough for Luke to get the first $5,000 he needed for the bookstore and then something for Brodie's cut. Phil was backed into a corner. And Luke agrees to turn whatever blackmail material he has back over to Phil. So, Phil agrees to pay, hoping that will be the end of it."

"So then why is Luke dead?"

"Because when the bank wanted another $10,000, Luke went back to the well. He tried to get it from Phil again. That's when Phil realized Luke could keep coming back forever. He agrees to pay him but has no intention of doing it. He meets Luke at the library to give him the money. Instead, he kills him, sets the fire, and hopes it will look like Luke died accidentally in a fire set by PPOK. That's why Phil was so amenable to my theory about PPOK. It fit perfectly into his plan. If the blame could be shifted onto someone from the group, then Phil is all clear."

"Okay, I'm with you. But then if Luke is the one who made the blackmail threats, why was Brodie killed?"

"Because blackmail is a dangerous game, as Luke found out. Brodie has to suspect Phil killed Luke. Which means he's in danger, too. But he can't resist taking one last big bite out of the apple. He asks Phil for a very large amount of money in exchange for giving Phil whatever evidence he has on him and leaving town. Phil agrees. He arranges to meet Brodie at the snowmobile trail, kills him, and his problems are over."

"I can't believe it! No, I *can* believe it, but how can we prove it if we don't even know what the secret is?"

"Yes, that's a pretty big challenge. But I have a tiny bit of hope on the secret front."

I told Miguel about the external hard drive and Brodie's failure to return it to Ellen.

"If the police find it in a search of Brodie's place, and if Luke stored a document or a compromising photo or whatever blackmail evidence he had on it, that could wrap things up pretty quickly. Plus there are some other supporting facts that could help build a case against Phil—at least for Brodie's murder."

"Like what?"

"Like the distance from the Haven to the ski trail by river is about five miles. A good skater—and Phil is an excellent skater, according to his wife—can do five miles in an hour or less. Luke's killer wore snowshoes. Phil has a pair of snowshoes in his garage. I literally bumped into them when I first talked to Brodie.

"Phil carries his snowshoes on his back, skates down the river, and then uses his snowshoes to get to the warming hut and wait to kill Brodie. Afterward, he walks back to the river and puts his skates on and goes back home. No car pulling out of the drive or coming back late at night for neighbors to see or hear. No snowmobile to wake everyone up when it comes home in the middle of the night either."

Miguel cut in. "I gave Charlie the photos of the snowshoe prints I took at the warming hut, and he said they will use them to compare to snowshoes of a suspect—when they have one. So maybe they can be matched to Phil's snowshoes."

"Yes, and maybe they were able to get a cast of the print, which would help even more."

The alarm on Miguel's phone went off, startling us.

"Sorry! I set it to remind me to go to the elementary school. I wish I didn't have to. I want to help you think some more. I could call and—"

"No, don't do that. I'm sure I'll still be here thinking when you finish. We can finesse things then, before I take it to Ross."

"Why not to Coop?"

"Ross is the one investigating Brodie's death. Plus I'm low-key mad at Coop right now. All along I've been very transparent with him about what we've done and found. But he told me barely anything about his cold case arson investigation. And he was focused on Phil from the start. If he'd shared that with me, we could've gotten here sooner."

"I hate when mom and dad fight," Miguel said.

"We're not fighting. I'm just mad. But Coop and I will have a discussion after this all comes out. Meanwhile, you go do your elementary school thing. I'll stay here and think."

"If you are sure..."

"I'm sure. Go."

57

After Miguel left, I ate a sandwich and thought about what to do next. Coop still hadn't called me back, which was frustrating but not that surprising. There's a lot going on at the start of a murder investigation. But I wanted to tell him what I'd figured out and see if he and Ross had found any links between Brodie and the fires at Jiggy's house and Phil's rental unit. That was a key element of my theory that Phil and Brodie's arson activity was the root cause that ultimately led to the murders of Luke and Brodie. And I finally felt in my bones that I'd landed on the right theory. Up to that point, I'd been floundering in deep water, grabbing onto ideas that sunk beneath me and left me feeling like I'd never reach Answer Island.

But how to convince Ross and Coop? If they had already linked Brodie to the fires, it would be a fairly easy segue to him as the burglar. But from there, could I convince them that Phil had killed twice to protect a secret I hadn't yet discovered? That could be a bridge too far without something more concrete than my firm conviction. I had to find out what the secret was. But how? Luke and Brodie were silenced, and Phil was not about to confess.

Then it hit me. Kimberly Stillman. She knew. She had to know—that's why she was in the grip of anxiety and panic attacks. She was near the breaking point. She could also be in danger. I had to talk to her as soon as possible.

I called Phil's office to make sure he wasn't working from home for the day. I needed to get to Kimberly alone.

"Stillman Realty and Property Management, this is Sarah. How may I direct your call?"

"Hi, Sarah. This is Leah Nash. Is Phil in? I dropped some paperwork off for him yesterday, and I have some additional information for him."

"I'm sorry, Miss Nash. Mr. Stillman is out of the office."

"Oh, dear. I really need to talk to him. Will he be back in later today?"

"I'm afraid not. He has a meeting in Madison today that he expects to take all morning. Then he's showing a client property in Omico and Hailwell, and he said not to expect him in the office until tomorrow. Can I take a message? He'll see it first thing in the morning."

"No, that's okay. I have his cell phone number. I'll try to reach him that way. Thank you."

"Oh, but that won't work! Mr. Stillman lost his cell phone yesterday. I'm in the process of getting him a replacement, but he won't have it until tomorrow. If it's really important, you could call Mrs. Myerson. I can give you her number. She's at the meeting with him, and she could let him know you need to reach him."

"Oh wow, he must be lost without his phone! No, Sarah I won't bother Mary Louise. Just leave Phil a note that I called, and I'll check in with him tomorrow. Thank you." And I ended the call.

"Yes!" I shouted out loud. For once, things were breaking my way. The coast was clear for a visit with Kimberly Stillman. I grabbed my purse and was zipping up my coat when Sam came zipping out of the bedroom and dove under the sofa—his favorite hiding place when someone comes to the door.

Then I heard a sharp knock. Not on the door I used most often, which leads to the parking lot. My visitor was rapping on the door that opens to the stairway leading to the front of the building. Courtnee must have sent someone up to see me. I really didn't have time for that nonsense right now.

I hurried down the hall, through my bedroom, and into my office. I pulled open the door without my usual look through the peephole. Which I regretted as soon as I saw my visitor.

Cole Granger.

～

"Cole, I'm on my way out, and I'm in a hurry. I don't have time right now. I'll give you a call later, okay?" I moved to close the door. But he was quicker. He pushed past me and stepped inside.

"I got somethin' you're gonna want to see. Now. Where's your laptop?"

I noticed then that he was holding something in one hand.

"Why? What have you got there?"

He went on as though I hadn't asked a question. "I s'pose you know that Brodie's dead."

I nodded. "I'm sorry. I didn't think the news was out yet. Miguel and I are the ones who found him. How did you hear?"

"Mama told me, but I was already suspectin' somethin' was up. He was supposed to fill in for a shift at JT's last night, and he never showed, so I had to take it instead. Then this mornin', my cousin Howie called lookin' for him. He didn't turn up for work at Way to Mow today either. I was just leavin' JT's when Howie called. I said I'd go by on my way home and give him hell for both of us. I expected to find him passed out on his drunk ass.

"But when I got to his place, he wasn't there. His snowmobile was gone, too. But his truck was in the driveway, so I took a look. There was a cooler full of Mountain Dew on the passenger seat and a bag of pork rinds next to the cooler, like he was all ready to go on a road trip. Then I saw the suitcase in the back and took a look inside. Thought I might get an idea of what the heck he was up to."

"What was in it?

"The kinda stuff you'd take for a trip down South—shorts, t-shirts, underwear, flip-flops, you know. And this here external hard drive. That kinda piqued my interest. Right then, Mama called and told me Brodie was dead. Kilt out on the snowmobile trail. She didn't know much else. Well, I knew it wouldn't be long before the cops come to search his place, so I grabbed the hard drive and went on home to look at it. You're goin' to wanta see what I found."

"You've never been more right in your life. Hand it over. I'll set it up."

Two minutes later, Cole was seated beside me at my desk while I opened the hard drive and clicked on the only file there.

"Holy shit, Cole!"

"Ain't nothin' holy about that shit, darlin'."

The video file we were watching didn't have high production values— the lighting wasn't great, the staging was clumsy, and the female actor had her back to the camera. But the performance was riveting. A half-naked Phil Stillman was full body embracing a partially clothed woman as he helped her disrobe. She turned, and I saw who it was. Brooke Timmins.

58

As the action got more intense, I hit pause.

"I've seen enough of this," I said. "I have to go and wash my eyeballs now."

"No, no. You got to see just a little more. That's when it gets real interestin'."

Cole reached over and fast-forwarded the video. When he stopped it, we were looking at a different couple, in a different room. Kimberly Stillman was lying on a bed, wearing lingerie. The man with her was buck naked, his back to us. I recognized him immediately by the pinky ring on his right hand and the ears which stood out like two open car doors. Cliff Timmins.

I shut the video off and turned to Cole.

"Cole, this is the closest I have ever come to actually liking you. This is it, the missing piece."

"What missin' piece?"

"I figured out most of what happened, but I couldn't get to the real motive. This is it. I know now why Luke was killed, and I know why Brodie was murdered, and I know who did it. I figured out that Phil must be hiding a big secret—and apparently, so are Cliff and Brooke. But I didn't know what it was. This video footage is it. Phil, Kimberly, Cliff, and Brooke—

they're swingers. They swap partners. It's not illegal, true. But there are a whole lot of people in Grantland County who don't want to see the Himmel Citizen of the Year and the leading contender for Judge Keene's seat engaging in wife-swapping with each other's wives!"

"You sound like you know what's goin' on here. It might be nice if you told the person what hired you. Not the wife-swappin', I understand that, but how did Brodie get this and why does it solve Luke's murder?"

"Even though I want to reaffirm that I am not working for you, in recognition of your excellent contribution to this investigation, I think I owe you an explanation. With the caveat that you do nothing with it. You do not approach anyone in the videos, you do not run and tell your mama, and, in fact, you leave this with me."

I moved quickly to unplug it from my computer and dropped it in my coat pocket.

"Wait a minute now. I found that there hard drive. Lemme at least make a copy so we can be sure nothin' gets lost."

"Oh, no. You did the right thing bringing it to me. But this hard drive is not coming into your possession again. It's critical evidence against Phil Stillman, not blackmail fodder for you."

"I have to say that your assumption that I have criminal intent offends me, Leah."

"Noted. But are you also agreeing to my terms—you don't talk to anyone in the video, or anybody else at all, until you hear from me. You sit tight and wait for justice to unfold."

"And how's that gonna happen? When you started, Luke was dead. Now Brodie is, too. It looks to me like you ain't as good at your job as people think."

"I'll give you that, considering how much I flip-flopped around on this case. But I've got it in hand now. Quit stalling. Promise me you won't share anything I tell you until I give you the word."

"Fine. Okay."

I gave him the theory that, thanks to his discovery, now appeared to stand on fairly firm legs, and he listened without interruption.

"That's it. I may be off on a few things, but I'm sure the gist of this is right."

"Well, you don't make the Granger boys come off too well—Brodie did break in, after all, and him and Luke did some blackmailin'. That hurts to know them boys acted that way. But I got to say, you just answered a lotta questions. Now, I'd sure like to see the others get what they deserve. Are you sure it was Phil that killed Luke and Brodie on his own? Maybe Timmins had somethin' to do with it, too."

"I'm sure he did, but probably more by steering the investigations to keep the truth about their little games secret. If Owen had been allowed to follow through on the Brodie-as-burglar angle, it might have prevented two deaths. It won't be easy to prove because Phil and Cliff have a lot of resources to protect themselves. There's no way Phil will confess to the murders, or that Cliff won't try to cover up whatever he did. And Brooke has the brains to help him. However, there's someone else who I'm pretty sure knows everything."

"Who's that?"

"Phil's wife, Kimberly. I saw her yesterday. She was extremely stressed and possibly frightened. I think she'll talk if I ask her the right questions. I'm going to the Haven right now to see her. When I'm done, the video, my theory, and what I learn from Kimberly goes right to the cops."

"Goin' to the Haven don't seem too smart, what with old Phil bein' more'n a touch homicide happy."

"I checked. He's in Madison and won't be back until tonight. But I've got to leave now. And so do you. Goodbye, Cole. Don't forget your promise. If you blab, it could mess up what we both want—Phil coming to justice."

The light snow of the morning and early afternoon had left little accumulation. But it had changed over to a light rain and sleet mix that made driving hazardous on the country roads I had to travel. Slow and steady is the key to staying out of a ditch in that kind of weather, I know. But my mind was racing as I tried to figure out the best way to approach Kimberly. Unconsciously I increased the speed of my car to keep pace with my thoughts. When I reached the turn-off for the Haven, a deer dashed out in front of me.

I immediately did two exactly wrong things. I slammed on the brakes, and I swerved to avoid him. My car fishtailed and then spun out of control. It crossed the centerline, hurtling off the road, scraping against scraggly pines. I fought to hold on to the steering wheel as the car bumped for what seemed like forever. Finally, it came to rest just short of crashing into the trunk of a looming large tree.

I sat for a minute, catching my breath and cursing my carelessness. If you live in Wisconsin and you do a significant amount of driving, you're going to have a car-deer encounter at some point. There's a reason I have the Bang Bang Bump Shop and Tow Service on speed dial. This wasn't my first, but it was my worst car-deer accident, and I should have known better. I tried the engine, but I couldn't get it to start. I got out and surveyed the damage. My passenger-side mirror was ripped off, there were some dents and a lot of scratches to the side of the car, but I had been luckier than I deserved.

"Bang Bang Bump Shop, if you need a tow, it's gonna be awhile."

"Timber, it's Leah. Sounds like the sleet brought you some business."

Tim Wolfe was a friend of mine from grade school, where given the wit of third graders, he'd been given the nickname Timber. It had stuck.

"Hey, Leah. Yeah, you could say that. And Roddy's out today. I just called Cole Granger in to work a few minutes ago."

"Cole? I didn't know he still worked for you."

"He doesn't regular, but he'll come in if we get swamped like today. So, what can I do for you?"

"I need a tow. I'm at the south entry to the Haven. I had a close encounter with a deer, and the deer won."

"You okay?"

"Yeah, I'm fine.

"Best case scenario, it's gonna be at least an hour, maybe two."

"No worries. I'm on my way to see a friend. I can walk from here. I'll leave the keys in the car. Just have the tow guy take it to your place, and I'll check on it tomorrow. I'll get a ride home."

"Sounds good, Leah. Gotta go, another call coming in."

I called Miguel next.

"Hey, can you pick me up in an hour or so?"

"Yes, where are you?"

I like it when people say yes to me without asking questions, and Miguel almost always does.

"I'm at the south entrance to the Haven right now. My car ran off the road. I'm fine, but it needs to be towed."

"Why are you at the Haven? You said you were going to be at home, thinking."

"New information and a change in plans. Timber's sending a tow truck, but he wasn't very optimistic about how long I'd have to wait. I'm going to see Kimberly. It's not far, so I'll walk. If you can pick me up there in an hour or so, that would be great."

"I can, but what is the new information?"

"I know Phil's secret. And it's not just his—Brooke and Cliff Timmins and Phil's wife Kimberly are all involved."

"What is it?"

"No, it'll be better in person. I hope to have more details after I see Kimberly."

"Wait! Just tell me a little bit what it is."

"Sorry, I know it's kind of mean, but I'm freezing out here, and it'll take too long to tell. You'll appreciate it more in person anyway. See you soon."

59

I had the equivalent of about six blocks to get to the Stillman house, but it was a slip-sliding walk, even in the hiking boots I wore. The wet sting of sleet in my face didn't make it any easier. By the time I reached the enclosed portico and rang the bell, I was shivering with cold. When there was no answer, I knocked loudly and rang the bell again.

I began to feel a little uneasy. I tried the door, and it opened. I took off my snow-covered boots. Before just barging into the main part of the house, I pulled out my phone and tried Kimberly's number. As it rang, I heard a corresponding faint ringtone coming from inside the house, but my call went to voicemail. Thoroughly alarmed, I hit redial as I opened the door and ran down the hall, following the sound of Kimberly's phone.

I ran quickly toward the den where we had first talked.

"Hello? Kimberly? Are you here? It's Leah Nash. Are you all right?"

The door to the den was open. Kimberly was lying on the couch, and an empty wineglass was on the coffee table beside her. An open prescription bottle on its side with several pills spilling out was next to it.

∼

I ran to the couch. Kimberly was on her back. I put my hand on her shoulder and shook her.

"Kimberly, wake up! Kimberly!"

I tapped her cheeks gently while continuing to call her name. I couldn't rouse her. I called 911.

"911, what is your emergency?"

"It's my friend. I think it's a drug overdose."

"What is your location?"

"I'm at 825 Haven Road. It's the Stillman house. Gray and white, the fourth house in when you take the south entrance.

"What is your friend's condition?"

"She's unconscious. I can't wake her up. There's an empty wineglass and a half-empty bottle of Xanax on the table."

"How old is your friend?"

"I don't know exactly. I think mid to late forties."

"How much Xanax did she take?"

"I don't know," I said, picking up the prescription bottle. "The bottle says it contains thirty pills. There are five left. But I don't know how many were in there when she took them."

"Do you know when that was?" he asked.

"I don't."

"Hold the line, I'm going to dispatch Emergency Medical Services to your location."

He came back on seconds later.

"Okay, I want you to put your friend in the recovery position. We want to keep that airway clear. Do you know how to do that?"

"No."

"That's okay. We'll take it a step at a time. It's not hard to do."

He walked me through rolling Kimberly onto her side and positioning her hand under her cheek and bending her top leg at the knee to keep her from rolling onto her stomach.

"Okay, it's done."

"Good job. The ambulance will be there in a few minutes. Now, what is your name and your contact information?"

I gave it to him, all the while patting Kimberly's arm. I knew she couldn't be aware of it, but it made me feel better.

The dispatcher stayed on the line with me until I heard the wail of the ambulance followed by the sound of tires crunching on the ice- and snow-covered driveway.

As I heard the front door open, I shouted out our location. "We're in here, straight down the hall, second door on the right."

I jumped aside as they entered with a gurney and began the work of saving Kimberly. I hoped.

I recognized the female half of the team as a friend of Ross's.

"Rita, is she going to be okay?"

"Can't say yet, Leah. Depends on a lot of things—how much she took, how long it's been in her system, any underlying conditions she might have. Is she a relation?

"No, just a friend, an acquaintance, really. Her name is Kimberly Stillman. Her husband is Phil Stillman."

"Stillman Realty?"

"That's the one.

"Do you have a cell phone number for her husband?"

"I do, but that won't help. He lost his phone and doesn't have a replacement yet. But I can give you his office number. He's out of town, but they'll be able to reach him." I scrolled through my contacts and gave it to Rita.

"Okay, we're ready to roll," her partner said.

"We'll get in touch with her husband. You did good, Leah," Rita said.

60

I looked at my watch. It was only 2:45. Although it had felt like hours, the whole thing from when I walked through the front door until the gurney rolled out had taken less than half an hour. But was that fast enough to save Kimberly's life? Rita's "can't say yet" wasn't much comfort.

For normal humane reasons, I hoped Kimberly would survive her suicide attempt, because I was pretty sure that's what it had been. For abnormal obsessed journalist reasons, I also hoped she'd survive to supply context for the video. I wanted to know if everyone in the group—Phil, Kimberly, Brooke, and Cliff—had been in on the murders.

Phil had done the killing, I was certain. But what did the rest of them know, and when did they know it?

I doubted that Kimberly had known about Luke's murder initially. If she had, she wouldn't have been so friendly and open the day I met her. Cliff and Brooke might not have known right away either, but Phil would have had to let Cliff know, after the fact—to get Cliff's help in keeping Owen at bay when he started investigating Luke's death. And what Cliff knew, Brooke would know, too.

A new question surfaced. Did everyone in the group know about the taping and agree to it? I turned that one over a few times in my head. I could see Kimberly doing basically whatever Phil wanted her to do, including recording their adult recreational activities with their friends. But Brooke and Cliff were another matter.

Brooke might have gotten into swinging out of boredom with Cliff. I couldn't blame her there. But she was smart enough to know that in this online-all-the-time world, anything filmed or photographed had the potential to wind up trending on social media. She wouldn't risk all the effort she'd put into making Cliff a circuit judge. And even if Cliff thought filming it was a fun idea, Brooke ran the show. She would never have allowed them to be filmed.

So, when did they find out?

The most logical order of events was that Brodie and Luke decided to hit the Stillmans for money, based on the video. But when Phil decided to kill Luke, he had to tell Cliff about it to get his help keeping the investigation of Luke's death from getting too close. Brooke would have been part of those conversations because Cliff didn't make a move without her.

Kimberly was different. She had ongoing anxiety issues, and she was more emotionally fragile than the others. They couldn't be sure how she'd react. She had probably been left in the dark while the other three plotted, until recently. And when she discovered that her husband, the man she loved, had gotten her tangled up in arson, murder, blackmail, and sex tapes, it had pushed her over the edge. That was the reason for the panic attacks, and that was the reason for her suicide attempt.

I got up from the chair I'd collapsed onto once the ambulance had left. I'd rather wait in the hall than in the den with Kimberly's empty wine bottle and half-gone pills. As I turned to go, my eyes fell on Phil's shelf of homemade DVDs next to the fireplace. I had a sudden thought. If taping and watching sexual encounters was Phil's jam, how likely was it that he'd restricted himself to making only one video? I pulled out a DVD case, hand-labeled "Bill's Retirement Lunch," and another titled "Dedication New Office Building."

If Phil was trying to hide his private collection in plain sight, those were pretty good names to ward off interest from anyone looking for a video to pass a snowy afternoon.

I popped "Bill's Retirement Lunch" into the DVD player attached to the television and hit play. It featured Phil and a woman I didn't know. I didn't have it in me to watch more than a few seconds. The cast of "Dedication New Office Building" was larger—four people I didn't know, though I recognized the setting as the same bedroom featured in the footage on the hard drive.

Okay, so the video that Brodie had wasn't a one-off. There was a good chance that all or most of the others on the shelf with extremely boring-sounding titles were in the same vein. I decided to take the two I'd viewed to share with Owen and Coop as evidence that my theory was correct. But first, I put them back on the shelf, their labels clearly showing, stepped back, and took a photo. It captured not only the rows of Phil's homemade DVDs, but also the Citizen of the Year Plaque mounted on the wall above them. Then I got a shot of the entire wall, showing the bookshelves to the right holding the buy-by-the-yard books, the TV and DVD player, and the left-hand side that held the homemade DVDs. It might be needed to establish that the videos had been found at Phil's and where, should they mysteriously disappear at any point.

I looked at my watch again—three o'clock. Miguel wouldn't arrive for another fifteen or twenty minutes. I had enough time to check out the master suite and verify that the blackmail video had been shot here in the house and the footage wasn't some kind of fake or setup. I went to find it.

61

I already knew where the formal living room was. I quickly discovered the dining room, a gourmet kitchen, a laundry room, a home office, and then at last I found the luxurious master bedroom suite. I surveyed the room from the doorway. The king-size bed with a bookcase headboard matched what I'd seen in the video of Brooke and Phil. The titles by authors Connelly, Baldacci, and Child fit what Kimberly had told me about Phil's reading tastes. This, no doubt, was Swinger Central.

I started to walk into the room for a closer look but stopped when I noticed a smoke alarm on the ceiling. It was positioned for a clear line of sight to the bed. I'd done a story a few years earlier about the surprising number of people who have spy cams in their homes—to check on pets when they're away, to monitor what a nanny is doing, to make sure house-keepers aren't snooping. And I'd learned that smoke alarms are a favorite place to stash hidden cameras. This smoke alarm might be real, or it might be a dummy outfitted to hold a tiny camera. All things considered, it was probably best if I wasn't recorded traipsing around the Stillman bedroom. I took a couple of photos from the doorway for comparison with the video, but I didn't go in.

When I finished it was almost 3:15. Miguel would be arriving soon. I got my coat from the den and headed for the portico to get my boots on. As I was tying them, I heard a car on the road. I looked out the window, expecting to see Miguel's yellow MiniCooper but felt a slight twinge of fear that it might be Phil's black SUV. It was neither. A Subaru coming from the other end of the Haven was driving toward the south entrance. For the first time, I thought about my car and wondered if Timber's tow truck had picked it up yet. I finished tying my boots and stood up. That's when I saw that the Subaru wasn't down the road in the distance. It was pulling into the driveway. And Brooke Timmins was at the wheel. Not the person I wanted to have find me here. I ran back inside, intent on exiting from the rear entrance.

I was hurrying down the hall when I heard a door slam at the back of the house and a voice call out.

"Brooke! Are you here?"

Phil!

Shit. They were coming at me from both ends of the house. I panicked for a second, then took the only option I had. I dove into the coat closet under the stairs, pulling the door shut milliseconds before Brooke's heels tapped on the hardwood floor. I couldn't see anything. But I could hear Phil approaching from the opposite direction. I reached for my phone and hit the record button, in case they said anything interesting.

"I saw you pull in," Phil said. "What are you doing here? Where's Kimberly? Is she—" he stopped.

"No, Phil. She's not dead. She's at the hospital. Your office called me because you told them you were showing me property this afternoon. They were trying to find you to tell you the tragic news that Kimberly had over-dosed and had been taken to the hospital by ambulance. We don't have time to go into it now. You need to be Kimberly's devoted husband and get to her bedside."

"Jesus, Brooke! What happened? Kimberly was already high on Xanax when I left this morning. All you had to do was get some alcohol and a few more pills down her. How could you mess that up?"

I nearly gasped out loud. Kimberly hadn't tried to kill herself. Brooke had tried to do it for her.

"How could *I* mess it up? This whole thing is your freaking mess. You made the video. You put all of us in the Grangers' greasy little hands. I'm the one who had to clean it up."

"You call killing Luke Granger and setting fire to the library *cleaning up*? You just made things worse."

That sent an even bigger jolt of surprise through me. *Brooke* had killed Luke, not Phil? That meant Luke hadn't gone back to Phil when he needed more money; he'd gone to the other couple in the video, Brooke and Cliff. And Brooke had taken action. I should have seen that before. Brooke was the president of the library board, she knew the setup in the storage area, she knew it was full of fire-starting fuel, and she knew enough about the security setup to make sure Luke turned off the two cameras there before she arrived.

"Don't even go there. If you had told me when Luke made his first blackmail demand to you, we could have stopped him right then. But no, you paid him off, never said a word to me or Cliff about the videos, and gave him the chance weeks later to come to us for a second payout. I did what you should have done in the first place. I took action to stop the problem."

"No, you dragged us all into a murder. You had no right to do that without telling me first. We could've figured something else out—or some other way to do it that wasn't so public!"

"Like what, Phil? If we really want to get to the root of things, you screwed up when you hired Brodie to set those fires for you in the first place. That gave him something to hold over you. That was stupid. But it was the recordings you made, without our consent, that dragged us all into the mess you made. So don't you dare tell me what I should or shouldn't have done. We're all in this together now, Phil. And if it goes to hell, you, and Cliff, and your dimwitted little wife are all going there with me. Right now, Luke is dead, Brodie is dead, and all we have to show for it is a hard drive with nothing on it."

I could feel the heat of her fury right through the closet door.

"It might not be as bad as we thought," Phil said.

"Oh, really? How do you figure that? As long as that video is out there, we're all at risk. You seemed to get that just fine when you called me in a panic this morning. Did you at least find your phone, or did you let the police scoop it up at the scene, and now they'll be knocking on your door any minute?"

"Could you just listen for a minute. Yes. I found my phone. I had to go all the way downriver, though. It was where I thought, on the ice, just a few yards from where I changed from my snowshoes back to my skates. The reason I think we might not have to worry about the video is that Brodie could have been bluffing. Maybe the reason the hard drive was empty is that Brodie didn't have the video."

For a few seconds, there was complete silence. Then Brooke exploded.

"What do you mean he could have been bluffing? Are you saying that you agreed to pay him $50,000 without even making him show you the video? You only talked to him over the phone? You're unbelievable. And I always thought that *Kimberly* was the stupid one!"

"Enough!"

Now it was Phil who was enraged. All of this yelling was excellent for the purpose of recording their fight on my phone.

"No, I didn't demand to see the video. I told you. He called me on the phone to make his threat. I knew Brodie was the reason Luke Granger had the video in the first place. It made sense that Brodie had a copy. You need to quit talking to me like I'm your lapdog Cliff, or you'll regret it. Do you understand me?"

Whoa. I was glad I was safe in my little hidey hole. Things were getting ugly out there. Suddenly, Brooke cried out.

"Ow, you're hurting me! Let go of my wrist! Please," she added, modifying her tone.

She continued at a much lower volume.

"Phil. We're both upset, but we can't hash this out now. When your office called me, I said that you'd just left for home. I told the woman that I'd drive out and give you the news myself, so I could be there to support you. You need to get to the hospital soon, or it's going to raise questions."

"Yes. You're right," said Phil, his voice calmer as well. "What did they tell you about her condition? Do you expect her to make it, because if she does . . ."

"I'm not worried about that. She was already half out of it on her own when I got here. I didn't have to work hard at all to get a few glasses of wine down her with a handful of pills. She won't even remember I was here. If she does, I'll just say I stopped by, she seemed sleepy, I didn't know she'd taken anything, or I never would have left her alone. I don't know how bad she is. I asked your receptionist when she called, but all the hospital told her was that Kimberly had been admitted and it was serious."

"*Serious*. What does that mean?"

"Get to the hospital and find out. I'll wait about half an hour, then Cliff and I will go the hospital as your close friends to support you. We can talk about next steps then."

"Right. You're right," Phil said. "Let's go."

Thank God. I needed them to quit arguing and get out of there before Miguel showed up. I could hear their footsteps moving toward the front door. I shut off the recorder on my phone and let out a sigh of relief. Quickly followed by an involuntary "Oh shit!" as my phone rang loudly with a call from Miguel.

"I'm in trouble. Bring help." I whispered urgently into the phone.

I shut it off just before Phil flung open the closet door and grabbed me by the arm.

62

I stumbled out into the hall. Both of them stared at me for a second, apparently rendered speechless by my surprise appearance.

My best option, my only option, really, was to stall and hope Miguel arrived with reinforcements soon. I commenced stalling.

"Phil, Brooke." I nodded at each. "I'll bet you're wondering why I called this meeting."

"Get her phone, Phil!" Brooke said.

"No need to grab. Here you go," I said.

I handed my phone to Phil politely and promptly. I didn't want to get in a tussle with him and risk him finding the hard drive stashed in my pocket and the DVDs I'd put in my purse.

"What are you doing here, Leah?" Phil asked.

"Well, I couldn't stop thinking about Kimberly. She was in such a bad way yesterday. Finally, I decided to stop thinking about her and just come out and check on her. She was unconscious when I got here. I called 911. You're welcome."

"Then why did we find you hiding in the closet, spying?" Brooke asked.

"I wasn't spying. I couldn't have if I wanted to. Which I didn't. Between the thickness of the wood and the coats in there blocking the sound, I couldn't even tell it was you two out here. All I could hear were muffled voices."

"That doesn't answer why you were in the closet at all," Brooke said.

"I was in the closet because as I was getting ready to leave, I heard a door slam in the back of the house. I knew it couldn't be you, Phil," I said, addressing him because he seemed slightly less hostile than Brooke. "When I called your office to give you some additional information about the *Times* board, your receptionist told me you were in Madison this morning and then you were showing properties to a client this afternoon. That's another reason I came to see Kimberly. With you out of town for the day, I thought it would be a good idea for someone to check on her. So I knew it couldn't be you coming in. I thought someone was breaking in. I jumped into the closet to hide until they left."

Phil looked at Brooke. For a second, I thought he might actually buy it. Brooke killed that hope—as well as my chance to keep stalling.

"She's lying, Phil. She's been snooping around for days. And she's doing it for Ellen Granger, Luke's mother. She knows something. Give me your purse," she said.

"Hey, I know I was stupid to hide, but you don't have any right to take my pu—"

As Brooke yanked the purse off my shoulder, it opened. The two DVDs I'd taken from Phil's den spilled out onto the floor.

"What are these?" she asked as she read the labels.

Phil grabbed them from her hands and turned to me.

"So you were just a Good Samaritan who happened to stop by to save Kimberly, and you don't know anything about anything? Then what are you doing with these?" he said, his voice a snarl of fury.

"I was just—" I started but didn't have any idea how to finish that sentence. Which was okay because Phil cut me off.

"Shut up," he said, his voice terse, and his face flushed with anger.

"Jesus, Phil! You still have these DVDs lying around? For God's sake, what are you, an addict? Get rid of them! Where are they? In the den? I'm going to do it right now!"

She started to leave. Phil grabbed her arm. "No. Don't worry about the DVDs now. We've got to figure out what do with her," he said.

"We have to get rid of her, of course," she said. "But we can't do it here." She turned to me. "How did you get here? Your car isn't in the driveway."

She was clearly tired of my delay tactics, but it was the only trick I had in my bag. What was taking Miguel so long? I should be hearing sirens in the distance by now. I tried dragging out my explanation.

"It's in a ditch at the south entrance. If you didn't see it, you must have come in the other way. I walked here. I was just going out to wait for the tow truck when you showed up. If I'm not there, the driver will be coming up to the house to get me any minute."

It was a stupid story, but fear was throttling my imagination.

Brooke shot it down immediately.

"I saw the car. I didn't know it was yours. But I saw a lot of cars in ditches on my way here. The tow truck driver isn't going to come and find you. He hasn't got the time. You told them you'd leave the keys in the car and find your own way home, didn't you?"

Damn she was smart, and quick.

"No," I lied. "I mean I did leave my keys in the car but, uh—"

"Stop talking," Brooke said. She turned to Phil. "We have to get rid of her," she repeated.

"I know that. Let me think a minute, will you?"

If Miguel didn't get here with help soon, it would be too late. They'd bundle me off somewhere, kill me, and who cared if they got caught in the end—I'd be dead.

Then an even worse thought struck me. Maybe Miguel wasn't coming at all. Maybe he hadn't heard my urgent whisper. I had been talking really low and then shut off the phone. If he hadn't been able to hear me and called me back, it would go to voicemail. A voicemail I'd never receive.

"Okay, I've got it," Phil said. "We stick with the plan. We just have to adjust it a little. Cliff will still tell Owen that given Brodie's death, he thinks now that Owen's original theory was basically right. Luke and Brodie fought over the takings from the burglaries. Brodie killed Luke. But the new angle is that Cole Granger was masterminding the burglary. He knew Brodie had killed Luke, and he knew Brodie was a loose cannon who could point the finger at him. So, Cole killed Brodie. The narrative doesn't have to change. We'll just add her into it," he said, pointing to me. "Cole killed her because she got too close to the truth."

It was an odd feeling to stand ignored as two people calmly worked out the logistics for my murder.

"Yes, that could work. Let's get her in the trunk of my car. I can drive her to our cottage. I'll call Cliff on the way, let him know what's happening. If Kimberly is dead when you get to the hospital, you can leave right away. If she's not, you'll have to stay for an hour or two, showing what a devoted husband you are. But then you can make an excuse about contacting family, or talking to her therapist, or whatever, and come to the cottage. We'll figure out how to finish things there."

"We have to get her out of here now, though, before the neighbors start driving by on the way home from work. There's some clothesline in the laundry room. You get it, and I'll make sure she stays put," Phil said.

It was chilling to hear Phil refer to me only as "her" and "she." He was depersonalizing me, to make it easier to kill me.

As Brooke left to get the rope, he stepped behind me, grabbed my arm and wrenched it behind my back and upward with a jerk.

"Hey!" I said as pain shot through my arm.

"Stand still or I'll do it again. This is going to end. Tonight. With you."

"Oh, it's going to end, Phil. But not the way you think."

I tried a Hail Mary play.

"Cole Granger has the hard drive with the video. And when you start rolling out your scheme to put the blame on him for all of this, he's not going to go down quietly. You and Brooke and Cliff— you'll all be caught. You'll all go to prison for the rest of your lives. And everyone is going to see your very special home movies."

"You're bluffing."

"Am I? Are you willing to spend the rest of your life in prison to find out? If I were you, and thank God I'm not, I'd pull all my available cash together and get as far away as I could from here. Right now."

"Shut up. You're screwed, and you know it."

Brooke came back with the clothesline.

"Do you need help tying her?" she asked.

"No, you go start the car and pop the trunk. I'll get her in, then you take off and I'll go to the hospital. There's one other thing. I don't want her phone records to show this as her last location. If you take Johnson Road to your cottage, it's longer, but you'll go right by that land the Grangers own. You know, where that old sugar shack is. You take her phone with you. When you get in the vicinity, run over it so it stops recording locations, then throw it away. That way the cell tower's last ping will show the Granger property as the last recorded place she was."

"That's a good tie-in to Cole Granger."

She took my phone from him and went out to start the car.

63

Phil tied my wrists together behind my back. When he was done, he grabbed the collar of my coat and frog-marched me to the door. As we stepped out, I heard the sound of an engine coming. A tow truck was barreling down the road toward the Stillman house.

Suddenly, it swerved and turned into the drive, headed straight for the back of Brooke's car. She saw it too. She threw her car in gear and hit the gas, but the tires spun on the ice, and she didn't go anywhere. I saw then that Cole Granger was in the driver's seat, and Miguel was sitting right beside him. Cole wasn't who I'd had in mind when I'd asked Miguel to bring reinforcements, but I was in no position to be picky.

"Looks like you're the one who's screwed, Phil," I said. "You should have taken off when I told you."

He flung me aside, and as I tumbled into the snow, I heard a deafening crash. Cole had rammed the truck into the back of Brooke's car. The impact moved the car forward at least twenty feet. The airbags had deployed, and Brooke was momentarily trapped inside. I could hear sirens in the distance.

I struggled to my feet—not an easy task with your hands tied behind your back. Miguel leaped out of the truck, ran toward me, and swept me into a bear hug.

Although I welcomed the warmth of his embrace, I couldn't return it with my hands still tied.

"Hang on there. You're my superhero, but can you untie me so I can give you a proper hug?"

"Yes, yes, right away! Are you okay?"

His fingers worked quickly on the clothesline. I gave him my best thank-you hug when he finished. The sirens were close now. As we turned to look, Coop's SUV was roaring down Haven Road, then swerving onto the Stillman driveway.

Something else caught my eye. "Look, Brooke is out of the car. She is trying to run!"

Ross jumped out of Coop's SUV as soon as it stopped and started running after her. Coop was running toward us, but he veered off course when Cole shouted something to him and pointed. That's when the sound of a snowmobile starting up filled the air.

"Holy cow, Phil's trying to make a run on a snowmobile," I shouted. "He's heading for the river!"

"Oh, that is not good. The river ice isn't thick enough yet for a snowmobile," Miguel said.

"You know what? I don't really care if Phil finds that out the hard way."

Ross caught up with Brooke easily. She'd fallen in the snow several times as she tried to get away. He had no trouble cuffing her, and she offered no resistance as he walked her to the sheriff's SUV, where he stored her before coming over to us.

Coop was running toward the river, his phone to his ear, no doubt calling for backup and the ice rescue team. But we could see that Phil's snowmobile was just hitting the river. There was nothing for us to do on that front. And if there were, I'm not sure I would have done it.

Cole had left the tow truck and came to join Miguel, Ross, and me.

"You got the hard drive?" he asked as he got closer.

"I'm fine, thanks for asking," I said.

"Hey, I just saved your life, didn't I? I can see you're fine. But that hard drive is gonna be pretty important to straightenin' everything out. I wanta be sure it's safe."

"Yes, you did. Thank you. And yes, I have it," I said, patting my coat pocket. "But I have to ask. What were you and Miguel doing together, and how did you turn into Batman and Robin in the nick of time?"

Before he could answer, a sound like the loud crack of a gunshot rent the air. Several more sharp, explosive noises followed as we all turned and raced toward the river. I outpaced the other three, propelled by overwhelming fear.

"Coop! Coop!" I shouted. I couldn't see him.

"There! He's over there by the willow tree, " Miguel said, catching up to me and pointing downriver.

I followed the direction of his hand and saw Coop partially obscured by the willow's drooping branches. On the river, Phil's snowmobile teetered on the edge of a jagged hole created as the ice gave way under the weight of the machine. Phil was struggling to get off, but his frantic efforts unbalanced the snowmobile. As the first police car arrived on the opposite shore, the snowmobile lunged downward, taking Phil with it as it disappeared into the dark depths.

"*¡Dios mío!*" Miguel exclaimed as he shivered beside me. "Do you think they will be able to rescue Phil?"

"I doubt it," Ross said. "By the time they get their gear set up and they're ready to go, Phil could be miles down the river under that ice. He might turn up in an ice cube sometime in the spring."

Miguel shuddered again.

"Ross, you have such a way with words," I said. "Miguel, they might be able to find him, but Ross is probably right. I don't think they'll be able to rescue him. I'm going down to talk to Coop." I ran in that direction, calling his name repeatedly.

He turned and held out his arms to me. I ran into them so hard I almost knocked us both down. He held me tightly for a minute, stroking the back of my hair.

"I'm fine. Are you?"

"Yes. I'm good. I'm fine," I said as I stepped away. "We thought we heard shooting. What happened?"

The rest of them caught up with me as Coop answered. "That was actually the ice cracking. I guess Phil's plan was to ride his machine across the river, then take off through the fields and eventually hit the trail. If he had a full tank, he could've gone a hundred miles or so without stopping. And he would've been damn hard to follow. He got better than halfway across when the ice started to break. It happened fast. One minute he was there, the next he and the machine went down."

The ice rescue team had begun to arrive across the river with their equipment as we talked.

"They've got their work cut out for them," Coop said. "It's going to be a search operation, I'm afraid. Not a rescue. And it's going to be a tough one. They can't take the airboat out. They're gonna have to use sonar, maybe drones. But the guys know what they're doing. And I know what I'm doing right now. Getting all of you down to the office. There's a lot of questions that need to be answered."

64

It was a very long late afternoon and early evening at the sheriff's office. I did get the pleasure of seeing Brooke Timmins escorted to a holding cell. Miguel, Cole, and I were interviewed separately and released.

Miguel left to write the first of many stories to come about the secret life and homicidal habits of some of the area's most prominent residents. Cole left to do whatever Granger things he does.

I went to Coop's office to wait for him. I called my mother back. I'd phoned her on the way into town, but I hadn't had time to do anything but reassure her that I was okay. I filled her in as much as I could. When I hung up, I leaned back in Coop's comfortable leather chair to close my eyes for a few minutes. I was just drifting off when the door banged open, and Ross walked in.

"Hey, Ross," I said, followed by a huge yawn. "Sorry, I'm kind of crashing now after all the excitement. Did you hear anything about Kimberly yet?"

"Yeah. Good news. She came around, but she's not with it enough to question today. I heard they're gonna keep her a coupla days to monitor things. She was pretty close to a goner, I guess. If you hadn't got there when you did, it sounds like she wouldn't be here."

"I'm glad she's okay. But man, how would you like to wake up and find out that your husband tried to kill you? Does Kimberly have any family? She's really going to need somebody."

"Yeah, she's got a sister in Florida. I guess she'll be here on Thursday night."

"I wish it was sooner. Social media—the press, too—will have a field day with this. Ross, what's going to happen to her? Legally, I mean."

"Depends on what her story is. What she knew, when she knew it, what she did."

"I hope she gets a good lawyer, and I hope she knows enough to help the case against Brooke and Cliff. What's going on with those two? I got to see Brooke headed for a holding cell. That was nice."

"They both lawyered up. Brooke's can't get here until tomorrow and neither can Cliff's. Doesn't matter that much because they can't get out on bail anyway, not until after they make first appearance in court. That won't happen until tomorrow. We're keepin' them separated, though, so they can't work on their stories together."

"That is sweet, sweet music to my ears, Ross. It must be driving Brooke insane that she can't get to Cliff and tell him what to do. Do you think they'll turn on each other? I bet Brooke will throw Cliff under the bus for a deal."

"I don't think she's gonna get offered one. You got her on tape sayin' she killed Luke. Not much wiggle room for dealing there. Cliff's the one with the better hand to play."

"I hope they both go down. Cliff is as bad as her, even if he didn't pull the trigger like she did. He's the damn prosecutor, the person who's supposed to uphold the law and make sure there are consequences for breaking it. Cliff didn't just break it, he smashed it to pieces helping Phil and Brooke cover up. Who's in charge in the prosecutor's office now—Kristin?"

"Yeah, but not for long. Timmins is suspended, but the governor has to make a temporary appointment. It'll probably be some retired prosecutor. For sure, the state Supremes will permanently remove Timmins. After that, there's a special election."

"I wonder if Kristin will run."

"I was thinkin' maybe Gabe would. He was a prosecutor back in New York, right?"

"Yeah, and he'd be good, for sure. But I think he's pretty happy in private practice. But we're kind of getting ahead of ourselves there. I'm just glad the Timmins era is over. Have they found Phil's body yet?"

"No. That current is strong under the ice. Phil's body could be way downriver by now."

His voice held a definite note of satisfaction. Which I understood completely.

But even though I had no sympathy for Phil, I couldn't stop a shudder thinking about how terrifying the last minutes of his life must have been. First the loud crack in the ice that told him he was in trouble. Then the fissures widening and shattering the surface. His snowmobile lurching downward as the ice gave way, and the final moment when the gaping hole sucked him into the blackness below.

Coop walked in then.

"Leaking to the press again, are you, Charlie?"

"I wish," I said before Ross could respond. "I'm hoping to get further with you, Coop. Are you ready to go home yet?"

"Yeah. I am. Tomorrow's another day, and it's going to be a busy one."

A little while later sitting in my apartment with Coop beside me, Sam on my lap, and a Jameson over ice in my hand, I finally felt the tension in my body let go. I sighed so deeply that Sam turned around to look at me, and Coop said, "Hey, you doing all right?"

"Yes. But I am mentally, emotionally, physically drained. And you should be glad of that."

"Why's that?"

"Because I'm too tired to be mad at you for holding out about Phil. If you had told me earlier that he was the guy you were investigating in your arson cold case, and that you thought Brodie was his fire starter, we could've figure this whole thing out together a lot sooner."

I expected him to raise his usual arguments about the integrity of a police investigation, balancing public interest and privacy rights of suspects, and how our personal relationship meant he had to be careful that it didn't look like his office got a free pass on press coverage, or that I got special favors because I owned the newspaper.

But he didn't.

"You're right."

"What?" I asked, sitting up straight so I could look at him, dislodging a disgruntled Sam in the process. "Am I so exhausted that I'm dreaming but don't know it? Because I swear you just said that you should have shared information about your cold case with me."

"You're not dreaming. I wanted to protect Phil's identity at the start because I didn't think it was fair to name him when all I had was an idea and some speculation. But when you started making connections between Brodie, the burglaries, and Phil, I could've been more open then. It might not have ended the way it did for Brodie and Phil, and nearly for Kimberly."

"Is this my early Christmas present? If so, let's make it the gift that keeps on giving. As in, for any future investigations where our interests cross, the standard rule is share, and the exception is rare. Seriously, it would mean a lot to me to know that you trust my judgment and my ability."

"I do, and I'll try to be better."

"I didn't say be better. I said do better. You already make my Top Five Favorite Men list. If you put in just a little more effort, you could hit the number one spot."

"Oh, really? I didn't realize I was in a ranking contest. Who's my competition?"

"Father Lindstrom, Miguel, your dad, and don't you ever tell him this . . . Ross."

"Who do I have to knock out of the top spot?"

"Father Lindstrom. He's been number one for years. But if you work at it, who knows? You're a very strong second. And you do have the ability to bring a little more to the game than he does."

"I see." He leaned in and kissed me. "Did you mean that?"

"I did. Do you have any more where that came from? Suddenly, I feel quite invigorated."

"Funny, I do, too. Let's see what I can do to improve my ranking."

~

I called Ellen Granger at seven o'clock the next morning, hoping she hadn't seen the story online. I also wanted to catch her before she left for work. She answered on the first ring.

"Leah, do you have news? You must have news if you're calling so early."

"I do, Ellen. But it's not the news you wanted to hear."

Without waiting for her response, I plunged ahead. I told her what had really happened to Luke and why, and that Brodie had met the same fate.

"I'm so sorry, Ellen."

She didn't say anything.

"Ellen? Are you there?"

"Yes, I'm here. I'm just . . . I can't, I can't quite take this in. It's so hard to think of Luke—he was such a sweet little boy—of him doing anything like that. I don't understand what made him do it—blackmail someone! He was a good man. He was smart, and he was kind, and—"

She broke down then and began to sob.

"Ellen, Ellen, please, listen. You're right, Luke was smart, and he was kind, and he was good. But he was a fallible human, too. He wanted that bookstore so bad, and he worked so hard for it. I think that when it looked like it was being snatched away, he got desperate. And desperate people do desperate things. What he did was bad, but that doesn't mean Luke was bad. He was, like most of us, a good person capable of doing bad things. This time, his desire was so strong it got in the way of his conscience, I guess."

As I waited while she struggled to get herself under control, my heart ached for her. She had lost her son, and she had lost her illusions, too. She'd created an image of Luke that was true, but it wasn't the whole truth. Now she had to learn to accept the whole of him, and it would be a very hard thing to do. I know, because I'd had to do it once myself, when I found out who my father really was.

"Leah, thank you for telling me. It's not your fault, but I wish I'd never asked you to help."

She hung up without letting me say goodbye. I felt awful. Sam came and sat beside me. For once, his warm, purring presence didn't help.

～

When I called Ava, the conversation was a little less fraught with pain, though it was still tough.

"Leah! Thank you, thank you, thank you! Captain Fike came to see me. He told me my alibi checked out. I'm in the clear. I can hardly believe it."

"I'm glad for you, Ava. Have you talked to Ray?"

"Not yet. I will when he gets home tonight." Her voice had become considerably more subdued.

"I'm sure that will be a hard conversation, but—"

"I know. I have to do it. He deserves the truth, but he doesn't deserve to be hurt the way I know he's going to be when I tell him. I talked to Mandy already. She's pretty angry with me for the way I've treated Ray. That makes two of us. I'm pretty angry at myself."

"What are you going to do?"

"You mean after? I'm not sure. I know Mandy will forgive me. I'm not sure Ray can. I've been thinking about him all night."

"Well, for what it's worth, he loves you a lot, Ava. Enough, I think, to forgive you . . . and to let you go."

"That's it, though. I'm not sure now that I want him to—let me go, I mean. When I told her about Luke, Mandy asked me what kind of an idiot I am. She said it's not that easy to find someone who loves you the way that Ray loves me. That what matters isn't that Ray likes swimming and I like hiking. What matters is that he's kind, and smart, and honest, and understanding. And you know what? She's right."

"I'm sure he is all those things, Ava. But if you don't love him, maybe it's you who needs to be the one to let go. Ray should have someone who loves him, too. You didn't ask, but I'll tell you anyway. A one-sided relationship isn't a good thing for either of you."

"But maybe it won't be one-sided if I get my head on straight. If Ray wants to, I was thinking maybe we could go to couples counseling or something and find out what we both want."

Privately, I was thinking that if I were Ray, I'd be all about making a clean break from someone who had deceived me the way Ava had deceived Ray. But this wasn't about me, and though I wouldn't have done what Ava had, I could understand how it had happened.

"Maybe he'll want to, but the first step is being totally honest with him. I know that won't be easy, but I know you'll do it. I hope things work out the way they should for you and Ray. Good luck, Ava. I mean that."

65

"So, they tell me I'm still alive because of you. I should say thank you, I guess. The thing is, I don't know what I'm alive for," Kimberly Stillman said as I walked into her hospital room on Thursday afternoon.

"Hey, you've just been through extreme medical and emotional trauma. Things will get better. Give yourself some time."

She smiled faintly. "You sound like my sister. She'll be here tonight. She wants to stay with me and make sure I'm all right. She's afraid I'm going to go home and kill myself, I guess."

"She's worried about you. You can understand that, right?"

"Yes, I can. But I wasn't trying to kill myself. I was just trying to calm myself, and I took too much medication. Detective Ross said Brooke and Phil were happy to help me with that."

"But it didn't work, and now you've got a chance to make a better life for yourself."

"Do I? I'm not sure the police agree with that. I've told them everything, but I don't know if they believe me."

"Do you have an attorney?"

"No. I don't want to hide anything. I just want to answer all the questions the police have and try to make up for my part in this whole mess. I don't want to try and get away with anything. I want to take responsibility for myself. It's about time, don't you think?"

"What I think is that you need a lawyer, Kimberly. You need someone to look out for your interests."

"I feel like maybe I don't deserve one. How could I have been so stupid? Leah, I really didn't know what was happening. I mean I knew some things, but not anything about the murders. Not until almost the end. I should have gone to the police. Not very long ago, Brooke said that I was a dumb little shit. A dumb, weak little shit. She was right. I might have saved Brodie if I had just pulled myself together instead of falling apart. I don't blame you if you don't believe me. I can hardly believe myself."

She blinked hard, to keep the tears in her eyes from spilling over.

"I don't disbelieve you, Kimberly. I don't really know what your story is. Do you want to tell me?"

She took the tissue I handed her, wiped her eyes, and blew her nose. Then she nodded. "Yes, Maybe it will help me sort it out in my own head."

"Okay, well, it starts about a year and a half ago. Phil told me he wasn't satisfied with our life—sexually, I mean. He said he loved me, but he needed more excitement. He said he had a married friend who felt the same way and maybe the four of us could get together. I was shocked, and hurt, too. I didn't know Phil was unhappy. I didn't want to have sex with other people, but I was afraid he'd leave me if I didn't. I agreed. And he did seem happier, and he was really nice to me after we started. I never liked it, though. I just did it for him. But I swear I didn't know anything about him secretly recording people. Not until Luke Granger came to us with the video."

"Tell me about that."

"It was maybe a month or so after the burglary at our house. He just showed up and said he had something Phil and I should see. He played the video of me and Cliff and Phil and Brooke. I was shocked and embarrassed and horrified. Phil asked Luke where he got it. Luke said he bought a DVD player at a pop-up flea market in Milwaukee, and it was inside the player when he opened it up."

"Did you believe him?"

"I did. When our house was broken into, the DVD player from the den was one of the things taken. Phil watched a lot of DVDs there. He said he was under so much pressure at work he needed that time to unwind with a Scotch and a favorite old movie. But he was really insistent that the den was his space, and when he went in and closed the door, he didn't want to be disturbed. When Luke said he found the DVD in a used player, it suddenly hit me what kind of movies Phil had been watching. Luke said he'd sell it to us for $10,000 or he'd put it online. It was our choice."

"How did Phil react?"

"After Luke left, Phil told me that we had to pay it. If the video came out, it would ruin his reputation. It could ruin his business, too. He paid Luke, and Luke gave us the DVD."

"Did you tell Brooke and Cliff Timmins about it?"

"I wanted to. I didn't think they should be blindsided like we'd been. But Phil said no. He said we'd paid the money. We'd taken care of it, and why should we get them upset for nothing?"

"But it wasn't for nothing."

"No. A couple of weeks later, Brooke came over. Luke had kept a copy of the DVD. He asked them for money, too."

"Just Brooke came over, not Cliff?"

"No. Cliff was away. Brooke was furious. I didn't blame her. Phil tried to calm her down. But she was so angry. It was a horrible scene. But then a few days later, there was the fire at the library. Luke was killed, and I thought it was over."

"You didn't know that Brooke had killed Luke?"

"I didn't. I really didn't. Phil told me someone with the PPOK group was probably responsible. He said that karma got Luke, and that's what happens when you play games with someone else's life. But at least now we could put all that behind us. I told Phil I wasn't going to do any more swinger nights with him. I asked him if he had any other videos, and he swore he didn't."

"What about all the homemade DVDs in his den? You weren't suspicious of those once you knew about the hidden camera?"

"No. I thought they were what he said they were—his old hockey glory days, fishing trips he took, family videos of him and his parents, stuff like that. It never occurred to me that he would just leave the sex ones right out there on his shelf. I sure wouldn't have invited you in there if I knew he had them right in plain sight."

"When did you find out that Brooke had killed Luke?"

"This past Monday. The Timmins' car was there when I got back from shopping. As I walked into the kitchen, I heard Cliff say that Owen Fike was still looking at Brodie, even though Cliff had told him to focus on Ava. I asked who Ava was and why Captain Fike was looking at Brodie. Brooke just exploded and started yelling at me. She said she was tired of me being such a dumb little shit while the rest of them took care of everything. She said I should grow up, and if I couldn't grow up, I should shut up."

"What did you do?"

"I got mad right back at her. She always treated me like I was stupid. I said I had a right to ask questions in my own house, and I had a right to know what they were talking about. That's when she told me Phil should have taken care of Luke when he came to us for money. Because he didn't, she had to. And now that Brodie had a copy of the video, we had a whole new problem to take care of—and she wasn't going to be the one to do it this time."

"Did she say who was—and how?"

"No, because I had a full-blown panic attack right there. I'd been struggling with my anxiety since Luke showed up. And it just hit me like a volcano right there in the kitchen. Phil took me upstairs and gave me a double dose of Xanax. I was exhausted from the attack, and I fell asleep. I didn't wake up until morning. I went to see my doctor, and he gave me a stronger prescription to help with the panic attacks."

"That was on Tuesday, when I saw you at Phil's office?"

"Yes. I'd been on my way there when I had another attack. I had to talk to Phil about Brodie and the video and what they were going to do. Phil said he couldn't talk to me then, but he'd tell me everything when he got home. He said not to worry, Brooke was just spouting off. He would handle it—and her."

"Did he tell you everything like he said he was going to when he got home?"

She looked away.

"Kimberly? What is it?"

She shook her head. "I was so upset when I got home. I knew I should call the police. But I was afraid they wouldn't believe me. Cliff is the prosecutor. I'm just a dumb housewife with mental problems. I had some wine, and I took some Xanax. Phil phoned and said he wouldn't be home until eight. I took an Ambien, and I went to bed. In the morning, I told Phil we had to talk. He promised he'd come home early. He brought me a couple of pills and told me to take them so I didn't have a panic attack and that I should just stay home until he got back."

"Do you remember Brooke coming over?"

"Vaguely. I was pretty groggy, but I remember she said she felt terrible for yelling at me. That it wasn't my fault. Everything would be fine, they had a handle on it now. She offered me some wine, and that's about all I remember."

"Did you tell the police everything you just told me?'

"Yes. I don't know if they believed me. Do you, Leah?"

"I do, Kimberly."

"What do you think will happen to me?"

"What I think is that you need to get a lawyer. If you don't know who to call, try Gabe Hoffman. He's here in town, and he's very good. He'll look out for you."

"You know when Phil first asked if I would go to a swinger night with him, I said no. But he said it wasn't going to change anything. It would just add a little spice to our marriage. That we needed a little fun and games in our life. That it wasn't anything real, it was just fun and games."

66

I didn't really feel like going to Miguel's holidays party on Saturday, given everything that had happened recently, but I knew he'd be very disappointed if I didn't show up. But as Coop and I walked up Miguel's sidewalk, our path lit by little solar lights shaped like tiny Christmas trees, I felt my spirits rise. I could hear the Christmas music playing even before Miguel flung the door open. He greeted us with an exuberant "Merry, Happy, St. Nicholas Day, Hannukah, Kwanzaa, Winter Solstice, Christmas, Boxing Day, and New Year's Eve!"

Coop laughed. "Back at you, Miguel, but you're going to be worn out if you have to roll out that greeting for everyone who comes to the door."

"No, no. I love it. I feel the holiday energy, don't you? Come in, come in. There is wine, and punch, and soda, and water. And in the secret corner of my cupboard, there is Jameson for Leah. Mrs. Schimelman is here, and she made so much good food! And my friend Marianne is playing the piano, and well, just come in and see everyone. You can put your coats on my bed."

I waved at my mother, who was standing at the piano, waiting until enough people had entreated her to sing her Christmas medley. She has a really great voice, and she loves to sing. But she also enjoys having people coax her into it. Little do they know that they couldn't stop her if they tried.

"Hey, I see Mike Waller over there. I want to talk to him before someone else grabs him. Would you take my coat for me?" Coop asked.

"Sure, but I'll expect a tip later."

"No problem."

It took me a while to get to Miguel's bedroom because I kept running into people I knew, some of whom I hadn't seen since Miguel's last holiday party. Finally I made it there and put our coats on the bed. As I turned to leave, I literally bumped into someone I hadn't seen in a lot longer than that.

"Connor? What are you doing here?"

"Leah! You're looking good. Purple's a great color on you. Miguel invited me," he added.

"You look good, too," I said. He was tanned from his days in the Florida sun. He wore a dark green sweater with a white, button-down shirt and dark pants. His light blond hair was still in a crew cut that was just a bit longer than usual on top. But what made him look really great to me was his wide smile and the clarity in his green eyes.

"I didn't mean what are you doing at Miguel's party. I meant what are you doing here, in Himmel? Miguel's soirees are always fun, but still, it's a bit of a drive from Florida to attend, isn't it?"

"I can answer that, Leah," said a gravelly voice. Maggie McConnell stepped out from behind Connor, wearing what she almost always wears: a white blouse, black blazer, and black pants. Though I noticed she had made a concession to the holidays by pinning some holly to her lapel.

"You can, Maggie?" I asked, puzzled.

"Yep. I hired him."

"But—"

I had mentioned the idea of Connor as the executive director of the nonprofit incarnation of the *Times* to Maggie. But I'd said that the board would post the job and it would be at least a few months before that would happen. I was surprised that she'd jumped the gun like that without talking to me first.

"Troy let me know on Wednesday that he needs to take a leave for a while. His grandfather is having knee surgery on Monday. His mother signed up for nursing duty, but she fell and cracked two ribs this past Tuesday. Now they both need help. That means Troy is going to be gone for at least a few weeks. We can't function with Miguel as the only full-time reporter. I figured you were so high on Connor that this would be a good chance for me to see what I think. I gave him a call, offered him a temporary spot, and—"

"And I jumped on it. Don't worry. I know this isn't a guaranteed stepping stone to the executive director position. But I figured this was a way to see if I'm a good fit for Himmel, and if Himmel is a good fit for me. And frankly, I need the paycheck," Connor said.

"Well, way to problem-solve, Maggie. Connor, welcome aboard. Come with me. I'll take you around to meet everybody."

As we circled the room, I soon lost Connor. He has Miguel's gift for making friends. He didn't need my help. Coop had spotted me and was headed in my direction, but people kept stopping him to tell him what the sheriff's office should be doing. I saw Kristin and Gabe come through the door and watched as they stopped under the mistletoe for a kiss. They looked really happy, and that made me feel all warm and fuzzy inside. Ross and Jennifer came in behind them. That made me happy, too, because Jennifer had been dreading coming to her first big party alone, without John. It was nice of Ross to come with her for moral support.

Miguel materialized next to me. I turned to smile at him and saw that he was holding a glass of wine in one hand and a sprig of mistletoe. He lifted the mistletoe over my head and bent down to kiss me on the cheek.

"Happy holidays, *chica*."

"Happy holidays to you, too, Miguel," I said. "Hey, did you see that Ross and Jen came together? I'm glad. I've been a little worried about her not getting out and doing things. Ross needs to do something fun once in a while, too. He's stepped up a lot to help Jennifer out with her boys. I think she really appreciates his friendship. It's good for him, too."

"I know. Oh, look, they are both getting very appreciative!" Miguel said.

When I turned to looked where he was pointing, I saw that Ross and Jennifer had made a stop under the mistletoe, too. Their kiss seemed way more than friendly. I turned open-mouthed to Miguel.

"Jennifer and Ross? They're dating? When did that happen? More to the point, why did it happen? Jennifer and Ross?" I repeated in disbelief.

He grinned. "I told you there would be a surprise for you at my party, remember? How do you like it?"

"I- I'm not sure. Jennifer and Ross? I never would have put them together."

"That's why you must leave matchmaking to Dr. Love."

"But Ross? Really? He's fifteen years older than Jennifer. And he's so crabby, and Jennifer's so fun and bubbly. And he's, well, he's Ross."

"Do they seem happy to you?"

I looked at them as Ross laughed at something Jennifer said and she touched his arm.

"Well, yes, I guess they do."

"Then what else is there?"

"You know, Dr. Love, you're right. I hope they stay happy."

Coop appeared beside me then with two glasses of wine. He held one out to me.

"Thanks. Did you see? Jennifer and Ross are here together? I mean, *together* together," I added.

"I did."

"You don't sound very surprised. Wait a minute. Did you know about this already?"

"Yes. Charlie asked me if I thought he should invite Jennifer to come to the party with him. He was afraid she'd say no, and then it would make things awkward between them."

"I assume you told him to go for it?"

"I told him that in my experience, it's better to take the risk and make the ask, than it is to worry and wonder about it and maybe lose your chance."

"You know what? That's my experience, too. Good advice."

Coop said, "Miguel, can I borrow that mistletoe you're holding?"

"No," he said. "I will hold it for you, so you can make the most of it."

After we did, Miguel excused himself.

I looked around the room then, at the people I knew and loved, at the ones that I knew and didn't love, and at all the others in between. Everyone was smiling, talking, drinking, laughing. The happiness in the room was palpable.

I turned to Coop.

"All we're missing is Tiny Tim to say, 'God bless us, every one!'"

"I think your Tiny Tim is there," he said with a smile, pointing to Miguel, who had moved to the center of the room.

"Everyone! A toast," he said, lifting his glass.

We all followed suit and lifted ours.

"To friends, to laughter, to the year to come. May all your holidays be filled with love, hope, and happy memories. Cheers!"

"Cheers!" everyone said in unison.

Miguel's friend Marianne began playing "White Christmas" on the piano, my mother started singing, and the crowd joined in. Coop squeezed my hand, and I smiled up at him. I felt a strong wave of gratitude and joy rush through me. It was followed immediately by the faint flutter of fear I sometimes get when things are going too well. But in the midst of so much happiness, I pushed it down and ignored it.

I shouldn't have. It turned out to be the faint portent of some very dark days ahead.

DANGEROUS BETRAYALS: Leah Nash #12

She's tracking a killer, but who is tracking her?

Former journalist, now fledgling mystery writer, Leah Nash receives a heartfelt email from Marianne, a reader she's never met. Marianne's sister Celia is in a Wisconsin prison for the murder of her married lover, Eric Ferguson. She begs Leah to save Celia from serving life for a crime she didn't commit.

However, Leah is pretty sure Celia *did* kill Eric. The case against her was very strong and the jury delivered the guilty verdict in less than an hour. But Marianne's desperation strikes a chord in Leah, because of the deep-seated guilt she feels over failing to save her own sister years earlier. She finds it impossible to turn Marianne down.

Peeling back the layers of Eric's complicated life, Leah uncovers multiple suspects who had reasons to want Eric dead. All of them—Eric's betrayed wife, his resentful sister, a bankrupted neighbor, a political adversary, and a cuckolded husband—are concealing secrets. But which one is also hiding the heart of a killer? As Leah navigates a maze of lies and alibis, each clue only deepens the mystery.

Leah becomes so enmeshed in saving Celia that when she begins to receive odd, anonymous messages, she attributes them to a fan with boundary issues. The county sheriff, who happens to be her boyfriend, isn't so sure. But as Leah works to prove Celia's innocence and bring the real killer to light, is a stalker waiting to close in for the final act?

**Get your copy today at
severnriverbooks.com**

ACKNOWLEDGMENTS

Thanks go to the staff at the Alma Public Library who answered all my questions with patience and shared some funny and touching stories about working in a library (none of which wound up in *this* story, but they were definitely keepers for the future). Thanks also to my beta readers who provided the encouragement and honest feedback I needed. And, as always, my biggest thank you goes to my husband, Gary Rayburn, who keeps everything running at home while I'm running the mean streets of Himmel, Wisconsin.

ABOUT THE AUTHOR

Susan Hunter is a charter member of Introverts International (which meets the 12th of Never at an undisclosed location). She has worked as a reporter and managing editor, during which time she received a first place UPI award for investigative reporting and a Michigan Press Association first place award for enterprise/feature reporting.

Susan has also taught composition at the college level, written advertising copy, newsletters, press releases, speeches, web copy, academic papers and memos. Lots and lots of memos. She lives in rural Michigan with her husband Gary, who is a man of action, not words.

During certain times of the day, she can also be found wandering the mean streets of small-town Himmel, Wisconsin, looking for clues, stopping for a meal at the Elite Cafe, dropping off a story lead at the *Himmel Times Weekly*, or meeting friends for a drink at McClain's Bar and Grill.

Printed in the United States
by Baker & Taylor Publisher Services

Printed in the United States
by Baker & Taylor Publisher Services